KISSED BY

A few dozen times? A ... him at the image of her kissing a long line of men. If he thought about it rationally, at the age of twenty and two it would have been more surprising if Mairead had *not* been kissed a few times. She was beautiful and probably highly sought by many as a potential wife. But Hamish was incapable of rational thought with her so close. The heat of her hand was making his blood boil and her fresh scent was causing his body to make demands of its own. All he could think was that he needed to erase the memory of every man's touch but his own.

Powerless to stop himself, Hamish could not pull his gaze away from her lips as he slowly, inevitably, lowered his mouth to hers. His arms gathered her close in case she suddenly realized what was about to happen, because Mairead was not going anywhere. She wanted to know if the passion of their kiss had been a fluke and he was not going to keep her wondering any longer. . . .

Books by Michele Sinclair

THE HIGHLANDER'S BRIDE

TO WED A HIGHLANDER

DESIRING THE HIGHLANDER

THE CHRISTMAS KNIGHT

TEMPTING THE HIGHLANDER

A WOMAN MADE FOR PLEASURE

SEDUCING THE HIGHLANDER

A WOMAN MADE FOR SIN

NEVER KISS A HIGHLANDER

HIGHLAND HUNGER
(with Hannah Howell and Jackie Ivie)

Published by Kensington Publishing Corporation

NEVER KISS A HIGHLANDER

MICHELE SINCLAIR

ZEBRA BOOKS
KENSINGTON PUBLISHING CORP.
http://www.kensingtonbooks.com

ZEBRA BOOKS are published by

Kensington Publishing Corp.
119 West 40th Street
New York, NY 10018

All Kensington titles, imprints, and distributed lines are available at special quantity discounts for bulk purchases for sales promotion, premiums, fund-raising, educational, or institutional use.

Special book excerpts or customized printings can also be created to fit specific needs. For details, write or phone the office of the Kensington Sales Manager: Attn.: Sales Department. Kensington Publishing Corp., 119 West 40th Street, New York, NY 10018. Phone: 1-800-221-2647.

First Printing: August 2017
ISBN-13: 978-1-4201-3880-1
ISBN-10: 1-4201-3880-4

eISBN-13: 978-1-4201-3881-8
eISBN-10: 1-4201-3881-2

10 9 8 7 6 5 4 3 2 1

Printed in the United States of America

This book goes to several people. First, to my friend's beautiful daughter Selah, who helped inspire my vision for the heroine and her sister. It also goes to Emma and Harmon, my reason for all that I do. And last I dedicate this book to some very special women who bolster me continually when I am down. I was recently reminded just how truly remarkable friendships can be when I met a couple of snobbish soccer moms at practice. (Yes, I'm a proud soccer mom.) Now, these women are NOT mothers of anyone on my daughter's team. There were many teams practicing and I was where several moms wait and watch. I was floored when I was told without words—you readers know how we women can excel at nonverbal communication—that I was not welcome, even as a temporary addition for the afternoon. Wow! It seems some ladies (I use the term loosely) never outgrow certain behaviors they probably perfected in middle and high school. And while such animosity can be crushing as a child, it only served to show me just what great friends I have, especially my fellow soccer moms. I have known most of these women for years, watching our daughters grow from small little ones missing their front teeth to the fierce players they are today. And so I dedicate this book to you, the Barcelona, Blue Flames, and Strikers Soccer Moms! I love every one of you. All those who have remained, who have come and gone, and who are new to our group. You are fantastic women, who genuinely welcome and accept all, which make us more than friends, but family. You are not just an inspiration to my daughter, but to me. I thank you. I could not be who I am, write my books, and remain somewhat sane without your continual support and endless kindness and generosity.

Chapter One

January 1317, McTiernay Castle

"Woman, did you not hear that?" Conor groaned as his wife ignored the muffled thump of the tower door closing.

Laurel ignored the question and continued to let her fingers explore the dark hairs of her husband's upper chest. She nibbled on his ear, ignoring the distinct sound of sluggish footsteps coming up the stairwell. Conor curled his fingers around her upper arms to push her away, but his body refused to comply any further. Forcing Laurel to stop her sensual assault was not an option—it was an impossibility. After nearly ten years of marriage, he still found her to be the most beguiling creature he had ever come across and remained just as incapable of resisting her charms as he had on the day they met.

Laurel pressed her lips against the warmth of his cheek and then slowly leaned back. She tossed a lock of her pale gold hair over her shoulder and feigned an evil glare. "My hearing is just fine," she whispered softly as she ran her slim finger along the line of his jaw, "and trust me when I say that if you call me 'woman' one more time, yours won't be."

Conor cocked a dark eyebrow and grinned at her. "Meaning what?" he challenged for provoking Laurel never got old . . . if anything, her unpredictable reactions over the years had made their relationship only more enjoyable.

Laurel's storm-colored eyes sparkled as they peered momentarily into his misty gray ones. Putting her cheek against his, she purred, "I mean that I'll be forced to bring you back to your senses, my love, and the ringing in your ears afterward might affect your hearing for a while." Then she tilted her head and recommenced her sensual assault, trailing promise-filled kisses along his jawline.

Biting back another moan, Conor clinched his fists in her hair, fighting his inclination to ignore the approaching footsteps and resume his own seductive caresses. Her pale skin beckoned to be touched and he was tempted to send an angry shout-out for whoever it was to go away. The odd command would secure his immediate wish to be alone with his wife. Unfortunately, based on previous experience, it would also instigate relentless gossip. By sunset, every clansman within miles would know of his and Laurel's latest place to rendezvous. And a secret spot that is permeated with giggles and obvious avoidance tended to spoil the fun.

"Laird?" The deep voice echoed in the stairwell. Whoever it was had paused just as Laurel nipped his neck causing Conor to groan loudly with need. The interloper cleared his throat and called out, "Laird? Are you well?"

"Mo chreach!" Conor muttered under his breath, suddenly recognizing the voice. "Aye! I'm coming down!" he shouted, hoping to buy some time to pull himself away from Laurel's ministrations and gather a semblance of self-control.

"No need, Laird, I'm almost there." The unwelcome reply held an undisguised hint of a chuckle.

"Damn it, Laurel!" Conor hissed. "It's Hamish and you don't have any clothes on!"

Laurel shrugged her shoulders and lightly dragged her fingers up his bare thigh. "You've lost most of yours as well," she whispered before slipping off his lap to search for her shift and bliaut, which were buried somewhere amidst all the piles of material.

Wearing only his leine, Conor was about to rise and quickly don his kilt when Laurel stood in front of him and pointed to his seat. He glanced down and realized he was sitting on the very garments she was looking for. He knew he should rise and give them to her, but he could only stare at his wife. She was everything a man could desire in a woman and every time he saw her stripped of all clothing that attempted to hide her beauty, it took his breath away. Tall and delicate-looking with ivory skin and long wavy pale gold hair, she looked like an angel.

Feeling himself growing hard once again, Conor decided to order Hamish to leave—immediately. To hell with the gossip. He and Laurel would just have to find another secret place to meet.

Unfortunately, he made the decision a second too late.

The door cracked open and Laurel immediately dove behind several barrels that were piled high with materials, blankets and other clothing supplies.

Hamish paused outside the entrance for several seconds before rattling the door in hopes that he had given his laird and lady enough time to prepare themselves for his entrance. He had come up the stairs at a painfully slow pace while intentionally making enough noise so that regardless of what state they were in, they should have been ready to receive him.

Any other day, Hamish would have turned around and left upon hearing the muffled sounds as he had started his ascent up the stairwell. It had been impossible to understand anything Conor was saying, but his laird's tone had been both heated and laced with passion. The combination was a clear indication that he was not alone. Laurel was with him.

No two people fought or loved each other as much as Conor and his wife Laurel—although Hamish had to admit some of Conor's younger brothers came close with their own wives. Though deeply in love, Laird and Lady McTiernay were both stubborn and headstrong. Each refused to let their strong emotions for the other make them ever appear submissive. And Hamish knew the depth of their love better than most, for he had witnessed their relationship since the beginning. He had seen it spark and how that ember had only grown into a constant fire, which burned between them. It was a relationship not to be envied but emulated. And while Hamish had for many years longed to find someone with whom he could share a deep connection and commitment, the debacle of his last attempt left his heart incapable of such emotion.

He felt nothing. And the numbness that had consumed him for the past several months was not going away anytime soon. Not a single one of the multiple beauties the McTiernay wives had pushed into his path during the recent festivities leading up to Epiphany had created even a spark of a physical, emotional, or mental reaction.

Hamish knew deep down he was no longer capable of love. And strangely, he accepted it.

For others, especially McTiernays, love was a wondrous thing to be sought and coveted. For him, the emotion equaled misery. A fact he should have accepted years ago

with the betrayal of his first love. It had left him with only
one honorable choice—to leave his home and all his
birthrights, never to return. Now the very man who had
stolen her heart was insisting he return.

It was not the first time his younger brother had made
such a request, but Hamish vowed it would be the last.

His heart neither sought nor wanted revenge. But after
twelve years, it was time for his brother to leave what happened in the past and move on like he had. Unfortunately,
it had become obvious that could not be accomplished
until all involved parties once again came face-to-face with
one another.

Hamish would have preferred to delay the meeting
until summer, for he had no desire to travel to the northern edge of Scotland in January, the coldest and wettest
time of year. But the nature of his brother's request made
such a delay impossible. Robert might be willing to risk
innocent lives, but Hamish was not. He had not thought
ever to see the men and women of his clan again, but he
had still considered himself to be a MacBrieve. Clan loyalty required his return to help—this one time. However,
once he was ensured of their safety, it would be up to the
clansmen and women to require their leader and clan
chief—his brother—to act on their behalf. Hamish would
have fulfilled any obligation to them.

Hamish started to push the handle of the door and
heard Laurel's teasing voice followed by some scuffling.
He closed his eyes and momentarily wondered if he would
ever again crave a woman's touch. Months ago, after years
of narrowly missing his chance at finding love, Hamish
thought he had finally found love with not only a stunning
woman, but someone who also felt the same in return.
Instead, he discovered he had almost pledged himself

to a female whose internal depravity matched that of her external beauty.

Since then, he had not sought nor returned the attentions of the fairer sex. His energies, once split between his duties and finding a wife and settling down, now were solely focused on his responsibilities as one of the famed elite guards for one of the biggest, most powerful clans in Scotland. He trained with his fellow guards and then taught the newer recruits until exhaustion overtook him. It was not the life he always thought he would have, but it was a good one. And it gave his heart one thing it craved—peace.

Hamish took a deep breath and opened the door. Thankfully, he saw only Conor, though somewhat disheveled, sitting on a backless cross-frame chair with various fabric items piled around him. One of the more fanciful ones was draped across his lap. It was an odd sight, seeing his laird sitting in the middle of the tower room where Lady McTiernay stored anything textile related.

"Gabh mo leisgeul," Hamish said, semi-apologizing for what he knew to be less-than-welcome entry.

Conor looked up from pretending to examine the expensive gold material he was fingering. *"Thig a-steach,"* he answered, offering Hamish to come in farther. "I was, uh, just trying to decide on what type of, uh, fabric I should surprise Laurel with this year."

Hamish considered Conor's obvious lie and decided to play along, but only somewhat. Crossing his arms, he used his thumb to point at the material. "Isn't it kind of early to plan a trip to Aberdeen, especially with everyone still recovering from this year's feasts? Normally, preparing for the journey is something you do the week before you leave." Hamish glanced toward the window and the gray skies before adding, "And, um, April will not be here for another three months."

Conor ran his tongue along the inside of his cheek and stared Hamish in the eye. "You are right. But perhaps it was Laurel's idea—not mine—to prepare so early." Conor smothered a smile as he felt the heat of his wife's pointed stare. "Be glad you have no idea of just what it takes to keep a woman happy," he added, waving a corner of gold fabric while keeping the majority of it on his lap.

"Aye," Hamish replied with a lopsided grin that was almost completely hidden by his overgrown beard.

"And you won't know as long as you continue to grow that thing on your chin. Laurel finds it repulsive and while I normally don't even notice how a man chooses to present himself to the world, your beard forces even my eye to wince."

Hamish began to stroke the wiry red hairs and shrugged. As beards went, his was bushy and long, but it was its unkempt nature that made it a topic of conversation. Hamish did not care. "My ability to attract a woman no longer holds any importance to me."

Conor grimaced. "Laurel was afraid of that. The woman complained for years about your flirting, and now she moans about the lack of it these past few months. She should understand that time and the company of a good woman are all that you need."

"I don't think any amount of time can pick up the pieces of my heart after what happened. And the last thing I need or want is being forced to be in the company of a woman—good or otherwise." Hamish knew his tone was clipped, but he hoped it would convey that he wanted no advice on the subject.

"After your cold behavior during the celebrations, I doubt that is a problem. I'd be surprised if Laurel could find even one woman willing to be in *your* company," Conor murmured. He acted as if he was about to let the matter drop, when suddenly Conor leaned forward, his gray eyes intense. "Hamish, your heart may be in pieces, but those pieces mean there *is* hope. When I thought I lost Laurel a few years ago, my heart not only shattered, but those pieces disappeared. *That* is when there is no hope."

Hamish sighed. "I understand."

Conor shook his head and sat back up. Hamish might say he did not want a woman in his bed, but he did. "You do not, but I hope you do understand someday. For then you will truly know what it means to have a *sonuachar*."

Hamish pursed his lips. To know what it felt like to lose a soul mate would mean a woman would have had to return even a portion of his feelings. That had yet to happen. And since he suspected he was beyond the point of emotion, he doubted it ever would.

"You must have had a reason to see me other than talk of your beard and its negative effect on women," Conor posed.

"Aye. Regrettably, I just received word that I must immediately head north. One of Robert's men has paid me another visit with an urgent request to return home. Unfortunately, this time I cannot refuse."

That got Conor's attention and he studied the large Highlander before him. When Hamish had joined the McTiernays, he had been young, barely twenty, and eager to prove himself. He had been shedding one life and seeking the promise of a new one. Conor had offered him that chance. Now, after twelve years, Hamish was like another brother, even though no one would ever mistake him for a McTiernay.

Conor and his brothers all had dark hair and either gray or blue eyes. Hamish's features were far different. The thick, loose waves of his auburn hair hung to almost the middle of his back and his high cheekbones caused his face to look harsh and unrelenting in battle, but when relaxed and smiling, enormous dimples softened his features. Dark lashes highlighted the unusual shade of forest green of his eyes, which had the ability to grow dark and cold like the pit of night or brighten and shine with laughter. Though tall, Hamish lacked Conor's significant height, but his girth outsized the McTiernay laird and all his brothers. And when it came to battle, Conor had a slight advantage of speed; however, Hamish was made of granite. He knew how to wield a weapon with deadly accuracy and enormous power.

His skill with bladed weapons—whether it be claymore, dirk, or halberd—was one of the reasons Conor had asked Hamish to be part of his elite guard not long after he had joined them. Finn, the McTiernay commander, had initially been cautious, as Hamish refused to assume the name McTiernay, but Conor never had any doubt. The man was not just loyal, he was also incredibly smart. Which was why Conor suspected Hamish knew exactly why he was sitting in the middle of a bunch of fabrics.

Tossing the flimsy fabric aside and revealing his state of undress, Conor leaned forward and rested his elbows on his bare knees. "So your brother Robert has contacted you again. How many times does this make it? Three . . . four?"

"Five," Hamish corrected. "If you include when he told me about our father's death."

Hamish had hoped that refusing to return for their father's funeral would be a strong enough hint for even Robert to understand. The past had been written and nothing was going to change that. But his younger brother had refused to recognize the unstated message and within a year had sent a second entreaty for Hamish to return home. That time Hamish did not reply. A couple of years later, the herald who relayed the third request was under orders to stay until Hamish gave an answer, to which Hamish obliged—he already had a home and was glad Robert had one as well. Again two years passed before his brother decided to try again. That time he had been foolish enough to send three of his best men in an attempt to bring Hamish home using force. All three returned wounded with injuries painful enough to make it clear to Robert that if he tried such a tactic again, his soldiers would most likely rebel. His brother could send a dozen men, but such ploys would not work.

Conor twitched his lips and inhaled. "He wants you to come at *this* time of year? It will be a bitter journey. You could always wait for him to send a sixth plea for your company."

Hamish quirked a brow. His brother did not seek his company, but absolution. "Unfortunately, that is not an option and I've come to realize it would only delay the inevitable. Robert refuses to let go of the past and will not let me be free of it either until we speak."

Sitting back up, Conor shrugged. "You say Robert is your opposite in personality. And though I have never met your younger brother, I know of one characteristic you share—stubbornness."

Hamish grinned. "I'd take offense if it were not coming from a man who practices that very trait daily and is married to a woman who reinvented what it means to be obstinate." Hamish heard the soft click of someone's jaw snapping shut behind the barrels. Before Laurel could say anything, Hamish quickly said, "I will be returning as soon as the situation and weather permit."

Conor looked pointedly at Hamish. "What if Robert

asks you to stay? To be his commander? You and I both know that you would be a good one and have earned the opportunity to assume such responsibility."

"I have little doubt that is exactly what my brother wants," Hamish huffed, having been told by the herald the situation he was to address. "But Robert will soon learn that being his commander is not something I desire," he added coldly, once again wishing he could just refuse Robert for the fifth time and continue with his life. The only positive thing about his brother's latest request was its timing. After two weeks of holiday feasts and seeing the McTiernays so happy with their wives, Hamish needed a temporary change of scenery.

"You know I consider you to be a brother," said Conor.

Hamish studied the man whom he called laird but felt so much more for. "I think the same of you, Laird."

"Does the situation require any men? Perhaps you should take some with you."

Hamish exhaled and shook his head. "It's not a McTiernay problem. If blood is to be shed, it will belong to the MacBrieves, for it was their laird who created the situation."

Conor nodded in understanding, although he was not inclined to agree. If Hamish had a problem, then it was a McTiernay problem. "My brothers and I consider you family. Most of the men and women of this clan consider you to be one of them. You could be a McTiernay to others as well. You just need to accept the offer."

Hamish raised a brow at the veiled implication. "You do not need me to accept your name to know where my loyalty lies. However, in my father's eyes, it would mean that I had disavowed him and my birth clan. He may be dead, but I will not dishonor him that way. I may not choose to live with the clan I was born into, but I have no wish to publically disclaim them."

Conor shook his head. "Then you are right not to take the name McTiernay, but not for the reason you just gave," he said in a low voice that while soft, relayed the intensity he was feeling. "Claiming a clan should not be about your father, or even your birth. It shouldn't be about anyone but yourself, for no one else is swearing that fealty. In this, I'm sure, your father would not just understand but also agree. But know, the day you change your mind, the offer is there."

Hamish swallowed as emotion threatened to overtake him. He gave Conor a quick nod, appreciative of the man he both respected and loved. "I need to be going before the weather turns foul." After another quick nod, he turned and headed toward the door. Just as he passed the fabric-laden barrels, he added, "And before Laurel chases me out so that she can have you all to herself again."

"You knew I was here?" Laurel yelped.

Hamish grabbed the door and opened it. With a shrug, he grinned at Conor and replied, "What other reason would the laird have for sitting half naked in a room full of nothing but cloth?"

As Hamish closed the door, he heard a soft thump of something hitting the other side and Laurel shouting out, "Shave your beard!"

Once she heard Hamish exit the tower and was sure he was not about to step back in, Laurel ventured out of her hiding place. She had wrapped Conor's tartan around her chest while listening to his and Hamish's conversation. "He spoke as if he was not eager to go but sounded surprisingly willing."

Conor grunted and stared at the door. "I think that what happened last year with Wyenda and then Meriel affected him more than we realized."

"Perhaps," Laurel said halfheartedly, sauntering over to Conor's side.

"You don't think so? Rumors are that Hamish has been celibate ever since."

"Not surprising. You had no idea how hard it was to find anyone to overlook that beard!" Laurel faked a shiver. She and the other McTiernay wives had all tried to set Hamish up, and all the hard work to find decent, funny women who were willing to look past his ill-kept appearance had been pointless. Every attempt had failed miserably.

Conor reached out to grab Laurel's hand. "Whether it be design or not—Hamish choosing even temporarily a life of abstinence is definitely evidence of a broken heart."

Laurel bit her bottom lip and said, "'Tis evidence of it being emotionally bruised maybe. And I'm not saying his feelings for Wyenda or even Meriel were nonexistent. Just the opposite. I know he believed himself to be earnest, I'm just not convinced he actually loved them. I'm not sure Hamish has ever *really* been in love since I have known him."

Conor pulled Laurel onto his lap. "Aye, the man does tend to seek opportunities clearly destined for heartbreak, but I think this last time those women truly wounded him."

"I disagree," Laurel said as she began to play with the strings on the front of his leine. "For if either of those women had truly captured his heart, Hamish would have fought harder to keep them. In truth, I don't believe he has fully endeavored to win the affections of a single woman."

Conor placed a hand over hers, stilling her fingers. "Two men fighting over a lass for her heart is a young girl's notion of love. A real man has no desire to win a woman's affection. He wants it to be freely given. When it is not, then what is the purpose?"

"I concede." Laurel sighed. "But there is something nice about knowing a man considers you worth fighting for. Makes you want to reward the victor," she said with a wink.

Conor bent over and planted a long, lingering kiss on her lips. "I'll keep that in mind," he whispered, and began to tug at the knot of the securely wrapped tartan.

Laurel smiled as Conor began to get frustrated. She had tied the material especially tight, hoping to make it difficult to remove. It would give her time to tease him mercilessly as he sought to regain access to her body. She leaned over and began to place soft warm kisses along his neck. "Do you think Hamish will return to us?"

"He says he will."

"What if he does not? Shouldn't you have told him the truth about his family?" she asked, snaking her hand inside the opening of his leine to stroke his chest.

Conor stifled a groan and tried to focus on the knot. He was well aware of Laurel's true intent with the securely tethered plaid and her persistent line of questions. She was trying to win an argument from two weeks back. That of the two of them, he was more likely to lose all ability to keep a clear mind when sexually aroused. He disagreed. Laurel enjoyed believing that she was always in control, but he knew how to awaken her body and cause her to let go of all thought and just feel. He accepted the fact that he was also susceptible to such tactics, but Conor had no doubts that he could outlast her in a game of sexual manipulation.

He gave another yank on the knot, freeing the harnessed mass. "I did not say anything because his father asked me not to until circumstances dictated it was time. And you know those conditions have not been met."

Laurel leaned down and placed a prolonged kiss on his chest at the opening of his leine. As she began to move her lips upward along his neck, she murmured, "I suppose not. Family is so much more than birth. It's also more than choice—it is commitment."

When she reached his jaw, Laurel hovered her lips just over his and shifted her bottom so that it moved provocatively against him. The erotic assault made him even harder. Conor steeled himself and tried to remain focused as his hands cupped her breasts and began their sensual assault.

Laurel bit her bottom lip but could not suppress a moan as she leaned into his touch. "Do you . . . um . . . think you might have lost . . . um . . . another of your elite guard?"

He used his thumbs to coax her nipples until they were hard and straining. "If I did, there's a dozen men waiting to fill his spot," Conor mumbled before kissing the tip of her chin, then slowly making his way down her neck.

Laurel instinctively arched against him, hoping she could outlast him as the pleasure he was creating within her was excruciatingly tantalizing. "Sounds as if you don't think Hamish will be coming back—" she said, barely getting the last word out.

Conor's mouth lingered in the crook where her neck met her shoulders. "Let's just say in the past few years, when a McTiernay goes on a trip, it never goes quite the way he expects."

Laurel closed her eyes and smiled. "True, but that's because you McTiernays have been lucky enough to find extraordinary women."

Focused on getting to his objective, Conor did not

argue. "And Hamish does fall in love faster than anyone I know."

She felt him flick the tip of one nipple with his tongue. She sucked in a deep breath and fought for something coherent to say. "Ah . . . but no woman will have him with that beard. He looks . . . so unappealing, which I suspect is the reason why he has grown it. For protection." Conor answered by enveloping her into his moist heat, rousing a melting sweetness within her. She strained against his mouth and moaned again. She was either going to have to find the willpower to pull away or concede defeat. Talking was becoming increasingly difficult.

As he turned his attention to her other breast, Conor countered, "I've heard some women like men with beards."

Laurel speared her fingers into Conor's hair and pulled his head back so that she could begin her own assault. "Perhaps," she whispered into his ear, "but no woman likes a beard that hampers the abilities of a man's mouth. And I like your face too much to let you cover it." With a smile, she began to suckle on his earlobe.

He stiffened and held her tighter. "Then, maybe I'll just allow you to shave me, woman."

Laurel gave him a light bite. "*Allow* me?" she asked as she pulled back slightly with her eyes narrowed. "Perhaps when I do *choose* to give you a shave, I give you a nick or two to teach you a lesson about calling me woman."

Conor leaned forward causing Laurel to fall back into his arms. "I call you woman because I am the only man who will ever know just what an incredible woman you are." He reached over and with the back of his free hand he caressed her cheek. "And you *are* my woman. All mine. And I love you more now than I did the day we married. You are everything to me. My *sonuachar*. My soul mate." She smiled adoringly and reached up to cup his cheek, but before she could say anything, he added, "And if you don't stop talking, I'm not going to have enough time to prove it before Maegan returns with the children ending our private afternoon together."

Eternal love filled Laurel's deep blue eyes and she pulled him toward her for another kiss, pausing only just before their lips met. "I guess we will have to see who is right another day."

Conor's mouth closed roughly over hers, searing her lips and ending any ability to continue their conversation. He would never get enough of her. He could spend another fifty years with his English beauty and it would still not be enough.

Chapter Two

Northern Edge of Scotland, Just South of Farr Bay

Hamish reached the top of the hill and gave a slight tug on the reins for the horse to stop. Swinging his leg over the animal's back end, he kept one hand on the saddle and used the other to prevent the furs around his shoulders from falling as he dropped to his feet. The wind had increased and the temperatures would drop below freezing upon nightfall at this altitude.

Letting go of the saddle, he lifted his hand to shield his eyes from the afternoon sun. A twinge went up his back, a telling sign that he had been riding for several hours and that his gait had been too slow. But he had finally arrived at the northern stretch of Scotland. To his left were the Kyle of Tongue and the four rocky peaks of the granite mountain Ben Loyal. To his right lay rocky, rolling terrain interspersed with occasional snow-capped peaks and crags. Before him were the bays of Torrisdale and Farr. It was along their shores he had once called home.

Hamish inhaled deeply. At least the sea had not changed. The blue water still pounded the jutted cliffs that stretched out into the bay. He was not close enough to hear the crashing sounds of the waves, but he was near enough to smell the seawater. He had not realized just how much he missed the ocean. Its loss was just one of many small prices he had paid when he had decided to leave. And now he was going to have to pay it again, for he fully intended to return to the McTiernays as soon as possible. There was nothing here that could entice him to stay, and much to keep him away from the place he now called home.

Hamish unhooked the water bag on his saddle and took a swallow. It was still early in the afternoon, but it would not be long before the night sky was over him. This time of year, daylight hours were few. The sun only appeared for about seven hours, rising and setting long after a typical workday started and finished. And when the sun was in the sky, it was often hidden behind gray clouds during the winter months. With the ocean lapping its shores, northern Scotland was not just dark and cold; it came with an overabundance of rain, sleet, and blustery wind. One was lucky to experience sunshine three days in a row.

The mud in the valleys and snow in the mountains required travel to be done in the daylight. Hamish had another hour, maybe two, before the sun disappeared behind the horizon, but he was in no hurry to his destination. The herald had to have arrived by now with word of his return for Hamish had ordered him and his traveling companion to go back as soon as he had made his decision. And though Hamish had left soon after he had dismissed the heralds, he had not been in a hurry and had decided to take a small detour and check on some of the more northern farmsteads on McTiernay lands. He had even considered visiting Conor's brother Cole on his way north, as the stop would give him more time to think. But thinking would change nothing. It would only postpone the inevitable.

Until he confronted his brother, Robert would not let him live in peace.

Hamish reattached the water bag to his saddle and let go of the horse's reins so the animal could seek out one of the many large water puddles and take its own fill. As the horse moved aside, Hamish looked out and stared at the one place he had hoped never to see again—Foinaven Castle.

Two years younger than Hamish, Robert was not just a beloved brother, but the unquestionable genius of the MacBrieve family. Hamish and his father had often jested that of the three of them, it was Robert who was the true MacBrieve. Like his grandfather and great-grandfather, he had inherited the MacBrieve gift for fixing anything from castle fortifications to enhancing everyday devices. Hamish and his father, on the other hand, were natural leaders and fighters and never able to understand how Robert could spend countless hours staring at an object, trying to see how it worked and how it could be improved. And yet, Hamish had felt both pride and envy of his brother's ability to quickly resolve riddles and build contraptions that worked from what seemed to be nothing but rocks and string. Unfortunately, Robert's brilliance was limited to inanimate objects. When it came to understanding individuals and discerning their true motivations, his younger brother remained perpetually naïve. He refused to see the world as it was and instead interpreted situations and people as he wished them to be—inherently good, honest, and accommodating.

Less than a week ago, Robert's herald arrived and his missive had made it clear that his brother had not changed. But as a leader of a Highland clan, such ideals were not just reckless but dangerous.

During the last twelve years, Robert had tried four

times to get Hamish to return home, each time making the situation sound a little more pressing and serious. Repeatedly Hamish had made it clear that he held no lingering animosity, but Robert wanted more. He wanted reconciliation. Hamish, however, had no desire to be inflicted with seeing the first woman to whom he had given his heart fawning over his brother.

None of that mattered for the nature behind Robert's latest request had made it impossible for Hamish to outright refuse. His brother had foolishly decided to send the majority of the clan's guard—including his commander—to Jedburgh Abbey to serve as an escort to the castle's newly appointed priest. Robert was hoping Hamish would come for a visit and help ensure the safety of the clan in the interim.

Hamish had little choice but to agree.

Despite the number of years he had been away, Hamish had never forgotten the men and women Robert was now responsible for were his people. Clansmen that he had been raised from birth to rule and protect. His decision to forego that privilege did not change his desire to know his clansmen prospered and were safe. Robert had gambled on that desire, creating a situation that would compel Hamish's agreement to come home. But if his brother believed that offering him the position of commander, a place of honor and responsibility, would entice him to stay, he would soon learn otherwise.

There was not a single thing Robert could say or offer that would result in Hamish's remaining at Foinaven.

Hamish stretched and studied the skies. The wind was picking up and by the smell of the air, the coming rain would be heavy. Sleeping outside tonight would be a bitter and uncomfortable experience, but it could not be helped. It was too late to reach Foinaven before dark and unwise to travel in these hills with no light and in the pouring rain. All that was left to decide was which was more important— finding food or finding shelter.

To the west were a few rock formations that would provide shelter from the wind and a little from the rain. To the northeast was Lochlan Duinte, an ancient monument that overlooked River Naver. It would provide little protection from foul weather, but the surrounding vegetation offered a better chance of catching some food. Hamish looked out at the horizon and debated his choices.

Just east of the river, Foinaven Castle lay on an elevated stretch of land just south of Farr Bay. Parts of the bay were treacherous, with a seacoast comprised of very high cliffs and deep fjords with ragged inlets of sandy beaches. Hamish could not help but stare and take in all the changes that had been made to the stronghold in the past twelve years.

When he had left, the castle had been but a single stone tower and the beginnings of a stone keep surrounded by an oblong wooden wall that conformed to the contours of the landscape. Now the timber had been replaced and stone made up the curtain wall as well as many of the buildings that lined the northernmost wall. The only thing that had remained unchanged from his memory was the main tower. It still stood alone in the middle of the lower portion of the walled courtyard, unconnected to any of the outer walls.

The village that lay just outside the castle had grown considerably since he had left. Houses, barns, sheds, and animal pens clustered around the center forcing the farmers that lived in the village to walk a good distance to reach their fields and pastures. Foinaven had become a castle any laird would be proud of and it could have been his.

Originally part of the Morrison clan on the Isle of Lewis, the MacBrieves functioned as judges, issuing brieves on the island. As a result, they held much power and influence, despite their few numbers. However, Hamish's great-grandfather was the second son to the clan chief and had wanted a different life. With an innate ability to build and engineer various devices, he saw little chance of using his skills as a judge. He also knew he was not alone in feeling confined on the island. The clan was never allowed to grow in size due to the constant aggressive nature of their neighbors. As a result, his great-grandfather had left, leading a small group of MacBrieve clansmen to the mainland to make a new life.

By the time his father had assumed lairdship over their clan, their numbers had grown significantly and they had formed a permanent village just south of Armadale Bay. Their blockhouse served as an isolated, defensive strong point and under his father's leadership, their clan became known for its strong warriors, who possessed the lethal ability to defend their home, families, and lands. But his father had aspired to more and merging with the Mac-Mhathains had provided the opportunity to not just grow in numbers, but also the chance to become a powerful and influential clan.

Hamish was to have helped his father realize that dream. Instead, he had given that honor to his brother.

Hamish closed his eyes and searched his heart. It spoke the same message as it always had. No resentment, no bitterness—only sadness and loss. If life presented the same situation again, Hamish knew he would make the same choices he had made so long ago.

With a shake of his head to clear his mind, Hamish

called for his horse and reminded himself that he lacked for nothing. He had a home and a prized position with one of the most powerful clans in the Highlands. He was able to be himself and felt at ease living with the McTiernays. And maybe someday it could be more. Love was not a necessary ingredient to get married and have a family. It was preferred, but after what he had gone through this last year, he had decided being compatible was far more important. It was something to consider. He could be alone for the rest of his life or maybe he could follow the same advice he was soon going to give his brother—move on.

Hamish guided his horse down the outcropping and heard a loud whistle to his right. Halting his progress, he looked to see who it was and the reason behind the piercing sound. A second later, a large, muscular man with a distinct profile and dark brown hair, slightly graying around the temples, came into view. He was signaling to a boy much farther away to help keep the free-range kyloe from wandering too far in their search for food.

Unlike most livestock, long-horned, long-haired Highland cattle could survive northern Scotland's harsh nature, rainfall, and very strong winds with minimal care. But they did have to be corralled often, especially in the winter when the search for food urged them to go beyond their preferred pastures.

Hamish stared at the father for several seconds before realizing he recognized him. The man was Amon and had been a respected warrior and part of his father's elite guard. He had been the one assigned to teach Hamish how to handle a sword and it was Amon's training enabled Hamish to be victorious in battle. Seeing Amon dressed as a farmer was surprising, as his former mentor had at one time lived and breathed the life of a soldier.

Hamish hollered down and waved when Amon turned in his direction. Similarly, after several seconds, Amon's deep blue eyes widened with recognition and he motioned for Hamish to come near.

Getting off his horse, Hamish greeted the older man with a smile. Amon grinned back and pulled him into a fierce, brief embrace. "It is you! So the herald was not spreading false rumors of your return. I thought he was mad with cold, but it seems I was wrong. Hamish Mac-Brieve has finally returned—something I had not thought I would live to see." Then he pointed into the distance at Foinaven Castle. "Your father and brother finished it a few years after you left."

Hamish nodded. "I saw."

Amon inhaled. "I imagine Menzies MacMhathain and your father are letting go a sigh of relief now that you have come home."

"I doubt it. I intend to be merely a visitor. And a brief one at that," Hamish said through gritted teeth.

"I see," Amon said quietly.

The man said nothing more, but Hamish understood all too well what his old mentor was conveying. Menzies MacMhathain had been a strong leader and done much for his people. What he wanted most was to ensure his clan's prosperity and the well-being of his family. With only two girls and no sons, Laird MacMhathain's dying request was for Hamish to wed his eldest daughter, uniting the Mac-Brieve and MacMhathain clan through marriage. Hamish had agreed, never expecting that upon meeting Selah he would become completely captivated by her.

Hamish had believed the feeling mutual and for a short

while, his life had been idyllic. He and Selah had talked and laughed and even kissed on occasion. Never did Hamish suspect that her affections would shift to another when he left for a monthlong trip with his father to visit the neighboring clans. But upon his return, Selah had told him that she had fallen deeply in love with someone else—his brother, Robert.

Immediately Hamish had confronted Robert, who quickly denied any physical involvement and vowed nothing would come of his and Selah's unexpected friendship. Hamish had thought to put the matter aside, court Selah, and regain her love. But when he overheard her impassioned response to his brother's tear-filled good-bye, Hamish had known that Selah and he would never be happy together. So he had made the only honorable choice available to him. He released her from her promise. But in giving up Selah, Hamish had also relinquished his claim to Foinaven Castle and the possibility of becoming laird. Those privileges came not to the eldest MacBrieve but to whoever married MacMhathain's eldest daughter.

The decision also resulted in his giving up his home and the only life he ever knew.

While Hamish loved his brother, he had no taste for daily suffering. Hamish also knew that his father would never accept Robert and Selah's budding relationship if he remained at Foinaven. The pressure his father would apply on the two of them to comply with the original desires of Selah's father would increase until one of them capitulated. In the end, it would have left everyone miserable with no path to happiness. So he had left, hoping his father would understand, having been deeply in love with his mother. Through hardships, both had been known to say that as long as they had each other and their boys, nothing couldn't be overcome. Hopefully, his father saw that being laird was not enough to overcome the knowledge of being second in your wife's heart.

After joining the McTiernays, Hamish had sent word to Robert and his father that he was content and had found a clan to which he felt akin. He wished his brother well and encouraged his father to prepare Robert for the role as he had spent years grooming him.

"Are they still together?" Hamish asked, still keeping his gaze on Foinaven.

Amon nodded. "They are and very happy from all accounts, despite the years it took for your father to finally agree to their union. I'm not sure he ever was truly convinced that you were not returning."

"That was one of many reasons why I stayed away. He needed to be focused on guiding Robert in the ways to lead our clansmen."

Amon stayed quiet, refusing to say aloud that his father had not been able to alter Robert's unrealistic ideas of leadership. His brother had never been the fighter Hamish was. Oh, Robert could use a sword, but his nature was that of a pacifist. And so it was not until their father's dying breath did he relinquish leadership of the two clans to Robert.

Amon waved for his son to join them. "I hope you had not planned to reach Foinaven by nightfall," Amon stated.

Hamish shook his head. "Not in this weather or without light."

"Wise. This area has maimed many mounts from fools riding after sunset." When the young boy reached them, Amon smiled proudly and wrapped his arm around the child's shoulders. The boy's hair had more red, but he had the same prominent nose and deep-set blue eyes of his father. "This is my son Jothree, who I suspect is enormously eager to hear stories of the famed McTiernays and some of the battles you have seen. Come home with us. I don't have an extra bed, but the barn is warmer than it looks and if you still possess even a little bit of that charm and flattery you threw about in your youth, my wife, Lynnea, will make you a large, hot meal that would satisfy a king."

"Shelter and food? Such a temptation is hard to resist," Hamish replied, and then looked down at his muddy feet and legs. "But after three days' travel, I'm unfit company."

"There's a small stream that runs by the house. Bitterly cold but not for the fierce McTiernay warrior all the tall tales have you be," Amon said with undisguised mirth and a wink.

Hamish rolled his eyes and followed. Being reasonably clean again sounded heavenly—especially if the cold bath was followed by a warm fire and food. "Then my company you shall have," Hamish replied with a smile as he squatted down to look the young boy in the eye. "And how old are you, lad?"

"I'll be eight the day after Candlemas," came the exuberant reply. "My sister won't turn seven until a week later so I always get to be the oldest."

Hamish fought the pang in his heart. If he and Selah had married, they might have had a son Jothree's age. "'Tis very true, young Jothree. I remember how important it was when I was your age that my younger brother could never claim to be the same age as me," Hamish replied as he stood back up. He looked at Amon and said, "Lynnea, you say? I must meet this daring woman who convinced you to give up being a warrior to live a life on the land."

"And so you shall for she would skin me alive if I did not bring you to meet her. We live not far from here,"

Amon said, pointing to a large cottage nestled near some trees and a running brook.

Unable to eat another delicious bite, Hamish leaned back from the table and winked at the woman sitting across from him. "I can see why you married her, Amon. She is not only beautiful but an excellent cook," he said, patting his stomach.

Lynnea tucked a loose lock of her red-brown hair behind her ear and flashed him a wicked smile before glancing at her husband. "He is so charming, Amon, it is a wonder that not every woman Hamish runs into doesn't fall into his arms. I mean it," she added in a teasing tone, "if it wasn't for that beard, I'd almost be tempted to fall into them myself hearing such flattery." She stood and gave her husband a lingering peck on the cheek. "Almost tempted."

Hamish chuckled, delighted his old friend had found such an enjoyable wife. "Alas, a loss that I am sadly familiar with, and yet Lynnea, you let yourself be captured by this rough and weathered man. The reasons of which escape me."

Lynnea flashed her husband a knowing smile. Tall and possessing a full figure, she knew she was not a classic beauty like that of Lady MacBrieve, but she was pretty in her own way and Amon had eyes for no one else since he had met her. "I fear I cannot take credit for my fortune. For that, I blame my father. Amon followed me home one day, claiming something nonsensical about seeing to my safety. I thought my father would chase him away like he did all my other suitors—"

Amon sat up suddenly. "Other suitors?"

Lynnea waved her hand. "Aye, other suitors. Anyway, my father took one look at Amon and decided his strength and bullying ways would be excellent help around harvest." With a glint in her eye that would show even the most casual observer her love, she said, "And my father was right. You should hear Amon yell at the cattle. They obey no one better than he."

Amon chortled and grabbed her wrist as she tried to sashay by him, pulling her onto his lap. "Aye, it is true. But lucky for you, I just so happened was willing to do anything to make you mine."

Lynnea rolled her eyes, gave him a quick peck on the lips, and scooted off his lap. "Just as sappy as the day we wed."

Amon grinned at Hamish, who sat relaxed, enjoying their banter, and studied his onetime protégé. Hamish had grown in size and he carried himself with ease and confidence. And while he was kind and amiable, he no longer seemed to possess his boyhood aptitude for harmless flirtation. It was a shame for it had endeared all around him. What was left seemed to be a friendly, but very unemotional, calculating man. Only a fool would assume Hamish was merely a large soldier who could wield the sword. The man always had a keen mind and Amon wagered that it had only grown sharper in the company of the famed McTiernays.

Lynnea moved to gather the plates from the table. "I know that you want to muse over the past with Amon, but do not think I have forgotten that you have yet to tell me the real reason behind your leaving Foinaven and just why after twelve years you have decided to return."

Hamish looked at Amon and then back at Lynnea. "I doubt I could tell you anything you don't already know.

On those two particular topics, I'm sure the gossips have it right."

Amon slapped his knee and stood up. "Why don't we get out of the way, while they clean up," he said, and pointed to two worn chairs in a sitting area at the far end of the room upon which were Hamish's drying clothes. He had done his best to wash them, glad he had brought his new tartan and leine as a spare to wear until traveling garb had dried.

They moved the garments aside, sat down, and within seconds Jothree and his younger sister, Fulanna, joined them. Amon looked at them both and then pointed to their mother, hinting they should be helping. Lynnea quickly said, "It is fine, Amon. It is not often the children get to meet a great Highland warrior."

Amon compressed his lips and said with a huff, "I was a great Highland warrior once myself, *mo chroì*."

"Fine, then it's not often the children get the chance to speak with a legendary Highland warrior."

Hamish puffed out his chest with feigned pride. Amon rolled his eyes and grumbled, "If you knew him better, you wouldn't think him such a prize, Lynnea."

Jothree gave his father a look of disbelief then turned his puzzled expression toward Hamish. "Is it true what Da said? That when Laird MacMhathain died, he made you his heir."

Hamish glanced at Amon. "Your da says that, does he? Well, that is not exactly accurate. Being neighbors, Laird MacMhathain and my father knew and respected each other. He was good to his people and a strong warrior, but it was not until we fought alongside each other in support of William Wallace did our mutual admiration truly grow."

Jothree came close and sat down beside his little sister. "Da said he died fighting England."

Hamish nodded. The Battle of Roslin had been one of many in the fight to keep English rule and authority out of Scotland, but it was the one battle that had been most pivotal in Hamish's life. "It was a cold day and we had been fighting for two long days, but we were winning and that knowledge gave us strength to continue for a third and final day. Unfortunately, in the final hours, right before the English were defeated, Laird MacMhathain was struck with an arrow, right here," he said softly, pointing to a place near his heart. "MacMhathain had no male heir, so his dying request was for a MacBrieve to marry his eldest daughter. This would bind the MacMhathain and MacBrieve clans via matrimony and ensure his people would be protected. The merger would give both clans more power and security."

"But then why didn't you marry Lady MacBrieve?" Fulanna pressed.

Hamish took in a breath and then let go, deciding the truth was the best answer. "Because she loved my brother."

Unfortunately, the simplicity of the statement did not satisfy little Fulanna. Her thin arms were crossed and her dark brows were furrowed. It was clear to all in the room that she was about to unleash a slew of questions. Hamish sat ready for the oncoming barrage, fully prepared for what was about to happen after many encounters with Conor and Laurel's youngest and very inquisitive daughter.

Amon, however, decided to avoid the penetrating questions his six-year-old tended to ask and quickly picked Fulanna up to put her on his knee, thereby deflecting her line of thought. Changing the topic to one he was more interested in, he asked, "What do you know of Robert's commander, Ulrick?"

Hamish inhaled and leaned back in the chair, intertwining his fingers across his chest. "He's . . . why I'm here."

Amon's brows shot up. "So you know of him. By reputation or personally?"

Hamish frowned, deciding not to hide his ill feelings about the man. "Personally."

Ulrick had been a mercenary during the war and they had fought together a handful of times. The man was more than moderately talented with the sword and though not nearly as gifted in strategy as the McTiernays, he was capable. He also enjoyed intimidating those around him, not an unusual trait, and when appropriately applied, a useful one. But Ulrick was also the foulest form of man. Hamish had no proof, but he suspected that Ulrick was behind some of the horrors widows endured after the fighting was over. Given true power, however, Hamish believed the man could be very cruel and possibly dangerous.

Even before his life as a mercenary, Ulrick was loyal only to himself. Many a time, Hamish had witnessed him refusing to help another when it was not to his advantage. On the other hand, Ulrick seized upon anything that inflated his unhealthy dose of pride, including claiming victories that were earned by others. The combination of Ulrick's narcissism, cruel nature, and a constant longing for more power made the man unpredictable. One never knew what would set him off or how he would retaliate. And Hamish suspected his brother had come to understand this too late and was seeking a peaceful way to replace him as commander. If that was the expectation, Robert would soon be disappointed.

Hamish had no intentions of ever allowing anyone to use him in such a way. Plus, there was nothing that could entice him to submit to his brother. And he suspected Ulrick had little desire to keep the title of commander. Based on the little he remembered of the man, he suspected that Ulrick's real goal was to overthrow his brother and take his place as laird.

Amon gently pushed Fulanna off his knee and said, "Go help your mother. You too, Jothree." Both their faces and shoulders drooped, but when they saw their father was serious, neither argued and instead shuffled to the other side of the room where their mother was humming and working.

Once out of easy earshot, Amon sat back and said, "If you know Ulrick, then you know his motives are questionable. Why else would he take so many men with him if not to prevent someone like yourself from gaining their allegiance?"

"It also gives him the advantage of returning with an army."

Amon snorted. "One he's no doubt growing."

"The herald said he left to escort the new priest."

Amon snorted again, before he realized that Hamish was grinning underneath his bushy beard. "'Tis no priest Ulrick's seeking. The man's probably making promises to every mercenary in Scotland to get them to join him. He has no coin now, but he will if Robert does not have an army waiting that can stop him."

Hamish heard the hint but said nothing.

Disliking the silent response, Amon continued. "I'm not sure how a visit from you alone will end Ulrick's aspirations. So I am assuming Laird McTiernay is willing to help."

Hamish shrugged. "He offered."

Amon's brows drew downward in a frown when Hamish said no more. "And how long will it take McTiernay to rally his men and provide aid?" Amon pressed. "Or are they here already, taking shelter in the mountains?"

For several seconds, Hamish did not answer. For most clans, it would take some time to mobilize and equip men for battle with arms and food. Conor, however, always had a couple hundred soldiers ready to fight and they could live off the land regardless of the time of year. But Hamish had no right to request Conor to lend him his men. McTiernays fought for McTiernays or their allies . . . not another guardsman who was born a MacBrieve. But even if bringing a few dozen McTiernay soldiers was the solution, the result would only be temporary. Ulrick would only return when they left. And Hamish would have thought Amon to have known that.

Hamish took in a deep breath and shook his head. "None rode with me nor do I have intentions to ask for Conor for his help."

Amon studied Hamish and then grinned. "Fine by me as this situation requires not a McTiernay army, but McTiernay ingenuity." Scooting to the edge of his chair, he rested his elbows on his knees and leaned closer. "You are too much like your father. You would not be here if you did not have a plan."

Hamish twitched his lips. Amon was right. He was like his father, plus he had lived with McTiernays too long to have come without at least one idea. "More likely two or three plans."

Amon shook his head, but his smile only grew. "Are you willing to share them?"

Hamish snorted. "With you. Only you, though. But be

careful, you might just be playing a role in one or two of them."

Amon threw up his arms and then with a nod toward his wife, said, "I'm willing but doubt I can be of any help now that I'm just a farmer."

"I cannot see you giving up the sword for a woman. Even one as lovely and kind as Lynnea."

Amon's jaw tensed. "What Lynnea said earlier was true. I fell in love with her and her father did desire my help with the land as she was his only child. By marrying her, I inherited all that he had when he passed. But that had nothing to do with why I was forced to give up the life of being a warrior and Robert's second-in-command."

Amon had Hamish's full attention. "Forced? I would not think that was possible."

"I am not alone," Amon said defensively. "Soon after Ulrick was named commander, none of your father's trusted guard remained for very long. Ulrick intentionally alienated Robert's loyalty, stating that men like me who desired to train and remain vigilant sought only war, not peace," he scoffed, and Hamish knew why.

Almost every man who had experienced the horrors of battle treasured peace above all things. They knew what sacrifices it took for their families to have that coveted peace in their lives. "Most of your father's men litter the hills, away from Foinaven, trying to make a living off the land and keep their family fed."

Hamish was somewhat shocked by what Amon was saying. "If my brother still possesses the soft heart he had in his youth, there is no way he would have allowed Ulrick to force you or anyone else from their position, even if it was as part of the army."

"Situation forced us to leave. Robert gave no order, but he did not try to stop us either."

Hamish blinked, letting what Amon told him sink in. "Maybe Robert has changed more than I thought."

Amon shook his head and stood up to get some mead. Grabbing two mugs, he poured the honey wine into the cups and handed one to Hamish. "Robert has not changed. Your brother's heart is the kind, conciliatory one as you remember, maybe even more so. Just look around tomorrow. You will see the numbers around Foinaven have grown enormously because of it. He accepts every clan and any Highlander who wishes to leech off the castle's protection. How else do you think we ended up with Ulrick?"

"I must admit I was wondering. I would have thought Robert to put you or someone like yourself as commander, not an outsider."

"Your brother cannot turn away a soul. They might not have anything to give in return and yet he stretches out a welcoming hand," Amon stated, waving his arm about to emphasize his point. "It was not too bad, until a couple years ago. The last group was fairly unruly and refused to subscribe to clan rules. But instead of asking me to take my men and kick them off our lands, Robert decided to follow Ulrick's advice and make him a co-commander, thinking that would elicit their loyalty."

Fool, Hamish thought, wishing he did not have his beard as he rubbed his jaw trying to relieve an itch. It was warm and served its purpose, but sometimes, it could be annoying and uncomfortable.

Amon took a deep breath for control, then let it escape slowly. "It's not that I don't like Robert. *Mo chreach*, everyone likes both him and Lady MacBrieve. But that does not make him a capable leader."

"He must have some support from the people. Without it, a laird has no power. So if Robert's still in charge,

I have to assume he is leading in a way that most people desire, even if it is not to your or my preference."

"Mayhap. But I would argue people support what is easy and enables them to be lazy. Robert believes his position gives him loyalty, when in reality it gives him none. People will turn on him the moment they realize that his promises of security are empty. Right now they are under the illusion that Ulrick is strong, and therefore they are secure. But they don't know Ulrick. Those like myself who were in your father's guard, however, quickly understood Ulrick's aspirations for power would not be satisfied. Our combined clan is large, but the army is far from powerful and it would never be strong under Robert's leadership. It was not long before Ulrick realized that there were several of us who would not stand by and let him take advantage of Robert's nature. So he carefully made it impossible for us to remain. One by one he maneuvered good men into leaving until I had no choice but to leave myself. And while I have no proof, I have no doubt that when Ulrick returns, your brother's days of being in charge of this clan will be limited. Unless, that is, you know of a way to prevent him from doing so."

Hamish studied his old comrade for several seconds, thinking it very opportune they had met up before his arrival. He believed Amon, but what his old mentor had revealed meant the men who he knew to be loyal to his father were no longer near Foinaven, let alone part of the army. Such information changed what he was going to do, but not necessarily for the worse.

"I have no intentions of letting Ulrick return to Foinaven in any permanent capacity. I know the man and what he is capable of," Hamish confirmed out loud. Seeing the hopeful demeanor surge back into Amon, Hamish quickly added, "I'm here this time to make sure Robert understands how this situation came about and to give my birth clan a chance to rectify its mistakes in supporting such a man. But whatever remedy I choose to use against Ulrick will not keep another man like him from having the same aspirations. If Robert continues to lead in a way that jeopardizes his position with this clan, then he and this clan will find itself in jeopardy once again. And if that happens, I will not come nor will I feel guilty about staying away."

"I guess any hopes that your plan includes bolstering Robert's leadership style are unlikely."

Hamish's jaw tightened. "More than unlikely. Unrealistic."

Amon nodded in understanding. "Well, then, by the time a similar situation arises, I'll have to pray that the clan can come together, understand that a benevolent leader is not necessarily a good one, and do what it must." Amon sat back and blew out a long sigh. "Meanwhile, tell me of your plan and I hope it takes in consideration Robert's leadership style. Your brother won't be eager to support any plan that includes arms."

"I assume from your meaning Robert still believes talking with one's enemy is the best method to elicit cooperation."

Amon nodded. "Aye. Personally, I like the idea of applying peaceable means to solve disputes. Costs less and involves no bloodshed. But only a fool talks without the willingness and the ability to fight. We have been fortunate since your father's death and many clansmen have come to actually believe Robert's benign approach works. When Ulrick returns, it is going to become clear that is not the case. Such weakness is going to be exploited. Even from those Robert considers friends and allies," Amon finished, unable to suppress the sneer in his voice.

"No allies, then?"

Amon shook his head. "Not ones that can be relied on.

The relationships haven't been cultivated since the time of your father."

Hamish assumed as much and would have been surprised if any alliance still existed for what could Robert offer that would entice a powerful laird into an alliance?

"The only nearby ally worth having would be the Mackays," Amon continued, "and they are more apt to becoming an enemy."

Hamish grimaced. He had never met Laird Mackay, but the man was reported to be ruthless, powerful, and slow to trust anyone. An easily understood position based on their clan's history. Mackay was not someone anyone wanted as a potential threat. Hamish needed to address Ulrick quickly before word spread of irresolute leadership at Foinaven.

"Well, what you have imparted does change things a bit, but I believe for the better. The only thing I am concerned about is time."

Amon tapped his steepled fingers and stared at the ceiling as he listened to Hamish go over his plan. "Could work. Definitely not without your involvement, but with your name and reputation . . . it might. It does need time to put it together though and Ulrick's return is hard to predict. He could be back next week or next month."

Hamish caught his friend's eye and gave him an assured shake of the head. "Not as hard to predict as you would think."

"How so?"

Hamish propped his right leg on his left knee and said, "The mercenaries Ulrick is seeking live where the money and action is. That's along Scotland's southern border. It'll take time to find and then convince them to ride so far north on only the promise of getting paid."

Amon finished his drink. "The one way your brother was identical to your father was money. Both held incredibly tight to their purse. So the money Ulrick is promising exists. Convincing mercenaries to leave their life temporarily for easy coin and a better bed during the winter months may not be difficult."

"True, but also consider what time of year it is and what you would do if you were Ulrick."

Amon's blue eyes narrowed for a moment and then widened. "I'm an idiot. You are right. We *do* know when the bastard intends to be back." The ride to the Lowlands to gather mercenary support that live near the border and return would take a little less than a month in the winter. More if the weather was bad, less if the weather was good.

"Candlemas."

Amon nodded. The holiday took place two days into February and celebrated the presentation of Jesus. It also marked the beginning of the next planting season. "'Tis not a lot of time for what you plan to do. But it's enough."

Hamish smiled and downed the contents of his mug, lifting it so that Amon could pour more mead into it. "Who knows? It might even be a little fun."

Amon nodded. "The most fun I will have had in some time."

Chapter Three

Foinaven Castle

Selah peered over her sister's shoulder and out the window to the busy courtyard below. She softly clicked her tongue. "The crowds on market day have grown the past few months. Have they not? I'm surprised anyone can find what they are looking for." She moved back to her chair to resume her needlepoint.

Mairead smiled inwardly. Her sister would never outright say that she was wasting her time by trying to find a single person in the packed courtyard, but that is what she had meant. To all who met her, Selah was the kindest of souls, never having a reproach or an ill thought about anyone or anything. And while it was true that her sister was incapable of hurting anyone intentionally, to assume she was incapable of faultfinding was a serious misjudgment, for Selah harbored the same critical thoughts as anyone. She was just a master at repressing and rephrasing her honest opinion. It was the same with her husband, Robert, who led this motley band of clansmen. Neither of them could outright say a harsh word to someone, even if they had earned their scorn and disapproval.

One just had to look at Selah to know that Mairead was not the only one anticipating Hamish's arrival. Her sister had bound hair and dressed herself as a properly married woman. Her barbette was neatly tucked around her chin and pinned at the top of her head, the ends hidden under her prettiest filet. She was not wearing a veil, but one only had to glance at her to know her marital status.

Mairead thought the ensemble incredibly restrictive and completely unnecessary. When she married, nothing would get her to wear one of those headdresses. Everyone had seen her hair either loose or in a simple braid for years. The idea that marriage required noblewomen to hide their hair made no sense and she would refuse to succumb to such nonsense. Especially when it meant constant discomfort.

A moment later Mairead felt a twinge in her neck due to the weight of the complicated braid pulled into an intricate knot. Instantly she felt regret at being such a hypocrite and reached up to rub her neck. "You do not have to wait with me, Selah."

"I do not mind."

Mairead gave her older sister a knowing look. "You do not fool me. You followed me in here and have done little but needle me about looking out the window, while sneaking a peek yourself. Your actions only prove your interest in whether Hamish has arrived is just as great as mine. I'm just not making you admit it out loud," Mairead said saucily.

Eight years separated them in age and because their mother died of illness a year after their father, Selah had been her guardian, mentor, and counselor since she was eleven. She had taught Mairead all she knew on what it was to be a woman, a friend, and someday a wife. Her efforts were appreciated and many of the lessons taken to heart, but their personalities were too dissimilar for Mairead to adhere to—or even believe in—all the advice Selah continually bestowed.

While her sister was predisposed to be unusually compassionate, Mairead was inclined to be candid. Sometimes Selah hinted that she might be a little too honest. If she was, Mairead blamed Selah and her husband, Robert. Growing up constantly trying to interpret what they truly thought had been tiresome. Mairead wanted no one to misinterpret her opinion.

"I do not know what you mean. I only came to keep you company while little Rab is napping. He rose rather early this morning," Selah replied, neither confirming nor denying her anticipation.

Mairead grimaced and quickly turned away before Selah could see. Her five-year-old nephew was not the only one who had been awakened by his father's hacking cough. All in the keep had been. "How is Robert doing?"

"Resting finally," Selah said with a sigh, trying not to sound worried. "I just pray that he will stay in bed this year until it passes."

Mairead nodded and looked back out the window at the busy courtyard below. Every year, her sister's husband became ill when the cold weather came. This year had been no different. The day after Epiphany, Robert worked with a sore throat, and as expected a couple days later, he had a hacking cough and found it difficult to breathe. It usually lasted two or three weeks—if he rested—and then he would be well again until the next year.

"Does the constant drumming help you search?" Selah asked as she forcefully plunged her needle down into the cloth, signaling that the noise irritated her.

Mairead gripped the side of the window frame to still

her fingers. "The sun has been up for nearly three hours and it is almost time for the midday meal."

"And how is that relevant to your search?"

Mairead glanced back over her shoulder with a scowl. "It means that Hamish should have arrived by now. I could have ridden to Amon's and returned twice by now."

Selah shrugged. "Perhaps Davros only thought he saw Hamish. He has never actually met Robert's brother. It could have been someone else entering Amon's home last night."

Mairead knew Selah was needling her. "Davros has the eyesight of one of his falcons and he said the man had the same height and coloring as Robert. He was also on horseback, had been traveling, and was carrying a sword. It *was* Hamish," Mairead exerted. Then with a touch of cynicism, she added, "Which also means your and Robert's ridiculous plan to get his brother to come home worked."

Selah bristled. "I completely support my husband's decision on what to do concerning his brother," she said crisply, a clear hint that she thought Mairead's condemnation a step too far.

Mairead rolled her eyes. She did not want to argue with Selah. Neither did she want to live with the results of her inept brother-in-law's actions. However, his latest plea to have Hamish return home was one that she not only secretly supported but also had prayed for. When the herald had returned letting them know that Hamish had sent him ahead to warn them of his arrival, her heart had soared. Not with joy, but relief. For nothing short of Hamish and his army could save them all from a horrible fate.

Mairead tilted her head to lean against the window frame and continued to study the busy courtyard. In the early morning hours, as many temporary structures that could fit within the castle walls had been erected. It seemed like the whole village had come to Foinaven to trade, barter, and buy goods. The crowds were now so thick it made it difficult to identify those whom she knew very well, let alone a man she had not seen in years.

Mairead had been only ten when Hamish had decided to leave Foinaven, his family, and his claim to lead the newly combined MacBrieve/MacMhathain clan. But the years had not erased her memory of him or the kindness he had shown her. It had been Hamish who had told her of her father's death. He had taken her out and shown her how to skip stones along the water, answering all her questions even though her mother thought ten years old was too young to understand such loss. The following year, when her mother passed away, it was the memory of his words she had used for comfort and strength.

Hamish had told Mairead to stop trying to imitate her sister and just enjoy being the person she was. That the light-colored freckles sprinkled along her nose and cheeks made her appear more interesting, and her propensity for "unnecessary truthfulness" would someday be appreciated by a self-reliant man, who would find the trait far more appealing than meekness. She had known that what he said at the time had been just to make her feel better, but nevertheless, she had clung to his words throughout the years, especially in periods of self-doubt.

Hamish had been huge and strong, able to make anyone who threatened him or those he loved tremble with fear. He had shown her that men were capable of both strength and kindness.

Then he had left, only to never come back. And despite her young age, she had understood why.

Throughout the years, tidbits about Hamish trickled in

from time to time. Traveling merchants always brought news of the larger clans—the McTiernays in particular—knowing Robert's interest. The fact that Hamish remained unwed after twelve years mystified her sister and brother-in-law. But not Mairead.

It was clear part of Hamish still loved Selah. Nothing else explained both his prolonged absence and his remaining a bachelor for so long. It also meant that Hamish would not stay but leave as soon as he could—and for the very same reason he had departed more than a decade ago.

All this Mairead understood and accepted as inevitable. But it did not matter, for Hamish was bringing with him hope and the chance to actually save not just the clan, but herself.

"I think I might go down there," Mairead said, and lifted her head off the windowsill. When she did, several dark gold strands of the intricate weave along the back of her nape got caught on a crevice and were pulled free. "This is why it is pointless for me to do my hair!" she groused. "I spent a good hour in a chair this morning letting Annot yank on my scalp for nothing. I should have just tied it back like I always do."

Seeing Mairead reach up to take the whole thing down, Selah jumped to her feet and exclaimed, "Stop! It is not that bad. Give me a chance to fix it before you do something rash."

Mairead ignored her sister and kept working at the tresses until they were free. She swung her head back and forth, feeling relief now that the heavy mass was loose about her shoulders.

"Come here," Selah said, pointing to the chair she had just occupied.

Mairead's eyes narrowed with distrust. "It's too uncomfortable and you and I both know that it would not stay.

Something would cause it to come down again. My hair is impossible. I've accepted it. So should you."

"At least sit and let me brush it out. Right now it is a mess and you would never have allowed Annot near your hair this morning if you were so disinterested in your appearance."

Mairead pursed her lips, then pushed Selah's needlework aside and sat down. Immediately Selah retrieved a brush and began to fuss. "Your hair is so beautiful. It's such a rich color and seems to shine on its own. Even when you leave it down, as it is now, you could attract any man you wanted . . . if you but tried."

Normally Mairead would have mocked the idea. Mostly because catching a man's eye had never been an issue, though Mairead sometimes wondered how many of the men who had sought her affections actually liked her, or just sought what a marriage to her might give them. It was an immaterial point as she had never met anyone whom she could share what her sister had with Robert— true love.

"I have no desire in attracting a man," Mairead lied, unwilling to answer the questions to follow if her sister suspected the truth.

Selah scoffed. "You're allowing me to brush your hair and I noticed that right after Davros told us that he saw Hamish entering Amon's last night, you went and found Annot to have her work on your hair. And you changed into your most flattering gown."

Feeling caught, Mairead licked her lips. She still refused to admit to her sister the real nature of her intentions. Selah could never know the threat Ulrick had made just before he left. She would feel responsible to do something and whatever conciliatory thing Robert and she devised, Mairead was positive it would only make things worse.

Though she hated it, Mairead had no choice. She had to continue to lie. "It is not what you are thinking, Selah. I simply wanted to look my best for Robert's sake as well as yours when Hamish arrived."

Mairead looked down to avoid looking at her sister and smoothed out the gown. She remembered vividly the response she got the last time she wore it. That night and the week after, she had received much male attention— even a couple offers of marriage. They had not been the first to seek her hand, nor had they been her last. If marriage were all it took to save her, there was always a widower in the need of a mother for his children.

No, the man she married could not just be anyone. He had to be someone whom Ulrick would be afraid of. And if this gown she was wearing could still elicit the same power of appeal, that someone would be arriving today.

The ankle-length chainse was a shimmering gold and had a rich green-colored, knee-length bliaut over it that brought out the color of her eyes. A band of intricate needlework circled the long sleeves of the tunic. The golden color enhanced the tawny strands of her hair and complemented her olive skin tone, but the cut also highlighted her curvaceous figure—which made Mairead feel at unease.

She and Selah were undoubtedly sisters. Both were of the same height, possessed golden brown hair and hazel eyes, but where Selah's skin was flawless, Mairead had freckles scattered along her nose and cheeks. Where Selah's hair was straight, Mairead's was wild and untamable, but at least she could braid it down her back. Her shapeliness, however, was impossible to disguise. It was the one thing that kept anyone from mistaking one from the other—even at a distance. Where Selah's thin frame made her appear delicate and graceful, Mairead possessed a much fuller figure, with curves and breasts that were forever getting in the way.

"I would not be surprised if one of Hamish's men took one look at you and spirited you away from Foinaven."

"Selah . . ." Mairead said hesitantly.

Selah shook her head. "I'm in earnest. In this dress, you are going to catch the eye of every man coming with Hamish. It is possible that one of them might catch yours as well," Selah said as she continued to brush the wayward strands.

Mairead sat completely still, wondering if she was really that transparent.

"If it happens, just remember to charm the man a little, and I promise he will be yours," Selah encouraged. "It only took a few days with Robert to know he was my destiny. When the right man comes along, you will know it too. Don't resist it, little sister. I want you to be happy and this might be your chance."

Mairead blinked. How could she be so blind? Was this the reason behind Robert's insane idea to send Ulrick off and cause their clan to be so vulnerable? To get Hamish to return with eligible men for Mairead to marry? It was ludicrous, but then so was sending off the majority of one's army to fetch a priest.

Pride shouted for her to refuse to participate. She would marry someday, but on her terms and not for convenience. She wanted someone she could trust. Someone she could rely on to be dependable and make hard decisions and stand behind them. She wanted someone she did not have to guide and encourage or worry if a strongly worded phrase would cause them to retreat. She wanted someone she could be proud of, whom she could support and love. In return, she wanted to be appreciated and respected. Most of all she wanted what Selah had with Robert. A partner who understood and loved her and someone she loved in return.

But that dream was not to be and her pride had to accept that destiny had other plans. If anything, she was fortunate that Selah and Robert had created this opportunity. She might have wanted a man to love, but what she needed was a man who lived far away. Such as a man who lived with the McTiernays.

Mairead started to squirm and Selah reached out to clutch the sides of her face to keep her still. Mairead sighed with resignation as she felt the familiar tugs on her scalp. Selah was braiding her hair. Mairead was shocked when less than a handful of minutes later, her sister took a step back.

"There," Selah said, and smiled at her handiwork. "I just brought the sides back to allow everyone see your lovely face. Not a man in sight could resist you."

Mairead patted the back of her hair. Two braids on each side were tied together allowing her hair to fall in waves down her back. "More than likely, the only males who'll find me irresistible will be the merchants, which makes a pretty gown and fixing my hair a waste of time. They would think I was attractive with matted hair and rotten teeth."

Selah ignored her. And pulled free one small lock from one of the braids so that it fell down the side of her cheek. "Even better."

Mairead darted her eyes upward, still unconvinced. "I'm just going down to talk with Davros, Selah. And he cares not about my hair." And before Selah could reply, Mairead escaped to the hall. Closing her eyes, she leaned against the closed door, finally free to feel the fear she felt inside.

Taking a deep breath, she began her descent, reminding herself that all she needed to find was one man in Hamish's army willing to marry her and take her back with him.

Mairead suddenly stopped her descent. Her thinking had been completely wrong.

Oh, she was right about having to let her dream of marrying for true love go, but that was not the only one she had. There were others—one of which she had given up on. She did not have to leave her beloved home and family. She could stay at Foinaven and even help ensure her family remained at its head.

All she needed was a Highland warrior from a powerful Highland clan. Several such men would be arriving with Hamish. How hard could it be to convince one of them to marry her?

Hamish tried to think of another song—any chant or verse—to replace the one he had been humming all morning. He did not know the words, but little Fulanna had been singing it this morning and the haunting melody refused to stop plaguing his thoughts.

He gazed up ahead. Foinaven was not far now and he soon would be within its walls. His stomach growled reminding him that it was at least an hour, probably more like two, past the time for midday meal. Normally he would have stopped to eat, but he was already much later in arriving than he had intended.

He and Amon had left early in the morning to meet with several of the men who used to be part of his father's

guard. Their discussions had been enlightening and only
supported what Amon had told him the night before. They
had spoken of their frustrations with Ulrick and his tactics
and many offered suggestions, most of which included
some variation of sending for help from the McTiernays
and permanently taking over as commander. Hamish had
made it abundantly clear that he refused to entertain any
ideas of this nature.

Living with the McTiernays, Hamish had learned to
always have many options when walking into a situation.
He may have come north alone, but he had not come
devoid of ideas. He was here to free his brother from
Ulrick's clutches and give his clansmen a chance at security. Afterward, it would be their responsibility to ensure
this one-time-only opportunity was not wasted. Amon
agreed with Hamish's desire to keep his plan confiden-
tial while secretly helping it come to fruition until the time
came to let others know.

Hamish approached the castle and paused to stare
incredulously at the point of entry through Foinaven's curtain wall. The stone walls themselves were thick, solid,
and extremely well built. They were tall and formidable
and Hamish would have been impressed if the protection
they provided was not completely negated by a massive
weakness—two large wooden doors that were currently
wide open, allowing anyone entry. There was no barbican,
no portcullis, not even a gatehouse that could effectively
keep anyone inside safe from those outside.

Hamish let go a deep sigh as people stepped aside to
avoid him as they moved freely in and out of the castle.
Such defense structures were meaningless if throngs of
people were allowed to come and go inside at will.
Hamish wondered at the point of having a castle, let alone

an expensive stone one, with such a weakness. He found it difficult to believe his father would have agreed to such a key requirement to the castle's security.

Hamish gave a small shake to his head and slid off his horse. The ground was soft from last night's rain and hissed a squishy sound. It was immediately followed by the feel of cold mud oozing between the seams of his shoes and along his toes. He looked down and grimaced. He was already filthy from the morning's activities, but he had been able to keep his feet somewhat dry until now.

This time of year meant rain, which in turn meant mud and a choice of a daily bath or dirty feet at night. He was tired of the latter and the feeling of sludge between his toes was something he particularly disliked. Luckily, at Foinaven he could replace a frigid dip in the river with a bath of heated water in a fire-warmed room. It was probably the only perk he would actually enjoy while at Foinaven.

Giving a small tug on the reins, he led his horse through the castle entry and began to weave his way toward the stables. The stable boy spied him and after several seconds finally ambled his way over to get the horse.

Hamish again told himself to hold his tongue—that any lack of responsiveness regarding Robert's staff was not of any importance to him. "Is the courtyard always this crowded?" he asked the lad.

The stable boy scrunched his nose in confusion. "It's market day," he grunted, and took the reins Hamish was extending. The bandy-legged lad was older than Hamish originally thought. He had long, straggly, ginger hair and bloodshot eyes, which indicated that his lack of speed was not due to lack of will or pride but lack of sleep.

Hamish untied his saddle bags, swung them over his shoulder, and pulled free his sword. "Get started on cleaning my horse and giving him something to eat. After I get something to douse my own hunger, I'll come back to help you."

Red-streaked eyes stared incredulously at Hamish for a minute, but then realizing that he was serious, the young man straightened his back and produced a wary half smile. "Aye, sir."

"Your name?"

"My name?" the lad asked as if no one had ever done so before. "It's, uh, Adiran."

Hamish turned to leave. "Feed my horse first, Adiran," he said over his shoulder. He knew the boy did not really believe he would return, and Hamish doubted the young boy had the energy to clean and attend to his horse properly.

Stepping back into the bustling, overly packed court-yard, Hamish looked up into the sky and flexed his foot. The mud between the toes of his left foot included small pebbles, which were extremely annoying. It looked like the clouds were going to pass, taking with them the possibility of rain—at least for the next several hours. Others must have realized it as well for it seemed all in the vicinity had come to haggle and buy and sell. There was very little room to maneuver in the crowded bailey, making it difficult to get back to where the kitchens were located, assuming they were still at the north end adjacent to the great hall. There Hamish hoped he could find not just food, but also the chance to remove a layer or two of grime from his body.

The layout of Foinaven looked to be unchanged since when he left. Its rugged inland landscape was formed from isolated sandstone peaks forcing the castle walls to conform to the undulations of the hill. The flattest parts of land, and therefore easiest to build large structures, were against the northern and western walls. That fact had not changed in twelve years. What had was the increased number of structures, the replacement of wood with stone, and the sheer number of people both in and outside of its walls.

Hamish began to maneuver his way through the throng, taking full advantage of his size and height to motivate people into moving out of his way. All types of merchants seemed eager to sell or barter every type of good from leather, woven material, candles, soap, stuff for horses, to tools for work or home. Hamish even spied several people next to a cart looking at what appeared to be basic furniture. His stomach, however, was far more interested in finding good food.

Dried meat was all around him, but after days of such fare, he wanted something different. His nose was telling him that somewhere nearby was fresh bread. His stomach rumbled again and he was about to stop and ask just who was selling the bread, when a small stall caught his attention.

Along the stall's corner wall hung leathers, tools, and various items used to erect the temporary structure. An L-shape bench completed the merchant's stand. Propped into a hole at the corner and each end was a long, thick stick that stood three feet into the air. A thin rope connected the sticks, upon which hung sparrows, a couple of herons, a rabbit, and one very large goose. The merchant was most likely an archer or a falconer, but he was also married, for small game and fowl were not all he sold. Three loaves of bread were on the bench, just below the trussed birds. And more important, they smelled fresh and their golden crusts proved they were not overbaked. But the best indication of their quality was the number of spaces between the loaves. Several had already been sold.

Hamish readjusted the bags on his shoulder and stepped

sideways to avoid being clobbered by two people jostling a barrel down the narrow path. He was about to make his way to the merchant when he stopped cold. The falconer was not alone. He was talking to a woman, who was leaning over the bench, giving Hamish the perfect view of the lower half of her profile. Suddenly food was the lesser of things his body craved.

Hamish twitched his lips, surprised at the unexpected jolt of desire. It had been a long time since he had craved a woman's touch and he had truly begun to wonder if he ever would again. Maybe time did eventually heal all wounds. Then again, maybe time had nothing to do with it. Hamish could not recall ever seeing a female body with luscious curves so perfectly proportioned.

Angled the way she was, it was hard to guess her height, but envisioning the long legs hidden beneath her bliaut, he suspected she was slightly taller than average. Hamish flexed his fingers as he watched the play of the green gown over her curved buttocks as she swung her hips slightly back and forth. Unlike tall females who possessed a thin, willowy shape, the lady before him had breasts and hips ample enough for a man to thoroughly enjoy. If a pretty face and a quick mind came with that shapely body, she would be his vision of a perfect woman.

Mo chreach! What was wrong with him? Of course it would be *here*, at Foinaven of all places, for his body suddenly to return to life and demand attention. Hamish took in a deep breath and exhaled, reminding himself that the most he had time for was to learn the woman's name. He certainly was not going to remain long enough for anything more.

Hamish closed his eyes and fought to regain control. He had spent months without a woman and his body could wait another few more weeks until he was back home to seek a female's company. Besides, had he not painfully learned that women—especially the kind who looked that good from the back—were nothing but trouble?

He opened his eyes just as a ray of rare sunlight caught her dark gold hair as it fell down her back in loose waves. Unbound meant she was most likely unwed and available. Hamish looked up to the sky. He had long suspected God was not vengeful or fearsome as some priests would have their followers believe, but instead quite mischievous. He was certainly having fun now. The woman probably had a high-pitched voice that could make vultures fly away in terror.

Feeling somewhat barely back in control, Hamish walked toward the merchant, trying unsuccessfully to keep his eyes from looking at the delicate arch of the woman's back. The thought of her sinful curves and how they moved was going to keep him awake tonight, and probably a few others.

Hamish blinked as his toe came into contact with something. He righted himself just in time, barely avoiding stepping on a young girl sitting just underneath the falconer's bench with her legs outstretched. Seeing him and how he almost crushed her limbs, the child pulled them up to her chest and hugged them. Her huge, fear-filled brown eyes traveled slowly up Hamish's body, taking in the large weapon in his hand, until they met his green ones. He smiled, but her expression remained unchanged as she stared at him. Hamish realized why and could almost hear Laurel yell at him to shave his beard.

He put away his sword and then winked at the child, pointing at the colored pebbles she had dropped near her leg. The girl glanced down and, seeing the rocks, grabbed them in her hands. Within a couple of seconds, she forgot he was even there and began to play, with her legs once again stretched out to hamper those walking by.

Hamish slightly parted two of the game birds so he could gain the falconer's attention, and hopefully sneak a look at the woman. Unfortunately, the man was standing right in the line of view. Hamish bit his bottom lip and fought the temptation to move down a little. Why let reality disturb the fantasy? He didn't need to know she had an overly large pug nose between two wide-set uneven eyes.

Hamish was about to ask the man about the bread, but before he could utter a word, the falconer said, "I tell you I have not seen Hamish within these castle gates." The man's tone was weary as if he had given the same answer several times that day.

"Thanks, Davros, but if you do see him, please let me know." Hamish felt his jaw drop. Her voice was just as lovely as her figure. Rather than drive men away, it had a lilting quality that could lure a man's soul and more astonishingly, she had been looking for him. "Oh, and tell your lovely wife I said hello and hope to see her soon."

"I'll tell her, and I'll also tell her about you being so gussied up today. Jeán'll be interested in knowing why. Though it's not hard to guess."

Hamish heard a fake gasp of shock. "Davros, I have no idea what you are talking about. 'Tis a dress I have not worn in some time, but all else needed to be washed," she said emphatically, but Hamish could tell the merchant did not believe a word. Neither did he.

Hamish closed his eyes. Their conversation indicated she was indeed not married, and hoping, of all things, to attract his attention.

"Can I help you?"

Hamish reopened his eyes as the merchant slid the birds farther apart on the string. Brilliant blue eyes spied him and immediately sparkled with recognition. Hamish, on the other hand, could not ever remember seeing the man before.

The falconer was on the short side, but his hands were large and calloused and looked like they belonged on a man much larger. The wrinkles on his face were evidence of hours squinting and made him look much older than Hamish suspected he actually was. With the exception of a few gray strands near his temples, the man's hair was still a vibrant jet black, hinting at his true age.

Hamish pushed forward a coin and glanced to see if the woman had left. She had not, but God definitely had a sense of humor, for she had turned around and was now leaning back on the makeshift counter looking out at the crowd. "I was hoping to buy a loaf."

The man took the coin and with a chuckle said, "Your eyes are not on the bread."

Hamish raised his gaze to study the man. Seeing only friendliness reflected in the man's blue eyes, he returned the falconer's smile. "'Tis bread I'm wanting, but I'll admit that I cannot imagine it being as tasty as that."

Davros picked up a loaf and handed it to Hamish. "Take the bread, but beware. That over there," he said, pointing to Mairead with his thumb over his shoulder, "may look like a sweet morsel, but most find her to be a bit sour."

Hamish took the bread and immediately pulled off a piece. "Perhaps she's just been waiting for some sweet words and a pair of strong arms, friend," he said, popping it into his mouth.

Immediately the woman's back went rigid. She then

stood straight up, indicating she had not only heard but also understood Hamish's comment. He expected her to quickly walk away, but instead, she turned the corner to address him face-to-face. Hamish looked at the falconer. The man just grinned and gave him a shrug that said he had given him fair warning.

Hamish turned and all thoughts of appeasing flattery vanished with nothing in their place. He should have known. He could practically hear God's laughter. Of course she would be gorgeous. The one time not a single McTiernay was within miles to challenge him for a beautiful woman's attentions would be here at Foinaven. A place he was soon to leave and never return to again. And not even the most beautiful woman he had ever seen was going to change that.

It also did not seem to matter what he felt about her because it was clear she did not return his sentiments.

When she had turned the corner, the woman had her finger up and her mouth was open, no doubt in preparation to release a scathing comment. However, one look at him had stopped her.

She finally closed her mouth and lowered her hand. Hamish could tell the moment she remembered just why she had turned to face him. Her hands curled into fists, which she placed on her hips. "Why is it that men desire their women to be attractive but never think to make themselves more appealing in return? Do you think we are so desperate that it only takes a few sweet words for us to fall into a pair of strong—*and filthy*—arms?"

Hamish opened his mouth to reply, but she waved a finger to stop him. "Do not bother to speak. I would not be able to hear a word you say. I am too distracted by that nest you are wearing on your chin. It looks like it has been out in the rain and the snow for the past two months and I can smell you from here."

Instead of being affronted, Hamish leaned back and started to laugh. The woman had spirit. "True, but unlike you, I am not aiming to catch another's eye." He let his eyes travel down her form and back up, blatant appreciation shining in their green depths. "In my experience, when a woman puts on her finest gown, she has one goal. She is out to catch a man."

Davros coughed and with a chortle said, "He has a point." Mairead turned her head and glared at him. Davros just shrugged. "But in your case, it'll take more than a dress."

Hamish found the merchant's assessment hard to believe and was about to say so when the woman hissed, "I do not need a dress to find a man to marry."

Hamish smirked and waggled his eyebrows. "Probably not, but I suspect you are hoping it will help capture a certain man's attention."

Mairead's hazel eyes shot wide open and Hamish knew he had assessed the situation correctly. She took a step forward. Her eyes crinkled as she studied him, which surprisingly accentuated her other facial features. Next time Father Lanaghly preached about how God loved everyone and they were all created equally, Hamish fully intended to relay the cruelty of this moment. He may have been visually disappointing to Mairead, but he could not say the same about her.

She did not possess the classic features of beauty such as high cheekbones and porcelain skin, but she was breathtaking all the same. Sprinkled along her small upturned nose and pink cheeks were faint freckles. Her gold and green eyes were rimmed with long dark lashes and the fire that sparkled in their depths spoke of a quick mind and fiery, irrepressible spirit. It was her mouth, however, that was most appealing. Made for kissing, it looked soft and supple with the lower lip slightly fuller than the upper, begging to be suckled. Altogether, she was the kind of woman a man went to war for. In another time, place, and circumstance, Hamish would have even fought a McTiernay to have the chance to win her.

"Hamish?" she asked softly, taking another step closer.

"That is the name I was born with," he said teasingly.

Mairead pointed a finger at him and started shaking her head. "No. You cannot be him. Hamish is . . . a fearsome warrior. He is courageous and kind and . . . handsome. You"—she paused to lick her lips—"are only large . . . rude . . . and dirty."

Hamish looked down and made a show of inspecting himself, examining the nicks and scrapes along his out-stretched arms. "Aye, I am not as pleasing to look at as usual. It's hard for us courageous warriors to be handsome all of the time. But then"—he paused to give her a wink—"maybe I just need the help of a woman's touch."

Mairead's mouth fell open. She glanced at Davros, whose blue eyes momentarily widened at the suggestion. But after a second, he only shrugged, eager to discover what was going to happen next.

Her eyes snapped back to Hamish as her shock mor-phed into anger. "First my sister and now me?"

Sister? Hamish stared at the woman. He could not re-member being with a woman from this far north ever visiting the McTiernays. Just who was she?

His puzzlement must have been obvious for she an-nounced crisply, "I'm Mairead. Selah's younger sister. And you . . . you bearded eyesore," she stuttered as she marched up to him, "are *nothing* like how I remem—" Mairead's eyes opened wide and her arms flew in the air.

Upon hearing just who had stirred his body to life after being dormant for so long, Hamish had frozen with shock. He realized too late that Mairead had failed to see the little girl's outstretched legs. He instinctively reached out just as she tripped, but Mairead was too far away. He was unable to catch her before she fell—face-first—into the cold mud.

Mairead pulled herself up on all fours. Hamish bent down to help her up, but when she looked at him, he decided against the offer. Raw fury poured out of her hazel eyes, making them incredibly appealing.

Hamish swallowed. He needed to get control of his growing desire and remember just who was glaring at him. And more important, just who her sister was.

"I might be nothing like you remember, but you, little Mairead," he said with a chuckle and a wink, "are exactly the same!"

Mairead shook with fury born mostly from embarrassment. She may not have been sweet and docile like her sister, but that did not mean she was prone to losing her self-control—and that was exactly what had happened. And it would happen again if she ran into anyone before she was able to duck into her chambers.

Mairead reached her floor and peeked out of the stairwell to the narrow hall. Thankfully, no one was in sight. She ran to her room and closed the door, sighing with relief. Then, without warning, the emotions associated with every mortifying moment hit her again. Her shoulders slumped and she slid down the door, letting the tears begin to fall once more.

Crying. Of all the things she could have done while lying in the mud in the wake of such humiliation. Why had her emotional state and body selected crying? Her only consolation was the horror and guilt her tears had created in Hamish MacBrieve's eyes when he had finally assisted her back to her feet. Weeping was a pathetic way to win the upper hand. It symbolized all that she was not, and yet, in this case, it had been her biggest ally.

No one argued when she entered the kitchens and ordered for everyone to vacate so that a maid could prepare her bath right there in the room with the ovens. Hellie, the head cook, looked sympathetic and nodded in understanding, causing her graying, once-pale blond ringlets to bob enthusiastically. Being a kind woman, she then reassured Mairead that it was an ideal time for a break, being it was so early in the afternoon. The meat still had a few more hours to roast and many of the staff were eager to go out in the market. One of her helpers had even nervously thanked her for not asking them to haul buckets of water up to her room. Mairead groaned as she rested her head against her knees. Everyone had been so stunned by her physical state they had searched for anything to say that would keep her from breaking down completely in front of them.

Wiping her cheeks, Mairead could feel the grime being smeared on her skin. She had tried to use her sleeves to remove as much dirt as possible, but her gown was so muddy it had made things worse. Only a bath would remove the muck embedded in her eyebrows and hair. After taking a deep, calming breath, she rose to her feet and poured some water in a bowl to clean her hands. She refused to soil her spare gown just by carrying it to the kitchens.

After selecting a clean set of clothes, Mairead paused

to peek out the window, searching for the source of her misery. She sighed with relief as she saw Hamish working with Adiran cleaning a horse just outside the stables, which were thankfully located on the western wall, opposite from the kitchens. She took another deep breath and glared at the back of his head, feeling some of her self-confidence return. She might have fallen in the mud. She might have broken into tears. But both her disheveled and emotional states were temporary and excusable. Hamish, however, was going to remain looking scraggly and unkempt, for that beard had been left unattended for far too long.

When she had realized who he was, she had been shocked. He looked so different from what she remembered. But from this distance, his movements triggered her memories of him. Hamish held himself in a manner unlike any other man. He was completely at ease and yet also fully in command of all that was around him. She had no doubt that, if he wished, Hamish could remove the massive sword sheathed at his hip and either injure or kill a would-be attacker before they got off one strike regardless of where he was or what he was doing. She bit her bottom lip, imagining Hamish in fighting mode. That would be something spectacular to see—even in his ratty state.

Feeling the mud crackle as it dried along her hairline, Mairead left the window and grabbed a brush and some soap to add to her load before quickly making her way back to the kitchens. Once again, she encountered no one in the keep and all eyes in the courtyard purposefully looked away. Upon seeing Mairead in the kitchens, one of the cooks added three kettles of boiling water to the water already in the tin contraption that was on the floor next to the large hearth. Hellie then quickly shooed everyone out of the room, leaving Mairead finally, and blissfully, alone. She wasted no time stripping every nasty garment off and immersing herself into the warm waters.

Her brother-in-law was a born tinker. He was always taking the most commonplace objects and looking for ways to improve or even reinvent them. Luckily, her sister loved warm baths. The river was always frigid, even in the summer. In the winter, the water was so cold most resorted to a simple sponge bath, for it was difficult, let alone very uncomfortable, to wash in a barrel. After hearing her and Selah complain one night, Robert had spent the next several days with the blacksmith. The end product was what he called a bathing bowl. The metal, somewhat oval container was not very large, but one could sit in it—though the bather's knees had to remain bent. The ability to relax in the warm water brought a level of bliss that was hard to describe.

Mairead could not recall ever needing its calming effects more.

Mairead MacMhathain.

Every woman who had ever entered Hamish's life, even briefly, was either a version of heaven or hell. Laurel and Meriel fit the former whereas Selah and most recently Wyenda absolutely fell into the latter. Just knowing Mairead's name should have ended the debate as to which category she fell into. But seeing the wet, beckoning vision before him, Hamish changed his mind.

Mairead unquestionably belonged to both.

When he had spied her sneaking into the kitchens, he had hustled over hoping to get a chance to speak with her before she ran back up to her rooms to clean up. He had assumed she was requesting water be brought up for a bath, but when he entered, he was surprised to find the large room was empty. Long tables were piled with various food items in various steps of preparation, but not a single person—cook, baker, or even scullery maid—was in sight. Hamish could not recall any castle's kitchens ever being so eerily silent. The McTiernay cook, Fiona, was always yelling at someone at this time of day.

Believing he had been mistaken and that Mairead had disappeared into another building, Hamish was about to leave when he had heard a moan coming from the back room where the oven hearths were located. Curious, he went to see who had made the noise and why, but again, no one was in sight.

He was about to turn around and exit the room when a head popped up out of a large, odd-shaped metal basin. Keeping her eyes closed, Mairead let out an audible, heartfelt sigh and leaned back so that the base of her head rested on the tub's edge.

Hamish found himself rooted to where he stood, unable to move or speak. Though he could only see the creamy skin of her shoulders and the upper curves of her chest, he knew she was completely naked. His breathing quickened and it sounded so loud to his own ears, he felt sure Mairead could also hear him. But if she was aware of his presence, she did not act like it. Instead, she lifted her leg into the air and began to run the small cloth along her calf and slowly up over her knee. Hamish swallowed, feeling every muscle in his body harden with sudden, painful desire.

Mairead finished with her left leg and was about to wash the other when out of the corner of her eye she saw him. She squealed and dropped low in the water. *"Mo chreach! Yer aff yer heid!"*

Hamish could only stare, mentally agreeing with her accusation. He *had* lost his head and if he found out that any other man had ever seen her in such a state, he would ensure they would literally lose theirs as well.

Mairead could not believe this was happening. She thought she had already reached the epitome of possible embarrassment, but she was wrong. Slunk down as far as she could in the water, she waited for Hamish to quickly apologize and depart, leaving her alone with her mortification, but the damn man just stood there staring as if he was waiting for something.

After several more silent seconds, whatever embarrassment Mairead felt turned into fury. "Why are you still here? Are you trying to torment me? Because I already know you are a *toll-tòine*. I need no more proof."

Hearing her curse snapped Hamish out of his shock and he immediately recognized her insult was justified. He was blatantly staring at her as if he were a young lad and Mairead were his first glimpse of a woman. In some ways, he believed she was, for never before had he seen true female perfection. Every honorable bone in his body knew he should move and do as she asked and disappear from sight, and yet, something inside him resisted. Hamish recognized it was a hopeless battle. There was no way he was leaving knowing that she was in here alone for another man to accidentally find. The best he could do was turn around.

Mairead had to be having some kind of nightmare. She had to have fallen asleep and her mind was toying with her, creating what had to be the worst possible conclusion to what had already been a horrible afternoon. She closed her eyes and slowly reopened them. Her stomach turned over. Hamish was still there. The only change was that he had turned around and was now leaning against the table

between him and the bathing bowl. The man obviously
had no intention of leaving. "What is wrong with you? Do
you want to find yourself at the altar by nightfall?" she
screeched.

Hamish blinked. He had not considered what would
happen if someone found out that he was in here while she
was bathing. What surprised him was that he found the
idea almost appealing. *Almost.* The idea of Mairead in his
bed was more than a little tempting. But as his *wife?* Certainly not. His primary reason for coming north was to cut
all ties with his brother and his wife—not create new and
even stronger ones. No situation, even this precarious one,
could induce him to change that goal. And no one, not
even Conor McTiernay, had the power to force him into
marriage.

But Hamish had no intentions of telling Mairead that.

"Your mind *really is* focused on marriage," Hamish
chortled, thankful his voice did not convey the physical
tension he felt in his lower regions. "Good luck, but you
should give up including me in those dreams, *m'aingeal.*
Even if you ask really nicely, I will say always no."

Mairead gaped at his back. "I must be having a nightmare and it is *you* who are dreaming, if you thought for
one moment I would ever want to marry someone like
you. And . . . and . . . what in the devil's own are you
doing?" Mairead stammered as she watched Hamish
remove his sword and then lean over to pick up a carrot. A
second later a loud crunch filled the air.

Hamish asked himself that very question. He swallowed and said, "Thought that was obvious. I was coming
in here to look for food and where I could get a bath. Now
I guess I'm guarding you," he answered, glad to have

thought of something plausible to explain his continued presence.

When he had laid his sword on the table, his peripheral vision had cursed him with another glimpse of just what he was "guarding." She had shifted to a more comfortable position and now sat farther up in the bowl. Her wet hair hung in dark waves down her back and shoulders, and her chest rose and fell with every breath. Hamish had gathered every bit of control he had to turn around and look away.

"You are . . . you're . . . *gun chiall*!"

Hamish crossed his arms and smiled to himself. "I'm back at Foinaven, a place I vowed never to return to, in the dead of winter, arguing with my naked sister-in-law in the middle of the day as she bathes in the castle kitchens. I think we're both insane."

Mairead squeezed the wet piece of cloth in her hand and toyed with the idea of throwing it at him. Feeling helpless made her even more outraged. *"Toll-tòine,"* she muttered.

"You already called me ass," he said in an infuriatingly agreeable tone of voice.

Mairead slapped her hand down hard in the water out of frustration, uncaring that water went everywhere, and let out a stream of curse words. Rather than being shocked, Hamish just laughed.

The muscle in the side of Mairead's jaw flexed. Hamish was nearly as dirty as she had been and she knew just how uncomfortable it was. "Unless you want to greet your brother, and my sister, in such a filthy state, I would think you might want to head toward the river before the sun sets. It would take more water than we have at Foinaven to get you clean."

Hamish heard her implication and wondered how many others thought he still had any interest in Selah. In truth, he had barely thought about her since arriving at Foinaven.

Her sister, on the other hand, was stirring something in him that was dangerous and forbidden. Deep down he knew he was once again on the path to pain for there was no way he was getting involved with anyone—let alone Mairead—while at Foinaven. But that pain could be easily avoided as long as he did not get emotionally involved. Meanwhile, it was great to feel alive again. To feel desire again. And he could think of nothing that made him feel more like a fully functional man than guarding Mairead as she finished her bath.

"I think I'll just wait and use that contraption you're in. If it got all that mud off you, then it can handle the little bit of dirt and sweat on me."

"Little?" Mairead scoffed under her breath. Hamish said nothing and the only sounds were him munching on the carrot. "Fine!" she said crisply. "But I refuse to let you rob me of my bath."

She then proceeded to the rest of her body all the while keeping an eye on Hamish, waiting for him to turn around and steal a peek. But after several minutes she realized he never would. *And why would he need to?* she asked herself. He had already seen everything there was to see. And obviously, he had little desire to see more of it.

Mairead watched as he extended his arms out and then massaged his neck. She stretched the same way after she trained the farm boys who desired an opportunity to learn how to use a sword—even if it was from a girl. She glanced down at the sword on the table. It had to be incredibly heavy for it was like him—huge. It was of course bigger than the small one she used, but she doubted any of the men around Foinaven could wield it. "Do you always carry that heavy thing around with you?"

Hamish finished swallowing the last of the carrot and said, "Only when I am busy protecting delectable damsels as they bathe."

Mairead rolled her eyes. "And that happens a lot, does it?"

After taking in a deep breath, he exhaled. "Not as often as I would wish, believe it or not."

"Well, I don't believe it," Mairead snorted. "Your reputation with women precedes you."

His face puckered and Hamish was glad he was facing away from her so that Mairead would not know that her comment had struck a nerve. What reputation with women could he have? Besides the one of failure? For it certainly was not one of conquest. Hell, for the past several months, rumors were that he was living the life of a monk. And they were true.

The silence to her accusation riled Mairead once again. Why would he deny his reputation with women? He was probably proud of it. "Do you always sneak peeks at helpless women as they bathe when all they want is just a few moments of peace? Don't you have something else you need to do? Shouldn't you be trying to find Robert and let him know that you have arrived?"

Hamish lifted his right arm and waved a finger. "Well, um, traveling this time of year has made me rather dirty, which you have suggested more than once that I rectify. To which I agree—especially before I see either my brother or his wife after being absent twelve years." He uncurled another finger. "Secondly, I doubt you have ever been helpless, Mairead. And as far as sneaking a peek—" He inhaled to pause for effect, and then blew it out and uncurled the third and final finger, before dropping his hand back to his side. "I feel no need or incentive to 'sneak a peek.' You have nothing I haven't seen before."

Mairead glared at his back. "I suspect your experience with women is limited to spying. Not even women who *like* beards would let that hairy monster on your chin get remotely close to them."

Hamish's jaw tightened. His facial hair was wiry and grew incredibly thick so that after a couple of weeks of no trimming or maintenance, it was definitely an eyesore. After four months, it had become the ideal female repellent. Still, he did not like the idea that Mairead thought he was actually naïve when it came to women. He may not know how to capture a woman's heart, but he absolutely knew how to make a woman's body sing with pleasure.

"Trust me. I know how to please a woman and have made many a female smile for days after a few hours in my company. You're just fortunate there are far more enticing things to nibble on in this room than you."

He was lying, of course. Not even a starving pauper would find a royal meal more enticing than Mairead in her current nude, wet state. Even a eunuch would prefer to stare than eat.

Mairead tried to think of a cutting retort, but nothing came to mind. She licked her lips and crossed her arms, placing them on the side of the bowl to rest her chin. From the back, Hamish's physique was the most enticing she had ever seen. His leine pulled across his broad shoulders outlining the tension in his muscles and hinting of his enormous strength. She had never seen a man look more powerful . . . or sensuous.

"Are you going to stare at me or finish bathing? It's not fair if I don't get to stare at you in return."

Mairead flushed and shrank back into the cooling water. There was no way he could have known she was looking at him. "I thought I had nothing you had not seen before."

Hamish swallowed and gripped the edge of the table in an effort to retain the last shreds of his self-control. He was not about to reveal that he had been watching her reflection in the copper pot on the table across from him. His eyes had been practically glued to her shimmering form, wondering what she was thinking. Her facial expression had lost all of its anger and for a moment she looked like she was having an erotic daydream. He had been forced to say something to annoy her for if she licked her lips one more time, he would not still be wondering what they tasted like.

The water sloshed and he knew by the sound she had stood up and was stepping out of the bowl to dry off. If he had any sense, he would announce that guard duty was done and dash out of the room. But once again he was riveted to where he stood. Thankfully, she had moved so that she was no longer being reflected in the pot. The vividness of his imagination was almost excruciating, but deep down, he knew that the image his mind was conjuring was nothing close to the real thing. If he actually saw proof of that, no amount of honor would have kept him from turning around and acting upon his desires.

Hamish gripped the edge of the table harder and prayed to God she would soon end his torture.

"—tonight? There is plenty of room in the bastion with most of the men gone. I am sure Selah and Robert would welcome them to stay there."

Hamish blinked. He had missed something. "Them? Who?" he asked, clearly puzzled.

"Your men," Mairead repeated. "Those large warriors who made the journey with you."

Hamish crinkled his brow. "No one traveled with me. I came to Foinaven alone."

Mairead stepped into view. She had finished tying one side of her bliaut and was working on the other. "What do you mean? Was there a delay? When do you expect them to arrive?"

Hamish crossed his arms and peered down at Mairead's expectant expression. He forced himself to focus on their conversation and not on her lips. "There is no delay. There are no men. And there will be no men. Robert only asked for me and so only I came," he replied simply.

"You're serious," Mairead whispered, feeling like someone had just punched her in the stomach. "I just assumed you knew about Ulrick. That he was the real reason you made the journey. I must tell you ab—"

Hamish put up his hand to stop her. "I know about Ulrick and he *is* the real reason why I'm here."

Mairead furrowed her brow and began tying off the last string on her bliaut. Once done, she threw her hands in the air. "I thought . . . I had heard . . ."

"Heard what?"

Mairead took a deep breath and then exhaled. "We were to understand you and Laird McTiernay were fairly close. So I had assumed he would offer men to come with you, especially if you knew of our situation."

"I know enough and Conor did offer."

Relief spread through Mairead. All hope was not lost. "Then you can send word—"

Hamish shook his head, cutting her off. "I told him no and I have no intentions of changing my mind." He held her gaze for several seconds, his own dark green eyes devoid of humor. The sudden absence of his easygoing demeanor sent a shiver up her spine. "Now that you are dressed and no longer are in any danger of being caught unawares, I'm going to take my bath. You are welcome to stay and be my chaperone, but I'll understand if you have other things to which you must attend."

He saw her jaw tightened and knew by her silent reaction that he had hit a nerve. *Mo chreach* was Mairead breathtaking when she was angry.

The green in her hazel eyes blazed. Her back straightened, which created a rigidity of her shoulders that accentuated her already enticing figure. The effect was making her damn near irresistible. For a second, he feared she might actually call his bluff and stay. But without another word, she just turned and walked proudly out the door just as the last vessels of his composure slipped away.

He wondered if she knew just how close she had come to being thoroughly kissed.

"Rab, it's time for you to go find your mother or Noma. I need a few minutes to talk to your uncle alone."

The young boy stared for a moment at his father, who was lying propped up on pillows in bed before leaving to seek his nursemaid. Though Rab was only five years old, the resemblance between father and son was unmistakable. Rab had the MacBrieve dark auburn hair and while it was hard to make out what his physique would someday be, his thin frame hinted that he would be tall and lean. Rab also had Robert's high forehead, dark thick lashes around much paler green eyes, and round cheeks, all proving which MacBrieve brother was Rab's father.

Robert started to cough forcing him to sit up for a second. When done, he slumped back against his pillows and massaged his temples. "I'm so sorry to be receiving you like this. It is not how I planned to welcome you home," he said apologetically for the fourth time since Hamish had entered the room.

"Think on it no more. Good company and food can be enjoyed in any setting," Hamish said, studying his brother as he continued to sit in a chair several feet away.

"I admit to feeling awful, but I come down with this illness around this time every year and it is more of an annoyance than anything. I can't breathe, I'm constantly sniffling making me sound as pitiful as I look, and this damn cough—" Robert's explanation was cut off by another short spasm.

Hamish was very familiar with the aggravation of his brother's plight, having experienced something similar a few years ago. It had taken about a week for his head to stop feeling like it weighed as much as a boulder and for him to finally breathe again, but the respite was slight. For it was followed by nonstop sniffling and a sore throat exacerbated by constant coughing. And while Robert was right that the illness was typically not life-threatening and just highly uncomfortable, it was not always so. Hamish had heard of it lingering in some people's lungs and the result then was almost always fatal.

"You have a fine son, though I think I scare him. He has hardly said two words in my presence."

Robert leaned back again and managed a smile. "He's shy and is constantly assessing all he sees, but once he becomes comfortable with you he will ask so many questions, your mind will spin."

"So he's like you in temperament as well as in looks."

Robert returned Hamish's smile. "Aye. It is strange to see a miniature version of yourself. He has even begun taking things apart, though he has yet to figure out that he must also learn how to put them back together." Robert took the cloth in his left hand and ran it against his very red nose. "I hope you have a passel of sons yourself someday. Though I am surprised you do not have them already."

Hamish quirked an eyebrow. "I actually like my freedom, but that doesn't mean I am against the idea of someday knowing what it is like to be a father. Meanwhile, I'm glad you and Selah are truly happy."

Surprisingly, Hamish was being completely honest, for seeing Selah and Robert together at dinner had not been the emotional hardship he envisioned it would be. Whatever feelings he had had for Selah had long since died, and in their place was not animosity but ease and acceptance.

"Selah looks well," Hamish added, "and you have a fine son. Things worked out as they were meant to."

Born with all the features of a classic beauty, Selah was the lovely and sweet-natured woman he remembered. Robert on the other hand looked much older and Hamish could see the results of stress that came with leading a clan.

Selah had refused to let Robert leave the warmth of his rooms in the keep, but neither did she want to deprive her husband of participating in welcoming his older brother home. As a compromise, they had all agreed to have dinner in Robert's dayroom with him.

Mairead had been late joining them and avoided making eye contact for almost the whole meal. She had pointedly chatted with Selah about various situations of the castle—including the need to make changes to the kitchen staff.

Hamish was glad someone recognized that the quality of the meal was significantly lacking. The bread was unusually hard and he personally had prepared more tasty meat using a stick and a campfire. But Selah had ended any discussion about replacing one or two of the more un-cooperative cooks almost as soon as it began. The concept of dismissing those not doing their job satisfactorily was repugnant to her. She worried for their families and re-fused to threaten their livelihoods.

Thankfully, about this time Robert announced his energy had depleted to the point he needed to lie back down. Taking advantage of the opportunity to escape the ongoing argument between the women, Hamish had quickly suggested he join him. Robert had readily agreed and nudged his son to stay with his mother.

Now that it was just the two of them, this was the first chance Hamish had to converse with his brother alone. Suddenly the distance created by the last twelve years could be felt once more.

"Why?" Robert asked, looking Hamish directly in the eye.

Hamish leaned forward and rested his elbows on his knees. He was not going to pretend he did not understand the question. "Though I admit to being cross with fate for a while, I never was angry with you or Selah. But you had to understand why I could not stay."

"Aye," Robert acknowledged wearily. "I understood. But not why it had to be for so long."

Hamish sat back up and clenched his jaw. "There was no reason for me to return."

"Father's funeral was not a reason?"

"He was dead, Robert. He would have had no knowl-edge of my being there or not. You had become laird and I did not want anyone to question your right to being chieftain."

"What about later? My other entreaties to come?"

Hamish scoffed. "Entreaties? Did you forget that I damn near killed one of your men who actually thought he could physically force me to return with him?"

Robert closed his eyes and sighed. "He admitted to being a little overzealous. I unwisely asked to bring you with him by any means possible."

"He was a fool."

"I'm sure in your eyes he was one. But he was trying to honor my request."

Hamish took in a deep breath, tempted to call his brother a fool as well. He probably should wait to bring up his brother's latest request until Robert was feeling better, but delaying the inevitable would change nothing. "What were you thinking when you let Ulrick leave with most of your men?"

His brother waved a hand dismissively. "I had my reasons and I still believe they were good ones."

"If you think that I'm here to take Ulrick's place," Hamish cautioned, shaking his head, "you are mistaken."

Robert laughed, but only for a second before it changed to a hacking cough. When it subsided, he leaned back against his pillows once again and sighed. "I would welcome you here by my side, leading the men, being my permanent commander, but after twelve years of your not wanting to be in my presence for even a visit, I am not under any delusion that you are here to accept such an offer."

Hamish eyed his younger brother thoughtfully. "Not permanent, maybe, but don't deny you are seeking my help in the interim as commander."

Robert sniffled and grunted as he wiped his nose again. "I do and I am not above using my sickness to help persuade you of my need. But I promise I understand its temporary nature."

Hamish pursed his lips. "Is that all or is there more you want from me? Because I suspect you need help in removing the commander you currently have."

His brother nodded solemnly and closed his eyes. "Ulrick is a problem. I thought making him commander would suffice his need to be in control. Unfortunately, he does not work well with people." He opened his eyes again and held Hamish's gaze. "You must know that I am disinclined to send any man or woman away from Foinaven, but it is time for Ulrick to find a new home. It would be better not just for us, but for him."

Hamish arched a brow in surprise. "Ulrick does not merely want control, Robert. He longs for power. He seeks to replace you, not a home."

"You cannot know that."

Hamish's eyes became wide and he bobbed his head. "I don't just know that . . . everyone around you does! All but you can see Ulrick's intentions. How can you not accept that?"

"By offering a man the opportunity to change, there is the chance he can and will. Condemning him allows no flexibility. No hope. I don't want to teach Rab to look for the ill in people because he will always find it. It takes effort to find and nurture the good."

"Then I should leave now. I know Ulrick too well to waste my time looking for the good in him. What good there was disappeared long ago leaving only his desire for personal gain."

"That is the reason why I asked you to come and why you must stay. You understand Ulrick. Therefore, you can negotiate with him," Robert countered, just before another coughing attack.

Negotiate? Hamish had to have heard wrong. "I am not a negotiator."

"Damn cough," Robert muttered when it finally subsided. "You could be and Ulrick will only respond to one of his kind," Robert continued. "Someone he sees as an equal. He will talk with you."

Hamish fought the compulsion to drop his jaw and just stare at his younger brother. Robert *had* changed in the past twelve years, but not in the way Hamish hoped. Becoming responsible for lives had made his brother even *more* of a peacekeeper.

Robert still did not recognize that it was more dangerous and more of a folly to overlook or discount the threat some people pose. His brother had always believed there was good in everyone. Hamish did too, but that did not change the fact that for many people, the enticement of personal gain outweighed the common good. A good leader recognized with whom and how to exploit that trait so that not just the individual, but all could benefit. A good leader also knew how to identify those few who would never be satisfied. The ones who always wanted more and would be ruthless in getting it. Negotiation did not stop people like Ulrick. Only a show of greater force could trigger their survival instinct and get them to stand down.

"I'm not sure that I can be the commander you want. You and I see things too differently."

"I know we do, but you still came. So you must believe as I do that Ulrick needs to be handled."

Hamish stood quietly for a moment. What little strength

Robert had at the beginning of their conversation was nearly depleted. "If I stay, I will act as I think best."

Robert nodded. "That is all I am asking and I agree to let you handle the situation as you wish."

Hamish felt twenty pounds had lifted from his shoulders. "Then I will help you handle Ulrick when he returns."

Robert's body relaxed and he managed a smile without coughing. "Thank you. All I ask is that we do so peacefully, without bloodsh—"

This time it was not a cough cutting his brother off, but a sharp, angry shout from down the corridor. Hamish decided it was probably for the best that their conversation came to a temporary conclusion. His brother wanted a plan that involved no bloodshed. It was something Hamish desired as well, but it would be up to Ulrick to decide whether blood would be spilled. Not Hamish . . . and not Robert.

Meanwhile, Hamish had addressed the most immediate concerns. He would stay at Foinaven as commander only temporarily and then help banish Ulrick upon his return.

He only had to negotiate with his brother as to how.

"I would lower your voice," Selah suggested calmly. "For if you wake Rab, it will not be I or even Noma who goes in and deals with him until he falls back to sleep."

Mairead studied her sister's quiet demeanor and knew that she was not bluffing. Rab was a good little boy, but his mind was fast and it never stopped when awake. One could put him to bed, but unless someone was with him to ensure he stayed there, he would rise and find something to keep his mind occupied. Sleep only seemed to overtake him at the point of exhaustion and not before. If he woke now, his energy would be restored enough that it would be some time before he fell back to sleep.

"I never would have asked you why you were so quiet at dinner if I had known it would upset you. I would rather have remained curious," Selah said, and moved to sit on one of the chairs near the hearth.

The dayroom was centrally connected on the floor with easy access to her and Robert's bedchambers as well as her son's. It was not a large room, but its size made it easy to heat, making it Selah's favorite place to talk or even be alone. Mairead liked the room as well, but she preferred the great hall. It was where her memories of her father were the strongest. He used to sit by the fire and let flames calm his thoughts as she sat relaxed against him.

"I'm more than upset," Mairead grumbled, and began to pace once more, "and you should be too! I was bathing!"

"You said that before," Selah replied as she reached over to pick up a small piece of needlework she used to practice designs before creating them on a large tapestry. "You were in the kitchens covered in mud."

Mairead opened and closed her mouth twice at her sister's nonchalant reaction to all that she had said. "I cannot fathom your reaction right now. Unless rallying to my defense would reveal Hamish's return is troubling you far more than you want anyone to believe."

For the first time, Selah showed her own mounting frustration and put the cloth down in her lap and raised her eyes. "I'm not sure what you want me to say, Mairead. You act as if I should be outraged, but you have already assured me that nothing dishonorable happened. If anything, Hamish acted as what he claimed to be—your protector.

And you certainly needed one bathing in the kitchens where anyone could have walked in."

"You are deliberately misunderstanding what I am telling you."

"Trust me, it is not deliberate," Selah mumbled. "It is you who refuse to tell me what truly has you so upset."

Mairead paused and stared at the flames in the hearth. Her sister was right. She had been mad about Hamish refusing to leave, but that had nothing to do with her current angst. "Hamish is no longer the same person he was, Selah."

"None of us are, dear. Can you imagine how different you are to him? When he left you were ten and far less easily agitated."

"You should have heard him. I've never heard anyone so excessively arrogant."

Selah stopped her stitching and gathered her thoughts. "Remember when Robert was overseeing the construction of the corner towers? Everyone thought him so conceited, but they were just not used to working with a master builder who had reason to be so self-confident. I suspect that like Robert and masonry, Hamish knows what he is doing when it comes to Ulrick."

Mairead's eyes snapped to Selah's, but her sister did not flinch. "He came *alone*."

"Aye," Selah replied, "but he did come."

"But why did he not bring any men to help us?"

"I'll admit to assuming he would bring men with him, but Robert and I do not see how this is an issue. We do not need additional men. Plenty remained here to guard our gates and help those who need it, especially now that Hamish is here to assist them."

Mairead glared at Selah, unable to believe what she was hearing.

Selah was shocked by the intensity of her younger sister's gaze. Putting aside her needlework, she rose to her feet and placed a comforting hand on Mairead's arm. "Is that what has you so upset? That he came alone? I promise there will be other chances to meet eligible men."

Mairead closed her eyes. How could she say that she had no desire to marry when a man was exactly what she had been hoping to find? "Hamish may be huge and strong and the best warrior in all of Scotland, but he alone will not persuade Ulrick to leave Foinaven. It will require a show of force, an army sizeable and skilled enough to engage Ulrick when he returns."

Selah gave Mairead's arm a little squeeze. "Robert believes otherwise."

Then Robert is a fool, Mairead thought to herself. *And so am I for believing Hamish was going to be the salvation of not just Foinaven . . . but me.*

Mairead shuddered, recalling Ulrick's last words to her. She had seen the cold look in his eyes when he had said he wanted Foinaven and he wanted her, and nothing would prevent him from either goal.

Mairead might not be able to stop his army and she could not leave, but it *was* possible to keep Ulrick from using her to secure his position. Despite his threats, she could marry someone—she just needed to choose the right Highlander. He needed to be a man who could not only help defend Foinaven, but one who could protect himself from Ulrick's vengeance. Before Hamish arrived, she had only one viable option—the Mackays.

Clan Mackay lay on their western border and rumors held that they were ruthless warriors, who protected what was theirs through any means necessary. No one at Foinaven ever met any of the Mackays and most did not want to. Traveling merchants had told too many tales of how hostile they could be to anyone posing a threat to their people or the lands they occupied.

Unfortunately, marrying a stranger belonging to a ruthless clan was fraught with danger, for her husband could turn out to be someone just like Ulrick. He also might not be content to be commander and seek to overthrow Robert. Then *she* would be responsible for everyone's downfall, including her own.

She *had* to change Hamish's mind and ask for help.

Selah looked up and spied Hamish leaning on the doorframe. Mairead saw Selah's smile and glanced toward the door. As soon as she saw Hamish, standing there relaxed as if he had been there some time, her temper threatened to explode again. "Why am I surprised? Of course you are here. You probably listened to the entirety of our conversation."

"Only the last part about you being upset about my not bringing men so that you can find a suitable husband," Hamish replied with a wink, unable to stop himself.

Mairead's jaw went slack. "How many ways and times do I need to say this? I do not *want* a husband!" she shouted.

Selah clucked her tongue. "Remember little Rab," she whispered.

Mairead took a step toward him. "I do not *want* a husband," she reiterated, this time in a harsh whisper. "What I want is for Foinaven and its clansmen to be safe from Ulrick and his schemes to take over."

Hamish stared down into her hazel eyes and saw that she spoke the truth. "Then you no longer have to worry."

This time it was Selah who swallowed and looked at him anxiously. "So you agreed to stay and help Robert convince Ulrick that he should find another home?"

He matched her serious tone and replied, "I did."

Mairead took in a deep breath and exhaled. Her shoulders relaxed and she gave him a dazzling smile. He had not realized it, but this was the first time he had seen her smile. He thought her fiery temper made her tempting, but when she smiled, the world seemed to fade away.

"I assume it's too late to send word tonight, but I will have the herald ready for you in the morning to send word to Laird McTiernay."

Hamish crossed his arms and pretended to look puzzled. "Why? I already explained to you that I have no intentions of asking Conor McTiernay for help, and that especially includes any men."

"But you just said—"

Hamish felt his jaw tense. For a few seconds, sheer terror—not anger—had reflected in her eyes. That kind of fear was deeply personal. Was it concern for her sister and the future of the clan? Or something more?

"I said I would help Robert deal with Ulrick. And I promise that I don't need the McTiernays to help me with this task."

Task? Mairead mouthed. "You may be the best swordsman in all of Scotland, but that is going to be of little use when Ulrick returns with a few dozen mercenaries at his side."

Hamish could not help himself from grinning and rocked back on his heels. "Best swordsman in all of Scotland . . . I like the sound of that."

Selah chuckled. "If you thought Hamish was arrogant before, he definitely is now, thanks to your flattery."

Mairead glared at Hamish. "I wasn't flattering him, I was insulting him."

Hamish leaned down and whispered in her ear, "To be

insulted by the prettiest lass in Scotland is the best flattery I have ever received."

"I give up," Mairead replied, and headed toward the door. She paused at the door, glanced at him, and then looked back at her sister. "That is what I was trying to tell you. Hamish and his overconfidence are going to endanger us all."

Hamish watched her leave, completely intrigued. "She's feisty."

Selah narrowed her gaze. "And by the sparkle in your eye, I'm guessing you like feisty."

Hamish put his hand up to stop her from saying anything more. "I only admit to enjoying a woman who can argue her mind."

Selah licked her lips and studied him for a minute. "I'm glad that you understand Mairead is family, but right now I'm more concerned about Robert and what you told him. Can you do what you promised . . . um, regarding Ulrick?"

"We have yet to resolve all the details. But Selah, you must know whatever solution I put into place will not stop others in the future, not if Robert continues to lead the way he has been."

Selah gave him a kiss on the cheek and smiled. "Robert only needs you to handle Ulrick. He has the future firmly in hand."

An unexpected jolt of jealousy shot through Hamish. For the first time in twelve years he wished he had what Robert did. He longed not for Selah nor the feel of her soft lips on his skin.

He wished for something far more profound—that someone trusted and had the same level of faith in him.

* * *

"Selah," Hamish said, "it has been a long day and I would like to retire, but was hoping to change rooms."

Selah blinked at the odd request but quickly recovered. "Of course, there is a room next to Rab's the servants keep clean for he sometimes uses it to play in. But I warn you, he rises early and can be very loud. Mairead is on the other side of him and mentions it often. You really would be more comfortable on the first floor."

"Would it be too much of an imposition to ask for the room on the bottom floor?"

Selah remembered Hamish stopping there earlier that evening to peek into the storage space. People may have thought her to be the kindly sort who did not look for ulterior motives in others, but that did not mean she never recognized them. "It would not be an imposition at all, but it is so drafty and we use it primarily for storage. The courtyard is just on the other side of the wall. Even little Rab would offer less noise."

Hamish shrugged. His reasons for being on the bottom floor would make the sounds from a typical morning courtyard irrelevant. "The noise will not bother me and I noticed it already has a bed."

Selah remained hesitant. She would not call the simple wooden frame a bed. It certainly was not a comfortable one. "Well, aye, it does, but Hamish, it has not been cleaned for use in some time, and the mattress is made of straw. I am not even sure the room has any wood for a fire."

Selah widened her eyes and looked at him imploringly. Hamish could see again why he thought her to be so beautiful so many years ago. Her delicate features and serene and kind nature were indeed beautiful, but the pull and the allure she had over him were no longer there. He wondered if it would have dwindled if they had married so long ago. His gut told him to just be glad that Robert and she had fallen in love and were still happy.

"Selah, a soldier considers himself fortunate to rest his head on a straw mattress. Besides, I've been sleeping outside for days and last night took shelter in a barn. One more evening in the company of a little dirt will not be an issue."

Selah pursed her lips together. She was used to persuading people to her point of view, not the other way around. But Hamish would not budge. He just stood and looked pleadingly at her. At last, Selah bit back a smile. "You are not as charming as you believe you are."

"Ah, but you agree that I *am* charming."

"Aye, despite that awful beard of yours. Thankfully, my sister seems to be impervious to your efforts," Selah said. She then picked up a candle and slid between him and the doorframe to head for the stairwell.

Hamish laughed and turned to follow. "I suspect Mairead is well acquainted with men's flattery."

Just before she reached the stairwell, Selah stopped and looked at him. "She is. She has had much practice in recent years in deflecting fanciful comments coming from your kind."

Hamish said nothing and waited for Selah to continue. He was not surprised that Mairead had suitors. He was surprised to find that he was slightly jealous of the fact.

"Just remember that Mairead is my sister and that makes her part of your family."

Hamish took the last step and exited the staircase. "I know who she is," he said.

Mairead was many things, but he did not see her as a sister. But she was Selah's, ensuring any desire he had for Mairead would remain only that. He was absolutely not going to act on those desires.

"Good," Selah said, and stopped in front of a closed door. She placed a light hand on his arm. "Do not concern yourself about Mairead. She will come to appreciate your being here despite your lack of company. But you should know that you are at your most charming when you're not trying not to be. Just be yourself."

Hamish reached over and picked up her hand to kiss it. "I'll remember that."

Selah shook her head and said "I give up" as she opened the heavy door. There were several rooms on the ground floor, but this was the one he had peered into earlier. It was also the only one with a bed and a fireplace. The spaces of the others were smaller and built solely for storage of food, materials, and weapons. "It looks like I was mistaken. There are several large logs stacked near the hearth. It is cold and damp, but at least you will be able to make a fire." Selah paused and looked at all the dust. "Are you sure you would not like to stay somewhere else, just until tomorrow night?"

Again, Hamish shook his head and stepped into the room. "Selah, this is fine," he said with a satisfied sigh. "Besides, I think Mairead would prefer the additional distance between us. Now go. I know that you want to check on Robert before you retire."

It was obvious he was trying to get rid of her and Selah once again felt the stirrings of curiosity. But she refused to yield to the temptation to ask him. Mostly because she knew it would be a waste of time.

"Hamish?" she asked, lighting the candle on a small table near the center of the room.

"Hmm?"

"I . . . just wanted to thank you for coming. I know it was a lot to ask after what happened. I did love you. I never lied about that. I just . . . with Robert . . ."

Hamish looked her directly in the eye, knowing it had taken everything Selah had to bring up the topic. But he was glad she did. For just as his brother needed to hear Hamish felt no animosity toward him, Selah needed the same. "All really is well, Selah. I have learned the difference between love and being in love. And you were right to follow your heart."

"It's just in following my heart, I broke yours. I've always regretted hurting you. I never wanted that."

Hamish was tempted to say that what she did to him was far more than break his heart. She took his future and nothing she said now would change that. But then neither would pointing out that painful fact. It was done and one of the main reasons he had returned was to put the past behind them so they could all move on. "That wound was mended long ago. I'm happy for you and Robert, and I want you to be happy for me." Hamish came forward and took Selah's delicate hands into his own. "I am more than content with the McTiernays. They respect me as a fighter and the ladies even appreciate my charm," he said with a wink.

Selah felt something tight within her finally relax. She rose on her tiptoes and kissed him once more on his hairy cheek. "You are more than a fighter, Hamish. You've always been so much more. And I am so glad you have finally come home."

Hamish moved to the door and opened it a little wider, said good night for a final time, and then closed it. Another time he would point out that he was not home and that Foinaven had not been his home for a long time. He was merely a visitor.

Turning around, he walked toward the overly large fireplace and placed the candle on the simple wooden mantel. One poke proved the logs were rotten, but more important, that it had been a long time since the hearth had been used. Hamish quickly removed them, stepped inside, and began to slide his hand along the stones. After a couple minutes, he found a groove around a large stone and followed it. He smiled feeling the thick layer of grime. No one had been here in many years. The room did not require the sizeable hearth, but it seemed no one had ever been curious to find out just why it had one.

This room and its fireplace were one of the first things he and his father had built when they first started renovating the keep. Being new to Foinaven, they were unsure how welcome they would be and created a secret passageway leading from the castle to a tunnel, which ended just outside the village. Hamish wondered if his father had ever told anyone about it. Perhaps it had been forgotten. Hamish hoped one or both possibilities were true, for being able to come and go without anyone knowing was going to be very helpful in keeping much of his plan a secret. Secrecy added complications—just one of which would be trying to explain his absence—but it also added a level of freedom.

Hamish put his shoulder on the deceptive stone and pushed. He felt it shift and then shoved against it once more. It was large but not very thick, making it look far too heavy to move. Feeling the air on the other side, he stepped back into the room, grabbed a torch, and lit it using the candle. He then stepped back inside and examined the passageway to see if it was still clear. It was. Hamish followed it, burning cobwebs along the way until it ended.

Surprisingly, it was not overgrown brush that blocked the way out but a decaying barrel. Hamish nudged it with his knee. As suspected it was empty and easy to maneuver. Stepping out of the tunnel, he was relieved to see that the large boulder marking the exit was still there, but the massive rock was no longer outside of the village boundaries. Now it was definitely within them. Thankfully, the hour was late and no one was about.

Hamish looked around as best he could and decided the situation was not as bad as he first thought. The area around the boulder was being used to dump unwanted and broken items. Most looked like they had been there for a while. It was almost perfect. Carefully Hamish tilted a rotted cart so that it hid the opening without actually blocking it. Being in the shadows gave him easy access in and out, but it also enabled him to stay hidden and wait for the right time to join the village crowds without being seen.

Returning back to his room, he started a fire and sat on the edge of the bed, trying to ignore the stink from the fumes. Deciding it was worth it to be warm, he lay down and let his thoughts drift to all that had happened that day. One person in particular kept coming to mind: Mairead.

For some reason, he could not control his thoughts—or his words—whenever he was around her. After she left the kitchens, he had left as well, deciding to bathe in the river rather than the warm water. He told himself it was because her scented soap had caused the water to smell feminine. But, in truth, he required something far more frigid to get his body back under control.

After washing in the cold waters of River Naver, he had vowed to stop saying anything that would get things heated between them. It was not as if he wanted to flirt with Mairead. He had not flirted with anyone in months. He had been acting on some strange survival instinct. She had made him uneasy, and he had needed her to be just as uncomfortable.

Hamish rubbed his temples and focused on his brother. It had not taken more than a few minutes of conversation to realize Robert was exactly who he expected him to be—a well-intentioned but weak-willed leader. That discovery changed none of his plans, however. Hamish refused to put in permanent measures that would ensure Robert remained laird. That was his brother's responsibility. And unless he changed, someday—probably sooner than later—someone would seek and successfully take advantage of Robert and his pacifist style of leadership.

But it would not be Ulrick.

Hamish may have come alone, but despite what Mairead thought, a large army was not what was needed. Ulrick was about to discover just what one man who had lived and fought alongside the McTiernays could do.

Selah sat down at the small table and unpinned her braided hair from its knot. She began to finger the long braid, unraveling it from its weave, when Robert started coughing. By its thick sound, she knew he was also having trouble breathing. It happened every winter and he always got well, but that did not stop her from worrying.

"You are getting worse."

Robert drew in deep breaths and grimaced from the pain in his throat. How he hated this time of year. "My throat and chest, aye, are not improving as fast as I would like, but my heart and mind are finally at peace. Yours should be as well, *sonuachar*."

"Do you truly believe Hamish will stay?" Selah twisted so that she could look and see if he spoke the truth when he answered.

Robert's eyes were closed and he was leaning back against the propped-up pillows, but he was also smiling. "Aye, at least for now. I told you he would."

"It was still a great risk you took to get him here."

"There was very little risk, *sonuachar*. I have yet to meet a more honorable or loyal man than my brother. Who else would have stepped aside for us the way Hamish did?"

Selah wiggled out of her gown so that she stood only in her chemise. "I do not think there are many."

Robert sighed, which resulted in another brief coughing spasm. "Give up everything for the love and happiness of a younger brother? Nay, Selah. Only Hamish. That's why I knew he would come and why I knew he would help." He opened his eyes and held her gaze. "And that is why I know my plan will work. I know my brother."

"I believe you. Just as I believe you know how to take care of all our family's needs," she said, as she slipped under the covers and moved closer to her husband's prone form.

Robert patted her hand and said, "Indeed. I am a master mason. So trust me to build the perfect future for—" Before he could finish his thought, he began to cough again. This time, the fit lasted nearly a half a minute before he could breathe and lie back down again.

Selah sat up and looked down at him. "I just wish you could fix your poor body. Your being sick—"

"Could not have come at a better time," he finished for her. "It made it much easier to persuade Hamish into accepting the role as temporary commander. I consider this damn cough to be God's gift. He knows how stubborn Hamish can be. Just look how long it took for us to get him here."

"And the lengths you had to go to."

"I'm just glad he came when he did," Robert said, giving her hand a slight squeeze.

"And Mairead?"

"I've been building this plan for some time, but Mairead is the reason why we are doing it now. I have not forgotten that."

Selah lay back down at Robert's encouragement. "I just hope you have considered Hamish when it comes to her. The tension between them was palpable and it was not all anger that was sparking between them."

Robert opened his eyes and gazed at his wife. "Really?"

She nodded.

Robert smiled to himself. His plan could not be working better.

Chapter Four

Hamish stood next to the kitchen entrance and bit into the hard loaf of bread. The gloomy afternoon weather matched his mood. A pleasant cook was a rarity and none of them ever liked anyone coming in and out of their workspace, but at least the McTiernays' foul-tempered Fiona could prepare a decent meal. The most Hamish could say about the food at Foinaven was that it was edible. This was the second day he had returned from the morning's endeavors too late to even enjoy leftovers from the noon meal. It would not happen again. Dried beef, hard bread, and warm ale may fill his belly, but it did little to improve one's mood.

A breeze smelled of rain. Hamish looked up at the sky. It was growing thick with gray clouds and within an hour, two at most, it would be raining hard and for several hours. Thankfully, he had risen early and had been able to accomplish much of what he aimed to achieve. He had several more painfully early mornings to look forward to, but based on these first two outings, the results were worth it.

Even last night's meeting he had with his brother had

gone easier than anticipated. Almost too easy. Robert had quickly agreed that Hamish would only remain for a short period as acting commander. Any other duties, including clan decision-making or overseeing any staff, would be handled and managed by Selah and Mairead until Robert was well enough to resume his responsibilities. The only thing they did not discuss was his approach to the Ulrick situation. Robert did not ask for information and Hamish did not volunteer any. But that had not caused Hamish to feel uneasy.

He could not shake the niggling feeling that there was more to his brother's accommodating demeanor. He just hoped that it was not a ruse to buy time and later ask him for more. For if that was true, Robert was going to be disappointed.

Soft thunder rumbled from the distance and those working in the courtyard started to move their livestock and goods under shelter. Hamish was just about to step out and help one of the men load his cart when he heard the distinct sound of swords clashing nearby. He paused to listen and realized that it was coming from inside the great hall.

Hamish pivoted and entered the buttery, deciding to enter the hall via the screens passage, which was used by the servants for easy access to and from the kitchens. A luxury in some castles, the passage was a necessity at Foinaven, unless the laird enjoyed his meals drenched from exposure to foul weather.

Stepping out from behind the partition, Hamish ignored the sounds of scuffles and clanking swords and took a moment to look around. Since his arrival, all their meals had been in the keep so that Robert did not have to leave his rooms. Twelve years ago, the hall had been much smaller and constructed out of wood. Since then, it had been completely rebuilt out of stone and Hamish found himself surprisingly impressed. From the outside, the structure resembled most great halls, which were just wide rectangular rooms with high ceilings and little else to make them remarkable.

Foinaven's great hall was more simplistic than the one at McTiernay Castle, but it was also more than the boxlike shape that could be seen from the courtyard. Only when inside could the enormity of the room become apparent. The roof, nearly three stories high, was formed by several massive beams precisely angled and balanced on elaborately carved corbels. The northern side of the hall was to his right. It served as part of the curtain wall and was decorated with several clan banners—the MacBrieves and MacMhathains being the most prominent. To his left were two oversize wooden doors that opened to the courtyard and five large, square-shaped stained-glass windows, which let in more light than he would have thought. At the far end of the room was an enormous mantel that spanned nearly the entire width of the wall. Nestled within it were three fire pits, with the one in the center being the largest and the only one currently lit.

Hamish would have spent a few more minutes taking in the great hall surroundings if his attention had not been almost immediately refocused on the spectacle taking place. All the tables and benches had been dismantled or stacked off to the side to create enough room for what looked to be a dozen men in their late teens haphazardly clanking swords together. At first, Hamish thought it a farce, for no self-respecting Highlander would agree to train inside just to avoid some bad weather, let alone do so in the great hall. But after a few seconds watching their expressions, he knew that they were serious—and terrible.

Only a few attempted to move as they attacked and all of them thought too much. Each step taken was heavy and slow as if it was done by decision, not instinct. A marginally experienced swordsman could defeat any one of them without much effort.

The swords were dented, dull, and incapable of doing damage, making them worthless in a real battle. In addition, they were small—perhaps two-thirds the length of his broadsword. Based on the men's open stance, Hamish surmised none of the young men had even held a decent targe, let alone trained with one. The shield was just as important to training as the sword and could be a serious weapon in and of itself, if one knew how to use it. The only positive thing he could see was that their grip was accurate.

Hamish stepped fully into view and was about to call everyone's attention to stop the farce, when across the room he saw Mairead sparring with a lad who knew less than she did about sword fighting.

Hamish stood there and stared. *Mo chreach*, the sight of her lunging as she countered an attack caused his lower regions to uncontrollably flare to life. He did not think it possible, but Mairead looked even more striking in combat with a weapon.

The simple gown she wore enabled movement and accentuated her athletic body. Her golden brown hair was long and loose, restrained only by a single strap of leather in the back. It swung about her as she and a much taller boy shuffled around each other, periodically stabbing the air in an effort to throw the other off. Mairead had a solid grip, but her stance and parry movements had no purpose. Like the others in the room, her basic sword skills and combat approaches were enormously lacking.

Seeing Mairead fighting an armed man unsettled him.
Aye, he had a penchant for beautiful women whose personality favored assertion and not compliance, but his
protective instincts told him to snatch the weapon out of
the young man's hand and make him realize what a reckless idea it was to train with a woman. Then he wanted to
order everyone out of the room so that he could show
Mairead just what a woman should be doing with a man.

Hamish took a deep breath, rubbed the back of his neck,
and fought back the unwelcome need growing within him.
Never again would he abstain from enjoying a woman's
company for so long. There was no other explanation for
these constant lascivious thoughts.

Mairead spotted him. She looked surprised for only a
moment, then he saw the determination in her expression.
He knew then that this was not just a farce, but a setup,
and of Mairead's doing. The woman had thought a pathetic display of skill would demonstrate Foinaven's inability to protect itself. In turn, he would reach out to
Conor and ask for help. Like most women, Mairead was
willing to manipulate and lie to attain her goal. He should
have known that no one so beautiful could be trusted.

With a smirk, Hamish realized the group had been in
there training for some time and Mairead planned to keep
them there, waiting for him, until he arrived. They could
continue until they collapsed from exhaustion as far as he
was concerned.

Hamish took a step back and was about to duck behind
the partition to disappear the same way he had entered
when he heard a loud scoff. "What we are doing here, old
man, is hard enough without bored servants skulking
about."

Hamish raised a brow at the insult. He could not decide
whether the insult was more amusing or annoying. Crossing his arms, he stared at the older, lanky lad.

The boy's sparring partner grabbed his arm. "Be careful, Jaime," he hissed, worry blanketing every feature of his face. "He might be one of Ulrick's men."

Jaime shook his arm free. "If he were any good, he would have left with the rest of them. And he came from there," he said, pointing to the servants' entrance.

His friend took another look at Hamish and retreated a step. "He doesn't look like any servant I've ever seen."

Refusing to admit that his friend had a point, Jaime pursed his lips and pointed to the back door. "Whoever you are, you were not invited and are unwelcome."

Hamish narrowed his eyes and then shrugged his shoulders. "I *was* leaving when you chose to insult me."

The boy glared. The sparring partner swallowed, and the others close enough to hear what was happening had halted all movement.

"Hamish!"

All eyes, including Hamish's, immediately shifted to the soft female cry.

Mairead had not seen Hamish enter, but when she heard his deep baritone voice, her heart had stopped with fear. Underneath its jovial quality was something dark, cold, and very lethal, forcing her to shout out and get his attention.

Hamish glanced in her direction and without a word, once again turned to leave.

"Wait!" she called out, and then lifted up her gown and ran to where he stood.

Mairead had seen him the previous day only during dinner, and it had been brief. Robert had been coughing so much he retired soon after they started their meal. Little Rab had wanted to be with his father and rather than sitting with only Selah and Mairead for company, Hamish heaped meat onto his plate, grabbed a mug, and took his leave. No one saw him during the morning and where he ate his noonday meals, no one could say.

Just before Hamish could disappear behind the partition, Mairead reached his side and grabbed his arm, preventing him from leaving without stopping to physically remove her hand. She captured his gaze, hoping he would speak first, but just what it was she wanted him to say escaped her.

The Hamish of her childhood had been a kind older brother, but the man right before her was nothing of the sort. The way he looked at her was not at all brotherly. Desire smoldered in his dark green gaze along with an unmistaken element of distrust. The combination was creating havoc on her senses.

Flustered, she gestured to the men, all of whom were now standing and watching them. "Don't you have anything to say?"

Hamish pulled his chin inward, pretending to be confused. "You look very pretty," he said in his most charming tone. "I prefer your hair down and this simple dress to the fancier ones you have been wearing."

Mairead felt her heart race and for a second, she was taken in by his flattery. But only for a second. She refused to be rattled by him. Hamish may be a renowned flirt, but she was not inexperienced in the art. If he meant to redirect her thoughts, he was going to discover that she was not so easily manipulated. She had brought these men in here to achieve a goal and she would not be goaded into anger or dissuaded off her mission.

"That is not what I meant."

"No?"

Mairead swung her arm out, gesturing to the small group gathering around them. "I meant as interim commander do you not have any advice that can help these men with their training?"

Hamish arched a brow. Mairead's anger had disappeared and in its place was a disturbing look of expectancy. Aye, she created the situation, but it was not out of ill will. It was out of something else . . . hope. Mairead was hoping he would seek Conor for help.

For a moment, Hamish wished she had looked at *him* and saw hope. That he—not those he knew—could remove her fears. But she had not, nor was it likely she ever would. "It would take much more than two or three weeks of lessons to improve these lads." Then, lowering his voice, he added, "And I am fairly certain you are aware of that."

Mairead put her hands on her hips and pursed her lips. Pieces of her hair had come loose, framing her face in such a way as to make him imagine what she might look like after a night of being in his arms. Some small, sane part of himself screamed to step away and look elsewhere, but his eyes defied the good advice. Instead, they perused her body.

In return, Mairead did the unthinkable. Without breaking her gaze, she took a step even closer. "If you cannot train them, then at least give them advice."

His sheer size loomed over her. Women this close to him were either in his embrace or seeking ways to get some distance. Not Mairead. If anything, their proximity seemed to encourage within her a self-assuredness.

Hamish's jaw began to hurt it was so tense. She had jutted her chin out and straightened her shoulders in defiance, unaware that the move caused her gown to stretch tight around her breasts. The green in her hazel eyes sparkled with challenge. She was not trying to be beautiful and it only added to making her damn near irresistible.

Mo chreach! He was turning into a McTiernay. They fought with their wives all the time . . . but at least they got to kiss their women after the battle.

In truth, Hamish had always been baffled by McTiernay relationships. Verbally sparring with women was not something most men enjoyed doing. But Conor and Laurel argued ferociously *and* quite regularly. Each was incredibly stubborn and steadfastly determined to coerce the other into accepting their point of view. To Hamish, their arguments seemed pointless for rarely could either claim true victory. But he was finally beginning to recognize the side benefits that came with such heated debates. Those benefits, however, also came with a very permanent price when the woman was unwed and the younger sister of your brother's wife. And Hamish planned on returning just as he came—alone.

"I see not men who lack training," he replied, refusing to keep his voice low. "I see would-be farmers playing with real, if not pitiful, swords. So the only advice I have is to go back to using sticks before someone gets hurt."

Jaime, the taller boy who had thought Hamish a servant, had heard enough. He did not care if Hamish was their temporary commander or not; he was no longer going to stand by idly and be insulted.

He stepped forward, shifting everyone's focus to him. His grip on his sword was so tight, Hamish could see the whites of his knuckles. "You know *nothing* about my skills and abilities." Jaime's anger was unmistakable.

Hamish let his gaze float up and down the young man's frame and twitched his lips. His dark hair fell unkempt significantly past his shoulders and the numerous freckles made him initially appear harmless. But he was as tall as Hamish and his frame was already rather muscular, most likely from hard labor. And his dark brown eyes glowered with indignation. The young man knew nothing about how to fight, but Hamish liked his courage. "A Highlander warrior in the making, are you?"

Jaime gave a single curt nod, anger still radiating from every pore.

"Then you must be decent at the pike." The boy's eyes narrowed. "No? Then are you comfortable with the spear?" A tic started in the boy's jaw and Hamish knew the young man's so-called training had been limited to the makeshift sword he held in his hand. "Have you ever even *thrown* an axe hammer?"

Hamish paused. Silence filled the room. He quickly scanned the faces and returned his scrutiny back to the one who had the gumption to at least try to defend his honor. Hamish knew his words were incendiary, but he needed to end this sham—not for just today, but forever. What was happening within these walls was practically a crime. They were doing little more than prepping themselves to get killed.

Jaime stepped forward. "Fight me."

Hamish's eyes widened upon hearing the unexpected challenge. He studied the lad and grinned. Jaime's courage and pride were the first signs that at least one of them might someday be a true Highland warrior. "You cannot wield a weapon, but I admire your *meanmna*."

Hamish's smile only infuriated Jaime further. "I know I'll lose. But it won't be as easy to beat me as you think."

Hamish was silent for a moment. Out of the corner of his eye he could see everyone watching and wondering just how Jaime would fare against him. Mairead was not among them. She knew. A muscle in Hamish's jaw flexed at the reminder that Mairead was just using these men. It needed to end.

Hamish rolled his eyes, knowing it would bait the young man into an attack, even though Hamish appeared weaponless.

It worked.

The moment Jaime made his move, Hamish reached for his dirk sheathed at his waist. In one smooth movement, he freed it and lunged forward. The moment he hit the blade near the hilt, the sword went flying just as Jaime lost his balance and fell to the ground. All gasped as they realized the tall youth was on the ground with Hamish's blade at his throat.

Hamish waited for a second before he saw the acknowledgment of defeat in the young man's eyes. "I heard him"—he pointed to his sparring partner—"call you Jaime. Is that your name?"

"Aye," the tall lad replied shakily.

Hamish re-sheathed his dirk and held out a hand to help the young man back to his feet. "I'd focus on farming."

Gone was Jaime's confidence. He now looked defeated and disheartened along with the rest of the men in the room. It was as if they just realized how completely unskilled they were against a true opponent. The drastic shift bothered Hamish. Confidence needed to be earned, but to snuff out the little these men had through embarrassment was not an honorable method of proving a point. These young men wanted to be trained and should at least be given the chance. But to give that to them now would only encourage Mairead in her pursuit to manipulate him. She had arranged for their humiliation and she was going to have to live with the guilt of achieving her goal.

Hamish looked each young man in the eye. "I've accepted my brother's request to take over as temporary commander for Ulrick until he returns. Under that authority, I will decide on what training is done, by whom, and where. Until then, all such activity in the great hall is to cease and you are to return and resume what you normally do to help support your family."

Without any argument, every young man grabbed his things and left the hall. Their shoulders were slumped and most looked embarrassed. Mairead, however, was outraged. Hamish even more so.

He did not like the disdain he saw in her eyes when it was she who had intentionally orchestrated this mockery to manipulate him. "Any guilt to be felt is yours, Mairead, not mine. *You* arranged this absurd display. *You* gathered these men knowing their skills were lacking—significantly more than they believed. But what is worse, is that *you* intended to humiliate them to promote *your* cause. You've claimed I changed. Know this, you have too."

Mairead was at a loss for words and she did feel responsible for what had happened. However, she still thought it somewhat justified. "I was hoping that you see the desperation of our situation. But never," she whispered with vehemence laced in each syllable, "*never* did I think you would demonstrate their absence of any skill in such a humbling way."

Hamish cursed under his breath. Mairead was speaking the truth. The shock in those boys' eyes had filled hers, too. She had also believed them to be more skilled than they were. Probably even believed herself to be decent with a sword. "Do yourself a favor and don't pick up that little sword of yours if you ever come under attack. You would only be giving the enemy a weapon to use against you."

"You think me weak and incapable because I am a woman?" Mairead asked coolly, finally finding her voice.

She had been numb, but her emotions were returning with force.

A shot of desire, wild and hot, roared through Hamish's veins. Eyes blazing green, Mairead refused to yield or back down, even when she knew he had accurately called her on her feeble attempts to manipulate him. Any other woman, including Laurel, would be feeling at least some remorse. But not Mairead.

He crossed his arms to keep him from pulling her close and kissing her into submission. "On the contrary. I like the idea of a woman being able to defend herself. Watching her pull back a bow and let go an arrow can be very erotic," he drawled out, "*if* she knows what she is doing."

Mairead's thoughts raced through her head. She told herself not to care what Hamish thought or said. He was a large, hairy oaf who lacked any gentlemanly behavior. But for some reason, his opinion about her ability with a sword did matter.

She took a step closer, stopping just shy of touching him. She looked him straight in the eye and said, "I prefer the sword."

Hamish said nothing.

Mairead's cheeks were flushed and her scent was slowly undoing him. Once again her breasts were heaving with each breath she took. Hamish knew he should leave and get away from her while he still could. Swallowing, he pointed to the door. "Leave, Mairead, before I do something foolish."

"Why should that be any different?" Mairead taunted, ignoring the undercurrent of fury going through Hamish. The man's entire body was taut with warning, but she refused to heed it. "What could be more foolish than coming here to take Ulrick on alone?"

"Stay and find out," Hamish answered through gritted teeth.

Mairead glared at him once more. The man could be angry all he wanted, but she had reason to be angry too. *"Toll-tòine,"* she hissed as she tried to step around him.

Hamish's hand snatched her arm. He leaned down so that his lips almost touched her cheeks. "You might want to be careful when calling a man an arse, *aingeal*. It gives him ideas."

And then without hesitation, Hamish captured her head in his hands and crushed her mouth against his own. Her lips were sweet as honey and softer than anything he had ever known. Anger momentarily forgotten, need took over. Slowly Hamish let his tongue caress her lips and when he felt her resistance soften, he nudged her chin down with his thumb, and let his tongue slip inside before Mairead could guess his intent.

Mairead involuntarily moved closer to his warmth, unaware that her arms were moving to slide around his neck until her fingers delved into his thick hair. She had been kissed before—several times between her attempts to find love and her sister's continual crusade for her to find a husband—but no one had ever stirred one of the feelings ricocheting through her body that Hamish was creating. Her mind tried to fight the desire flooding through her, but her body refused to obey. The longer his lips caressed her, the less will she had. When she had felt the pressure from his thumb, she could only close her eyes and let her lips part for him.

Hamish felt a shudder the moment Mairead yielded to his desires. Instinctively he deepened the kiss, pulling her even closer. His primal urges flared to life and set his body ablaze. All he could think about was what it would feel like to have her in his bed and the velvety warmth of her skin pressed fully against his.

A loud crash of thunder shook the building and yanked him back to reality. With the last of his strength, he lifted his mouth from hers and looked down into her shimmering eyes. The emerald and gold pools reflected passion, along with a mixture of confusion and vulnerability.

Hamish softly caressed her bottom lip with his thumb. He had wanted to kiss her practically since the moment he had seen her and now that he had, he just craved her more. "I knew those lips would be good for kissing," he murmured.

The words broke the spell he had woven around her and Mairead instinctively took a step back. Her eyes grew wide as she realized just what had happened and with whom. She turned and rushed to the main doors of the great hall. But she did not open them. She just stood there, holding on to the handles, fighting to regain a little of her pride.

She turned around to look over her shoulder to find Hamish staring at her. Encouraged, she mustered her most casual tone and said, "You may have enjoyed that kiss, Hamish, but I have had many others far more pleasant. All I will remember from this experience is the feel of that frightening mess you call a beard."

Only after he heard the thump of the door did Hamish squeeze his eyes shut. Her little speech did not deceive him. Mairead had enjoyed it every bit as much as he did. And yet, that knowledge was not enough to prevent a surge of irrational jealousy.

Many others, Mairead had said.

Just how many men had she kissed?

* * *

Hamish finished putting a thin layer of oil along the blade of his broadsword and began to stroke the metal back and forth at an angle against the whetstone he had on his lap. To some, polishing a sword was an onerous chore that had to be done, but he found the repetitive movement relaxing, allowing his mind to flow back to the events of the day and plan for the morrow. And tonight, he had much to think about.

Hamish flipped the blade over and pushed thoughts of Mairead aside, and instead tried to focus on dinner and some of the unexpected conclusions he had made. Selah had informed him that Robert was not up to eating, so dinner had been small, limited to only himself, Selah, his nephew, and Mairead. They had dined in the great hall, which little Rab enjoyed. He had finally decided his uncle was someone who could be trusted and had shed his shy personality.

The boy reminded Hamish of Robert as a youth in both looks and mannerisms. He was eager to learn everything and very intelligent, understanding far more than Hamish would have assumed a child could at such a young age. Like Robert did when he was young, Rab used everyone's spoons, bowls, and plates to build a tower that defied gravity and stood upright until he was forced to dismantle it when the servants brought out their food. Without question, Rab was another true MacBrieve, loving to tinker with anything in arm's reach while asking questions on random topics.

After what Mairead tried to do in the great hall, it was not a surprise that she took advantage of the child's inquisitive nature. After some simple prodding, Rab began a string of questions on battles and with Mairead's help, even asked a few on how Hamish would defend a castle. Fortunately, being only five, Rab easily accepted the insubstantial answers being offered. He then tried to talk about what he knew of castles. Thank goodness Selah had been there to help because in the end, Hamish had learned far more than Mairead had.

The masonry of the great hall and some of the more intricate stonework of the castle were actually designed by Robert. He had apprenticed under another mason, who upon seeing his genius, allowed him to start designing some areas himself and to oversee the construction of the curtain wall. The two had grown very close and when it came time for the mason to leave, he knew that Robert would not be able to leave with him. So he declared Robert's apprenticeship to be over a year early.

At one time, Robert had planned to build a gatehouse that connected the tower to the curtain wall, but after his father's death, he had decided to just complete the wall. He wanted Foinaven to be a place that welcomed clansmen, not shut them out. Hamish had downed a full mug of ale hearing that one, wondering how two brothers' viewpoints could be so different.

Hamish flipped the blade again and reviewed his plan to deal with Ulrick. It was not a very complicated one— he learned from the McTiernays that most good ones weren't. What they were was inconspicuous. And his definitely was.

A key factor to its success, however, was its initial secrecy. Right now everything Hamish was working on could be considered part of a commander's responsibility. And while Robert had ultimate authority, if he knew certain aspects too soon, he might overrule Hamish's ideas and decide they were unnecessary. But with time, Hamish could build the appropriate lure to ensure Robert not only approved of the plan but hopefully was involved.

Until then, he expected Mairead to try various ways to learn his plan. The woman obviously was incredibly stubborn and would not give up on her idea of using Conor's army. Which meant she was going to be around— a lot.

Balancing his sword on his right knee, Hamish raked his left hand through his loose hair. It was rare that he found himself truly regretting something he did. Life was too short to constantly second-guess one's decisions and actions. And deep down, he felt no guilt about kissing Mairead. But he did regret it. For now that he had experienced her soft, full lips, all he wanted was to feel and taste them again.

Hamish could not remember ever being plagued with thoughts of a woman to this degree. The only explanation he could muster for the intensity behind his desire was his self-inflicted, prolonged abstention from female companionship. Unfortunately, that was something he would not be able to rectify until back on McTiernay land. He certainly was not going to entertain the notion of finding someone to release his physical frustrations while at Foinaven. Not only was he not sure who would welcome such advances without any promise of commitment, the only woman he desired right now was the one woman he absolutely refused to have.

Hamish put aside the whetstone and tested the blade with a piece of straw, verifying its sharp edge. Grabbing a rag, he dipped it in some water and then in a cup of vinegar, and began to rub the blade, thinking about the dull, tarnished sword one of the young men had left behind in the great hall.

After Mairead had announced she had kissed his beard and not him, he had needed something to do. So he had aided the servants in restoring order to the hall. The purpose had been twofold. He had genuinely wanted to help as he had been the motivation behind Mairead's request to dismantle all of the tables, but it had also given him the opportunity to casually probe the servants about what they knew of Ulrick, Robert, and their quality of life.

Most said very little, which was fine, for their body language had conveyed more than what their words would have. They did not fear for their positions for they knew neither Robert nor Selah would ever order their removal. And while they spoke little about Robert, Hamish got the impression it was less out of respect and more because Robert was his brother. Ulrick, however, brought a different reaction.

Answers about Ulrick were always brief and very respectful. Not a single person said anything that could not be said in front of Ulrick himself. And that alone proved several things. Even the servants who loved Laurel and Conor mumbled their frustrations when they were not within earshot. These people were afraid to even whisper. Their eyes would dart around before each reply, which only verified what Hamish suspected.

Foinaven had a mole. And probably more than one.

He had considered telling Selah tonight about his thoughts but decided it would have been pointless. She was incapable of believing someone might seek to harm her or Robert, especially after they had shown such kindness to all. Hamish wondered how he had ever loved a woman like her, but he had.

For years, Selah had been the one with whom he had compared every other woman. He had believed her to be his great love. His lost chance at happiness. And she was exactly as he remembered. She spoke the same, moved the same—even had the same sweet, gentle laugh. And yet, he truly was not attracted to her. More so, he could not fathom what it was he had loved about her twelve years ago.

Looking back, he understood why he thought he had loved Selah. At the time, she was the most beautiful woman he had ever seen. With her easy nature and kind spirit, it was natural to think he had been in love. But Hamish now doubted that it was love he had felt. He had just been too young to realize his feelings were mostly of lust and a sprinkling of awe that someone like her would even fancy him.

Hell, maybe he had never really loved *any* woman. Maybe he was not capable of the emotion. It was not like Selah was the only beautiful lady he had ever met and fallen for. Aye, the McTiernays had an infuriating habit of marrying them before he had a chance to capture their hearts. But he was certain that love existed. He had witnessed couples who were really in love. Conor and Laurel, Cole and Ellenor, even the twins had managed to find enviable women to share their lives. They were partners who challenged each other but were also fiercely loyal and supportive. Their relationships were highly passionate and possessive in nature.

Things he had never experienced with any woman.

Things he knew no woman had ever felt about him.

The soft sound of a door opening and closing stalled the depressing direction of his thoughts. He did not need to turn around to know it was Mairead. Something inside him smiled.

Mairead stepped inside the large room and froze upon seeing Hamish sitting by the hearth. Part of her wanted to leave and scurry back to her chambers, but another part urged her to go in and sit down anyway. The great hall was her favorite room at Foinaven. Robert had designed the crossed ceiling beams in a pattern to reflect her mother's favorite mountain, which the castle was named after. Mairead usually finished her day sitting quietly and alone in front of the large fireplace curled up in a chair until the last of embers died out, mulling over her frustrations.

Most of the time they involved Selah and her sister's refusal to do what was necessary to get the castle staff to do their jobs. Many of them, especially those assigned to the kitchens, were just in the wrong position. Poor Hellie was actually a very good cook, but her timid disposition allowed those around her to ignore her instructions or worse, bully her into following theirs. The situation required Selah's intervention, but she just would not support Mairead's solution—replace the servants with ones who could actually do the job. It was the same in positions throughout Foinaven, just in lesser degrees. But the castle and its staff were not on her mind tonight—her thoughts had been consumed by one particularly aggravating man.

After Epiphany, Ulrick and his threats had been all she could think about . . . until Hamish arrived. Since then, she had felt more confused, out of control, and helpless than ever. She also had this strange sensation of hope. That if she could just get Hamish to understand what was needed, all would be well. So far she had tried arguing, silence, yelling, and pleading to persuade Hamish to send for support. She had even resorted to an ultimate low— manipulation. But it was not until dinner tonight did she realize the true folly of her approach.

When Selah asked about the women in Hamish's life and why he had yet to marry, he had given her an answer, but it had been scant on the details. His personally aimed jests might have fooled her sister, but Mairead sensed that Hamish had been hurt deeply by not just Selah, but several women in his life. And when he nonchalantly discussed the one who had deceived him, Mairead had felt herself grow tense and angry. For that vile woman had done one of the worst things a person can do to another—she had made Hamish doubt himself.

That was why he had been so angry this afternoon with her. Her heart had been in the right place, but from Hamish's point of view, she had tried to play him for the fool by gathering those boys in just to force him into admitting Foinaven needed additional help. If the positions were reversed, she would have been furious too.

Still, Hamish was wrong about not sending for more help and she had come to the great hall to think of a way to talk to him about the situation. It was clear that he had no intentions of asking Laird McTiernay for help, but Mairead could not understand why. Maybe if she did, then she would be in a better position to make a counterargument, and explain just why Foinaven needed more than just what Hamish alone could provide. If he could grasp just how short-staffed the castle guard was, as well as how inexperienced, Hamish would have to agree that he did not have the means to protect this clan and his brother's position as leader from Ulrick when he returned.

Mairead stood quietly and watched Hamish work on the long, deadly blade on his lap. The muscles in his back rippled with each stroke. Those women who so callously rejected him were fools. Aye, Hamish was not very handsome to look at, but Mairead had had enough suitors to know that he offered things few men could—protection, strength, and intelligence. Plus, despite what she had said, he *could* kiss.

He was the first man she had met who possessed all the qualities she wanted in a man. Unfortunately, he also possessed a few aggravating characteristics as well. Still, if he were anyone but Robert's older brother, she would consider pursuing him as a possible husband—after convincing him to shave off that beard. But their family connection made the idea of them as a couple impossible. Not because her sister was married to his brother, that would be odd but definitely surmountable. His rejection of Foinaven and his family, however, was not. To permanently cut all ties with her sister and her home was . . . unacceptable.

And yet when he had kissed her all that had been forgotten.

She had told Hamish that she had experienced many other kisses that were far more pleasant. That had been a lie. A big one. She had kissed and had been kissed several times over the years, but not one had stirred her emotionally. Until this afternoon, she had found the activity merely a semi-pleasant way to pass the time. She certainly had never understood why some people found kissing so entertaining. Now she fully understood. Hamish's kiss had created sensations in her body she had never known to exist.

Since his guarding her while she bathed, Mairead had wondered what it would be like to kiss him. It did not mean she was attracted to him, for she never did like beards, but Hamish did have an incredible body that pulled at a woman sexually. Naïvely, she had assumed his kiss would be like others of her experience, but when she had succumbed to his embrace and kissed him back, all thoughts had ceased. She honestly had not been able to think. Gone were Selah and Foinaven and all her responsibilities. Even Ulrick was a distant memory.

Afterward, Mairead had chided herself for assuming Hamish's kiss would be like any other. Practically from the moment they had met, she had seen the desire in his eyes and it had stirred something primal within her. And when they kissed, her body had come alive to the point that even now, hours later, it continued to yearn for something that could never be.

Hamish dropped the wet rag on the floor and bent over to pick up a thick, dry cloth to finish polishing the blade's edge. "I know you caught me staring at your sister tonight, but I have no interest in Selah and have not had any for many years."

Mairead jumped at the sound of Hamish's voice. She had not realized he had been aware of her presence. If he believed she had been thinking about him and Selah just now, Mairead was not going to correct him. For she was *not* going to let him know the true direction of her thoughts.

"I believe you," Mairead finally offered, stepping out from the shadows. And she really did.

He *had* been staring at Selah through much of dinner. And it had caused Mairead to study him, examining his expression and trying to decipher what he felt for her sister. There was a serious side to Hamish she suspected few saw because they never bothered to look past his flirtatious mask. Like his younger brother's, Hamish's mind never stopped. It was constantly working. Examining questions and exploring the possible answers prior to asking them. Mairead had seen it tonight, when he talked about his inability to find love as well as when he had studied her sister. There had been no desire reflected in the depth of his dark green eyes, only curiosity and perhaps a little bewilderment.

"I do not think you would have been happy with Selah. She confuses you. I'm guessing that most women do."

Hearing the accuracy of her conclusion, Hamish stopped polishing and mumbled, "*All* men find *all* women confusing." Mairead strolled up to his side. "Is there something you need?" he asked, and then made the mistake of glancing at her. Mairead was impossibly beautiful. Her hair was completely free from restraints and the dark gold waves tumbled down her back, drawing attention to her perfectly rounded bottom. Without warning, need tore through him like a dull knife.

Mairead shrugged her shoulders. "I come in here at night sometimes before I retire to think. In this big space, I don't feel confined and my thoughts seem to find peace where they cannot anywhere else."

"I can leave," Hamish said reluctantly, even though he knew it would be a wise move.

He bent over to grab his things and Mairead instinctively reached out to stop him. Her fingers wrapped around his forearm. She could feel the sinew of his muscles and their strength. Her heart began to pound and she quickly released him. Needing to sit down, she took a step to her right and sat in the chair next to his, glad there was a small table situated between them. "Please don't leave. No one else is ever in here at this time, so I did not expect to find you. But it would be nice to have your company. That is if you don't mind having mine."

Hamish did not move. Mairead was hard to predict. She had used deceptive tactics this afternoon, had been dismissive about his kiss, and both manipulative and contemplative during dinner. Now she was being exceptionally pleasant. The woman was just as puzzling as she was alluring. And though Hamish knew he should just take the opportunity and leave, his curiosity forced him to stay. He nodded and resumed polishing his sword.

Mairead used her chin to point at what he was doing and asked, "Is this something you do often?" The work looked not difficult but tedious. And yet, Hamish's expression was relaxed, not that of one forced to complete a chore. "I just . . . well, you look . . . content."

Hamish paused for a fraction of a second before continuing to move the cloth along the metal so that it gleamed a little more with each stroke. Only one other woman had recognized the calming effects his nightly ritual had on him. Her ability to see into the real him had almost captured his heart. Opening himself up to Mairead would be a mistake. "No use owning a sword if it is not maintained."

Mairead tucked her feet underneath her, situated her elbow on the chair's arm, and then rested her chin on her hand. "I guess at the McTiernays, polishing a sword is something everyone does. Not here. I expect a lot of things are different here at Foinaven." She took a deep breath and sighed. "Do you miss your home? With the McTiernays, I mean?"

"I do," Hamish answered honestly. Then he looked her directly in the eye and said, "They trust me."

Mairead refused to flinch. Instead, she narrowed her own gaze. "I trust you."

Hamish scoffed and returned his focus to the blade in his lap. "No you don't."

Mairead pursed her lips together in frustration. She wanted to argue but couldn't. "Aye, you're right," she grudgingly admitted. "But I want to."

Hamish inhaled and bit back a curse. Her scent could

make the lower regions of a dead man come alive. It was a mixture of fresh meadows and flowers and the effect it had on him was powerful. Just one whiff and not only did he want to bed her, but part of him was compelled to tell her anything. But that part of him was just going to have to wait for satisfaction until he returned to the Mc-Tiernays.

He kept his gaze on the blade as he moved the cloth down its length. "But you won't trust me until I tell you my plan, which negates the value of having someone's trust." He paused to look her in the eye. "You and I both know that you don't want to know the plan, Mairead. You want to control it."

"That's not true!"

Hamish kept his gaze steady. "Then trust me."

Mairead opened and closed her mouth several times before she finally admitted that she could not. "I want to. I really do, but I just cannot fathom how *any* plan that does not involve confronting Ulrick with an equal, if not more powerful force, will convince him to leave Foinaven and never come back. Strength and power are the only things he respects."

Hamish put down his rag and set aside the polished sword. He shifted in his chair so that he could give her his undivided attention. Mairead honestly thought a McTiernay army was the solution. What she needed to realize was that he had brought something much better—McTiernay knowledge and experience. "Let's say I am persuaded to your way of thinking and I send word for Conor to send at least a hundred of his men. What is the plan then?"

Mairead crinkled her brow. What else was there to think about? "That's it. Nothing more would be needed. A hundred McTiernay soldiers would be more than enough to confront Ulrick when he returns."

"I agree. However, where exactly do you envision this confrontation taking place?"

Mairead blinked. The answer was obvious. "I expect it would be near or just outside the castle."

Hamish nodded in agreement. "So we would wait with our hundred men and confront Ulrick next to the village, where anyone in the clan—men, women, even children—could come, see, and possibly get involved, such as those lads training in here today."

Mairead adjusted her posture, suddenly feeling uncomfortable. "We would tell everyone to stay away."

"I'm sure we would and let's say that even worked. A simple instruction is issued, all obey, and not a single soul from the village gets involved when Ulrick arrives," Hamish stated without pushback. "What's next? How do you see Ulrick reacting to seeing a hundred McTiernay soldiers outside of Foinaven?"

"I don't understand."

"I'm asking you to think it through. Do you really believe Ulrick—someone who is battle-seasoned and power-hungry—would yield without a fight? That he would see our borrowed army and then simply call out and have his newly attained mercenaries drop their weapons and surrender without even *trying* to attain his goal? Do you think those mercenaries would leave without payment? No, I can see by your expression you know as well as I do that would not happen. If Ulrick and his men were confronted in such a way, there *would* be a battle." Hamish paused and pointed to the village located just on the other side of the great hall's walls. "And it would not just be Ulrick and a handful of mercenaries fighting experienced

McTiernay warriors. Remember many of your clansmen ride with Ulrick and when they die—because many would—you would have their wives and children to console and take care of afterward."

Mairead's shoulders slumped as she envisioned the horrific picture Hamish was painting. "Oh my God," she whispered.

"That is why I am not resisting Robert's 'no bloodshed' request. That route you so desperately want me to take only holds misery for everyone."

Tears formed in Mairead's eyes, which had grown dark with fear. "He knew this," she said so softly, Hamish could barely hear her. "Ulrick knew that we would never risk so many lives. We are doomed."

Hamish arched an eyebrow. "I wouldn't be here if I thought that."

Mairead shook her head and stared at her fingers tightly interlaced. "What can be done?" she asked rhetorically.

Hamish leaned forward and when she finally looked at him, he let his smile grow into a wide grin. "Well, I learned from the McTiernays that you never fight those you can outsmart."

Mairead bit her bottom lip. Her furrowed brow indicated her lingering doubt, but her hazel eyes brightened. She still believed there was hope. "There is a way to outsmart Ulrick?"

Hamish shrugged. He believed he could outsmart pretty much any man. He smacked his hands on his knees, then rose to his feet, picked up his sword, and gathered all of his things into a sack. "You will have to wait and see."

Mairead blinked. "What does that mean?"

Hamish slung the sack over his left shoulder. "I mean

that for the first time I see in your eyes a glimmer of trust. You are finally starting to believe that I might have thought this through and have a plan. That it's conceivable I can do more than just wave a heavy sword around. That I just might be intelligent, as well as arrogant, and know what I'm doing. All you want now is proof. But I'm not going to let you in on my plan. I think I'll just keep that to myself."

Mairead's mouth opened and closed several times before she realized what she was doing and clamped her lips shut. She *hated* that he was right. She hated that she had no clue what his plan could be, and mostly she hated that there was no way she was going to convince him to tell her. But she was going to try anyway.

Mairead stood up and stared at him right in the eye. "An honorable man, Hamish MacBrieve, would not keep such a plan a secret, knowing that my family and clan were at stake."

Hamish slid his free hand up along her arm to her shoulder and then gently cupped the back of her neck before leaning down. "And if I am not an honorable man, Mairead MacMhathain," he whispered into her ear, "then what is to stop me from kissing you and doing possibly much more?"

A quiver of desire went down Mairead's back as she held her breath. Hamish was doing it again. He was making her lose control, focus, and all ability to think. And he had not even kissed her yet. This was exactly what she had promised herself she would not let happen again.

And she was going to keep that vow.

Mairead mustered all her willpower and tilted her head toward his. She placed a soft kiss on his cheek and then whispered back, "There's your kiss. And just because you refuse to tell me your plan does not mean I won't find out what it is. I may be naïve to the ways of battle, but I am an extremely clever, not to mention stubborn woman. I will haunt your every move and I will learn just what it is."

Hamish backed up a step and laughed out loud, praying it disguised his racing heart. "I wish you luck with your endeavors because I imagine it will be very entertaining to watch you try."

Then without another word, he headed for the great hall's main doors and exited them without looking back even once.

Chapter Five

Mairead pulled the tartan around her to help with the biting cold. The wind had picked up since this morning, and the clouds overhead were accumulating. Soon it would be dark and the cooler night air would definitely bring rain. She entered the keep, leaned against the stone wall, and closed her eyes, fighting the inclination to bang her head out of frustration.

Despite what Hamish thought, Mairead did trust him. And she did think he was highly intelligent. And not only did she believe he had a plan to deal with Ulrick, she also thought it more than probable it would work. But those beliefs were not nearly enough to calm her troubled thoughts. Hamish's plan, whatever it was, solved one of her problems—keeping Ulrick from taking over the clan and ousting her sister from her home. However, whether his plan might also resolve her other problem was unknown. If it did not, she still had to find a way to protect herself. Yet if the result of Hamish's plan rendered Ulrick unable to threaten her or anyone else again, that changed everything. It would mean she was free to choose her future—a privilege she swore never to take lightly again.

Mairead had lain awake thinking about the possible methods a skilled warrior like Hamish might employ to confront Ulrick. Hamish might not have meant to give her clues to what he had in mind, but he had. His plan aimed to avoid bloodshed—or at least minimize it. It was clear that it did not require an army and his comments suggested that any confrontation would not happen close to Foinaven. Based on that final fact alone, Mairead could only surmise that Hamish planned to surprise Ulrick prior to his arrival, probably on the outskirts of their land. Without even a small contingent of fellow soldiers, it was not going to be battle, but one-on-one. Hamish must have intended this fight to be between just him and Ulrick.

At first, the image of them battling face-to-face horrified Mairead. Hamish getting injured—or even killed—was unthinkable. However, the more she mulled over the idea, the more her fears dissipated. Because no matter how she envisioned the fight, Hamish was always the victor. She had seen Ulrick train and Hamish's brief encounter with Jaime gave her enough to compare speed and skills. Hamish would win, and he knew it—which made such a fight the only logical plan possible.

She just needed some way to prove it.

Upon waking this morning, Mairead realized she did not need to understand the details of what Hamish had in mind—just the basics. Just enough to verify his plan would take care of not just her family—but permanently remove Ulrick as a threat, thereby securing her freedom to marry when and whom she chose. To learn that level of information ought to be simple for it would not take much to confirm her assumptions. She had mistakenly thought that nothing was faster—or easier—than eavesdropping.

Mairead pushed herself off the stone wall, searching for some of the positive spirit she had from earlier that morning. Her plan could still work. It just would not be nearly as easy as she had assumed. Like most men, Hamish was being incredibly uncooperative, even when he did not mean to be.

Mairead began a slow ascent up the keep's stairs, thinking upon the day's events and vowing that the next time she and Hamish met, she would be doing the outwitting. This morning, she had quickly met with the most critical of the castle staff and gave them their daily instructions, including how any follow up or noncritical staff should go to the Lady of the Castle. Selah would not like it. Mairead had always handled much of the responsibilities, especially anything that was remotely confrontational. But since Robert had become ill, Selah had foisted practically all the remaining castle responsibilities onto Mairead's shoulders as well, only to fuss later at decisions Mairead made that were not in line with her ways of doing things. But Selah's management style was avoidance and therefore time-consuming, and Mairead had things to do.

She had planned to spend the first part of the morning observing Hamish and had immediately gone to find him, thinking he would be in discussions with one of his guards. But no one had seen him. Even the soldiers she had assumed he was with had not spoken with him. Mairead had just come to the conclusion that she must have missed him when Hellie informed her that if it was like the previous two mornings, he was still in his bedchambers! Hours after everyone had risen! What was he doing in the mornings? With all the noise about, it could not be sleeping.

Mairead eyed the keep's door for almost another half an hour before she finally gave up and went to meet with the farmers who supplied the majority of food to the castle's guard. Candlemas was fast approaching and the day after the feast marked the beginning of the growing season. Everyone needed to be prepared.

These particular decisions were usually something Robert handled, but her knowledge on castle and general clan needs meant she was usually involved in the discussion. Her brother-in-law was a very passive man when it came to fighting, but he excelled at anything financial and always seemed to find a resolution that made everyone happy. It was one of the primary reasons so many had flocked to Foinaven and stayed, despite Robert's overall weak leadership style.

Today, Mairead was very glad Robert had requested her presence the past couple of years. Overall the meeting had gone smoothly and quickly, despite her being a woman. No doubt because there was not enough time to wait for Robert to recover and everyone knew that these decisions and agreements had to be made.

She had been about to begin the short trek back to the castle to spy on what she had hoped was an awake and active Hamish when she stopped short. He was standing by the village well—far from where she assumed he would be—at the castle, either still in his bedchambers or with the guards swapping stories. But what caught her by surprise was that he was not alone.

Quickly Mairead had ducked around the corner behind the cottage from which she had just emerged and peeked out to see what Hamish was doing. She was not quite close enough to hear what he was saying, but she knew it had nothing to do with his plans for handling Ulrick. He was smiling and chatting with two women who looked completely uninterested in getting water. It was not long before their small group started to grow. Doors opened and several more clanswomen headed to the well, all carrying empty water buckets they had no intention of filling.

Mairead had kept hidden, watching the spectacle that Hamish was not just causing, but enjoying. Almost half of the women who had gathered were unmarried, and most of them were younger than her. What did they see in him? Aye, the man was large, but he was hardly attractive! But deep down, Mairead knew the answer. Something about Hamish drew a woman to him. And to her mortification, she was not completely immune. But unlike the foolish women flocking to his side, she had no difficulty controlling those impulses. His mysterious allure did not negate the fact that he was the most frustrating, uncooperative, and secretive man she had ever met!

Mairead had forced herself to look away. Closing her eyes, she fought back the compulsion to stomp out and snatch Hamish from those possessive, seducing looks and smiles. But that act would make everyone think she was jealous—including Hamish. And it was most certainly not jealousy she felt. If she had to name her emotion it would be resentment. Aye, they were keeping him from her goal. For as long as he was with them, it was pointless spying on him!

Several high-pitched voices coming toward her had caused Mairead's eyes to pop open with alarm. Immediately, she had changed her expression and had tried to look deep in thought, but it had not mattered. She doubted if a single one of them even saw her as they passed by, all talking over one another about their encounter with Hamish. Mairead had only been able to pick out bits and pieces. Some of the single women were arguing with those already married whether Hamish meant something more with his compliments, for it seemed he had been flirtatious with all of them. The one thing that all of them had agreed was that he was the biggest and most thrilling Highlander they had ever met.

After all of them had passed by, Mairead had slowly looked around the corner for another glimpse. Hamish had left the well's edge and thankfully started to saunter away from where she was hidden. Able to keep from being spotted, Mairead had covertly followed him for several minutes, unable to decide whether she was envious or pleased with what she was witnessing.

Clansmen and women who would normally never stop to talk to anyone—let alone a stranger—did so, again and again. Foinaven was a collection of clans pulled together out of necessity. It created an atmosphere that could not be characterized as distrust, but wariness. People were cautious around those they saw every day. But to out-siders? They were between unfriendly and hostile. And yet, Hamish had moved with ease and his welcoming de-meanor seemed to invite passersby to say hello. It made no sense. Aye, he was a MacBrieve and came from this region, but most of the clansmen stopping to talk with him had not been with the clan twelve years ago. Something Hamish did or said somehow convinced one person after another, regardless of age or gender, to stop and engage him in a minute of conversation.

When Hamish returned to the castle, his puzzling be-havior only got more baffling as he went from engaging and friendly to unaffected, silent observer!

One of the farmers who had come to deliver meat from that morning's butchering directed his mule to turn too sharply, causing the empty cart to fall over. It not only startled the jenny, the accident also freed it, enabling the bucking animal to run all over the place, wrecking any-thing in its path. Instead of helping the stable boy and the

hobbling farmer to rein the animal in, Hamish just moved
to the side to keep out of the lad's way. Mairead had felt her
jaw actually drop in shock.

When the bottler and the castle carpenter argued,
Mairead found herself praying it would come to physical
blows, thinking only a man of Hamish's size could stop
them. The argument never did escalate beyond a string of
heated words and when it was over, Mairead wondered if
it was fortunate that her prayer had been unanswered. The
two men might have pummeled each other into bloody
masses with Hamish on the sidelines thinking "that's how
men work out their differences."

Then there was the last incident where Mairead had
been *sure* Hamish was going to intervene. Several older
children were playing chase nearby, causing a ruckus to
all those working in the vicinity. Despite shouts by their
elders for them to stop, they continued dodging in and out
of stalls and jumping over crates and barrels all the while
ignoring all cries for them to behave. Hamish just avoided
them as he headed to the kitchens, only to emerge with a
partial loaf of bread. Within minutes he was back in the
middle of the courtyard, by himself, quietly eating his
bread, just watching the fracas be resolved by one of the
older servants.

Most of those bustling around the castle sent him several cautious glances, their mannerisms a mixture of wariness and curiosity. Like she, they wondered why he just
casually stood nearby, never interfering. But the longer
Hamish remained, looking unconcerned with much of
what was going on around him, the more everyone returned to their daily routine with no concerns about his
interfering in their affairs.

Mairead had not been able to see Hamish's eyes due to
the distance and her vantage point, but she could tell that

he was studying everything and everyone. Probably had been since the moment he walked into Foinaven. And yet no one realized that Hamish was mentally logging every detail of their lives. And while she was impressed at his ability to observe life in Foinaven as if he were not there, it still grated her that he was not doing more.

Foinaven and its people were desperate for strong leadership—even if just for a few days or weeks until Robert recovered. And Hamish could give that to them, but not if he continued to refuse to offer guidance or establish order on the even simplest of things!

When another cart came in disrupting her line of sight, Mairead had decided she needed a better vantage point and had taken a step back in order to maneuver closer to the stables. She froze when her back came into contact with something large, bulky, and warm. She inhaled, knowing immediately not what—but who—it was.

Turning around, Mairead stared at Hamish's chest, refusing to look up. She wondered just how long he had been aware of her watching him. Forcing herself to answer his gaze, she tried her best to put on a slightly surprised but relaxed expression. It immediately turned into a grimace.

Hamish was bestowing on her one of his largest and most triumphant grins. No longer was there any doubt whether he had seen her following him around. Only question was when had he caught her and her gut said it had been some time ago. Along with everyone else he had been observing, she had somehow captured his attention.

Seeing her scowl, Hamish widened his grin. "I'm going to talk to the candlemaker and ask him for some additional candles for my room. Want to introduce me? Or do you prefer watching me from a distance?"

Mairead had forced herself to unclench her jaw and

smile back. "The candlemaker's name is Conley. You can find him in the north wing over there," she said, pointing across the courtyard, "next to the silversmith."

"Coming?" He used his thumb to point where she told him to go.

"Um, I'm too busy standing here doing nothing but stare at people. The importance of which is something I am sure you understand," Mairead replied, refusing to pretend she had not been watching him. Impossibly, his smile only grew. She bet she could count all his teeth.

Hamish rocked back on his heels. "Well, just in case you are tempted to follow me again, when I leave the candlemaker, I'm going to the buttery and get a drink, and then I'm going to visit Robert." He then crossed his arms and leaned down to whisper, "I won't be meeting the guards until the morning and I'll start with those in the towers. You can follow me if you want again tomorrow, but up by the battlements might make it pretty difficult to eavesdrop."

Then he had winked at her.

Just the memory of it made Mairead want to bang her head on the stone wall. The man defined what it meant to be infuriating. She was not sure how Hamish did it, but he always seemed to be one step ahead. Mairead did not consider herself to be a controlling person, but typically she was the one who knew all that was around her. Inexplicably, Hamish now had that power and if she did not find some means to yank that control back, her sanity would soon be in jeopardy.

Mairead paused just as she was about to push open the door to her chamber. A smile she had not felt all day curled her lips as an idea came to mind. It was not the cleverest of ideas, but it could not be any worse than eavesdropping had proven to be.

Best part was that even if it did not work, it would teach Hamish what it was like to be at the mercy of something he could not control.

Hamish heard the door open and smiled to himself as he heard Mairead's footsteps come toward the large hearth. He had just finished polishing his sword, which had been desperately in need of his attention. The entire time he had been working the metal back to a deadly shine, he had been thinking about her and their short encounter that afternoon.

He had asked Mairead to join him to see the candlemaker for two reasons. Partially, because making her realize that she had been caught spying would rankle her. As anticipated, her eyes had come alive and she had bristled with energy. Mairead was naturally pretty, but mad, she was gorgeous. However, the main reason he had wanted to aggravate her was something he would never let anyone—especially Mairead—know. The woman was incredibly good at spying.

It has been by pure chance that he had observed her behind him. Hamish doubted anyone else in the castle had known she was in the courtyard. Once he had realized what she was doing, he had decided to see just how good she was at reconnoitering. What he discovered was both impressive and disconcerting. Mairead was a natural. She moved neither too late or too early and she always had a place to go where she could remain hidden and yet have a line of sight to him. It was a miracle he had spotted her.

He could not afford to let her continue this latest strategy of hers. Sooner or later it would work and everyone would be aware of details before he was ready. Just when his brother learned certain aspects of his plan were critical to its success. Hamish's best option had been to make Mairead believe her spying was a hopeless act and to give it up.

He had thought it had worked too when she had left his side in the courtyard. At dinner, however, he was not so sure. Mairead had cheerfully enjoyed their less than tasty meal, oozing with a blend of satisfaction and confidence. Her expression was identical to the one Laurel McTiernay wore when she was about to teach Conor a lesson. Hamish's instincts all screamed that he was about to be taught something he had no intention of learning. And yet he could not wait to discover what it was.

Hamish hummed as he heard Mairead enter the great hall. Seems it would not have to wait. When her footsteps neared, he pointed to the chair she had sat in last time as he glanced over his shoulder. He was about to ask her to join him when he saw that Mairead was carrying a small bag in her hand. She was swinging it back and forth and the mischievous smile she wore should have made him wary. Instead, he found himself entranced.

She had changed into a simple dark green bliaut that hugged her curves perfectly. Her hair was no longer in a complicated knot but down, hanging over her shoulder in a very loose braid. He had thought Mairead could not be more beautiful than when she was angry, but the woman standing before him now took his breath away. Her hazel eyes snapped with excitement and in the firelight, she practically glowed with anticipation. The scent of her fragrant soap settled around him and he knew that if she came within arm's reach, he would be unable to stop himself from pulling her into his lap and kissing her. And in his current state of mind, she would only have to offer a fragment of the passion she displayed a couple days ago before he disclosed anything she wanted to know.

Hamish cleared his throat. "What do you have there?" he asked, setting aside his sword and cleaning tools.

Mairead bit her bottom lip and wiggled her eyebrows. She moved the small side table so that it was in between the two hearth chairs and then dumped out the contents of the bag. "For someone who prefers to be in control—" Hamish coughed into his hand, causing her to glance his way. Seeing his left brow in a high arch, she quickly amended her statement. "For *two people* used to being in control, I thought it would be interesting to see what would happen if we let fate—not your obstinacy or my inquisitive nature—decide just what each other knows."

Hamish eyed Mairead carefully and then picked up the knucklebones to study them. "Determination and persistence. Fantastic qualities rarely found in a woman."

"What about curiosity?"

"Interesting choice of words. Most would call what you do spying."

Mairead stared at him pointedly and then glanced at the bones in his hands. She tried not to look too eager, but Hamish had yet to agree to play. "If you agree to play, I will have no reason to observe you anymore."

Hamish laughed as he rolled the playing pieces in his hand, realizing that if he did agree, her presence would be a sensual form of torture. And yet sending her away was impossible. It had been too long since he had felt anything and what Mairead stirred inside of him was something he was not willing to let go—at least not yet.

Nodding, he pointed at her chair again. "So what rules are we playing by?"

"Whoever wins the round gets to ask the other a question," Mairead stated simply.

His agreement had come suspiciously easily and much too quickly. It was unnecessary to say that the other must not only answer, but do so honestly. And until just a moment ago, she had not been afraid that Hamish would tell an untruth, but that he might not agree to play. Now she wondered what element of her brilliant plan was amiss. The smile Hamish was wearing was far too genuine.

"Count by knuckle or set?"

Mairead licked her lips and smiled. "Set of course."

"Who goes first?"

"You," Mairead answered. "You're the guest."

Hamish shrugged and then shook the four small bones in his hand before dropping them. Each sheep knuckle could land in a way that provided one of four results: flat, twisted, concave, or convex. There were various ways to play with the pieces. Counting by set meant that rather than each bone holding a value, the combination of all four determined one's score.

Mairead looked down and frowned. Hamish had rolled one of each shape—the highest scoring combination. She swept the bones into her hand and tossed them on the table. She rolled a dog—four concave shapes—which of course, was the lowest of all set values. She sat back and asked, "Your question?"

Hamish studied her and found himself wishing they were playing another type of knucklebone game—one that involved the removal of clothes. His lower body immediately reacted to the thought. He quickly adjusted his seat and said the first subject that popped into his mind. "Why do Foinaven kitchens function so poorly?"

The question took Mairead by surprise. She had thought he would ask about that afternoon and what she was doing in the courtyard to which she had already planned a truthful but innocuous reply. But no, his mind was like that of all other men—either on women or his stomach. She had hoped it would be her as the dress she chose normally attracted a man's attention, but it seemed Hamish was immune. "Is the food really that bad?"

Hamish blinked. One of Mairead's semi-loose curls had fully escaped and now hung across her forehead. "Um, well, I'm used to Fiona's cooking—she runs the McTiernay kitchens—and she is one of the best in the Highlands."

Mairead watched his face change to one of longing as he thought about the McTiernay cook and her food. "So, aye, it is that bad. At least compared to what you are used to."

Hamish suddenly felt a little guilty. "Aye, but there is a price to pay for good food. Fiona's a tyrant to all who enter her kitchens—it doesn't matter who. I have even seen her speak sharply to the laird."

Mairead furrowed her brow and then reached up to play with the loose curl, wrapping and unwrapping the strand around her index finger. "Hellie is a good cook, but she could never be a tyrant. She is too sweet natured to run the kitchen and its staff."

"True, Hellie is nothing like Fiona," Hamish said, trying to think about anything other than what Mairead was doing with her hair. "I remember her as a child. My father could bark and yell and she would just paste on a smile and tell him that all would be better soon."

Mairead tucked her feet underneath her and then absentmindedly began to play with the end of her braid. "Aye. She is still the same way. No matter how poorly anyone performs in the kitchens, she offers only words of encouragement." She paused and her face shifted to a frown. "Hellie would be able to prepare better food if she had better help. And for that Selah is to blame. Not one person in this castle fears what will happen if they do their job poorly—therefore most do."

Hamish winced. "People don't usually respond well to threats."

Mairead narrowed her eyes and issued him an "I know that" look. "Maybe not, but they don't respond at all to my sister's empty, softhearted pleas."

"True," Hamish agreed, sliding the bones into his hand.

"But it's more than just low expectations. Many are given responsibilities in things that they just despise doing. I've spoken to Selah about the situation, but she refuses to listen."

Hamish handed the bones to Mairead. "Your sister will never be a taskmaster, but perhaps if she were to learn that her efforts to keep the people in their positions were not felt as a kindness but something more akin to punishment, she might be a lot more open to changes in staff."

Mairead took the bones and watched Hamish as he sat back and stroked his mangy beard. His suggestion was straightforward and highly likely to work with Selah, and yet it had never occurred to her that an emotional plea would be far more effective than a logical one. Hamish surprised her and once again she found herself drawn to him in a way that she could not explain.

She tried to imagine him clean-shaven like he had been twelve years ago, but the young man she envisioned did not correspond to the one before her. The years had changed him and Mairead imagined that his face was now like that of his body, hard and chiseled. The mental sight of him shirtless formed and Mairead bit her bottom lip, wondering if it was close to reality.

"I'm waiting on you."

Mairead glanced down at the knucklebones in her hand and realized what he meant. She let them fall. "I was just thinking about what you said."

Hamish picked up the pieces and rolled them. He was not sure how much longer he would have lasted if she had kept staring at him so attentively. She had been studying him, almost as if she was trying to see him. And then, without warning, her eyes had darkened with desire.

He glanced down, hoping that he won. The combination value was just slightly less than Mairead's. He grimaced and decided that if he could not ask, he would prompt an answer another way. "I suspect you were thinking about me."

Mairead refused to acknowledge or deny the statement and pointed down at the winning set on the table. "Just why do you flirt with women?"

The question had not been the one she had intended to ask next, but she needed to end the current conversation and at the same time turn the tables and make him feel uncomfortable for once. Plus, she was actually extremely interested in the answer. The man never stopped flirting and Mairead found herself constantly battling her emotions because of it.

Hamish shifted in his seat at the unexpected inquiry. They both knew the purpose behind her request to play this game and her question should have been about Ulrick and his plan. As far as his flirting, it was just something he did, especially in situations like now, where he needed to regain control of the situation and his body. But in general, he did it merely because he enjoyed making women smile and seeing them blush. Nothing more.

He might not be a saint, but his reputation of being a ladies' man was highly exaggerated. His fellow soldiers thought he was just as friendly with women privately as he was publicly. Rather than correct them, Hamish used their mistaken impression to his advantage. It kept them from prying into his personal business and allowed him to be alone at night without being taunted. And when he wanted company, he was quite selective in whom he sought out. There were a handful of widows who were lonely too but only wanted some periodic company, not marriage. Hamish doubted he was the only one they saw, but the arrangement worked. At least until several months ago when he foolishly thought he was in love with Wyenda. Afterward, his desire for women had vanished and even now the prospect of going back to the widows held little appeal.

"Is it a complicated question?" Mairead prompted, her large hazel eyes blinking periodically as she stared at him.

Hamish returned her gaze, refusing to be rattled. "On the contrary." He collected the bones and then rolled them. "My answer is simple and therefore I'm not sure you will believe me. The truth is, I enjoy it."

Mairead gave him a pointed look. She thought about arguing for a better, more complete answer, but what she saw in the dark green depths made her realize there was not one. With an exasperated sigh, she rolled the bones.

Seeing he had the better hand, Hamish grinned. "My turn. Why should I stop flirting?"

Mairead snorted and rolled. "I doubt you could even if the King of Scotland himself demanded it of you."

Hamish picked up the pieces and clucked his tongue. "That was not an answer."

Mairead narrowed her eyes and remembered the young girl's comments from that morning. "Why flirt with women you have no feelings for? It is akin to lying, giving them hopes of something more when the only thing you are interested in is amusing yourself."

Hamish leaned forward. "First, it is not simply to amuse myself. Second, I have never been inclined to refrain from flattering a woman when it was deserved. Third, offering a few kind words is not a proposal of marriage. If anything, flirting helps when dealing with those of your frustrating sex. A playful comment can eliminate tension. And last, I have never known simple, well-intentioned words to ever hurt anyone." He dropped the bones.

"Kind words," Mairead mumbled to herself before counting the bones and gathering them in her hand. "Flattery never hurt anyone. Flirtation, however, is insincere. It's dishonest from one who never plans to marry."

Hamish quirked a brow.

Mairead began to repeat what she had heard that morning. *"Ah, lass, you are much too pretty to want attention from an old man like myself. I have no doubt that there are many young suitors eagerly seeking your hand."* Mairead rose a brow. "Was that not what you said to one of the girls at the well?"

Hamish felt his face redden, realizing Mairead had been following him even longer than he had suspected. His blush must have been noticeable because Mairead bit her bottom lip and began to giggle. He swallowed as he fought the compulsion to taste that lip himself. He had been doing well so far, enjoying her presence and how open and easy they were in each other's company. Friendship was something he had only briefly experienced with one other woman, but this was becoming deeper, far more compelling, which meant far more dangerous. A practical, cautioning voice began whispering to him to focus on the game, not on her.

Ignoring her muffled mirth, he cupped the four sheep knuckles in both his hands and shook them vigorously. His violent action caused Mairead's laughter to break free. Rather than being miffed that she was enjoying his discomfiture—though she was egregiously mistaken as to its cause—he fought from joining her. Her laughter had not the melodic quality some women possessed, which he admittedly had found quite alluring on certain occasions. Instead, hers was honest and the sincerity of it had an appeal all of its own.

"I doubt shaking them harder makes a difference," Mairead said, showing no guilt over her amusement.

Hamish continued shaking, but he spared her a single, highly arched eyebrow. "That is not *exactly* what I said." He dropped the bones, pointed at the winning result and then her. "Just why do you think I don't want to marry?"

As soon as he asked the question, he wished he could take it back. He had been thinking of Mairead when he had been pummeled with questions from all those women. She was so unlike them, which was why he suspected her string of suitors was quite long. And the thought had not set well with him this morning and it still didn't. But he did not want her thinking that he could become one of them.

Mairead looked down contemplatively at her losing combination of knucklebones before picking them up and rolling them. "The other night—you spoke of that woman Wyenda. It sounded like you had given up on ever marrying."

Her accurate assessment caused Hamish to be motionless for a second. He was glad the game gave him something to do. Thankfully he lost the round for he still was at a loss for words at how easily she seemed to read him.

Mairead smiled when she saw four convex shapes appear. The topics of marriage and flirting were interesting, but it was not the purpose of the game. She needed to bring it back to his plans for Ulrick; problem was he was well aware of her ultimate goal. But what he did not know was that tonight all she wanted was enough information to confirm her assumptions. For that, an indirect question would be far more successful.

"Why must you control everything?" she finally asked.

Hamish had leaned forward to pick up the bones but stopped and instead sat back. "Quite a peculiar thing for you to ask."

"You didn't answer my question."

Hamish shrugged. "I don't need to control everything. Not in the least. And my actions here at Foinaven prove that point exceedingly well. I did not control Selah, my brother, or my coming back here. And of all the people to say that I have a need to control everything, I find it incredibly odd coming from you. I have never met any female who desires control more. And trust me, I've met a few crazy women. Crevan McTiernay married one."

Mairead felt her jaw tighten as a frisson of anger raced through her. "And is he unhappy?"

Hamish pursed his lips and returned her stare. When it was clear that she would continue to wait for a reply, he said honestly, "Quite the contrary. Then again, Raelynd *trusts* Crevan."

"You say that as if I do not trust you."

"You don't."

Mairead scooted forward, but when she did, her hair tie got caught in one of the tacks used to upholster the chair. Frustrated, she pulled the tie, freeing her hair, and then looked up pleadingly. "Hamish, I do trust you. I do believe that you have a plan and that it will work. If I didn't, I wouldn't be using a game to learn more about what you have in mind, but every method and means I could devise to thwart your efforts."

Hamish could see she spoke honestly, and knowing that she really did trust him rattled him almost as much as seeing her hair fall all around her. With his eyes closed, he took a deep breath. He had always wanted a woman to believe in him, but Mairead obviously did not, otherwise she would not be pressing to find out just what his plans were.

"Why follow me then?" he asked, remembering the very first time he saw her and how upset she had been that he had come north alone. Before she could answer, he waved his hand dismissively. "Don't answer that." He reopened his eyes, caught her gaze, and held it. "What is this 'need to know' really about? Because I'm thinking this is less about my plans and more about yours and how I ruined them, unless you still are going to deny you were hoping to meet a potential husband the day I arrived."

Mairead stared at him for almost a minute, barely breathing. "Perhaps I am just ready to settle down."

Hamish continued to hold her gaze for another minute. He did not for a moment believe that her motivation was simply a yearning to be a wife and mother. Over the years, he had met plenty of women who fit that description and Mairead was not eagerly looking for a husband . . . and yet she *had* been seeking one when he had arrived. So if Mairead did not want to marry, why had she been compelled to find a husband? It did not make sense, for no one compelled Mairead to do anything. But something was inducing her inordinately strong desire to learn about his plans with Ulrick and he wanted to know what it was.

For the level of her angst was certainly not due to a simple lack of knowing.

They continued bantering back and forth for a while, each carefully scripting questions and cleverly avoiding answering those they didn't want to. They found themselves not only to be enjoying the game, but also each other's company. Hamish learned as much about her by the questions she refused to answer as the ones she did and wondered if Mairead was similar in her discoveries about him. Her questions were incredibly clever and he consistently was trying to outmaneuver her with his answers. While each answer he provided seemed nondescript by itself, he suspected that his efforts were about as successful as hers.

When he thought about it, he now knew more about Mairead than any other woman—including those he had spent a few hours with for countless days. Granted most of those hours had been spent focused on more physical needs, but the talking they had done had been more about the clan or the weather. Not about themselves. And more terrifying was that in some ways Mairead now knew him better than anyone. I mean his friends and fellow soldiers knew the basic things—important things—like how he fought, enjoyed looking at a pretty face, and how much ale he could enjoy and still be functional in the morning. But personal things? Like his favorite color, time of day and year. Not just what his favorite foods were, but why it was his favorite and many other things that went far deeper— like what he thought about when he was by himself and where he liked to go when he wanted to be alone. And though he never outright stated his feelings on what had happened twelve years ago, an astute person could construe his feelings and Mairead was very, very astute.

Hamish may have been able to keep her in the dark about his plans, but he was in dangerous territory about himself. The game needed to end.

He picked up the knucklebones and began to shake them. "Last roll. If you win, ask the question you really want to know. If I win, then be prepared to tell me why you were husband hunting if you have no desire to marry."

Mairead gulped as Hamish let go. She had hoped she had escaped that subject as he had not brought it up again. In the hours they had been playing, she had told him much about herself. A few times she had wondered if she had told him too much.

Mairead looked down at the table. Her heart stuttered. Not a single convex shape landed and his roll would be difficult to beat. He gave the bones a nudge so Mairead could reach them. She rolled, held her breath, and then sighed in relief seeing the coveted shapes appear. She got to choose the topic. And it would not be about why or whom she intended to marry.

Mairead knew what she wanted it to be, but asking what his plans were would be a wasted question. There were so many ways to answer that question honestly without divulging a thing. But maybe a more pointed inquiry might be best. Something that not only plagued her curiosity but if she was right, its answer might just give her the insight she needed. "Just what do you do in your bedchambers in the morning?"

Hamish inhaled, immediately regretting it as her scent filled him. The woman was eating through all of his defenses. He rose to his feet and moved to pick up his things.

Realizing that Hamish was not just standing to stretch his legs, Mairead jerked to her feet and closed the distance between them. "You're leaving? But you didn't answer my question."

Hamish made the mistake of looking down into her hazel eyes. They had grown large and liquid and her honey-colored hair gleamed in the firelight, swinging around her waist with every movement she made. He had to get out of the hall. Immediately. The desire he had worked so hard to suppress was about to take control and if their last kiss was an indicator, Mairead might not stop him if it did. "I'm tired and someone I know believes I rise late enough as it is."

Mairead stared into his eyes. Their deep green color had grown so dark it was like looking into fathomless pools, swirling with emotion. Every nerve ending had awakened to their unspoken message of want and desire, causing an unfamiliar feeling to build deep inside her. Disregarding the voice in her head telling her to be care-ful, she listened to the one that was jumping up and down, reminding her that he did not answer her question. So in-stead of taking a step back, she did the opposite and moved even closer.

Moving to her tippy toes, she lightly clutched his arm for support and closed the remaining distance. "Your re-fusal means that I am right. You rise early, probably ear-lier than everyone." Then leaning in close, she murmured into his ear, "I believe you are secretly plotting something in your chambers, no doubt related to your plans. Some-day I will learn what they are."

Hamish stood completely still as her heels returned to the floor. It took everything he had to fight for some modicum of control. But he refused to let her know how much she affected him and reached out to caress her cheek. "No need to wait. I'll tell you right now exactly what I am doing in my chambers."

Mairead's eyes closed, reveling in his touch.

Hamish knew he was playing with fire, but he could not stop himself. "I am only doing what everyone else does in their chambers," Hamish replied. A second later, her eyes flew open and her jaw dropped as his implied meaning was understood. Before she could say a word, he leaned down and she could feel his soft beard against her skin. He whispered in her ear, "I sleep. Nothing else. Until tomorrow, *m'aingeal*." Then he gave her a light kiss on the cheek.

With the feel of his warm lips still on her skin, Mairead's heart began to pound so furiously against the walls of her chest she felt lightheaded. She reached out to clutch the back of the chair Hamish had been sitting in for balance. Between his tender kiss and the invitation to try again tomorrow, her mind was racing.

In the past few hours, she had revealed more about herself than she had intended. Nothing secret. Nothing important, but altogether Hamish knew her in a way few did. But he had known her even before they had played. *Determination and persistence. Fantastic qualities rarely found in a woman.* Hamish had meant what he said. He actually admired her stubbornness.

Mairead waited until Hamish disappeared out the door before collapsing in the chair. She had been a fool. She had spent all afternoon, dinner, and most of this evening convinced that whatever strange attraction she had for Hamish was under control. If anything, his unexplainable lure was only growing, drawing her to him.

If the man could read her before, now after their little "game" he could probably predict her own thoughts and actions. That alone was enough to terrify her, and it would, if it were anyone else. With Hamish, rather than feeling judged, she felt accepted. She had been surprisingly comfortable telling him about herself. But what was more profound was what she had learned about him. He, too, had given her a peek of who he really was. An intelligent, complex man who was far more introspective than he let others—even those close to him—believe. A man who was deeply affected by the circumstances of those around him and despite his words and actions, he was still extremely loyal and connected to this clan and his brother.

The more she learned, the more she wanted to know despite the risk it posed. For she was on the verge of losing her heart to a man who knew her like no other would. A man who made her feel strong and feminine at the same time. A man whose pull she could not deny.

A man who, in the end, would break her heart with his inevitable departure.

Chapter Six

Mairead gave up the pretense of finding something to do around the keep's entrance and began to pace in front of Hamish's door. The sun had risen almost an hour ago and based on what Hellie had told her, he was still in his chambers and had yet to join the world. The old cook was usually the first person he visited and he had yet to make an appearance at her door.

Mairead wondered if Hamish was sitting in his room intentionally, knowing the agitation it would cause. Only a deaf man could be sleeping right now. On the bottom floor, the noise from the courtyard would make slumber impossible. As the center point for nine clans, Foinaven was always active, especially during the few daylight hours available in the winter months.

What could he be doing? Mairead wanted to shout out loud. An image sprang to mind and a frisson of jealousy flashed through her. On impulse, she went to the door and whispered, "If you are really doing what every other man does in his chambers, it means you are not alone."

Hearing no answer, she let out a frustrated groan and resumed her pacing.

Last night, she had lain awake for what felt like hours. Her mind had hopelessly sought a stratagem that would get her the answers she sought without overtly being in his company. But before she could crystalize an idea, her thoughts would drift back to the last few moments she had spent with Hamish.

The man was perplexing to the point of insanity. Each time she was near him, he jumbled her emotions. Last night, Mairead had even thought she might be losing her heart to him. Thank goodness she had awoken more clear-headed. The man was not at all attractive. He enjoyed aggravating her. He was impossible. Arrogant. And even if he was not all of that, he was family. She just wished she could remember that last fact whenever she was in his presence.

Truth was, she could not think of Hamish as a brother. He brought out all kinds of instincts in her and none of them were that of a sibling. Moreover, it was clear that he did not view her as a sister either. So what *had* she been thinking when she had whispered in his ear? Because her actions were practically a dare and he had not backed away from the challenge.

Mairead stopped her pacing.

His kiss had been his *second* reaction to her overture. His first had been something more akin to panic. The more she thought about it, Hamish always became flirtatious when uncomfortable. Such knowledge could be very advantageous if used appropriately. With careful probing and a few coquettish comments of her own, Hamish might accidentally reveal the nature of his plans—maybe without even knowing it. She would ask various questions and gauge his response. When her inquiries came close to the truth, Hamish's flirtatious means of misdirection would almost certainly become more overt and more outrageous.

She had only to look at his recent behavior for verification of her theory. Each touch, comment, and kiss had all been in an effort to discombobulate her. They had not been real or meant anything to him. They had just been a distraction. The knowledge hurt a little, but Mairead vowed to use that pain to help shield her from his future attempts to manipulate her in such a manner. In fact, today such tactics would not work in his favor—but hers.

"Hamish MacBrieve," she whispered to herself, "you are about to meet your match."

Hamish grimaced at his unintended handiwork as he stared at his reflection in the piece of glass. He had found it in the myriad of things stored in the corner of the room and decided to really look at himself and see if all the remarks women had been saying about his beard were true. The second he had seen his face staring back at him he had realized Laurel and Mairead had been kind with their comments. Since Epiphany, his beard had gone from merely overgrown to a misshaped mass that looked laughable. Foul he could deal with, even dreadful or menacing, but ridiculous? No.

Thankfully, when he spotted the glass, he had also seen a broken pair of spring scissors. It had taken little effort to sharpen the edges and reconnect the thin, flexible piece of curved metal that held the blades in alignment, but eventually his efforts paid off and the scissors worked . . . too well. When he had tested them on himself, he had accidentally sliced a large chunk of his beard.

And he knew whom to blame. Mairead.

This morning he had risen nearly three hours before dawn to ensure he returned in time to keep from rousing hers and anyone else's suspicions. But his success of the past few mornings meant there was much to do. More than the three hours he had allowed. Plus, once finished, he had been in serious need of another bath. If he had returned with mud and dirt caked on the majority of his body, the laundress would have notified Mairead. Her curiosity would have been sparked and he would have had to endure a litany of questions he was not going to answer. It had left little choice but to take another time-consuming detour for a freezing dunk in the river.

By the time he had snuck back into his chambers, he had grown exceedingly chilled. He had started a fire, stretched out his wet clothes to dry, and thrown on his newest leine. It was when he had reached for his tartan that he had spied the broken piece of glass and scissors. He was just about to make the first snip to trim his beard, when he heard her whisper, "If you are really doing what every other man does in his chambers, it means you are not alone."

The insinuation was as unmistakable as the distinct ring of jealousy in her tone. The knowledge that Mairead might feel something deeper for him caused an unexpected shiver to ripple through him just as he had closed the now very sharp blades. He was fortunate he had only sliced off a large swath of facial hair and not part of his actual cheek.

However, the error had forced him to make a choice. He had meant to give himself a trim. Whereas shaving removed a protective barrier he had hoped to keep in place. Without his despised beard, his ability to stay away from Mairead was going to be much more difficult. His only other option was to leave the hole. Hamish envisioned Mairead's face morphing into hysterics the moment he stepped out the door.

Without further thought, he began to snip off the rest of his beard and shaved. When finished, he sat back to study his handiwork in the glass. His skin was understandably slightly pink and tender, but he did look far more present-able. Inspired, Hamish pulled his pony tail to the side and cut off the ragged ends so that his hair no longer hung past his shoulders in various lengths. When done, he felt a lot more like his old self. Next time he encountered Mairead, it would be *she* who would need to fight to remain in con-trol for *Hamish was back.*

He was once again a charmer of women and the man every female, young or old, loved to be around. So none of them ever came close to falling in love with him, they were still charmed by his attentions. Even Laurel was sus-ceptible to a well-placed smile. And Mairead MacMhathain would be no different. Next time he saw her, he would flash her his most devastating grin. Then after she swooned at the sight of his dimples, she would turn into just another ordinary female. Her appeal would disappear and he would finally have control of his body once again.

Whistling, Hamish tucked in his shirt and adjusted his pleats so they fit securely under his leather belt. His stom-ach growled. Before he met with Robert, he definitely needed to grab something from the kitchens. He hoped Hellie had saved one of the tastier morsels for him. Step-ping outside, he turned toward the direction of the buttery but had barely taken three steps before his path was blocked. The scent of fresh meadows and flowers hit him and he could not help but inhale.

* * *

The moment Hamish emerged from his chambers Mairead had quickly spun around and moved to intercept him. For the last hour, she had been rehearsing what she was going to say, but the moment her eyes fell on Hamish's clean-shaven face not a single word of it came to mind.

Power and strength radiated from him in waves. He was a massive, self-confident presence with a unique blend of authority and relaxation. The combination was incredibly compelling and she was far from immune.

His height and strength had always been obvious, but his new leine, unmarred with stains, fit him perfectly, molding his chest and making the muscles of his shoulders and arms even more apparent. The ripples visible beneath the fabric made her fingers yearn to know just what they felt like. Though still pulled back in a ponytail, his shorter auburn locks looked thick and healthy and beckoned to be played with. But what held her completely transfixed was his face. Without the bushy beard hiding his features, Hamish was, simply put, beautiful. She could never remember using the term before regarding the opposite sex, but seeing Hamish MacBrieve well dressed and shaven was like seeing her secret fantasy of what an ideal Highlander should be come to life. He was so intensely and overwhelmingly male. And she was not the only one to notice.

"You're staring, *m'aingeal*."

Mairead clenched her jaw and closed her eyes. The arrogant chuckle had been unmistakable. She *had* been staring. She had not been able to help it. She was just lucky her mouth had not dropped wide open as well.

With a deep breath, she forced herself to gather her wits and focus. Her own plan depended on her being immune to his charms. She was in serious trouble if she could not even look at Hamish without fear of drooling all over herself and him! Besides, the damn man had ruined every idea she had had so far and he was not going to wreck this one as well just because he decided to shave and reveal his dimples. If anything, it should make her sweet-filled words easier to deliver. Besides, she, too, had taken great care with her own appearance this morning and Hamish's current expression made it obvious that he was not unappreciative of her effort.

Mairead reopened her eyes and slightly arched her right brow. "Of course I was staring. I was shocked to finally be able to see your face. It's such a drastic departure from what you have been looking like that I think I'm entitled to gape a little. But that doesn't explain why *you* are staring at *me*."

Hamish blinked at the unexpected retort and at the fact that she was right! Mairead was supposed to be susceptible to *him*—not the other way around. But did the woman have to smell so good? And her dark gold hair, the way it was pinned on top of her head with little ringlets falling free, could tempt even the most honorable men. Not to mention the gown she wore; while simple, it had a low bodice that showed off her figure and toyed with a man's ability to think. Her beauty was no longer supposed to affect him this way!

Hamish went on the offensive and gave her his most dazzling smile. "I stare because not another woman compares to you." He could see it bothered her that she had run from the truth whereas he openly admitted it. "Don't fret. Your pretty eyes can feast on me for as long as they like, *aingeal*."

Mairead bit her bottom lip. Hard. She needed the pain to keep her mind clear, but Hamish was making it hard.

Angel. It was not just the endearment, it was how he said it. Soft and warm. Like he meant it. If she was not careful, she was going to be susceptible to his means of flirtatious persuasion and not the other way around. It was time for Hamish to be on the defensive.

Releasing her bottom lip, she intentionally and slowly licked it. Simultaneously she let her gaze drift down his entire body and then back up to linger on his mouth. "You must really want another kiss to be willing to shave and don a new outfit just for me."

Hamish could not stop the tremor of desire coursing through him as her eyes devoured him. Any second he was going to have to turn around and go back into his chambers to keep the world from knowing the effect she had on him. Mairead was obviously employing a new tactic. That she would do so was expected, but *this* particular tactic was not. Worse, her flirting was working . . . at least in part.

After his parting taunt last night, he should have foreseen that she would have changed her approach to discovering his plans to deal with Ulrick with something less direct. However, he wondered if she knew just how much danger she was putting herself in. For her flirting, if she continued it, would eventually work. However, it was going to achieve a far different goal than she had in mind. He could only withstand Mairead's carnal looks and sensual words for so long before he kissed her again and in such a way that she would never be satisfied by any other man.

Her new approach was dangerous on one level but not in the least on another. Did she really think that being charming would make him susceptible to divulging just anything? If so, she was going to be disappointed. He was a *master* at the art of flirting. He usually did not use it as a ploy to achieve his own agenda, but this was an exception. He could not remember being so eager to flirt with a woman.

Leaning down so their faces were only inches apart, he purred, "You like playing with fire."

She smiled up at him, pretending to be completely unfazed. "I do. In fact, I love to play with it. And if I ever found the right man, imagine the *hours* of fun we would have."

Hamish forced his jaw to unclench. *Ó mo chreach*, she was good. Lucky for him he was better. "You forget. I don't have to imagine. And if *you* are craving one of my kisses, all you need to do is ask. I'm more than willing to comply, *m'aingeal seòlta beag*."

Mairead swallowed at his newest endearment. His breathy tone made "cunning little angel" sound like a compliment, but it was also a hint that he had already figured out her plan and was keen to see it fail. His green eyes had grown dark, daring her to continue the game she had started. Mairead needed no more convincing to know she was not going to be able to use flirtation to trick Hamish into giving away any tidbits about his plan. However, she also knew that the man was not completely unaffected by her actions. She might eventually have to admit defeat, but it did not have to be now.

"I don't believe you," she said softly, both surprised and elated that her voice was smooth and steady. "I think it *was* me who inspired you to shave." Her lips curled upward, with just a hint of challenge.

Hamish returned her smile with one of his own. "Perhaps you are right, *aingeal*. But then who could blame me? God made a mouth like yours for a man to kiss."

Mairead fought the compulsion to prove him right and

instead slightly shrugged her shoulders. "It is unfortunate for you men then, as the Lord gave this mouth to me to do with as I will. And after kissing half the men around here, I can say with confidence, my lips prefer to be left alone."

Without warning, sparks of jealousy ignited in Hamish. She had to be exaggerating and he wanted to demand to know exactly how many men she had kissed, but he knew the answer would not matter. For it riled him that even one other man knew what she tasted like. "If you really feel that way, then that only means you have never been properly kissed."

"Hmm," Mairead said with a sigh. Then she tapped her finger against her chin and asked, "Are you also including the one you gave me?"

She was goading him and he was seconds away from reminding her of just how good it felt to be held in his arms. "I think you were more rattled by it than you let yourself admit."

Mairead's hazel eyes widened. "Oh, but I was rattled. Robert is married to *my* sister, which practically makes me *your* sister." The reminder was less aimed at him and more at herself for she was close to doing something incredibly foolish—like throwing herself into his arms—despite the people mulling about and the inevitable consequences.

"I may be many things," Hamish growled, "but *I am not your brother*."

Mairead swallowed. His tone was intimidating . . . which meant her words had actually hit a nerve. It was only fair, she told herself. He had hit several of hers. "But we *are* family."

"By marriage only." Hamish snatched her hand and pulled her close. "Your pulse is racing, proving you are not as disinterested as you sound. But do not worry, *m'aingeal anamúil*, I will not kiss you again . . . at least not until you ask."

Hamish then took a step back and let her wrist go. Mairead rubbed it, hoping it would hush the unwelcome, impractical, and very inappropriate inner voice begging her to ask him for just one kiss. Forcing the crazed thought away, Mairead produced the most stunning smile she could muster. "I expect you to keep that promise despite the torment it is going to cause you. Just imagine what my lips would feel like now that you could actually kiss them."

Hamish's green eyes grew brighter and he felt his own heart stammer for a second. Mairead was playing with fire and she knew it. She knew there was no way he would yield to their desires, at least not in their current public forum. The clever minx was getting back at him for recognizing her latest ploy and, in a way, he admired her all the more for it. She truly was every bit the feisty angel he just named her to be. Worse, she was correct that his vow to stay away was undoubtedly going to be torture.

With a clap of his hands, Hamish said nonchalantly, "As you have made it clear that nothing more interesting is going to happen here, or at least not in the near future, I am going to get something to eat and then see Robert."

Mairead had caught his look of anticipation of a challenge and wondered if her own hazel depths reflected the same eagerness. When he moved around her, she turned and fell into step beside him, "You will need more than your charm to see Robert today. My sister would not let even little Rab in this morning, despite his sweet pleas."

Hamish pursed his lips at the news. "Until when?"

"I'm unsure. Selah came down a while ago, relieved that Robert had finally gone to sleep. She had made it clear that whoever woke him would find themselves living outside of the castle walls until he was well again. That's why most are avoiding being near the keep. Everyone is making themselves scarce less they be blamed in case he awakes."

Mairead watched Hamish consider what she said and then glance up at the window that was Robert's room. She knew he was concerned for his brother but also knew that now was not the time for him to make inquiries. "If her decree included me—which it did—I'm certain it includes you as well." Mairead crossed her arms and flashed him a wicked, but victorious look. "I suggest the next time you decide to improve your appearance, you awaken much earlier. It obviously takes a good deal of time."

Hamish returned her triumphant look with one of his own. "Ah, but if I had, then I would have robbed you the joy of pacing by my door and wondering just who was in there with me."

Mairead momentarily froze. He *had* heard her when she had whispered about what else he could be doing in his room. Of course he had! He had been in there chipping away at the monstrosity growing from his face at the time.

Anger replaced mortification and Mairead felt her hands ball into fists at her sides as he pushed open the door that led into the kitchens. Just before he entered, he glanced back at her, wearing that sappy "I won" grin of his again.

Smile while you can, Hamish, for I will learn what I want to know, Mairead vowed to herself. *And then it will be me smiling at you.*

Hamish stepped into the kitchens, hoping Mairead would be gone by the time he came back out. Despite what he said, Mairead *was* family. But his problem had less to do with who Mairead was and more with what she was doing to him. And now that she was countering his comments with flirtatious ones of her own, conversations with her were even more enjoyable, and therefore even more dangerous.

Hamish felt his stomach turn just before it growled. He needed to divert his thoughts to something he could control—like eating. He turned the corner and was glad to see the tight ringlets of graying blond hair pulled into a frizzy knot. He coughed and immediately the petite, round figure turned. Hellie's plump face immediately lit up. "Hamish!"

"Thank God you are still here, Hellie," he said, and then gave a quick peck on her soft, wrinkled cheek. "Without you I think I would starve."

Hellie had been a cook for the MacBrieve clan for years and had quickly became a lead cook when they had come to Foinaven twelve years ago. She was older now, but her deep-set eyes remained a vibrant blue and she still wore an ever-present smile. Hamish knew the food from her kitchens would be the envy of all around if she could just muster the strong personality it took to lead those around her.

Hellie patted his clean-shaven cheek. "You look much better. The good Lord never intended you to hide your handsome face, otherwise he would not have given you those dimples. Here," she said, handing him a fairly large leg bone. "A growing boy needs his food. Now go play."

Hamish flashed her a disarming grin and took the bone. "I'm a man now, Hellie. I work, not play."

He then reached for a piece of bread, but Hellie gently swatted his hand. She then made a shooing gesture toward the door. "And I am an old woman now and know quite well that all men want only to play. Now go."

Hamish nodded in agreement and took a bite. It was good and juicy. He almost wanted to go in and get some more knowing that if he waited until the next meal, the meat would be dry and tough from being overcooked in an effort to keep it warm.

Instead, he exited the kitchens and was trying to decide just which of Robert's remaining soldiers he wanted to visit first when Mairead tapped his shoulder. "Hello."

Mo chreach. She had been waiting for him. Though part of him had hoped she wouldn't be, an even greater part was glad that she was. But she did not need to know that.

Hamish pasted on a frown and glanced to his side. Mairead was casually leaning against the wall. Her body was relaxed, but there was no mistaking the determination in her eyes. "You intend to follow me again?" he asked, surprised at how much he hoped she would say yes.

Mairead shook her head. "You made it clear that such efforts would be a waste."

Hamish shifted to join her against the wall and began to look around the courtyard. The last thing he needed her to see was his disappointment.

"So I've decided to do as you suggested yesterday," she continued, refusing to believe his disinterest. "I'm not going to follow you. I am going to join you."

Hamish stopped mid-bite. "I never said that."

Mairead shrugged, secretly clapping herself on the back for being right. Hamish might pretend to be indifferent to her presence, but he was anything but. The man did not want her with him probably because she would learn something he did not want her to know.

When Hamish had entered the kitchens, she had meditated on the prudency of spending the day with a man whom she had barely lasted ten minutes flirting with, but now she had no doubt. "You certainly implied it."

"I did not," Hamish countered, and then wrenched off a piece of meat. "Besides," he added after swallowing, "what I have planned for today would be boring."

"Are you still meeting with the guards?"

"Aye."

"Maybe it would be boring for some, but I think hearing you discover their strengths and abilities would be fascinating."

"I doubt it. In the end, you will have spent the day futilely learning nothing more about my plans than you already know."

Mairead tilted her head, bestowing on him a smile that made it clear she did not believe him. "It's a risk I am willing to take."

Hamish arched a brow.

Mairead shrugged her shoulders. "If you truly wish to visit the men alone, just tell me your plans and I promise to walk away right now."

Hamish started to laugh. "You would not. Doing that would only increase your curiosity."

Simply caving to an ultimatum rarely worked from what he had seen. The few times he had witnessed Conor try it with Laurel it almost always backfired. Probably because Conor never fully conceded, but it was also largely due to the fact that his answers tended to generate more questions and interest. Their discussions only ended when Laurel was ready for them to end, and not before. Conor said the trick was revealing only what was needed to satisfy a woman's curiosity. Either too little or too much information would result in her continuing interference and questioning. Unfortunately, until now, this "ability" was not one Hamish had ever needed to learn how to do.

Hamish was trying to think of something that would placate Mairead, at least for today, when Jaime spotted him and ran to his side. The tall, lanky young man proudly held up his newly sharpened sword for him to inspect. "I went to the smithy just as you suggested," he announced.

Mairead blinked and studied Jaime. Gone was the loathing that had at one time filled the lad's brown eyes. Now they shined with eagerness for approval. What had happened to change the young man who had been so angry and humiliated in the great hall to the one standing before her?

Hamish grasped the handle and maneuvered the large blade in the air. "Good balance. Nice length. Just don't forget what I told you," he said, handing the weapon back.

Jaime bobbed his head up and down. "We all remember every word and really appreciate everything, but I best get back to helping my father with the farm." Then with only a quick nod to Mairead acknowledging she was even there, Jaime hustled toward the castle gates.

Shocked, Mairead once again found herself opening and closing her mouth as she tried to understand exactly what she had just witnessed. "You went and found those men? You spoke with them?"

Hamish shrugged, thinking the answer obvious based on what Jaime had just said. "Aye."

She threw her hands in the air. "I honestly cannot believe they even *looked* at you after you were so cruel."

Hamish took another bite and wished he had some ale to wash the meat down. "I was not cruel," he finally countered. "I was honest. There is a difference. And I knew they all agreed with me. Even Jaime, despite his being so angry at the time."

"Still, that doesn't explain his complete change of attitude or why he decided he needed a new sword."

Hamish chomped off the last bite of meat and dropped the bone down in front of a hopeful dog, which quickly grabbed the prize and ran away from possible competition. "It's not that surprising. It is the right of every Highlander to own a decent sword and know how to use it. And despite what you thought, I did not want to discourage them. I just wanted to shake them up enough to realize that their current training methods would never bear anything fruitful. The untrained cannot teach one another the art of battle. Now it's their responsibility to go and find someone who can and will instruct them how to handle a sword."

"But why can't that be you?"

Hamish chuckled and shook his head. "Because it takes years and I'm only going to be here a short time, that's why."

"But then they will learn from Ulrick."

"I *knew* you didn't trust me," he said, his voice holding a tinge of exasperation. He wiped the grease from his hands on his tartan and began to walk toward the large, lone tower at the other end of the bailey.

"Fine, even if you do take care of Ulrick, once you leave, there will be no one else to train them," Mairead pressed. Then her face lit up and she scurried to catch up with him. "Unless, of course, your plan also addresses that situation."

Hamish chuckled to himself. She was good at wheedling information. "A good plan always includes many options."

Mairead lifted her skirt to help her walk faster and keep up with him despite his quick gait. "Do you mean that?"

He glanced down at her but did not slow his stride. "Aye."

Mairead could not believe it. Had Hamish really just admitted to the possibility of ensuring that someone—who was not Ulrick—would be left in charge of the men? Someone qualified enough to train Jaime and the others? Suddenly other possibilities opened up before her.

Hamish had made it clear that he was not seeking help from the McTiernays, but they were not the only powerful clan he knew. The McTiernays had allies. Maybe he knew of someone who wanted more than to be a soldier. Someone perfect for the position of commander and just needed the opportunity. If so, it reopened a possibility she had almost given up on. Marriage.

Hamish opened the tower door that led to the stairwell. He paused to let Mairead step in before him. "If you are thinking that a McTiernay army is one of my choices, I've told you before—"

Mairead held up her hand, stopping him from finishing his sentence. "After last night's discussion, I am in agreement with you and no longer believe a large army is the solution."

Hamish held her gaze for several seconds. Mairead's brilliant green and gold eyes did not waver. Nor did they sparkle with frustration. They instead radiated with confidence. "Speak your mind, *aingeal*. You obviously think you know something. You may not be smiling, but the glee shining from your eyes is practically lighting up this dark room."

Mairead did grin then. She could not help herself. "Why I know nothing of your plans, but if what you said about Jaime is true, then I just might have plans of my own."

Hamish's eyes narrowed. "And I suppose you are going

to refuse to tell me them just because I won't reveal my plans to you?"

Mairead shook her head. "Not at all. I do not have the ability or the resources to keep Ulrick from gaining power, but then you said to trust you on that."

Hamish squared his jaw and confirmed her statement with a simple "Aye."

"But when Ulrick is gone, Foinaven will need a new commander—a good one. And based on what you said just now about Jaime getting further training, you have one in mind."

Hamish crossed his arms. "I make no promises."

Mairead only smiled at him. "Of course not. Neither do I."

Another shot of jealousy slammed through Hamish for he knew exactly what she meant. "Just like that?" he asked sharply. "You honestly think a man will succumb to your whim and ask you to marry him just because you want it?"

"Don't make me sound petulant and spoiled," Mairead scolded. "I'm aware I don't hold that kind of allure for men, but I do know that marriage to me would give a commander several benefits."

Hamish had never heard such nonsense. Mairead possessed more allure than any woman should have. Such power over men was dangerous. But she was right about one thing. If Robert ever took ill one winter and passed away, or if the clan called for stronger leadership, succession to Mairead and her husband was probable. Almost certain if he were commander.

"And," Mairead continued, "I'm aware that a few well-placed compliments might not win me his affection. Perhaps you could help me."

"Help you?!" he choked.

Mairead nodded her head, widening her eyes so they appeared sincere. She knew it was only shock keeping him from realizing she was not serious, but until he caught on, she was going to have fun. "I mean I know that you meant nothing with your flirtatious comments, but I did catch your interest enough to want to kiss me. I just want to know what it was and how I can do so again."

Hamish just stared at her incredulously. He could not decide if she was serious, but fear made him answer as if she was. "Trust me. You do not need any help. You have plenty of allure." He inhaled. "You also have plenty of opinions," he muttered as he let the breath out.

"See?" Mairead's cheerful voice rang out. "You are helping already."

"Then that's all the help you're getting from me," he grounded out, "because if marriage is what you are really seeking, then I'm the last person from whom you want lessons. My methods tend to repel women."

"That is not at all surprising," Mairead replied too readily for his liking. Then after a long pause, she smiled at him and he knew he was in trouble before she even said a word. "So we have a deal."

"Deal?"

She nodded and looked at him as if it was obvious and already made. "I help you learn how to capture a woman's heart and in return, you will tell me just what Foinaven's future commander is looking for in a woman."

"You're assuming he isn't already married."

That stopped her. She had not thought of that. She looked up at him and concern lit her eye. "Is he?"

Hamish blinked. He didn't know. He had no idea who would be Foinaven's next commander. He knew whom he would choose, but Robert was not him and if things worked the way he hoped, there would be a handful of good men to choose from—most of whom were not married.

The concern on Mairead's face morphed into satisfaction when he said nothing. He knew that she had read from his expression that her crazy idea was possible. She sauntered by and he sought for something to say, but nothing came to him.

By the time she reached the tower stairwell and turned back to gesture for him to follow, Hamish was once again smiling. She had fooled him for a moment, but no longer. There was no way she could have been serious and he should have seen it from the moment she spoke such ludicrousness.

But nonetheless a deal had been struck.

Hamish began to hum to himself as he followed her up the stairwell. Very soon, Mairead was going to discover that her little impromptu and mischievous deal was real and one he intended to use in his favor.

Hours later, Mairead sat wrapped in a tartan trying not to freeze to death on a tower battlement. How Hamish could sit in the icy wind for hours and look warm when he had to be chilled to the bone was a mystery, but that he was doing so while gabbing about nonsense baffled her to the extreme. All day Hamish had been talking and swapping stories, never repeating even one.

After this group of men, they would have met with nearly all of the soldiers Ulrick had left behind to guard Foinaven. She knew a lot of them were not completely unskilled—Ulrick routinely had all the men train with him, but there was a reason they were left behind to hold sentry duties. Not one of them trusted Ulrick. But based on the questions Hamish had been posing all afternoon, he would never realize their skills or where their true loyalties lay.

She had assumed there would be some discussion about their fighting abilities, weapon preferences, Ulrick's methods, feelings about being left behind, or at the very least, questions about possible castle defenses. Yet Hamish had made not a single inquiry about anything that would help him prepare or at least understand how Ulrick might strike. All Hamish was interested in was women, food, and drink.

At first, Mairead thought his choice of topics had to do with her. She had vowed to haunt him so he, in return, intended to make her so miserable that she would give up and go away, leaving him to talk about the very things she was interested in hearing. But he had to have known that would not work. Her pride and obstinacy would refuse to allow her to be so easily swayed from her goal. But after wasting a whole morning and part of the afternoon, she was beginning to think that these conversations were what Hamish intended all along!

She was now convinced that her presence was not causing him to avoid subjects but just the opposite. If anything, her being there only helped. A revelation she had after trying to influence the conversation's direction for the umpteenth time. He took the opportunity to effortlessly turn the topic to something more enjoyable, such as who had done the most outrageous thing to stay awake while on night duty. After seeing Hamish's genuine interest in their much less interesting tales, the men forgot she was even there, becoming quite candid and open with their responses. She could only conclude that developing some level of comradery with these men was a part of Hamish's plan. But it had *not* been part of hers.

Mairead followed Hamish out of the tower and stretched her back. The last session had been the longest. "I think you met with all but the ones who were on duty last night."

Hamish followed her suit and cracked his neck. "I'll catch them another time. I'm not in any hurry."

Mairead fought the compulsion to roll her eyes at the idea of Hamish being in a rush to hear some nonsensical stories from a handful of unremarkable soldiers. "Well, it's nearly time for dinner. Selah is probably wondering where I am even though she knows I was with you for the day. Still, I must go and prepare, and—"

Two very distinct, very unhappy female voices across the courtyard stopped her mid-sentence. Mairead knew immediately who they were. Both women were a source of constant irritation. Fights occurred between them regularly and one was obviously about to erupt. Someone would have to step in and stop them. Hamish could do it, but based on what she had seen so far, he would do nothing more than stand and watch.

Mairead was not sure how she was going to force Hamish's involvement in clan matters; she only knew that she needed to find a way. But hearing the increasing volume of shrieks currently being exchanged, Mairead smiled as she was suddenly struck with an idea of just how she could make that happen.

"It won't be long now," Mairead forewarned cheerfully.

Hamish looked at her, his brow arched quizzically.

Mairead used her chin to point out two average-height, full-figured women facing each other across the yard and began to amble over to watch the show. "Ava and Sophie are sisters and responsible for cleaning the laundry generated in the keep, which includes me and now you. At least once a week, one of them accuses the other of not doing their fair share of the work or doing it poorly. It never fails to escalate until someone steps in and separates the two."

Mairead kept to herself that it always fell to her to be the person to separate them as everyone else was afraid of getting hurt. But today, she would simply refuse. Hamish would either have to watch the two women brutally attack each other or finally get involved.

As she predicted, the women's screams were now being accompanied with hair pulling, as Ava reached out and grabbed Sophie's brown braid. All-out war between the two women was moments away. "Aren't you going to do something?" Mairead finally asked, elbowing Hamish once again in his side.

"Why would I?" he asked back, his eyes locked on the two warring women with interest, not even bothering to look at her.

"Because," Mairead hissed, "they are arguing about *you*."

"I know," came his gleeful reply. This time Hamish spared a second to glance her way and she could see the proud grin across his face. "Who am I to decide which one gets to do my laundry?"

Men! Mairead thought to herself as she realized her folly. She should have realized that the show only would inflate his ego and therefore be the last thing he would want to see end. But then again, if attention was what Hamish enjoyed, Sophie and Ava were also ideally suited to meet those needs.

Mairead rocked back on her heels. "I highly advise you to stop them or you might not like the consequences."

Tilting his head, Hamish bent down and placed his lips close to her ear so that no one could overhear. "As part of our deal, I feel obligated to let you know that such coercion techniques are highly unattractive to a man."

Mairead blinked. Deal? What deal? As the memory of her whimsical pact came back to her, her eyes grew large with secret amusement. She kept her gaze on the two women and the physical violence they were inflicting upon each other. "And as part of that deal, I must tell you that listening to a woman's opinion cannot only be quite rewarding to capturing her heart, it most likely will save you from enormous discomfort."

Then before he could conceive of a rebuttal, she called out in a singsong voice, "Sophie! Ava! Guess what Hamish just told me?" Hearing his name, instantly the two women paused. Their hands still held a fistful of hair, neither letting go, but both wanted to hear what Mairead said next. "He just mentioned that he needs a chambermaid to assist him during his stay here and is hoping one of you will agree to take the role. But he needs your help deciding who it should be."

A great sense of satisfaction filled her upon seeing Hamish's face morph into one of horror as both Sophie and Ava shifted their full attention onto him.

Without another word, Mairead flashed him her most becoming smile, blew him a kiss, and sauntered off, intentionally swaying her hips as she moved.

Next time, Hamish, she thought to herself, *I would think twice about dismissing a woman's suggestions—especially* this *woman.*

* * *

Robert coughed and cleared his throat. "Selah tells me that you both are spending a lot of time together. Is this true?"

Mairead stared at her fork, trying to decide if she should stab her sister with it now or wait until later and do it in private. Could this day become any more unpredictable?

When she had left Hamish in the courtyard, she did not think anything could diminish her joy from teaching Hamish a lesson. Even Selah's attempts to make her feel guilty about being unavailable for most of the day had not worked. Her good mood though was short-lived. Just before dinner, she bumped into Ava wearing an expression Mairead could not remember the woman ever having.

Ava was happy. Very happy. And with much enthusiasm, she relayed how Hamish had quickly resolved the matter to both women's immense satisfaction. He originally suggested they take turns, but after talking with them for a few minutes he helped them realize that Ava longed for a break from doing the laundry and that Sophie had no interest in cleaning rooms. She actually enjoyed working with the other women at the river, despite the cold.

Mairead could not decide whether she was frustrated with Hamish's ability to charm his way out of impossible difficulties or relieved to learn that the regular tirades between the two women had finally come to at least a temporary end. By dinnertime, she had decided that the unlikely happy outcome only proved her motivations were well placed.

Hamish had a gift at turning situations to his advantage, if he so chose. Somehow she had to convince him that he needed to use those skills for the good of the clan. She knew Hamish would never stay, but that did not mean he could not leave a lasting impression on his brother. Robert was many things, including intelligent. He also had an earnest desire to do what was best for the clan. If he could see what a good leader like Hamish could accomplish, there was a good chance Robert might alter some of his methods and beliefs.

Mairead had hoped to launch her campaign at dinner, but her plans were usurped by Robert, who had insisted on joining them against Selah's wishes, stating he felt much better. Nothing could have been further from the truth. Based on his loud and persistent cough, her sister had been right. He should have remained in bed. Mairead had just been about to join Selah in her efforts to persuade Robert to return to his chambers when out of the blue he asked about her and Hamish. And for the life of her, she could not think of anything to say.

Thankfully, Hamish did not have such a problem. "Just what are you really asking about, Robert?"

Mairead swallowed. Hamish's posture was relaxed as he sat back against the chair, but his green eyes, normally so warm and full of brilliance, had grown cold, reminding her of marbled rock merchants brought over from the Isles of Iona and Skye. Such a look was terrifying, for Hamish had completely shut down his emotions. As a soldier, the ability made him capable of necessary but horrific deeds. But off the field, it meant he was capable of saying and doing just about anything. This included rising to his feet and leaving Foinaven forever without a single word or feeling of regret.

If Robert also saw the same precarious possibility looming, he did not show it. His own frame was weak and slumped, but his gaze held firm to Hamish's. "Only that people have seen you both together."

Mairead continued to stare at her fork. She was tempted to put it down and remind her sister that she had been quite clear about her plans to help Hamish and that of course people had seen them together. But she also knew that many had seen them that morning. She was positive that no one had overheard them based on where they were, but it was possible that they had deduced what she and Hamish were talking about based on a few of her reactions as well as his.

Hamish's anger, however, was growing. "How so?"

Robert waved a finger at them both. "Only that you have been seen close together on occasion and people are beginning to talk," he answered, stopping as a coughing spasm took hold.

Selah nodded and patted her husband's hand. "Most believe you are fighting as several remember your exchange in the courtyard that first day. I've assured everyone that you are on friendly terms and just trying to keep your voices low when near the keep because you do not wish to disturb Robert."

Mairead felt her hand relax. No one suspected the truth. If they had, this conversation would be much different.

"I remember you two being close when Mairead was a child," Selah continued. "It is only natural that the sibling affinity you once had to still remain."

Mairead finally put her fork down and tried to gather her racing thoughts. Nothing she felt for Hamish could be categorized as sibling-related, but that did not mean she was not going to cut all but minimal ties with him. She couldn't. She needed to spend time with the man to learn his plan and decide whether she was going to have to marry, leave, or do nothing.

Mairead looked up and caught Selah's gaze. "I have no

intention of ending the time I'm spending with Hamish. He met with your soldiers, but when it comes to understanding the needs of our clansmen, he needs much help and you, Selah, need to be with Robert. That leaves me."

Selah, hearing the logic along with the emphatic tone, nodded in agreement.

Hamish's eyes shifted from Robert to Mairead and instantly, their icy exterior melted and was replaced by an even darker look—one that heated her insides. "I've agreed to your company, but as far as your help? I've never needed it. Nor do I want it."

She returned his smoldering glare with one of her own. "After what I saw yesterday and today, you seem to be the most unwitting man ever to walk through these castle gates. You certainly don't know when to offer assistance and guidance to those in need."

Hamish squared his jaw. "Did you just call me unwitting?"

"Aye, I did. And I don't care if a few gossips wag their tongues, I made you a promise the other night and I intend to keep it."

Selah lifted her hand. "Mairead? What promise?"

Hamish snorted. "When you are wrong, *m'aingeal*, you are *really* wrong. If anyone is clueless around here it is you. I've only been here four days and I know more and have done more for Foinaven than you can conceive."

Mairead scoffed. "Oh, ho, I would like to conceive, but all you ever tell me is 'trust you.' And when I do, children cause chaos and two men almost kill each other!"

"What promise?" Selah tried again. "And what is this about men—"

"Kill each other?" Hamish bellowed, preventing Selah

from finishing her sentence. "Those men didn't even come close to touching each other."

"What about the mule practically destroying everything in the courtyard? Or did you just consider that entertainment?"

"What about Ava and Sophie? Wasn't it you who said they never got along? They practically are singing each other's praises at the moment."

"But for how long? Tomorrow, they—"

"I really would like to know about this promise—"

"You have no concept of—"

"Enough!" Robert shouted loudly, surprising everyone into silence, including himself. "Now that I've seen the two of you together myself, I'm satisfied. Now, before I begin to cough again and make you worry unnecessarily, dear," he said, squeezing Selah's hand and rising to his feet, "let us leave."

Relief filled Selah's features and she quickly got to her feet. "It is about time. I'm serious, Robert. Your cough is not getting better and it is because you refuse to stay in bed where it is warm."

"You're probably right, dear, but will it matter that my body is healthy if my mind has gone mad with boredom?"

Selah sighed and shook her head in surrender. "Mairead, I want to hear more about that promise, but until then will you check on Rab? He was so tired today after their outing. Noma put him down to sleep, but I want to make sure that if he wakes he has something to eat."

Mairead nodded. "I will take care of it." She immediately started preparing a small plate of food. When finished, she grabbed it and her own plate and started to leave.

"Refusing to eat when it is just you and me?" Hamish drawled out. "And I thought you were serious about haunting my every step."

Mairead stopped and turned around upon hearing the implied challenge. "If you want a woman's company, you will have far more success if you just ask her to stay. Consider that my last free lesson on women, Hamish Mac-Brieve. Our deal is now concluded."

Hamish watched her leave, knowing he should not have incited her company, but their discussions were challenging and lively and of all things honest. And based on the way her hips were swaying back and forth she felt the same.

Mo chreach, he liked it.

Chapter Seven

Hamish stepped out of the stables and looked up at the sky. It was going to be another cold and windy day. But the air did not smell like rain. Tomorrow the weather could bring rain that would not stop for days, which meant, windy or not, he needed to ride out and meet with Davros today. He might not have another opportunity.

He was about to step back inside and check on the stable boy's progress when he spied Mairead—the very woman he had been looking for—standing in the doorway of the keep's entrance with her back facing the courtyard. She stood there for several seconds and then he saw the deep green of her gown disappearing back inside the keep—but not to the right toward the stairwell, but to the left. The only room in that direction was his bed-chambers. Hamish crossed his arms and waited. After several minutes, he realized Mairead was not pacing by his door or even pounding on it. She had gone inside.

Stepping back inside the stables, Hamish told Adiran to ready a second horse after finishing with his. That he would be back in a few minutes for them both. The boy nodded, surprised that Hamish remembered his name.

Hamish headed across the courtyard with a spring in

his step, eager to find out what Mairead's reaction was going to be upon being caught. Hopefully, she felt guilty for snooping in his room uninvited. It would make it easier to persuade her to come with him on today's journey.

Last night, after Mairead had left to check on Rab, he had reconsidered what Robert had been hinting at and had decided to give up his nightly reflection in the great hall. He wished he could just as easily remove Mairead from his thoughts. She invaded his dreams and was the last person he thought of before falling asleep. He woke this morning calling himself a fool. Why should he abstain from Mairead's company? She was the primary reason being at Foinaven had not felt like a burden but . . . rather enjoyable. He did not just endure Mairead's company, he wanted it . . . he needed it. Aye, every moment he spent with her was going to make it harder when he left—alone. But if he was going to experience pain either way, he would rather it be later. At least then, he would be back home where she was not constantly around, reminding him of what he could not have.

Hamish was about to pass through the keep's entrance when Mairead came out, looking down as she dusted her hands off on her skirt. "Find what you need?"

Mairead's head snapped up, her eyes wide. She saw where his hand was pointing. "What makes you think I was in your chambers?"

Hamish stepped around her and pushed open the semi-closed door. He inhaled deeply through his nose and then said with a grin, "I can smell you."

Mairead watched in mortification as he went to the nearest table to grab his sword and a travel bundle. She wanted to deny the accusation, but it would be a lie and the big grin on his face made it clear that he was not guessing she had been in there. He knew. "What put you in such a jovial mood?" she asked, trying to change the topic.

Hamish shrugged. "I like the way you smell. Come visit anytime."

Mairead pursed her lips as he grinned at her again. The sincerity of both the grin and the invitation was almost overwhelming. "Stop smiling."

Hamish chuckled and then went to hold open the door. "Why? I always smile at you."

Mairead shook her head and followed him out into the courtyard. She crossed her arms. "Aye, you do. But this morning your smile is unnervingly candid. As if you are truly happy. Normally the curve of your mouth twitches, which I've figured out is a clear sign that you are up to something."

Much of the time Hamish liked that Mairead could read him so well, but right now was not one of them. If he was not careful, she would connect his genuinely happy demeanor to seeing her and the last thing he needed was to empower her with the knowledge of just how much he enjoyed her company. "Ah, but this time *you* were the one up to something. I wonder, just what of my many secrets did you find?"

Mairead let go a short, terse breath. "You know that I found nothing."

"I am well aware there was nothing to find. But I am curious as to what you *expected* to find. I mean what could I possibly have in my chambers regarding my plan for Ulrick?"

"Your plan?" Mairead scoffed. "I knew all along that would be fruitless. I was *hoping* to learn just what you do in there after the rest of the world has risen and started the day."

She had already probed Ava on the topic and the girl had been no help. Mairead had hoped that the temporary chambermaid just had not known what to look for, but after examining the room, she had to agree—there was nothing there one would not find in any man's bed-chambers. The few items Selah stored in the room looked basically untouched and everything else was as expected. Hamish had traveled with little and even if he did have more, there was nowhere in the room to hide it. "I won't give up. I will find out," she pressed, more to convince herself than him.

"I have little doubt that you will," he replied, and curled his index finger for her to follow him.

Mairead waited until he was halfway across the court-yard before she picked up her dress and ran to catch up with him. "False flattery will not distract me."

Hamish stopped in front of the stables and pulled out two fur wraps from the bundle. He held out one to her. "First, I was being sincere. Second, we have known each other for years. You were obstinate then and still are. And third . . ."—he lowered his voice to a sensual level that only she could hear—"when I'm trying to distract a woman, I employ much more pleasurable means."

Mairead grabbed the fur in her hands and was about to issue a retort when she was interrupted by two women passing by wishing Hamish a good morning in altogether too cheerful voice. Their overt friendliness irked her and she knew there was no reason for it to. Hamish was an extremely good-looking man and other women were bound to notice. It was natural that they flirt with him whenever they got the chance. But did they have to do it right in front her? It was like they knew she had no chance with him and considered her to be no competition.

"Jealous?"

Mairead's eyebrows shot up as she realized her emotions had been plastered all over her face. Pride took over, saving her with a quick retort. "I probably would be if it were not for all the male company *I've* had lately."

"I would normally encourage you to join those old farmers again, or even offer you the chance to continue with your search of my chambers, but today, I need your help." He waved to Adiran to bring the horses.

Saddled horses and a fur covering meant that Hamish intended to travel farther than the village. "Just where are we going?" Hamish did not answer. Instead, he cupped his hands to help her mount the smaller of the two horses. He then pulled the blanket around her and draped it so that it also shielded the exposed part of her legs. The attention he was giving her was unnerving for many reasons, most she refused to acknowledge. "Getting me bundled up is not enough to make me go with you. Where do you want to go?"

"To see Davros."

"Davros?" She blinked in surprise. "He doesn't like strangers."

"That's why I need your help. Besides, you were going there anyway. I distinctly remember on the day I arrived that you promised him to visit his wife."

Mairead narrowed her gaze. "Does the reason you want to meet with Davros have to do with your plan?"

He knew she was stubborn enough to refuse if he did not answer. "It might," he answered. It definitely did if Davros agreed to his proposal. Hamish knew that bringing her along would give Mairead tremendous insight into what he was ultimately devising, but he did need her help. From what he learned earlier that morning, Davros could be instrumental to his success. And just walking up to the man's front door was not advisable.

"Then you know my answer."

Hamish gave a light tug on the reins to avoid a group of children playing chase outside one of the village cottages. The path they were on would soon fork and both led to Davros. The left was a much longer, more circuitous route and followed the river. The right was the opposite. It was a significantly shorter, direct route, but it required one to go over several semi-large hills, a wide valley, and then a small forest. Hamish wanted to go left. Not because the other was more difficult, but because it came uncomfortably close to where he went early in the mornings. Soon he would bring Mairead in on his secret, but not yet. He had other things he needed to put in place first and there was just too great a chance that Mairead would do more than watch or ask questions. She would want to interfere.

Mairead pointed to her right. "There's a shortcut if we go south and cut across the valley, but this time of year it is muddy and the wind can be strong along the hills. This way," she said, pointing left, "follows the river before it bends north. It will take us a bit longer, but the path is wider. Farmers and merchants use it and their carts have broken down most of the rocks keeping the mud at a minimum." She shivered and pulled the fur around her tighter. "It's also warmer."

Hamish sent a silent prayer of thanks to heaven. "I'm in no hurry and besides that gown is one of my favorites. I wouldn't want to see it ruined due to a shortcut."

Mairead issued him a sideways glance. She was cold and not in the mood to be intentionally riled by duplicitous compliments. Hamish might like her gown, and it could even be one of his favorites, but its potential ruin was *not* the reason he had so readily agreed to go left. When they had neared the fork, the tension in his body was almost palpable. But the moment she hinted her preference for the longer route, his shoulders deflated and the expression on his face relaxed into the smug grin he still was wearing. And if going right hadn't been *very* muddy and were not so bitingly cold with today's winds, she would have tested her theory by turning around and going that way.

The obvious postulation was that Hamish had lied and the McTiernay army was hidden in that valley. It was big enough, and yet Mairead knew without any doubt that was not the case. In the last week, someone would have reported seeing strangers and the sudden influx of a hundred men or so would definitely have affected the ability for local clansmen to hunt and feed their families. Nothing beyond the normal complaints about the weather had been heard. No one was having to go significantly farther to find game, so it was not an army. But what then? Hamish *was* a MacBrieve. And they did like to build things. It was not much, but he had fixed those broken scissors. Maybe Hamish was working on something that would help secure the gates. It *was* Foinaven's largest weak point.

Mairead shrugged and told herself that she just needed to be a little patient now that she knew where to go for answers. She would soon be able to unravel Hamish's plans and decide her next steps.

"So how long has it been since Foinaven has had a steward?" Hamish prompted once they were alone and out of earshot from the village.

Mairead was surprised by the sudden question. They had been riding in silence, only talking when necessary.

She knew why she had been quiet—the air was bitter and she had buried most of her face in the furs. But now that they had turned north, the easterly wind was blocked by one of the larger hills in the area making talking far more feasible. Hamish had appeared to not be affected by the weather, but perhaps he was. Then again, maybe his silence had been due to a reluctance to give the village gossips any fodder. Whatever the reason, Mairead was glad for any conversation as it would make time pass much faster and the ride much more enjoyable.

"The last steward died shortly after your father," Mairead began. "Robert decided he could handle Foinaven's finances better than anyone he could hire and felt that Selah and I had the ability to oversee the servants."

Hamish pursed his lips together. He had known from the first night that Foinaven had no steward, but he had assumed that the role's vacancy was only temporary. That there had been no castle steward for some time, however, explained a lot.

To an untrained eye, Robert would seem correct—a steward was unnecessary. Foinaven appeared to be running smoothly. Servants were kept busy. Villagers enlisted help from craftsmen. Farmers, hunters, and the cooks could be seen hauling food in and out of storage areas. But what a good steward would recognize were the areas Foinaven lacked attention. Hamish was far from an expert on such matters, but even he knew that castles—even those erected in stone—required periodic maintenance. Based on Foinaven's size and number of buildings, the noise of repairs being made should be constant. He had not yet seen anything that posed an immediate threat, but there were several places where rot had taken hold and would soon be a problem if not rectified.

Being a master mason, Robert should have known this and been the first to recognize construction issues and initiate action. And he probably would have, if he had looked. But maintenance involved no creativity. It posed no new challenges. As a child, after Robert built something it had been impossible to get him to repeat it again, even if the item could be very beneficial to his father or the clan. The boredom of repetition always prevented him from finishing. In this, the years had not changed him, though the impact of his neglect was far greater.

The lack of a steward reached beyond structure to personnel and clan matters. If not for Mairead, things would be truly dire. Technically, Selah was responsible for overseeing many of the areas of the castle, but from his vantage point she added no value. She dictated what she wanted, but instead of the steward running around seeing to her desires, it was Mairead. It was possible that it only seemed that way because Selah was tending to Robert, but the dynamic between Mairead and the staff was too seasoned to be temporary.

He was about to probe more on the subject when loud, very angry shouts could be heard up ahead. Mairead looked at him. "It sounds like Seamus and Art," she said in disbelief. They had passed the village and were now near several large farms. Until the start of the planting season, most of the men relaxed indoors, avoiding the cold and enjoying time off from the long hours of hard work in the fields. "This is unlike them."

Mairead urged her horse into a trot and Hamish followed her, stopping only when they neared the two men. Both ignored their approach, refusing to break eye contact. With each shout, they drew a fraction closer toward each other, increasing the chances that one of them would soon throw a punch.

Hamish held his breath and then let it slowly go. He would hate to be hit by either man. Despite his own substantial girth, both men matched him in height and were even wider than he was. It mattered little that their size was due more to fat than muscle. The weight behind their punch would not only hurt the recipient, but possibly cause serious damage. A broken nose would heal, but a jaw hit just right snapped—a fate worse than death to some.

He thought Mairead would recognize the obvious danger, but before he realized what she was planning, she had slid off her mount and moved to stand between the two men. He was about to jump down and pull her out of harm's way, when he realized her presence might be working.

Mairead held her hands up on either side of her. "Art! Seamus! What has you so angry?"

"Ask him!" Seamus shouted, stabbing a finger over her shoulder toward Art.

Art's dark beady eyes became slits and his face turned red as he began to clench his fists. "I did nothing! Unless ye count catching this lazy *scraiste* trying to steal me wall."

"If that's a wall, then I'm skinny wee *caileag*."

Infuriated, Art moved forward and this time jabbed a finger at Seamus. "Then ye best be taking off that plaid and be puttin' on a little girl's dress because it was a wall yesterday, it's a wall today and it'll be a wall tomorrow!"

Mairead threw her hands in the air. "Art? What wall are you talking about?" From her puzzled expression, it was clear she did not remember there being a wall anywhere on or near his property.

Seamus gave out a single triumphant shout. "Even one of yer own doesn't think that *truagh* thing is a wall."

Art nudged Mairead out of the way so he could again get in Seamus's face. "Me wife's da built it and I'll not be hearing her screeching till the day I die because it was destroyed by the likes of a Faill."

"We Faills have been in these parts longer than ye MacMhathains and if ye heard me wife nagging all day about them rocks, ye'd be out there with me!"

Art's fists came up and immediately Seamus's followed. Mairead's eyes grew wide as she realized that her presence was no longer enough to prevent the men from fighting. She pointed behind her as she ran to Hamish, who was still sitting on his horse. "This time you have to do something!"

Hamish arched a single brow and reached down to pull out a leather water bag. He took a large gulp, gargled loudly, and then swallowed. Mairead's jaw dropped open, but the unexpected sound gained him both men's attention. Seeing his opportunity, Hamish threw it at Seamus, who instinctively unballed his fists and caught it. Hamish pointed at him and the bag and said, "Have some."

Seamus eyed Hamish for a second and then pulled the plug out to take a swig. His eyes widened and without thought he handed it to Art. Smelling its contents, the farmer immediately took it and downed several gulps. When done, he handed it back to Seamus and said, "Ahhhh, blessed ale. I've had nothing but weak mead fer near three weeks."

Seamus nodded and enjoyed a couple more swallows before capping the bag. When he was done, his thick brows once again formed a straight line as he leveled a glare, this time at Hamish, before tossing him what was left of the ale. "Sharing a drink does not change things."

Hearing the residual anger in the tone and Art's grunt, Mairead knew the argument was seconds away from reigniting. If Hamish did not resolve the matter, this time both men would come to blows. Anyone else, a fight would be undesirable, but with these two, the damage they could cause would be horrifying. "You are Robert's commander. Settle this," she hissed.

Hamish stared at her for a second and then with a shrug to his shoulders, he looked at Art and Seamus and said, "You're both farmers, right?"

"Aye," they both replied, each poised and ready to fight should the other try to sneak in a punch.

"That's what I thought," Hamish said with a nod. "What you men need this time of year is more ale. Go to Foinaven and make your way to the buttery. Tell them that I sent you and they are to give you both two large tankards, filled to the brim. Once you've finished, then go to the main tower in the courtyard and find something that will put holes through the first floor."

Each man dropped his fists and stared incredulously at Hamish. Hamish ignored them and instead focused on Mairead. "How many do you think? Five? Six?" Receiving no response, he nodded and looked back at the men. "Six it is. Punch six holes, three a piece, and make them about so big." Hamish raised his hands and made a circle touching his index fingers and thumbs together. "Once you're done, head home. Anytime between now and planting, your wives make a ridiculous request just to get you out of their sight, go back to the tower, and make another hole."

Hamish then reached over and gathered the reins to

Mairead's horse and handed them to her. She took them automatically and remounted her horse. Hamish nodded to the two men, nudged his mount in the flanks, and once again continued toward his intended goal—Davros's.

Mairead urged her mount to catch up and when she was sure no one was in earshot, tried to decide just which of the multitude of questions pouring through her mind to ask first. "Why would you go and tell Art and Seamus to pound holes in the tower floor?"

"You told me to."

Mairead opened her mouth, shocked that Hamish would make such an obviously false accusation. "I did not."

Hamish nodded his head. "Aye, you did. You said to *'do something'* so I did."

Mairead licked her lips and shook her head with disbelief. "You think Art and Seamus are going to walk all the way to Foinaven and spend the day cutting holes in the tower floor."

"Aye."

"Unbelievable."

"Not really. Most men really enjoy ale. A tankard of it? I guarantee you both men are on their way and neither of them are thinking about fighting . . . at least not with each other as that would only delay their drinking."

"And the holes?"

Hamish cocked his head and gave her a sideways glance. "I thought the activity would relieve some frustration. Any man caged in a house with a woman for too long is bound to get edgy."

"How awful, especially as confined men bring their women nothing but pure joy." Her sarcastic tone unmistakable.

Hamish chuckled. "I suspect not joy, but stress," he said

NEVER KISS A HIGHLANDER   201

sincerely. "No doubt that is why Seamus's wife sent him out to move the wall in the first place. With nothing to do but annoy her, she decided to give him something outside, time-consuming, and most important far from her. I would have thought all that obvious."

Mairead sat quietly absorbing what Hamish just said and how it sounded not just plausible, but likely. But Hamish's solution was not going to be liked by Robert when he finally recovered. "I'm curious to know how you expect to explain the state of the tower floors to my sister and your brother."

Hamish shot her one of his playful grins that accentuated his dimples. "I'll just tell him that this is what happens when I follow your advice and get involved with the affairs of the clan."

Mairead opened her mouth, but almost immediately snapped it shut. Hamish eyed her carefully. Whatever she was about to say, Mairead had changed her mind, and it was not out of fear of his reaction. Her expression had shifted from major frustration to ease and contentment. She held her head up high, allowing the breeze to catch her hair and whisk it around her face. She really was beautiful. And she was also quite confident. Something had given her an idea, but just what it could be, he could not fathom.

Hamish maneuvered his horse around another large puddle, trying to decide on whether to wheedle it out of her or pursue something Art had said. He decided on the latter. "What was all that about Faills and MacMhathains?"

Mairead furrowed her brow, confused by the question. "Nothing more than what you heard. Seamus is from the Faill clan and Art is a MacMhathain."

Disturbed by what Mairead was implying, Hamish rubbed his chin. He had been at Foinaven for nearly a week and seen at least half a dozen different plaids. He knew several small groups from other clans had joined Foinaven for protection and had assumed they still wore their old tartans because it was a costly—and therefore slow—process to replace them with MacBrieve colors. He was now beginning to think that was a very incorrect assumption. "Why are they not wearing the MacBrieve plaid?" he finally asked.

Mairead turned her head fully this time. Every feature indicated she was puzzled by the question. "Because they are not MacBrieves."

It was Hamish's turn to be confused. Twelve years ago, the idea of merging the MacMhathain and MacBrieve clans had seem daunting and his father had thought long and hard about how it should be done. Knowing that unity and loyalty were keys to success, he decided to use Foinaven as the tool to instill them in the clan. At the time, Foinaven had a single stone tower, but the rest was predominantly constructed out of wood. The courtyard was large, but there were relatively few buildings within the castle limits and the main village was located some distance away. Hamish had been young at the time, but as the next leader, he had been very involved in the initial decisions. It had been his idea to gradually move to a stone structure that provided not only significantly more security, but would be something all clansmen could participate in and be proud of. Seeing Foinaven today, even larger and more impressive than his initial vision, Hamish had assumed that is what had transpired.

"And how is that possible if Seamus and Art are pledged to a MacBrieve laird?"

Mairead's mouth opened, still baffled, before forming a small *O* as understanding dawned on her. "Robert is not the laird of everyone who lives at Foinaven. He is more of a . . . caretaker I guess."

Hamish blinked. What Mairead was saying was almost incomprehensible. It was certainly unacceptable.

"I thought you knew. I mean you know that Robert does not sleep in the solar," Mairead continued. "He refused to move in there when your father passed away as it symbolized a level of authority he refused to accept."

Hamish pursed his lips. "So what you are saying is there is in fact no MacBrieve laird."

Mairead bit her bottom lip and shook her head. "Not exactly. He is laird of the MacBrieve clan, just not of the others."

"And just how many 'others' are there?"

Mairead gave a slight tug on her reins to keep her horse next to Hamish's. "As of last year, there are families from six other clans. Mhic Eain, Ceiteach, Faill, Shyn, Larg, Munro, and of course MacBrieve and MacMhathain. Many relocated here because there was farmland available where there wasn't any within their clan's territory. One group came to escape the tyranny of their laird. Others are here because their laird died and their clan had grown too small to protect itself on its own."

Hamish was dumbfounded by what Mairead was saying. So many questions were coming to him at once he was not sure just what to ask first. So he started with her last—and probably most shocking—statement. "Am I to understand that the MacMhathains *never* merged with the MacBrieves?"

Mairead took in a deep breath and pulled the edges of her fur blanket closer together. "I am not sure I am the best to answer. I was young so I may not know all the reasons—"

"I suspect you understand them well enough," Hamish said tersely, cutting her off.

Mairead shrugged, but the gesture was hidden under the fur blanket. "I will tell you what I know, which is not much, but some of it does involve you."

Hamish straightened his back defensively.

"When you left, your father at first expected you to return and marry my sister as planned. I know he hoped for it for a long time. By the time he agreed to Selah and Robert's union and what that meant, the two clans had lived together under a single leadership for three years."

Hamish arched his left brow. "*Three* years?" He had no idea that his father had kept Robert and Selah apart.

"Aye," Mairead answered. "He felt that when my father died, he had intended *you* to be laird, not just the man who married Selah."

His father was in a way correct. It was all how one interpreted Menzies MacMhathain's dying request. He had asked him to marry Selah, thereby uniting the MacBrieve and MacMhathain clan. He had *then* asked Hamish if he would be their laird and ensure both clans' future and well-being. In Hamish's mind, being married to Selah was a requirement to being laird and uniting the two clans. Without it, many MacMhathains would question his loyalty and even his right to preside over Foinaven. The MacBrieves may have been the more powerful of the two clans army-wise, but the castle had been part of Menzies MacMhathain's legacy. It was important a MacMhathain helped continue to oversee it.

But it seemed his father had felt differently. If Hamish had returned when his father was alive, would he have made him laird despite Menzies MacMhathain's intentions?

Greeted only by silence, Mairead assumed he wanted

her to continue. "I do remember your father and brother fighting about it once. He wanted Robert to complete the agreement and take the title and unite the clans. Robert believed they were already united and that forcing any MacMhathain to become a MacBrieve would jeopardize their loyalty. After your father died and Robert took his place as leader, no one questioned Robert's authority. Things were prosperous at the time and no one wanted to change that. The English were attacking castles in the Lowlands and along Scotland's waist and all wanted to avoid the strife—as well as attention—a clan war might bring. It was not long before a handful of small clans came to Foinaven for security and were welcomed with no expectations in return. In time, more came and now we live peacefully for each other's mutual benefit."

Hamish could tell by Mairead's sarcastic tone at the very end that she disliked his brother's community concept, but probably not for the reasons he did. "You disagree?"

"There *are* advantages," she conceded. "Food is one and some of the clans specialize in certain skills that support trade."

"But you also recognize the disadvantages."

Mairead looked ahead, but tightened her grip on the saddle. "Your brother's philosophy is one that all should aspire to—peace. But he believes it can be achieved at all costs. Robert wants people to stay because of a sense of community. In his and Selah's minds, the approach has worked. However, neither will acknowledge the barriers it has erected."

Hamish knew that Robert was right in thinking that forcing people to join another clan would cause strife and resentment. But temporarily avoiding discomfort and some pain did not create loyalty. It only postponed it, and worse, it made the pain and hardship to be endured later much greater.

Robert did not understand that while fidelity and loyalty may look the same, it was not. Hamish had seen too many battles, too much bloodshed, and too many lives lost to pretend otherwise. He suspected by Mairead's posture that even without his life's experience, she felt the same. "You didn't answer my question."

"The MacBrieves are loyal to Foinaven as are the Mac-Mhathains, in part due to Robert and Selah, but also after twelve years, many of them have intermarried, making the bond between our clans very strong. With the others it is not the same. Most are too new in the area to have deep roots. They are here because they believe the English won't venture this far north if war should come again and though at times, life here is difficult due to the weather, there is also plenty of land to farm and there is easy access to fish in the sea."

"*And* an inordinately lenient leader who has an unheard of accommodating attitude," Hamish growled.

Mairead bit her bottom lip. She agreed with Hamish, but she had gotten to know these people and did not like the idea of forcing them to leave just because they were not of their clan. "Most of them are good and hardworking, needing the opportunities that Robert and Selah have given them; however, it is also true that they reap the benefits of a large community and clan."

"But fail to contribute to Foinaven's and therefore their protection," Hamish added. "Robert will never acknowledge that a man's ultimate loyalty is to himself and his family. It *certainly* is not to a clan he doesn't claim."

"Ulrick has made it worse." Mairead pressed her lips together until it hurt to keep from saying more. She felt guilty saying anything that went against her sister, but it was also nice being able to vocalize her true opinion about her brother-in-law's approach to leading a clan. And Hamish was probably the one and only person with whom she could ever do so. "Outside of a few of us—and that includes both MacBrieves and MacMhathains—no one is loyal to Foinaven. Ulrick has made things too distasteful and they know it will become worse if he takes over. He will declare himself laird and I suspect soon after many will leave."

Hamish took a deep breath and exhaled, relieved to hear of Mairead's disapproval. If she had supported Robert's ways, it would have detrimentally affected his ability to relate and talk with her. Though in the end, it would not matter as he intended to sever his relationships with Foinaven and its people. However, knowing that they thought alike on such matters gave him indescribable comfort. He also knew that on some level this meant his feelings for Mairead were growing.

"I doubt Robert knows how fortunate he has been," Hamish said more to himself.

If Foinaven had not been located so far north or if it had been in an area of any strategic value, the façade of being a large, united clan would have been discovered long ago. It was amazing no one before Ulrick had attempted to seize control. And the fact that Selah actually supported Robert sent a chill down Hamish's spine.

Once again, Hamish found himself to be *relieved* that Selah had rejected him. They would have been miserable together. The idea of creating a utopia-like society was a wonderful one, but it was unattainable. Every feeling human being alive at one time or another wished life worked that way. But it simply did not. Men's baser desires would eventually always come before the good of the community if their own happiness was not in some way tied to the greater good.

"I hope your plan with all of its options can also make Robert and Selah see reason."

"I have no desire to change Robert," Hamish said with a grimace. "And if my father could not convince Robert to join the clans under the MacBrieve name, I certainly do not possess the power."

Hamish was right. His father had tried for years and without success. Even she had once endeavored to get Selah and Robert to consider the advantages of uniting all the clans. But it had been a waste of time and energy.

Still, Mairead had wanted to argue that it was years later and Hamish's input might be welcome after being gone so long, but she knew it be pointless. Besides, there was no time to state her case. They had finally arrived.

"We're here," Mairead said, pointing to a small cottage up ahead.

Hamish took a bite, closed his eyes, and savored the moment. "Never let your wife cook for a McTiernay, Davros. They'll charm her right out of your arms and into one of their kitchens."

Jeán tucked a loose strand of hair behind her ear. Wrinkles were apparent around her eyes, but she was still a striking woman. Her once-dark auburn hair was now a glorious blend of faded copper and rosy-blond, accented by beautiful silvery-white streaks near her temples. And her large brown eyes were beaming from Hamish's compliment. "I just might run away with you, if you keep flattering me so."

Hamish opened his eyes, patted his stomach, and watched her melt upon seeing his dimples. His grin grew.

Finally! A woman who responded to his smile like he expected. "Then I shall sing your praises until you are mine."

Davros, completely unfazed by all the flattery being exchanged, pushed his empty plate forward and rested his elbows on the table. "It was another fine meal, *mo muirnín*. And you, young man," he said, pointing at Hamish, "may regret those words. I might just hand her over to you the next time she's in a mood."

Jeán rolled her eyes, not in the least worried by her husband's threat. "Did you notice that he only dares to make such comments *after* he's eaten?"

"Aye," Davros said proudly. "That's because you married yourself a smart man."

Mairead laughed out loud. She always enjoyed visiting Davros and Jeán. They expressed their love so differently than Robert and Selah, and yet she had no doubt that their bond was just as strong.

They were Munros and had traveled with a handful of families that had come to settle near Foinaven and make a fresh start after their son George was killed at the Battle of Bannockburn. That had been less than three years ago, but to Mairead it seemed like she had known the couple for much longer.

Growing up without parents had been difficult and Selah had done her best. When Mairead was young, Selah had been all things wonderful to her. But as she grew older and aspects of their personalities became more disparate, it had been Jeán and Davros who had helped her to understand Selah's viewpoint without losing her own. In many ways, they had become family. She was like the daughter they always wanted, but never had, and Mairead suspected they were angels her parents had sent to Earth to help guide her in their absence.

Davros pointed to Mairead but looked at Hamish. "Our Mairead has recently seemed to become quite interested in marriage. How about you?"

Out of the corner of his eye, Hamish saw Mairead blush. He did not think it possible someone could turn that red that fast. "I've always been interested in marriage, but alas whenever I thought I might have found the right woman, a McTiernay was around to steal her heart first."

Jeán narrowed her eyes skeptically. "From what I understand there are only seven McTiernay brothers and only five of them are married. So I find it hard to believe that they are the sole reason you are not married."

Hamish grinned. It was no surprise that Mairead liked the couple so much. He did too. Jeán's wit throughout the meal proved she was a highly intelligent woman and Hamish suspected that like Mairead, she could be quite tenacious on certain subjects. His gut said marriage was one of them and the fastest way to close the topic was with honesty. "McTiernays may not be the *only* reason, but women do seem to gravitate into their arms," he agreed. "And I did come close and was nearly married last year. I was almost ensnared by a stunning creature named Wyenda, whose beauty was just on the outside. So you see? Love has forsaken me and now my heart is so battered and bruised, I no longer think I'm capable of the emotion." His tone was sincere, with an intentional whiff of melancholy. He hoped it would enlist Jeán's sympathy and motivate her to move on to less personal subjects.

Mairead tried to catch Hamish's eyes, but he refused to look her way. She could not believe that Davros and Jeán were pursuing this line of questions. Obviously, Davros had not forgotten that she had been all dressed up on market day and had told Jeán what Mairead had been attempting. The couple knew her position on marriage—

that she did not want it. They were also well aware that even if she *was* inclined to be married, there was no one who had even made her heart stutter, let alone succumb to something like love. But by the way Davros and Jeán were looking at Hamish, they thought that had changed.

Jeán stood up and patted Hamish's hand. "Well, the past dictates the future only if you don't learn from it. Who knows? Maybe you will find a nice young lass here." Her hand just casually waved in Mairead's direction. "And even better, there are no McTiernays about to interfere."

Mairead groaned and covered her face with her hands. "Jeán, Hamish is here to deal with *Ulrick*, not to be set up by you two."

"Aye, and no smart woman would ever want to tie herself to me." Hamish hoped his tone conveyed just the right note of finality to it. He was ready to change the direction of the conversation. There was a reason he was here, and it had nothing to do with Mairead, marriage, or being entrapped by love. "As far as dealing with Ulrick, Mairead's been very helpful about introducing me to Foinaven's staff and while they are friendly, they seemed to be incredibly tight-lipped about their opinion of their commander."

Davros leaned back in his chair and entwined his fingers behind his head. "Not surprised. They probably should be quiet. More than one has sought his favor by conveying what they overheard or saw. I wouldn't be surprised if Ulrick has convinced a few to look out for his interests while he was away."

Hamish nodded. "I've already identified a few servants who fit that description."

Mairead frowned. She was not surprised that Ulrick had spies, but she did not think it possible to determine who they were. "What are their names?"

"Probably the ones you already suspect, but there were not as many as I would have thought."

With a snort, Davros unlinked his hands and tapped a finger on the table. "That's because most are smart enough to realize that such information comes at a price. It brings them to Ulrick's attention and afterward he is not understanding if you have nothing new to provide."

Hamish's brows furrowed. "That explains why I'm having a difficult time discovering who the moles are within the guard left behind than I did among the staff."

Mairead was confused. If Hamish had easily identified the spies within the castle's staff, why could he not do the same in the guard? "I don't understand."

"Think about it," Davros said before Hamish could answer. "All those who supported Ulrick left with him. The guards who remained he deemed expendable if he faced opposition upon his return."

"Still," Hamish said, raking his hand through his hair. "I doubt Ulrick would have left without at least one person behind to inform him on what happened during his absence."

"More than likely two or three," Davros said, nodding, thinking about what Hamish was implying. "And the guard is where he had the most influence."

Hamish bounced an index finger in agreement. "That wisdom of yours is exactly why I came to see you today."

Davros smiled. "Not sure how I can help you, but I don't mind answering a few questions."

Mairead's jaw went slack. "Why?" she asked in a forceful tone. "Just *why* are you so willing to talk to Hamish?"

Jeán's eyes widened. She looked at her husband, who just shrugged before returning her shocked gaze back to Mairead. "I must say I'm surprised that you object."

Mairead shook her head. "I don't. But I just do not

understand. Davros, you avoid talking to anyone in the guard and you most particularly *dislike* to answer questions. So why are you, *like everyone else*," her emphasis conveyed her exasperation, "completely willing to open up to Hamish when it is not in your nature?"

Davros fought from smiling. He could see why Mairead would be mystified, especially as he refused to answer many of her questions. But there was something about Hamish that he just trusted. It did not mean he would go to war for him or reveal any deep secrets, but it did compel him to conversations that he might not normally have had.

"First," Davros began, "I don't dislike answering questions. I dislike answering *ridiculous* questions. Most of the ones you pose are about your feelings or worse, someone else's feelings, or some other female thing I could care less about. Second, Hamish may be here to support his brother, but outside of that, I see him as a McTiernay with no allegiances to any person or clan in these parts."

Hamish did not respond and was glad that no one looked at him to add anything or denounce Davros's assessment. Truth was he was not sure how he felt about it. On many aspects Davros was correct. Based on his home, his philosophy, and where he felt most needed and accepted, he *was* a McTiernay. But he had been born a MacBrieve. He was proud that his father had been Laird MacBrieve and did not want anyone to think otherwise. It had not occurred to him that like Jeán and Davros and so many others at Foinaven, he had been living with one clan while still maintaining allegiances to another. Aye, he wore the McTiernay plaid, but did he too have divided loyalties?

Davros placed his hands on the table and rose to his feet. "Well, I know that Mairead came to say hello to Jeán as she promised. Let's move our conversation out to the byre, Hamish, so we don't disturb their time together."

Mairead's eyes grew large and displeasure rippled along her spine. She opened her mouth to state that she too was keenly interested in what he and Hamish were going to discuss and would not be left out of the conversation. But before she could utter more than a couple of incoherent words, Jeán grabbed her hand and squeezed. "That is very thoughtful, Davros. Mairead and I do have much to talk about."

Mairead's lips formed a thin line. "Why didn't you allow me to stop them? I wanted to hear what they were going to say."

Jeán patted Mairead's hand and relaxed again in her chair. "I could tell. Every time Ulrick was mentioned you began to fidget so much that even a *nothaist* could tell that you knew nothing of Hamish's plans and that none of your methods to learn them had worked. Let me guess. You spied on Hamish and when that did not work, you then attempted to trick him into telling you his plans. What else have you tried? Coercion? Persuasion?"

Mairead reached out, avoiding Jeán's knowing look, and clasped the half-full mug in front of her. "I tried all of those and I also threatened him. Today, hearing what Hamish had to say to Davros, was my best chance to learn at least his basic strategy. And you cannot convince me that you too are not interested in what it is."

Jeán smiled and went to pour some more water in Mairead's mug and refill her own. "Of course I am, but I only have to practice a little patience as Davros will tell me everything after you and Hamish are gone. Besides, if you *had* insisted on following, you and I both know that

Hamish would have left here without disclosing anything important." She sat back down and gave Mairead a mischievous smile. "And I had my own reasons for keeping you here with me."

Mairead eyed the older woman. Jeán's eyes were sparkling with controlled excitement and it gave Mairead a sudden sense of foreboding. "And just what are those reasons?"

"Why to learn more about Hamish of course." Jeán winked at Mairead, who in return rolled her eyes. "Do not pretend with me, Mairead. I saw you two look at each other. You have finally found someone who not only can meet your level of wit, but he is not at all intimidated by you. In fact, I think he actually enjoys tackling the challenges you pose. So, I approve."

Mairead's jaw dropped slightly. "You approve? Of *what*? Because if you think I am interested in Hamish, I can assure you, *nothing* could be further from the truth."

Jeán ignored Mairead and closed her eyes, tapping her mug with the tip of her finger. "Davros said Hamish was rather scruffy upon his arrival, but I must say I found the man to be *very* good-looking. If I were younger"—Jeán sighed—"and of course never met Davros, you would have to fight for him."

Mairead had to convince Jeán she was wrong. "You would be fighting with someone else because *I'm not interested*."

Jeán took a deep breath, closed her eyes, and exhaled with exaggerated contentment. "How do you not melt each time he smiles?"

Unease began to fill Mairead as she began to realize Jeán was not just teasing—she was serious. "I find it amazingly easy to do."

Jeán sighed and took a sip of water. "I wish Davros had dimples like that. Got to love a man with dimples."

"You wouldn't find them so attractive if you realized those dimples belonged to the most frustrating man alive," Mairead snapped. "He flashes them to every lady who passes by and they all just fall in line to do with whatever he pleases." Mairead prayed her words would alter Jeán's impression. "You know Ava and Sophie?" Jeán nodded. "Well, after a few words and smiles from Hamish, they now inexplicably get along. The man plays on women's feelings—and a key tool he uses are those dimples you love so much."

Instead of curbing Jeán's bubbly demeanor, it strengthened it. Her eyes grew bright and she could barely sit still she was so happy. "*Och!* Jealousy. Be careful, sounds like you are on the verge of falling in love with the man," she said, her singsong voice causing a large knot to form in Mairead's stomach.

Jeán had always had a mercurial personality. Typically, her character was the one she had sported during their noon meal—easygoing with bouts of clever words and insightfulness. When Mairead needed a listener, Jeán had provided support by just being there or by offering insight and wisdom. But when she clasped onto an idea— especially something she was excited about—Jeán became a dogged force of nature. She was unstoppable and confusing at the same time. And in the end, she somehow persuaded you to join her way of thinking. This was about to be one of those times if Mairead was not careful.

Jeán had moved from simmering glee to energetic and was now practically *frothing* with excitement. If Mairead did not end this misconception about her and Hamish, Jeán would have their wedding planned by the end of the day. She needed to understand that there was no bride and groom!

Jeán hummed and took another drink. "Don't worry, I'm sure if Hamish thought someone was vying for you, you would see several sparks fly."

"I'm not worried about Hamish." *I'm worried about you*, but Mairead had not the chance to finish her thought.

"You needn't be jealous. Aye, Hamish is the affable sort, but he flirts to hide his discomfort. I suspect he is much like my Davros and very selective about whom he spends his time with. And I understand you two have spent quite a bit of time together."

"We are *friends*, Jeán. Nothing more."

Jeán placed her mug on the table, her smile suddenly gone. Her brown eyes drilled into Mairead's hazel ones. "You can fool yourself, but not me, *cara*. Hamish looks beyond your beauty and sees you, all of you. What's more he likes what he sees and respects your opinion. Who else have you met who does that?"

"Davros, Robert, little Rab," Mairead quipped.

Jeán issued her a pointed stare. "You would be a fool to discount such gifts. It is so rare to find them in anyone, but in a good-looking, eligible man who clearly finds you attractive? It's a miracle. What I cannot understand is why you are spending your efforts learning about this plan of his instead of catching him."

Mairead suddenly wished Jeán went back to being bubbly. It was not emotionally healthy to consider Hamish in the light Jeán was painting him. "I won't deny there is an . . . attraction between us, but beyond that you are wrong. I have good reason to doubt Hamish cares about my opinion. The man doesn't trust me. He won't tell me anything—from his plans for Ulrick, which I have a right to know, to inconsequential things, like how he spends his mornings in his chambers."

Jeán raised an eyebrow at that part. "I suspect Hamish does nothing more than any of us do—sleep and dress."

Mairead snorted and crossed her arms. "He's in there for *hours*. Sleep and dress? I don't believe it."

Jeán crossed her arms and then raised her hand to tap her index finger against her chin. "Almost," she said quietly. "Clever. You *almost* distracted me there." She leaned forward. "Hamish may not trust you yet, but that is only because he doesn't realize how much he cares for you. That"—she paused and pointed to Mairead—"will require your help."

"He does not care—"

"I think you should kiss him."

Mairead stared openmouthed at her friend for several seconds. Jeán just stared back, her suggestion completely serious. Mairead threw her hands in the air. "Are you even listening to me?"

"To every word. When you return to Foinaven, bathe and have one of the chambermaids do your hair. Oh, and you can wear that one gown that—"

"Jeán, whatever you are thinking a bath and a gown would accomplish, you could not be more wrong. *We have already kissed* and nothing happened."

Jeán's eyes grew large and the excitement from a few minutes ago returned anew. "That why you are so scared. You liked it."

Mairead tried to look disgusted. "He had a beard at the time. I imagine it was the same as kissing the top of a man's head."

Jeán ignored her. "He liked it too I expect. So how many times have you kissed?"

"Only once!" Mairead exclaimed. "And it was just to shut me up. What's more, is that we both made a deal that it would not happen again."

"O' mo chreach! You both *really* liked it."

Mairead threw her hands up in the air. "And you *really* aren't listening to me."

Jeán shrugged. "You wouldn't either if you could hear what you are saying. If neither of you enjoyed the experience, a deal to prevent it from happening again would be pointless, no?"

Mairead knew she was gaping but was unable to come up with a valid argument. What Jeán said was true, but Mairead was not going to admit to it.

Jeán gave her a knowing grin. "You've probably thought of little else since you struck that silly deal. And I don't blame you. A man that good-looking as well as funny, intelligent, and caring. You'd be insane not to kiss him again. Besides, how else are you going to know how you really feel about him?"

Mairead pushed back her chair and stood up to pace, despite the small area. "I'm going to indulge you for just a moment. Let's say you are right. That I did enjoy his kiss and agree that he is somewhat close to the type of man I might want to spend my life with. I will even entertain the idea that he is attracted to me. But beyond that? You heard him talking about that woman Wycnda almost *ensnaring* him. He believes love only ends in tragedy. I don't want a man afraid to love, but one who will embrace it completely. But even if I didn't, it would not matter. *Hamish is leaving Foinaven.* And this time he will never return."

Jeán shrugged. "Then let him know that you are willing to go with him."

Mairead swallowed. Leaving Foinaven was just not

something she was willing to consider, but she was not about to tell Jeán that. It would start a stream of questions that would never cease until the woman knew everything. And *no one* needed to know these secrets. They were hers to handle alone. "And leave Foinaven? Never see my sister again?" Mairead finally responded. "Abandon her when she needs me?"

"People leave their homes and their families all the time. I left mine when I came here three years ago. I wanted a chance for new memories. Do not let family keep you from a chance to be happy. But we both know that Hamish and Robert are speaking again and his willingness to stay here for a few weeks means it would not be that difficult to convince him to return periodically for a visit. As far as Selah needing you, your sister is several years older and was the one who taught you most of what you know about running a castle. Aye, her approach is soft, but she knows what needs to be done. And there is always the option of hiring a steward."

Jeán paused to stand up and move to clutch Mairead's hands in her own. "Davros believes you were husband hunting the other day. Were you?"

Mairead looked at the ceiling to avoid looking Jeán in the eye. "Aye. But it is not what you think."

"If you want to tell me, I'll listen." Mairead shook her head and closed her eyes. Jeán squeezed her fingers. "Mairead, you sometimes get so focused on an idea that you find it hard to consider that there may be other alternatives." Mairead opened her eyes. What Jeán was saying was true. Had that not just happened a few days ago when she thought the only solution to Ulrick was an army? "Be broad-minded, Mairead, especially about yourself and your future. Be open to discovering your true feelings and only then decide what you want to do. Don't end a possibility too early. You and Hamish have a connection. I saw it. So did Davros, and you both feel it. What that means, could it turn into something more, is something you will need to find out."

Mairead swallowed. "How?"

Jeán gave Mairead's hands a final squeeze and let them go. "First, let Hamish know that you do trust him by *actually* trusting him. Let go this need to know his plan. I understand you feel vulnerable, but men want women who believe in *them*, not their plans." Then, with a grin and a playful wiggle of her brow, she said, "Next, you must kiss Hamish. And not just a peck but in a way that would make Davros blush. When it is over, there needs to be no doubt on how you feel about each other."

Mairead bit her bottom lip. How she wanted to give herself permission to just succumb to her desire to kiss Hamish, for it had not diminished in the least. If anything, it had grown. That was what worried her. Based on her response to his touch when she believed she was not attracted to him, kissing him now could be dangerous. For she was fairly certain that once she was in Hamish's embrace, she would lack the control to keep things merely at a kiss.

"I appreciate your listening," Hamish said as he followed Davros out the byre and back outside. The barn emitted a mixture of smells from all the birds kept in there. Hamish had been surprised that Davros had so many. Most independent falconers only had one or two birds; this falconer had ten.

Instead of heading back to the cottage, Davros turned

toward a clearing. He shielded his eyes. The sun had come out and the wind had died, warming the air by several degrees. He stared at the set of nearby hills. "Let me think. Now that you've explained what I've been seeing, I have much to think about. And that also includes just how your brother is going to react."

"You think Robert will cause problems?"

"I like Robert MacBrieve and his wife. He respects people and has the capacity to be both generous and frugal when appropriate. And yet while he cares, he has no experience with military matters or keeping a clan secure. A good clan leader can learn these things, but your brother lets his own personal philosophies cloud his ability to accept reality. And yet Robert *is* still the one with final say over Foinaven and its security. He is a major factor and one you cannot control."

That did not bother Hamish. "One never controls most elements of any situation, but that does not mean they are not predictable. The key is not to depend on any assumption. Plan, act, and always have options when things take a twist."

"And you are prepared for your brother?"

Hamish smiled reassuringly. "I wouldn't be here if I did not expect to succeed."

Davros pursed his lips and after a few seconds nodded. "Never thought I'd support a MacBrieve in a confrontation, but I believe you will succeed. Moreover, I want to be there when you do."

Hamish's smile widened, as he felt oddly triumphant to have convinced the falconer to join his cause. He leaned against a tree, glad the sun had made an appearance—even if it was only temporary. It was almost comfortable outside. "You called me a McTiernay just a little while ago."

Davros nodded but kept his gaze on the distance. "That I did."

"I'm not one, by the way. Rightfully, I am a MacBrieve."

"No one will know who you are until you do. But it does bolster my confidence thinking a McTiernay is spearheading this endeavor, not a MacBrieve."

Hamish knew he should be insulted by the somewhat insensitive comment. But he wasn't. "I guess I should not be surprised that you say that." Hamish had been born a MacBrieve but never felt like one. They were either administrative judges or builders like his brother. They were not a clan of warriors. "My father used to feel displaced at times. I remember him telling me once that it didn't matter whether we fit the MacBrieve mold, we would just change it. Our legacy of MacBrieves would be one of warriors and leaders—men of strength and honor. He did not realize his legacy would live through Robert, who has not needed to break the mold. He is a true MacBrieve."

It was Hamish who was the fraud. It was why he had always been more comfortable with the McTiernays. He loved Robert, but he had an indescribable bond with Conor and his brothers. Hamish understood them, and more important, they understood him.

"I'm glad you like Mairead."

Hamish blinked. He had been so focused on his inner monologue, he had not been listening to what Davros had been saying until the very end. But even without knowing how Davros had led up to such a statement, it was not difficult to discern what he was implying. And two could play that game. "I do in fact like her. Very much. She is fiercely loyal and very protective of those she loves. That is what makes her so willing to confront and challenge anyone she thinks is in the wrong."

"I think you enjoy the challenge."

"Why wouldn't I? I like being around anyone with spunk and find that few women have the gumption to say their thoughts. Most either sit quiet and obedient-like or just glare in silence."

Davros nodded and glanced back at Hamish. "You find a lot of women with gumption with the McTiernays, I take it."

Hamish had answered that question earlier, when they were eating. He had met only a few women who had the mettle Mairead possessed, and each time their hearts had all been swept away by a McTiernay. But this time it was not a McTiernay who was preventing him from pursuing Mairead. "We are just friends, Davros," he finally said.

"Friends," the falconer repeated as if mulling over the concept. "Hard to be just friends with someone who is your kind of woman. I know. I tried that with Jeán for a while."

Hamish was well aware of what Davros spoke. Just this past year, one of his closest friends, Craig McTiernay, had fought for months his feelings for the woman who later became his wife. If Craig had never admitted the truth, Hamish had little doubt that he would have sought Meriel to be his own, disregarding Wyenda without a second thought. Meriel had been the one to make him realize that a relationship with a woman could be much more than just physical.

"I'm not sure I have a 'kind' of woman. I can find something I like about almost any female, just as I can find things that I *don't* like about them. Things that I would not want to be tied to. Unfortunately, they seem to be the very things you don't discover until *after* you make a commitment."

Davros broke out into laughter. "You have no idea how right you are. The stuff that I learned about Jeán our first year of marriage . . ." Davros stopped mid-sentence and got lost in the memory for a minute before facing Hamish and saying, "But it is all worth it if the woman loves you and you love her in return."

"I have no doubt that what you say is true, but right now, Mairead's interest in me is limited to what I have planned for Ulrick."

"She will have to know sometime."

"But not yet," Hamish countered.

"I know she has been hounding you and I could only imagine some of the things she has done to trick you into divulging your plans."

"You know Mairead very well."

"I do," Davros agreed. "And a few times I have been tempted to teach her a lesson about being too pushy with her curiosity. Is that the reason you don't want to tell her about what is going on?"

"Not in the least. I would tell her if I could, for I suspect she has insights that would prove very helpful. But Mairead and Selah are close. They may disagree with each other on many things, but the risk of her confiding in her sister is too high."

"It's possible but unlikely. Still, Jeán and I will keep your secret."

"Thank you. I just wish you could help me with understanding why Mairead is so insistent on knowing my plans."

"Mairead has always been inquisitive, which is why I know how annoying it can be at times. Selah might be the lady of Foinaven, but it is Mairead who shoulders much responsibility. She is used to being the decision maker and knowing all that goes on."

Hamish did not disagree, but he did not believe that was the reason behind Mairead's persistence. It went beyond wanting the comfort of knowledge to something more akin to fear. But what about? She had believed him when he promised that Ulrick would not succeed in taking Foinaven away from Selah and Robert. "Whatever it is, I think it is linked to her desire to find a husband."

"That's a complicated leap."

Hamish agreed, but his gut still told him it was an accurate one.

Davros pointed to the cottage and signaled to Jeán that he saw her wave. "I wonder why men who are so capable of preparing for battle, examining all aspects from the improbable to the likely, do not do so when it comes to personal matters. They leap to assumptions and dismiss options, believing that certain impediments exist which prevent them from pursuing happiness, instead of just seeking the truth."

Davros waited until he caught Hamish's eye. "I do not know for sure how Mairead feels about you and I wonder if you even know how you feel about her. But I do know that Mairead is smart, steadfast, and generous as well as uncommonly beautiful, though she doesn't really know it. And if the right man wins her heart, she'll aggravate and delight him for years. But if she surrenders to the pressure of marrying someone who will not appreciate her bold ways and fondness for creating challenges, she will be miserable. Much more so than if she had just accepted the few things that made it seem impossible for her to be with the right man." Davros turned and walked back to the cabin.

Hamish stood unmoving and watched the falconer be welcomed by his wife at the door with a kiss. The man had seen much in his years and held a lot of wisdom. But he was wrong about Mairead not being afraid. And he was wrong about Mairead's interest in him.

Mairead might be searching for a husband, and while part of Hamish wished it were otherwise—she did not want it to be him. Oh, Mairead might have been interested if he were not leaving Foinaven, but her sights were on the next commander—a man who would have power and influence. And yet, if that were it alone, she would have already enticed someone to ask for her hand. No, there was something more and if Hamish were to guess, Mairead did not want to marry at all and was hoping to find a way to keep that from happening.

That was why she wanted to know about his plan; however, *that* was not enough to get him to confide in her. Too much was at risk.

But that *was* enough to make him decide it was time to do some probing of his own.

They had not traveled far from Davros's home when Mairead came to a stop at a fork in the route back to Foinaven. Hamish slowed his mount to a stop next to Mairead's. Once again they were faced with a choice of paths. To the right was the road they used to get to the cottage. Hamish suspected Davros only used it when he went to the river or on market days when he needed a cart. The path to the left was narrow in places in that it went through some woods, but when it emerged on the other side of the trees, it sank into a fairly steep valley. From there it was about an hour to Foinaven, a trek with which Hamish was intimately familiar.

Mairead turned her head and looked at him with an indiscernible expression. They both had said very little since they left the cottage. If her and Jeán's discussion was anything like the one he had with Davros, she was thinking of all that had been said—or *not* said, in his case.

Mairead pointed toward the wooded path. "I want to go this way and we both know it is not because it is the shorter route back. But I also know that you are not ready for me to see what is there." And without another word of explanation or argument, she pulled her reins to the right and aimed her horse toward the river.

Hamish sat stunned. His heart momentarily swelled with an indescribable emotion. A couple seconds later it vanished, replaced with wariness and suspicion. Mairead was way too stubborn to not *at least ask* to go the way she wanted. For her to immediately resign to his wishes she had something else in mind and he needed to be ready.

He urged his horse to catch up to Mairead's and then matched the unhurried speed she had set. "What are you planning?" He decided to take a direct approach. He doubted it would work, but if it did, it would save him a lot of time and energy. "You are far too stubborn to simply concede after you have made up your mind. And I don't believe that talking with Jeán for an hour changed that about you." *At least I hope not*, he added to himself.

"*I'm* stubborn?" Mairead half asked, half repeated with a snort. "That's amusing coming from you. Every person in northern Scotland has been told stories of how obstinate the McTiernays can be. And living with them for so long, trust me, you have become *exactly* like them."

Mairead gave him a sideways glance. The look in her big honey-and-green-colored eyes practically dared him to deny that he was any different. And for a second Hamish was once again transfixed. He finally broke free from her gaze. Then he began to chuckle. Soon he was full-out laughing for he finally understood just what Conor, Cole, Craig, and the rest of the McTiernay brothers had been up against for so long. "The McTiernays may have a *reputation* for being stubborn—and they would probably pummel me for saying this, but every one of them—well, the married ones at least—yield *all the damned time*."

Mairead shifted her jaw. "I'm assuming you mean to their wives."

Hamish nodded and quickly got his laughter under control for Mairead's expression did not hold nearly the amusement his did. If anything, it was rather chilly. He sucked in a short breath hoping that he had not accidentally plundered into unfamiliar and potentially volatile territory.

"Perhaps the McTiernay men are not *yielding* to their wives, Hamish. Perhaps, they are merely realizing that the women they cherish—and I suspect heavily rely on for support and advice—were *right*."

Hamish shifted in his saddle, suddenly somewhat uncomfortable. Mairead was miffed. But she was also wrong. Too many times he had inadvertently heard Laurel's "winning" justification during one of her and Conor's arguments. Hamish would never say her point of view was ludicrous—Laurel was a very smart woman and could outsmart most men if they were not careful—but there was only one reason Conor had "yielded" to some of her more absurd positions. He had simply been disinclined to argue.

Hamish just now realized that assumption had only been *partially* correct. Aye, Conor had been disinclined to argue, but not for the reason Hamish had always assumed.

Hamish took another sneak peek at Mairead. The woman was breathtaking when she was riled. The rigidity of her back accentuated her figure. The color of her skin glowed and her eyes blazed. But right now, Hamish did want to bask in the beauty of her anger. More than anything he longed to see her smile and know that he was the cause. Conor always used four choice words to create that very effect. "Perhaps you are right."

Immediately Mairead visibly relaxed and her soft mouth curved into a sensuous, mysterious half smile he could not quite figure out. But he liked it.

Mairead shifted the reins from her right hand to her left and after a long minute, she said softly, "Thank you."

"For what?"

Hamish watched as she contemplated her answer and her teeth began to play with her bottom lip. "I know you still think I am completely wrong about why men yield, but I really appreciate you for saying otherwise."

"And you wonder why men are confused by you creatures," Hamish mumbled under his breath.

Mairead crinkled her brow. "We are not that difficult to understand. Despite what you think, women rarely seek to win a verbal battle. What we want is not to be found right or wrong but *to be heard*. No one likes their opinions to be dismissed, and especially not without consideration."

Hamish tugged the reins to avoid a muddy hole. Women *absolutely* wanted to win arguments. Mairead may think otherwise, but it was only when she was victorious did she believe she had been heard. And it was not just women who were like that, men felt the same way. "I hear you, Mairead."

"Do you? Because I don't believe you have yet to really listen to me when it comes to your plans with Ulrick."

Immediately tension ran through Hamish and he instinctively raised his defenses to do battle. "I'm listening now," he said honestly. And he was. He always had . . . hadn't he?

Mairead's furrowed brow eased a bit. "You *think* my need to know your plans has to do with curiosity, a need for control, or a lack of trust in you, *but it is none of those things*. Out of the two of us, it is you who is lacking trust. There is obviously something in that valley you do not want me to see. For if I do, you believe I will be compelled to tell Selah and Robert. I don't believe I would and it hurts that you think I would, but not having any idea of what it could be, I guess I must allow that you may be right. Only something immoral would compel me to inform my sister and Robert as they are responsible for this clan. However, *I trust you* and know that you would never cross that line."

Hamish listened to all she had to say and this time he heard something he had not before. *You think my need to know your plans has to do with curiosity.* Hamish's tongue slid along the inside of his cheek. *Need* to know, Mairead had said. Not want. Once again, he had the feeling that this tied back to Mairead's reluctance to marry despite what she had done or said. "And I also trust you," he replied. "You now know where to go to learn about my plans and I am trusting you to wait until I am ready to show you. And I never believed your reasons for learning them were so shallow as mere curiosity or a simple need for control. I've always known they went far deeper. I wish you would tell me the truth. I might be able to help."

Mairead swallowed. Her reasons needed to remain her own. She was not sure what Hamish would do if he knew the nature of *all* Ulrick's threats, but she had no doubt that he would do *something*. And every scenario she came up with involved her relinquishing what little say she had over her future. All except one. Hamish killed Ulrick. If that happened it did not matter if Hamish knew in advance. But if Ulrick lived—which was the more probable outcome based on Robert's request for no bloodshed—

then Hamish would undoubtedly decide that he was honor bound to protect her. The only way to ensure that would be via marriage—either to some McTiernay he hand-picked or worse—Hamish would feel pressured to wed her himself.

Those options were not acceptable, they would not work, for leaving Foinaven was not an option. The only way Hamish might stay was if he loved her, and even then, she could not imagine it being enough to withstand working with Robert.

Mairead nudged her horse to turn toward the river. Once at the bank, she slid off its back and let it drink. She looked into the distance. The land grew flat so the sea was visible—though just barely. But she could feel it.

She waited until Hamish dismounted and stood beside her. She took a deep breath and held it for a second. Then let it go as she spoke. "You are right. There is much more to why I want to understand how you intend to deal with Ulrick. A lot has happened while you were away. Much of it has been good, but unsurprisingly, there have been some difficulties. I am hoping your plan might rectify a few of them." Mairead then looked him in the eye. "You will learn nothing more from me. Like you, I have a right to my secrets."

Hamish studied her for nearly a half a minute. Mairead's gaze never flinched and he knew she meant every word spoken. "Keep your secrets, Mairead. I will not pressure you into telling me, but if you ever do want me to listen, know that I will."

Mairead was both relieved and grateful that she would not have to fight him on this. She had seen him debating whether or not he should probe and just how hard. But in the end, he had opted to respect her wishes.

Mairead bent down and picked up a smooth rock and rolled it around in her hand. She eyed him again and then threw it. It skipped once and then sank into the water. "Just what was it that Davros said to you? I am not sure how to react to your being so cooperative."

"I suspect it was very similar to the conversation you had with Jeán."

Mairead picked up another rock and then put it down. She did that twice more before finally selecting one that was larger, but also flatter and more evenly balanced. "I doubt it, unless Davros also has a bizarre fixation with your dimples."

Hamish laughed out loud. "Um, I do not recall that subject coming up. However, I cannot believe my features were all you talked about for an hour."

Mairead shrugged and then reached back, and with a sharp flick of her wrist, let the rock fly. She smiled when it skipped several times before disappearing. "Depends on what you mean. Jeán *really* does like your dimples." Mairead paused and Hamish found himself thinking, *Do you?* But before he could finagle asking the question without being obvious, Mairead flashed him an impish grin. "But we did talk of more than just your smile. However, the topic of our conversation never strayed from *you.*"

A shot of nervous energy erupted in Hamish and he felt the sudden need to occupy his hands. Following her lead, he bent down and found a rock for skipping. "That is both telling and frustratingly vague."

He threw the rock. He was a master at skipping stones and was disappointed when a ripple caused by the current prematurely ended what should have been a good throw.

"You are still good," Mairead said. "Remember when you taught me?"

"Aye, though I wasn't sure you did."

"I remember everything you said to me back then," she whispered, and threw another stone. It too hit the water wrong and immediately sank. Frustrated, she picked up two more rocks and was about to try again when she felt Hamish's arms slide around her back to guide her movements.

Immediately Mairead's heart started beating faster. She knew what Jeán would say if she were there. *Turn around and kiss him.* And while Mairead wanted to do just that, too many women in Hamish's past had focused on only their needs. And when they decided he was not what they wanted, his heart had become a casualty. She refused to be like them. Aye, she needed to decipher what her true feelings were, but she was not going to play games in order to do so.

"Jeán thinks you are attracted to me." Mairead paused and glanced over her shoulder at Hamish. "Are you?"

Curled around her, Hamish was so close to her lips that it would have taken no effort to press them against his own. However, *not* doing so was unbelievably hard. "You already know the answer to that," he replied huskily.

Mairead pulled back so that she could turn around but did not completely step out of his grasp. "That's not an answer."

Hamish's green eyes grew dark with intensity. "Then, aye. Most sane men are attracted to a beautiful woman," he said flippantly. A muscle flicked angrily in her jaw. She took a step back forcing him to let her go.

Hamish could not blame her. He had known he was not going to be able to physically push her away, so he had said something to make her do it. Her anger he could handle. But it was not anger he had seen flash in her eyes just before she pulled away. It had been pain. He had hurt her and it wrenched him to know he was the cause.

He wished he could tell her the truth. Tell her that he craved her lips, that he had tasted nothing better in his life and how they haunted him every night. But saying such things would only cause more pain, because a simple kiss would not quench his thirst for her. It would only create more desire. And Mairead deserved a man who could give her more than a kiss.

Mairead stuck her chin up and waited until she was certain she had his undivided attention. "Would you kiss me again if I asked?"

Hamish swallowed. He had just reaffirmed that was something he was not going to do again . . . didn't he? "I . . . I am not sure that would be a good idea. For either of us."

Mairead took a step forward, reclosing the gap. "I'm asking for a kiss—nothing more."

Hamish shook his head, fighting his instincts so he could remain in control. He needed to ignore what she would feel like and focus on what would happen if he succumbed to her offer. He was losing the battle. "I *won't* be trapped into staying," he muttered in an accusing tone.

Mairead put a hand on his chest and looked him in the eye. "And I *won't* let the act of enjoying a mere kiss tie me to a man either. Hamish, I'm not thinking about the future right now. I just want to know if what I felt that day in the great hall was a fluke."

Every muscle in Hamish's body froze. His mind, however, was whirling out of control. He *knew* their kiss had affected her, but it was still shocking to hear Mairead admit it. And she was not seeking promises, just answers.

"A kiss is not a commitment, Hamish." Mairead let

go a small chuckle. "If it were, I would be married a few dozen times by now."

A few dozen times? A surge of jealousy shot through him at the image of her kissing a long line of men. If he thought about it rationally, at the age of twenty and two it would have been more surprising if Mairead had *not* been kissed a few times. She was beautiful and probably highly sought by many as a potential wife. But Hamish was incapable of rational thought with her so close. The heat of her hand was making his blood boil and her fresh scent was causing his body to make demands of its own. All he could think was that he needed to erase the memory of every man's touch but his own.

Powerless to stop himself, Hamish could not pull his gaze away from her lips as he slowly, inevitably, lowered his mouth to hers. His arms gathered her close in case she suddenly realized what was about to happen, because Mairead was not going anywhere. She wanted to know if the passion of their kiss had been a fluke and he was not going to keep her wondering any longer.

He brushed his tongue across her lips, silently urging her to open for him. When she did, Hamish invaded the sweet warmth he had been dreaming of for days. He kissed her long and soft and deep, capturing her tongue and drawing it into his own mouth. It seemed hardly possible, but she tasted better than he remembered. The more he sought, the more she gave him—her eager response perfectly matching his own fervor.

A shiver rolled through Mairead as she committed the kiss to memory. *This* was her first real kiss and it was more than she had ever dreamed it could be. She was unprepared for the feelings being created within her. She should be terrified. Hamish was searing her senses with intimate aggression that should make her run away. But each masterful stroke of his tongue only increased her desire.

The other day, Hamish had awoken feelings that were now burning out of control. She said she liked to play with fire, but kissing Hamish was like embracing an inferno. And yet, she wanted more.

Hamish groaned as Mairead began to move her hands up along his chest. She was returning his kiss with an innocent, but nonetheless intense level of passion he never sensed in another woman. When he felt her fingers clench his shoulders, his lower body similarly clenched with need. *Mo chreach*, Mairead was soft, warm, and inviting. She was everything he had ever dreamed of in a woman; consequently, kissing her was the most dangerous thing he had ever done. He was not just in danger of doing something that would lock them together forever but in danger of losing his heart. This time there would be no broken pieces to mend.

Mairead sensed Hamish was about to pull away and refused to let him. She twisted her fingers into his hair and held on. Jeán had wanted her to learn how she truly felt about Hamish. Mairead was not sure of anything at the moment. She had been unprepared for the feelings Hamish was igniting in her. Later she could analyze just what they meant, but right now all she wanted was to sink her soul into this kiss.

Hamish moved his hands to cradle her face as he drank hungrily from her lips. He could not get enough of her lips, her taste, her touch. He wanted to consume the essence of her vibrant spirit. He needed to get closer, to feel more of her, taste more of her.

The full force of his hunger broke over Mairead. The kiss was growing in intensity. It was now darker, more demanding, and far more blatantly erotic. It was as if

Hamish was unconsciously testing her desire. Mairead did not think; she only felt. And what she felt could be summed up in one word: "more." She leaned into him and with her fingers buried in the softness of his hair, she held his mouth to hers. She did not want this kiss to end.

Mairead moaned with pleasure into his mouth, stroking his tongue with her own, matching his wild, ravenous desire. Hamish's body was tight. He wanted to lose himself within her. Her breasts had contracted until her nipples were firm little nubs pressing urgently against his chest, begging to be touched. Without thought, his hands became as undisciplined as his mouth. He stroked a warm path from her shoulders to the base of her spine and then up her stomach until they cupped her breasts, reveling in their fullness.

Mairead shivered as he gently squeezed one nub. Even through the material, he could feel her respond and using both thumbs, he began to tease the hard peaks. She moaned but did not pull away, instead arching her back, encouraging him to continue.

As he feared, kissing Mairead did not quench his desires. It had stoked them to levels he could not control. Unfamiliar emotions began to churn him. Need tore through him, ripping away all his carefully constructed defenses and leaving only the agony of knowing she could never be more to him than she was at this moment. And yet he couldn't stop.

The hot, sweet, sensuous kiss went on and on, suffusing her body with an aching need for more. Hamish was making her body come alive and the more he touched her the more she wanted to be touched. To remove their clothing and feel his skin against hers. His arms were taut with muscle, and his body was excitingly harder than hers. Mairead clung to him in confusion and desire.

Gu sealladh orm, he could feel the fire growing in her. Her needs fed his and vice versa. To know this woman would be unlike any experience he would ever have. He wanted her and she wanted him and he was about to throw all reason aside when a piercing sound of two drunk men singing yanked him back to reality and—where he was, whom he was with, and just what he had been about to do.

All ye Highlanders lend an ear,
Come alang, come alang, wi' some ale a song,

When Hamish's lips released hers, it took several seconds for Mairead to realize just why he stopped.

For we've got er tale that ye never did hear
Of a mighty Highlander who's finally come home.

Mairead blinked and looked around. She saw no one, but she could hear a very drunk and a very out-of-tune Seamus and Abe coming. Soon they would be around the corner and in sight and her chest was still heaving with the effort it took to breathe. She would have thought she was the only one deeply affected by their kiss except for Hamish's own uneven intake of his breath.

Hamish made sure that Mairead could stand on her own and then stepped away from her. He collected the reins of both horses and handed one set to her. He was just about to mount his horse when the two men came into view. Both waved at Hamish and he walked toward them, providing a distraction and time for Mairead to fix her hair. However, he doubted either of them could focus well enough to recognize the telltale signs of what he and Mairead had just been doing.

"I see you found the ale. How's the tower floor?"

Abe threw an arm around Seamus's shoulders. "I thought you were *ar buile* for wanting holes in the tower floor. Still kind of do."

"Not me," Seamus said interrupting, "I'm thinking of building a floor in me barn just so I 'ave somethin' to pound on when me wife nags at me again."

With that Abe started singing again and Seamus joined him as they continued to stumble their way back home.

Hamish waited until they had turned the next bend before he went back to Mairead to ask her if she was ready to return to Foinaven. But when she had looked at him, he knew he was in trouble.

Her eyes were still misty with passion and her lips, red and swollen, beckoned to be kissed again. He thought her taste had haunted him before, but it was nothing like it would be. She was sweet and spicy and he would forever crave her taste. The effect she had on him was dangerous for he could see himself giving anything to have it again.

Hamish looked away. He wanted to think that he would have stopped their embrace before it had gone any further. But deep down he was not sure he would have. Even now, it was taking everything he had not to walk over and resume where they had left off.

He mounted his horse and tried to clear his mind, but it was not working. He needed space away from her or he would have no chance at regaining control over the emotions she had stirred within him. Why had he kissed her? Did he want to lose his heart to someone he could not have? Because he was on the verge of doing just that. And if Mairead felt even a tiny bit of what he did, then he was setting her up for heartache as well. They needed distance from each other and right now. He just prayed she understood that.

"The village is just around the corner," he said as Mairead mounted her own horse. With his thumb, he pointed in the direction Seamus and Abe had gone. "I think it might be best if I make sure those two make it back home and to their wives. Otherwise, they might pass out and freeze to death before anyone finds them. Are you able to travel the rest of the way yourself?"

Mairead nodded. She normally would have chafed at the question. But the way her emotions were spinning out of control, she was glad to finish the journey by herself. "I will see you later." And with those words, she urged her horse toward Foinaven.

Hamish had not missed how the tension in her shoulders had eased upon hearing his suggestion that they part. He should have been comforted by her ready agreement to travel alone.

But he wasn't.

Chapter Eight

Mairead woke with a start and sat straight up in bed. She shivered. Her feet were freezing. She reached for a blanket to pull around her, wondering why it was so very cold in her room. As she rubbed her eyes, her mind slowly stirred to life and she looked around. The almost-always-present clouds had yet to return, letting rare winter starlight stream through her bedchamber window. It was not very bright, but it was enough to see what she was wearing.

With a thump, Mairead fell back against her mattress. She was not sure what time it was, but if the temperature of the room was an indicator, the fire had gone out hours ago, which made it the middle of the night. That meant she had not only missed dinner, but everything else she had intended to do before she retired.

Selah had probably come to get her, but rather than waking her, decided to just let her sleep. Mairead rolled over. Sometimes she loved her sister's generosity, but this was not one of those moments. Selah should have woken her to help with Rab, handle dinner, and if necessary, deal with Hamish.

Mairead had stopped by Robert's chambers to say hello after she had returned from Davros's but had not been allowed to stay long. His condition had become worse and he was now running a low fever. A fever was not unexpected and though Robert always pulled through his illness every year, it was getting more and more troubling to hear him struggle to breathe. The only thing Mairead knew to do was pray and be there for her elder sister.

By the time she had finished talking with Selah and doing what she could to lift her sister's spirits, Hamish had still not returned. Knowing the evening meal would not be for at least two more hours, Mairead had decided to retire to her room to lie down. The day had been long and she was exhausted after being unable to sleep the last couple of nights. But mostly, she needed a quiet, private place to think . . . and to remember.

Never had she thought that within minutes of lying down she would fall asleep. But she had.

The last thing Mairead could remember was sitting on the bed and slipping off her shoes. She had been thinking about Hamish, about their kiss and what it meant, but before she had come to even one conclusion she must have fallen asleep. Mairead rolled so that she could stare at the ceiling and flopped an arm across her forehead as her memories of her dreams returned in flashes. In them, Hamish was kissing her again. In some, he just vanished, leaving her to shrink and eventually turn into dust. But in others, he had declared her to be his. He fought off Ulrick and then reclaimed his right to Foinaven, where they lived the rest of their lives happily together.

Mairead squeezed her eyes shut as the hazy memory of him kissing her to prove his love began to replay again. Flinging her arm to the side, she grabbed the pillow, put it over her face, and then screamed into it with frustration.

If only that future was even slightly possible. But it was not, and entertaining the idea that it could ever happen was pointless. And yet that knowledge did nothing to quench the passion Hamish had stirred in her.

Groaning, she rolled her legs off the bed and stood up to remove her outer clothes and become more comfortable. She threw two logs in the hearth and nudged the nearly dead embers until they sprung to life and caught the wood on fire. She then splashed some water on her face, brushed her hair, and returned to bed.

Snuggling down under the covers to get warm, Mairead curled up on her side and wondered if Hamish had been grappling with what happened between them the same way she was. Maybe, for he had been gone far longer than it would have taken to see Abe and Seamus home. But then again, she was not even sure when he returned. Maybe he had gone to the valley and never gave their kiss any thought for *she* had been the one to insist that it would be a simple kiss and it would change nothing.

Problem was, to her, what happened by the river was much more than just a kiss. It felt like she had found where she belonged. She suddenly knew where she could be happy every day for the rest of her life, where she would be safe and loved and free to be herself.

Mairead pulled the blankets and murmured curses at Jeán. Aye, a kiss proved that she was far more interested in Hamish than she had wanted to admit. But just how far did her emotions go? Was she in love with him? Mairead was not sure.

Desire by itself was not love and would always fade with time. But Mairead had been infatuated before and this was different. Those times she was enamored of one or two characteristics, but not the man as a whole. With Hamish, she craved all of him—even the things that drove her insane. She wanted him and just as he was. So was this love? She was afraid to answer without knowing how he felt about her. He desired her. But he had since the moment he had arrived. Had their kiss also caused him to rethink his feelings? Would he even allow himself the possibility of loving her?

Mairead closed her eyes. Her feelings were so raw and turbulent. No matter how she looked at them, they were impossible to define. Why was it easy to discern the feelings and character of others but difficult within herself? She never struggled to see the emotions that drove people, whether it be love, envy, or even hatred. Why could she not discern the truth of her own heart as easily?

Mairead bolted back to a sitting position. She really could easily recognize the motivations of others, it was just knowing what to look for. The matters of her heart may always be a mystery; however, the truth about people's loyalties did not have to be. She knew just how to help Hamish flesh out the moles in the guard.

Unfortunately—or fortunately, depending on how you looked at it—her idea required both her and Hamish to spend a significant amount of time together.

Hamish slid off his horse and entered the castle gates, wondering why Foinaven even had them. All an enemy needed was a few lit torches and the wooden barrier would cease to be.

He had gotten an especially early start that morning to give himself enough time to travel a little farther and meet with some people Davros thought might be influential in his plan. The falconer had been correct. They were exactly whom he was looking for, but he had not known where to look for them.

He entered the stables and handed the reins to the very lethargic stable boy. Adiran, who had helped him prep to leave, must not have gone back to sleep. Hamish could see it in the lad's eyes and suspected that same weariness could be viewed in his. But his fatigue was not caused by the early departure, the distance he had traveled, or even the stressful time he had dealing with those who did not know him, even by reputation. He could have never left— he knew that he would still feel this deep weariness.

It was all because of Mairead.

She was the one who convinced him a kiss would be nothing more than that. And he had let himself believe her. But it had been much more than a kiss. Kissing was something he had done much in his lifetime and never before had the activity made it difficult to do even the simplest of functions. But what made it worse was knowing that for Mairead it *had* been just a simple kiss.

When she had not come down for dinner, Selah had sent someone for her. Hamish had felt his jaw actually drop when the servant returned and said Mairead had retired early for the evening and was already asleep. Until then, he had thought the sparks that flew between them had been plaguing her thoughts as much as his own. Unfortunately, knowing that was not the case had not lessened the turmoil going on inside of him.

He wanted Mairead more than he had ever wanted any other woman. But it was more than a physical craving; he loved spending time with her. He loved looking at her, laughing with her. He even enjoyed arguing with her. If he had met her a year ago, he would have already pronounced to the world that he had fallen in love. And he would have been right. For he now knew that he never loved anyone before Mairead. Those rejections that had hurt so much at the time had wounded his pride—not his heart.

But with Mairead, his heart really was in jeopardy.

His only protection was to keep such feelings to himself. Because saying them aloud did not bring happiness; it only brought pain. No, this time before he succumbed to any emotion—especially to the ones building inside him—he was going to be absolutely positive they were returned. And right now, that was dubious.

She desired him. But did she love him? Could she love him enough to leave Foinaven, her beloved home, and the last of her family—her sister? Hamish was not sure any woman could love him enough to do that and not regret the decision.

Crash!

Hamish stepped back out into the courtyard to see several of the older boys wrestling with one another. Their faces were familiar for he had seen them running around and annoying the servants. Like their fathers, they were bored waiting for planting season. Being so young, they were teeming with energy and had no place to release it. Their mothers had probably chased them out of their homes and to keep from being yelled at, they had come to Foinaven to pass the time. Most found the havoc they created to entertain themselves extremely vexing, but Hamish found their presence fortuitous.

Hamish walked toward a rotund merchant. His plump face was bright red with fury and Hamish could not blame him. A half dozen boys had been wrestling with one another, rolling and tackling, unaware and uncaring of what was in their path. When one boy tackled another, the two collided into a parked cart, carrying a box of clay pots. The impact sent the pots flying and when they landed they all broke but one.

Upon seeing the merchant grab the back of two of the boys' leines, the rest of the lads stopped fighting and hid.

Hamish was not sure just what the merchant intended to do. He suspected the merchant did not know either.

Hamish arrived at the scene and gave his most withering look to both lads. "I'll deal with these two." His voice was cold and he saw both pairs of eyes grow wide with fear. "I'm standing in for Robert until he is well."

The merchant lived in the village and had seen and heard of Hamish as a soldier, but this was a matter of commerce, not battle. "These delinquents cost me this month's wages."

Hamish doubted it was a whole month, but the man did have a point. "I will have Mairead meet with you and see that you are appropriately compensated for your loss." Then Hamish looked down, staring hard at one lad and then the other. "Which means you will need to reimburse Foinaven for its loss."

One boy swallowed and fear completely took over the other at the thought of going home and telling their fathers. It was clear they knew neither of their families earned enough to pay for the pots.

Hamish gestured for the merchant to let them go. He did and then huffed as Hamish pulled them to the side so that he could go back to what he was doing before being interrupted. One boy glared at the other and just before he was shoved in retaliation, Hamish got their attention. "Just what are you two arguing over?"

"He," one boy said with a sneer, "says Ulrick could fight the Mackays when everyone knows they are the most fearsome warriors of the north."

"Are they now?" Hamish asked.

The other lad crossed his arms, gave a withering look to his opponent, and nodded. "My da says Ulrick could rip them to shreds. He says the Mackays are cowards that were off their lands. And his sister," he said, pointing to the other boy, "married one of them, making him a coward too."

"Ulrick is a cheater where the Mackays are the meanest Highlanders in all of Scotland. They gut people and leave their entrails to be eaten by vultures." The shout was followed by a shove and Hamish had to pull them both apart.

"First, it is true that the Mackays were forced out of Moray and resettled nearby." He looked at the first lad, who was indignant. "But that was long ago. I happen to know King Robert personally and can tell you that he is very appreciative to have such strong warriors on his side." The lad relaxed a little and gave him a nod.

Hamish turned to the other lad. "Your father is correct. Ulrick is a sly fighter and is willing to use any means to slay a foe. I have seen him many times to be ruthless in his approach. I cannot say that I find many of his tactics honorable, but they are usually successful."

The boy swallowed. Hamish had just told him that in a way he was right about Ulrick, but he got the feeling that he was fighting for the wrong side.

"I hope that was a worthwhile thing to fight about because you both will be spending some time repaying their costs." The boys looked at each other and then at Hamish blinking rapidly. They had thought they were going to have to go home and attempt to get the payment from their fathers. Severe punishment would certainly follow, but Hamish spoke as if *they* could pay him back, not their parents. "I think hauling rocks will keep you out of trouble," Hamish continued. "Not small ones either. And I want them in two piles, one on either side of the castle gates. I'll pay you wages, which will go to reimburse the pots, but once done, if you do a good job and work hard, you can stay on and keep the additional wages you earn."

Both boys had gone from afraid, to relieved, to shocked, and were now almost busting with excitement. "Aye, we will!" they both shouted simultaneously.

Before they could dart off and brag about what had happened, Hamish put up a hand to stop them. "And tell your friends that I saw them. I know who they are and they too have to help, for they contributed to the damage."

"You'll pay them?" one lad asked, still not quite believing that he was about to get wages.

"Aye. Now go and the next time I see any of your faces, you better be hauling rocks."

Both boys nodded in agreement and then immediately ran off to find their friends.

"*Keep* their *wages*?" The question came from the merchant who had been lurking behind him. Hamish was unsurprised. The man had looked disappointed when Hamish had pulled the lads aside. He had wanted to hear them being punished and threatened, not rewarded.

"They will be earning it."

The merchant blew out his already chubby cheeks. "Aye, hauling rocks is laborious, but they need to learn a lesson."

Hamish thought about teaching the merchant a lesson on eavesdropping but decided that it was not worth it. "What would you prefer? Punished lads seeking ways for revenge? Or lads learning the value of a hard day's work while keeping them *and their friends* from causing men like you any trouble."

The merchant twitched his lips and then after a moment shrugged before going back to his cart and broken pots.

Hamish headed for the keep, feeling much better. He

had intended the boys to start collecting rocks a couple of days ago when he had last seen them causing problems, but he had been unable to. Mairead had been there and would have thought his actions were a direct result of her meddling. He valued her input, but he was not about to let her think that she could dictate his actions. That precedent would haunt him for years.

Years? He closed his eyes shut. What was he thinking? When had he started thinking of their relationship in years? When had he started thinking of her and him in a relationship?

What he needed was distance. Maybe he should go tell Selah and Robert that he was going to spend a couple of days with Amon and his family. Hopefully, a little time would give him the perspective he needed.

"Hamish?"

Hamish's eyes snapped open. Mairead was exiting the keep and heading straight for him. God, she looked radiant. Positive energy poured out of her. She looked fresh and vibrant. Certainly not like a woman who had any difficulty sleeping.

"Hamish?" she repeated as she came to stand before him.

He made a mistake and inhaled. "What?!" he bellowed, and moved to go around her. He knew he had no reason to bark at her, but women who smelled like her should be locked up.

Mairead froze with her mouth open in shock. She only came back to her senses when she realized he was about to enter the keep and disappear into his room. She ran and caught up with him just in time. As she grabbed on to his forearm, he stopped. "I know that you are frustrated," she said, "but I can help."

Aye, she could help. Starting with letting go. "I'm not frustrated."

"Of course you are," Mairead pressed. She then lowered her voice. "But I can help. I know how to identify just which guards are moles for Ulrick."

That's why she thought he was grumpy? The moles? And he had thought she could read him so well. Then again, Hamish was relieved that in this case she could not. For he certainly did not want her knowing that he had barely slept last night because his mind could not stop thinking about her. A problem she obviously had not shared, based on her irritating cheerfulness. He *really* needed to put space between them and get some clarity.

"Explain," he said in a low voice, his gut warning him that he should just leave. That by even listening to her he was about to get himself into trouble.

Ten minutes later, Hamish entered his chambers. His gut had been right. And while Mairead's idea would probably work, it meant that he was going to have to spend the entire afternoon with her.

So much for perspective and clarity.

Mairead leaned her small sword against the stone fence next to where Hamish was standing and then hopped up to sit on the waist-high stone wall. She was breathing hard and was glad to be able to sit. The stone hedge was one of many the farmers used to delineate boundaries, to corral livestock and mark farmland. She had actually helped build this particular wall almost ten years ago. Made of granite cleared from the fields, the double dyke consisted of two stone walls built parallel to each other that was then filled with smaller rocks and covered with a smooth, rounded cope stone.

Most farmers erected single dyke walls by simply piling stones on top of one another. It was quicker, but it also meant that every couple of years they would have to take precious time to fix, and oftentimes completely rebuild, large sections again. Then Robert had offered an alternative that he had learned as an apprentice. He showed the farmers how to construct the wall using an interlocking pattern so that the weight of the stones created enough pressure to keep them in place. No mortar was needed to create stability and it required very little maintenance. The wall looked the same as it did the year it was built and Mairead suspected that unless someone took it down, it could potentially be there for hundreds of years.

Hamish kept his eyes anywhere but on Mairead. She was still breathing heavily and it was very distracting. He also knew that he was not the only one to notice. "I have a water bag attached to my saddle."

Mairead nodded and went to go get it. Her latest sparring partner watched as she sauntered up to the horse. Hamish coughed and forced his face to remain impassive, when he really wanted to punch the man for appreciating some of Mairead's most delectable attributes.

"Anything else?" the man asked.

Hamish unclenched his jaw. "Aye. You did well. You can return." It was a lie, of course. Any soldier who could not defeat Mairead within seconds was near worthless in battle and Mairead had sparred with him for almost three minutes.

They had told all the guards to meet out in the large field just outside Foinaven in small groups. That Mairead was insisting she show Hamish the skills of the soldiers.

He had suggested they face each other, but Mairead had insisted on sparring with them.

The man flicked his wrist, swinging the two-handed longsword in the air. "You impressed?"

Hamish looked at the weapon. It was dull and dented, but it would not have mattered if it was fresh from the silversmith. The man wielding it was a poor soldier. But like most of the ones Hamish had seen, the man had the potential to be fairly good, with the right training. "It's evident that you've held the weapon before."

The man grinned, taking Hamish's words as a compliment. He lowered the blade and shifted his gaze back to Hamish. "And if I was lacking in skill?"

Hamish shrugged indifferently. "Then that would be the problem of Foinaven's permanent commander. Not mine." He pointed to the group in the distance. "You can tell the next two to come up."

The guard glanced at Mairead, who was pushing the stopper back into the water bag. "You want two? Not one?" he asked continuing to blatantly stare at her.

Hamish felt his anger rise but outwardly forced himself to remain relaxed. "I've appeased Mairead enough," he said nonchalantly. The man was trouble and Hamish had no inclination to teach him a lesson and stifle the man's arrogance. "If we do not speed this thing up, we will be out here in the rain and I'm cold enough."

The guard flashed him a crooked smile, then returned his gaze to Mairead. When she looked at him, he gave her a nod and turned around to stroll back toward Foinaven. As he passed the dwindling group, he gestured and the next two men started coming toward them.

Hamish glanced at Mairead, glad she had taken her time. Her delay had been intentional. She knew the guard was going to say something and elected to be out of earshot when he did. Hamish still could not believe he let her spar with the man, but Mairead would not be dissuaded. He could tell the men were refraining from using their full strength, but Mairead had made them work nonetheless.

She was fast and accurate and had great balance and focus, but it was clear that she lacked the strength and weight to wield even a lighter, shorter sword against a man. Mairead knew it though and had resorted to distraction to help her odds—and it had worked. The woman had flirted, and laughed, and teased with each one of them. When she flirted with the first man, it had taken everything Hamish had to keep from ending this insane idea of hers. But Hamish refused to let her know that he was jealous—more than he had ever been in his life. And secondly, her idea was working.

Mairead re-hooked the water bottle and then came back to lean on the wall next to him. "Lumley is definitely one of Ulrick's men."

"Aye." The man was a weasel. Hamish had sensed it a few days ago when he had met with all the men. Most had been wary to talk in the beginning, but not only had Lumley been eager to talk, he had asked bold questions for just a guard. Hamish answered them, which made the man even more cocky. His ill-placed arrogance did not concern Hamish. The more overconfident he was, the easier it would be to use him later. Arrogant men tended not to be suspicious.

"He hangs around a lot with Jollis."

Hamish nodded. "You were right. I can definitely see the difference in how Lumley attacked versus the two men before him." He patted the wall next to him, hinting for her to sit down. "And now that I know what to look for, you don't need to prove yourself with a sword anymore."

Mairead grimaced but hopped back onto the wall. She was tired and was not sure that she could have continued even if Hamish was asking her to stop. "And did I?" He arched a brow at her. "Did I prove myself?" she explained.

Hamish took a deep breath and crossed his arms. He was entering dangerous territory, but his gut said that he needed to be honest. If she continued down this path, she would only hurt herself and arm an attacker if she ever really did try to use the sword in defense. "You lack strength and stamina, and it is clear that you have never been properly trained, but"—he raised his hand to stop her from getting defensive—"I have to admit that I am also impressed. You have speed and instinct. And believe it or not, I support the idea of a woman mastering use of a weapon. A sword, however . . ." He pushed himself off the wall and walked toward the two more men who came into view, not finishing his thought.

Mairead listened as he gave them the same encouraging speech as he had given the others, telling them why they were there and that it would not take long. Hamish rejoined her and the two began to spar. Almost immediately she knew neither of them had spent any time being trained by anyone—let alone Ulrick.

"We can safely discount those two," Hamish muttered, before halting them and instructing them to send the next pair.

Those trained by Ulrick definitely had certain habits the others lacked. They were subtle, techniques Hamish would have thought to look for if Mairead had not suggested it. Ulrick's men liked to attack first and always at the leg, not anywhere high on the body. They seemed to parry effectively, but once an opponent knew their moves, it was easy to deflect as they knew only a handful of maneuvers. It was one of the reasons Mairead had been able to perform as well as she had. She could predict what they were going to do. And those who had not trained under Ulrick were so poor at fighting that Mairead would have beaten them if she had the strength and stamina.

For the next couple of hours, they watched the guard spar and Mairead was pleasantly surprised to find herself enjoying the afternoon. She had expected the tension between her and Hamish to be high after the kiss yesterday and at first she had been right. Both had felt uncomfortable and neither had been inclined to talk about what had happened or what it meant. Both still struggled with defining what it was that they wanted in the light of the obvious passion they shared. And until they could, neither had anything to say.

It was that silent mutual agreement that enabled them to leap past the previous afternoon's events and onto safer subjects. And once they started talking, their conversation easily flowed from one topic to the next. She loved that he laughed at her warped sense of humor and in return he showed his own droll wit. They seemed to be able to talk about anything . . . with one exception. And each was privately grateful that the other did not want to explore it at this time.

Hamish looked at the last two men coming into view. "Any more after them?"

Mairead gave a quick shake of her head. "They are all that is left and neither are Ulrick's men. They lack skill and discipline. I don't know why Ulrick kept them as part of the guard." Hamish knew. Ulrick needed men to leave behind. "Now that you know who the moles are, what are you going to do?"

Hamish barked out a laugh. "You will *never* give up, will you?"

Mairead rolled her eyes. "I don't think I can," she admitted. She was no longer trying to trick him into revealing anything for it was no longer necessary. She knew where to go for answers but would not betray his trust. He would show her when he was ready. But that did not mean it was in her nature to ignore secrets. She hated not being included.

His elbow nudged her knee. "Remember—I like a persistent woman."

Mairead produced a small smile and raised her brows high. Then with a smirk she said, "As long as she trusts you."

"Aye. As long as there is trust." He chuckled softly. Then signaled for the two men to spar. As expected, the two were more of a danger to themselves than to others. Hamish quickly halted them and told them that the weather was causing him to end things faster. Both men looked relieved and began the trek back to Foinaven.

Mairead watched them leave, somewhat sad that their afternoon was over and that there was no longer any reason for them to spend so much time together. "What are you going to do about Ulrick's men?"

"Nothing."

"Nothing?" Mairead repeated incredulously. Then wondered why she was surprised. She would have been looking for potential "accidents" to send a message to anyone else who was thinking about squealing to Ulrick. So *of course* Hamish intended to do just the opposite.

Without thinking, Hamish grabbed her waist and helped

her down off the wall. "I never did intend to do anything. I just wanted to know who not to trust when the time came."

A loud crack of thunder followed by a long rumble filled the air. Hamish went to go get his horse. He had hoped to have time after they were done to ride out to the valley before nightfall, but the weather had other plans and was growing colder. Lightning lit up the sky and the following boom was almost deafening. "We need to get back before one of those finds us," Hamish said, and without asking for permission, swung her onto his horse and then jumped up onto the saddle.

Mairead shivered and Hamish pulled her back into his arms. They felt wonderful and she wanted nothing more than to lean back and nestle into his chest. She needed to focus on something else. "With Jollis, that makes four."

"Aye, that's one more than I expected."

"Do you think we caught them all?"

"Most likely. Three of them I was already suspicious of. If there are more, we will discover them now that we know who most of them are."

Mairead nodded, loving the vibration as he spoke. She wanted to hear more and thought of just the question to ask—something she had been dying to know most of the afternoon. But before she could even utter the first word, Hamish urged the horse into a gallop and talking became impossible.

They had left for Foinaven about five minutes late. They were still outside the gates when the rain, which had been blissfully absent the past couple of days, seemed to be making up for lost time. By the time they reached the stables, they both were soaked.

Hamish swung his leg over and then helped Mairead

down, who immediately dashed back into the courtyard toward the keep. He handed Adiran his reins and gave the lad a few instructions before heading in the same direction. He entered the main keep entrance and stopped short when he nearly ran into Mairead. He had thought she had gone to her room to dry off and get into warm, dry clothes. It was what he intended to do, but she was clearly waiting for him.

Mairead hugged herself. Having grown up in the north, she was acclimated to the cold and it normally did not bother her, but the combination of being wet and the wind hitting her in the face as they rode back had chilled her to the point her teeth were chattering. She had been dashing toward the keep when she realized that she had yet to ask her question. And she wanted an answer to it more than she wanted to be warm again.

"Wh-wh-what were you g-g-oing to say ab-b-out w-women using swords?" she finally got out. She was not sure why it mattered so much to her, but it did.

"You need to go upstairs and get dry clothes on."

Mairead squeezed herself tighter. "I w-w-ill, but f-f-f-first I w-w-w-ant to know what you were g-g-going to say."

Hamish blinked. He had no idea what she was talking about. "When?"

Mairead rolled her eyes in exasperation. "You said that I had s-s-some skill with a sword, that y-y-you like women who know how to use a w-w-weapon. Then y-y-you said 'however.'" Her hazel eyes glared at him. "I now hate that w-w-word by the way."

Hamish pointed to the stairwell. "Get dry. We can talk about this later tonight."

Mairead gave a single but violent shake to her head.

"T-t-tell me now." She did not want to wait until dinner for chances were high that Selah and little Rab would be there and Hamish had already told her that she would have the great hall to herself. "Tell me," she pressed.

Hamish thought about carrying Mairead up to her room, but the stubborn glint in her eyes spoke volumes. She would just march back out. Answering her was the quickest way to get her warm. "It is nothing to freeze over," he huffed. "I think women should know how to use a weapon, but . . ." He looked at her. His brow furrowed deeply as he debated his next words, but he was also cold and wanted to go change. ". . . listen. Don't get mad, but why the sword?"

Mairead's eyes became wide with indignation. Her jaw dropped. "You don't think a woman can wield a sword?"

"Not a claymore." Hamish knew of only one woman— Colin McTiernay's wife—who was decent with a sword, but it had also been especially made for her. Even so, Hamish had always thought the idea of women and swords ridiculous. "Most men find them difficult to use, but that is not my point. Even if you could become proficient, when would you use such a skill? If you are going to put energy and time into mastering a weapon, why not one that you would use, such as a bow and arrow? It's not my strength, but lucky for you, it is Davros's. I'm sure he would be willing to teach you."

Mairead's gaze narrowed and he knew that she did not welcome the suggestion. "Just think about it. What's the point of learning a weapon if you can never apply your skill?"

Mairead shivered again and he pointed to the stairs. "Get dry and warm, lest you become like Robert." This time his voice brokered no room for disagreement.

Mairead spun on her heel and rushed up the stairs. She ran to her chambers, glad she had seen no one. It was still a couple hours before nightfall, but the heavy clouds made it seem like it had already arrived. The small fire was struggling to remain alive and Mairead quickly tossed a couple more logs into the hearth before stripping.

Her mind was no longer even thinking about being wet and cold. What Hamish said rattled her far more than being caught outside in the rain. He had been trying to be nice, but she still heard what he meant. *Even if I could get proficient.* She had never thought herself an expert with the sword, but she had thought herself decent. She had held off several men for quite a while. But now she wondered if that just indicated they were even worse than she knew. What did she know of a true warrior's skill? The only time she had seen one in action, besides Ulrick was Hamish, when he disarmed Jaime. But if she really was not any good, that meant she was vulnerable.

And that was the last thing she needed to be.

All this time she had been wanting to know what Hamish had planned for Ulrick, hoping she might be protected as well. She had even considered marrying a stranger so that he might keep Ulrick from coming after her. Even last night, she had dreamed that Hamish stayed at Foinaven, shielding her from harm.

She had it all wrong. She didn't need someone else to protect her. She needed the ability to protect herself.

Hamish was right. She had been training on the wrong weapon. A sword, even a bow and arrow—these were for offense, to hunt or attack.

Knives, however, were different. Ideal for close-quarter fighting, the *biodag* was a stabbing weapon and the perfect means to defend oneself. If she was going to learn how to use another weapon, it would be the dirk and there was only one person she wanted to train her.

But how was she going to convince Hamish to work with her and teach her what she needed to know without telling him why?

Selah helped move the pillow to a more comfortable position behind Robert. "You sound better, but you don't look any better."

Robert nodded, his eyes closed. He was exhausted, but they both knew from past years that he was finally on the mend. His fever had broken in the early morning hours and he had been able to eat food and drink a good bit of water. He opened his eyes and when they fell on Selah, they softened. "What has been happening?"

Selah sat down next to him. "Little Rab is his normal self. He is worried about you, but I have assured him that you will be better soon."

Robert sighed and successfully fought the need to cough. His throat felt like it was on fire whenever he did. "I miss him." He took comfort in Selah's loving gaze. "Is that strange to miss your five-year-old son?" Selah smiled and shook her head. "He is so creative and sees the world through such innocent eyes. Eyes I once had." His throat constricted and the coughing spasm he had fought finally won.

Selah laced her fingers with his and tried not to look worried. "Your fever broke, but you still have a ways to go before you are better. Remember that before you decide to jump out of bed. That healer we sent for a couple of years ago was very clear. This cough will go away, but it becomes deadly if you do not allow yourself to completely heal."

Robert squeezed her hand. "'Deadly' is such an unbecoming word for you, dear."

"I'm not waffling on this, Robert."

He smiled, hearing her serious tone. "You must admit that the timing of my illness has worked in our favor."

A short, exasperated breath escaped her. "In your favor, not mine. I do not like to hear you in so much pain."

Robert took back his hand to cover a cough. He relaxed against the pillows. "It's worth it if my plan is working."

Selah pursed her lips in frustration. "That is because you did not see Hamish tonight. Something is bothering him."

"I think you mean some*one*."

"Well, it is to the point that I think he might decide to leave." Robert looked at her then, the intensity of his eyes growing. Selah nodded. "We might be forced to tell him everything we know to keep him here."

Robert's gaze relaxed. "Not yet." His tone was filled with assurance, but Selah was not comforted. "Listen to me. Hamish will do what is right. He did twelve years ago and he will do so again. He is too honorable to do anything less."

"He is an honorable warrior, I agree, but this is different."

"Nay. It is the same, Hamish has just demonstrated it more as a warrior."

"You are just as honorable, Robert."

He gave her a reassuring smile. "I can lift a sword and wield it to defend my home, but I am a MacBrieve. We are builders, farmers, and judges and we are good with money, but Hamish is like the McTiernays. *That* is why I know he will do what is right. Trust me. My plan will work."

Selah bit her bottom lip. "What about Mairead?"

"I thought you said she was in love with him."

Selah wringed her hands. "Aye, she is. You only have to look at her to see just how much she loves him, but she *refuses* to admit it. And Hamish is just as bad. Why do you think I'm afraid he might leave? They are both doing everything they can to resist their feelings, not succumb to them. I . . . I . . . I think it just happened too fast."

Robert cocked a brow. "It only took one look for me," he reminded her.

"And for me, but we *accepted* it. I doubt if either Hamish or Mairead has admitted the truth to themselves, let alone each other. They will still be in denial by the time Ulrick arrives."

Robert took a deep breath and waited for Selah to look at him once more. He needed her to remain hopeful. "Hamish and Mairead may deny what they feel, but if they are really in love, they will not be able to resist for long. And when they finally do admit their feelings, are you ready for what will happen? You and she will no longer be living together at Foinaven. It is even possible you might not see Mairead for a long while."

Selah swallowed and then stood up. She went to the window and looked down into the courtyard. The rain had persisted for hours but had finally stopped an hour ago. "We knew when we started this that things would change for everyone. I want my sister to be happy."

"She will be, my dear. I promise. And it won't be much longer. Another week, I suspect. By then, hopefully I will be out of this bed and attending a wedding. Then we can focus on our true goal."

Selah pulled her eyes from the courtyard and shifted her gaze back to Robert. "I wish I had your faith, but right now I am not sure if *any* of our goals will be achieved. You were not at dinner. You did not see them."

Robert patted the spot next to him on the bed. "There is always a messy stage when building anything, but out of that mess comes the most beautiful creation. And what we are about to create, *sonuachar*, is something beautiful and long lasting. I am doing this for all of us."

Selah sat down and when he opened his arms, she leaned into his embrace. "And if we are wrong about Mairead and Hamish? What then?"

Robert shrugged. "Then I will tell him the truth. Mairead *will* be protected. I promise you."

Selah said nothing and took comfort from once again being in Robert's arms. She hoped he was right. If they had to tell Hamish the truth, it would change everything. Aye, Mairead would be protected physically, but her heart would be destroyed.

"Tha gaol agam ort," Robert whispered. "Trust me, my love."

"I do, *a ghrà mo chroì*, I do."

Chapter Nine

Mairead licked her lips and closed her eyes in an attempt to strengthen her resolve. She rapped her knuckles lightly on Hamish's door afraid to knock any louder. It was very early and no sound was coming from the courtyard, but that would change if anyone heard her.

She feared getting caught, but it was more important that she speak to Hamish. If she did not catch him before he left, she might not see him all day, and dinner was questionable. The man was determined to avoid her. She had hoped that had changed yesterday afternoon, but his chilly demeanor at dinner made it clear that if anything, he was more determined to keep her at a distance.

Mairead knocked again and then stopped to listen but did not hear any movement. Hesitating for only a moment, Mairead put her hand on the door and pushed. She gasped when it nudged forward for she had expected the door to be barred from the inside.

Mairead stepped inside and shivered. The room was dark and very cold. No embers glowed in the fireplace, which meant he had either not lit a fire or it had gone out hours ago. Had they not restocked his wood?

"Hamish?" Her tone was soft, but it should have awoken him, and yet there was no response. The man was either the heaviest of sleepers or he was awake, wondering what she would do next. He certainly could not be watching her. Without any windows or light from a fire, she could see only around the entrance and even that was difficult as shadows created from the torches hid more than their light revealed.

Mairead took another step, remembering that there was a table with some candles. Feeling around, she found both. Grabbing a candle, she went out, used a torch to light it, and came back in, closing the door behind her. No one was up yet, but they would be soon and she did not want to answer questions if someone decided to be curious.

Holding the candle in front of her, she looked around the room. Hamish was not a heavy sleeper. He was not even there. The room was empty. The bed was mussed, proving he had slept there, but at some point in the night he had risen and left. She did not wonder where he went. Mairead was almost certain that if she rode out to a certain valley, she would find him there.

Mairead sighed. Hamish not being here answered several questions. The man must leave and return in the middle of the night, because he always emerged from this room in the later morning hours. If she was right, he would be back any minute.

Mairead found a holder for the candle and then looked around for something to sit on. Seeing nothing, she sat down on the edge of the bed to wait. If Hamish was mad finding her in his room, she would just tell him that it was his own fault. She had been prepared to ask him for dirk training after dinner, but they were not even halfway through the meal before he excused himself. She and Selah had just gaped in silence as he loaded up his plate, grabbed a mug full of ale, and then headed out the door, stating it was time he ate with the guards. Mairead suspected that this was going to happen every night going forward. And since he was also refusing to meet in the great hall, she had little choice but to corner him this early in the morning.

A cool breeze swirled around her, causing Mairead to shiver. She glanced back at the door and verified that it was closed. So where was the breeze coming from? She rubbed her arms and again felt the movement of air. It felt like it was coming from the hearth. Mairead stood up and again felt the air stir. Grabbing the candle she went to go stand by the fireplace. It flickered and almost went out till she put up her hand to shield it.

Breezes could be felt from the fireplace, but usually only from the top floors and it had to be much windier outside than it was right now. But this hearth was on the first floor.

Carefully protecting the little flame, Mairead studied the hearth. It lacked the ornate mantel that was in some of the keep's main rooms, but it was like any other for the most part. She shuffled back and realized that she had never realized just how huge it was though. It was even bigger than the one in the solar, making it the largest in the keep. It was so big, she could almost walk inside it. Without thought, she moved forward and stuck her head into the charred structure. Immediately she felt the cool air and turned toward the source. Her eyes grew large. There was a large crack in the wall.

Completely focused on what she was seeing, Mairead stepped fully inside the hearth and then moved closer to examine the crack. She quickly deduced it was not a crack, but an opening. Using one hand, she pried it open, surprised it took little effort. She once again held out the candle, which now illuminated a narrow but traversable passageway.

Mairead stood there shocked. She had it all wrong. Hamish would not be back any minute. He had probably just left.

She began to chuckle. *I sleep,* Hamish had said. She had been asking the wrong question. But Mairead now had a new one. How did Hamish know there was a secret passageway? Mairead felt both impressed and frustrated. It must have been here twelve years ago. All this time, and she had never known. Did Selah? Did Robert? She highly doubted it.

Mairead bit her bottom lip and grinned, delighted with her discovery. She then followed the narrow tunnel to where it exited out near the village. Several discarded items were piled near the exit and she made sure nothing was disturbed and that she had remained unseen. After returning to his chambers, Mairead left and went back to her room, being careful not to make any loud noise.

Back safely inside her own bedchambers, she quietly closed the door and then quickly began to undress. If she was lucky, she could catch a couple of hours sleep for she was going to need them.

Nestled back in the covers, Mairead closed her eyes. She was still grinning.

She no longer needed luck to convince Hamish to teach her how to defend herself with a dirk. She now had all the leverage she needed.

Mairead's eyes flashed with a sudden shower of angry sparks upon hearing his refusal. "If you don't, then I will tell Selah and Robert about the secret passageway leading to the village from the hearth in your room. I might even tell them about the valley and that you have intentionally kept them in the dark about your plans."

Hamish stared down at her without expression, without moving a muscle. The lines around his eyes and mouth etched deeper than ever before as his lips curled into a smile that held no humor . . . only menace. "Then do it."

The biting words sent a chill through Mairead and she knew she had gone too far.

Hamish spun on his heel and was headed out the great hall doors. The noon meal was over and she had convinced Selah to leave early, giving her a chance to speak with Hamish privately. He had recognized what she was doing and attempted to leave as well, but Mairead had stopped him. Then she had tried everything, asking, persuading, even begging him to agree to train her on how to use the dirk. When nothing worked, she had made the threat. And she wished she could take it back.

Regret assailed her and she ran to block his path. "I'm sorry, Hamish. Really. I did not mean . . . I just need your help."

His green eyes had grown dark and cold, and they bore down on her. "Understand this. I could leave right now and it will not be my home or my life uprooted in a few weeks. It will be yours."

A thin chill hung on the edge of his words. He had spoken them too gently, too softly. He had meant every word and it set her on the edge. She was about to lose everything when all she wanted was a way to protect herself when he left.

Hamish gave Mairead one last hard look and stepped around her. She closed her eyes as grief and despair tore at her heart. She had seen in his eyes what she had done. To her family, to herself, but mostly to Hamish. Her threat had decimated the trust that had been growing between them. She was now one of the many women who had disappointed him. And it killed her. He needed to know that she did not mean it.

"Hamish, wait!" she called out again. He did not stop. She ran up to him and caught his arm just as it reached out to open the door.

Hamish looked down. "Let go."

Mairead shook her head. Tears slipped down her cheeks. "Please listen to me first. *Please*," she begged. "I would *never* betray you. I was just desperate for your help. For you to understand. I thought it was the only way. But I would not have gone to Robert or Selah. I swear it."

Hamish turned to face her. He grabbed her upper arms and gave her a shake. "*What*, Mairead, just what do I need to understand that would make you risk your sister, Robert, little Rab, your *home*?"

Mairead closed her eyes, her heart aching with pain. "I just needed you to realize how much I need your help. There is no one else who can teach me what I need to know. You saw the guards yesterday. None of them has the ability and even if they did, I don't trust them. And you said I couldn't protect myself with the sword. And that is all I want. To be able to protect myself, so I said something stupid to get you to agree. But I never meant it. Please don't leave."

The anger in his countenance began to dissipate. "You need to be trained that badly?"

Mairead gulped. "I do."

Hamish took a deep breath and slowly exhaled. His anger was returning tenfold, but this time it was not aimed at Mairead. "You are being threatened."

Mairead bit her bottom lip and then nodded. To say different would be pointless. "I was and no, Robert and Selah do not know about it. Nor do I want them to know.

Their way of handling things . . . well, it just wouldn't work." Hamish did not doubt it. Robert would probably advocate talking. "So please do not tell them. Please believe that I have my reasons."

Mairead's hazel eyes held so much despair that he could no longer look in them. This latest request, her fear, her persistence, her damn marriage-seeking quest . . . it all now made sense. Never had he been so mad.

Hamish grabbed the handle and without another word, left.

Chapter Ten

Mairead stared at the small knife in Hamish's hand and tried hard to listen to what he was telling her. But she really did not want to learn to attack someone. She wanted to be able to defend herself, which is why she had asked to be trained on the dirk—not the *sgian dubh*. Known as the black knife due to the color of the bog wood in its handle, the small knife did not feel substantial enough to stop someone. It was made for cutting and slicing things, not for fighting. The dirk, on the other hand, was almost twenty inches and though it was nothing like a sword, it could at least do some damage. But Hamish had been adamant. No dirk. He would only train her on the *sgian dubh* and since she did not want to do anything that might cause him to change his mind, Mairead had quickly agreed.

She had been frightened when she heard a bang on her door early that morning. Only one person could have a reason to rouse her that early—Robert had relapsed. She had flown to the door in only her chemise, thinking it was Selah on the other side. Seeing Hamish, looking somber and still a little angry, she had stiffened, unable to move or speak.

He had taken a long look at her, his gaze traveling up and down her barely clothed frame, but when his eyes recaptured hers, they still held no warmth. Mairead felt terror then for she knew he had stopped by just to tell her he was leaving and she would not see him again. That his secret was now hers to tell, for keeping it no longer mattered. She had held her breath waiting for his crushing words, when he agreed to train her. Shock simply did not cover the range of emotions she felt.

"After the noon meal, meet me by the river where it bends sharp just north of the village. There is an odd-shaped boulder there. Do you know it?"

All Mairead had been able to do was nod. She knew the rock he was talking about. It was a large chunk of granite jutting out from the ground that had been exposed by the wind and the rain. It was near a part of River Naver that was fairly close to Foinaven but difficult to access, due to the thick, tall weeds and thistles that grew in clumps along the shoreline. When she finally emerged on the other side of the brush, Mairead realized it was an ideal spot for training. It was remote, private, protected from the wind and a large portion of the beach was exposed.

As Mairead watched Hamish move the small knife, several footprints in the sand caught her attention. They led to the water's edge and she guessed that this was where Hamish went to bathe.

"Are you paying attention?" The tone was sharp, causing Mairead's eyes to snap back to what Hamish was doing.

Hamish grimaced at her lack of focus. Ever since he had left her in the great hall he had been stewing. Learning that Mairead feared for her safety had sent him to the edge of reason. Mairead's words and her beseeching look had haunted him all day and night. Everything in him screamed to resolve the problem and fix it so that she never had to be afraid again. It took him hours before he realized that no matter what he decided to do, Mairead was right about one thing. She needed to be trained and not by anyone else. Not by Davros or even Amon. *He* needed to ensure she had the ability and the means to defend herself at all times, which meant knowing how to fight with a *sgian dubh,* not a dirk. A dirk was big and could not be hidden. But a black knife could be strapped to an arm or a leg and be on her at all times.

But protecting Mairead was not going to end with knife training. Hamish intended to do whatever was necessary to ensure she never used what he was teaching her. His next steps would be decided after he learned the name of the man she feared.

"Focus, Mairead. It was you who wanted this so badly, so prove it." Hamish frowned. He was barking instructions and being anything but kind and friendly, but he was finding it difficult to rein in his anger.

Seeing he had her full attention, Hamish forced his tone to soften. He needed her to listen, not be afraid of him. "The first thing you need to understand is that a dagger is the most intimate of all weapons. Spears as well as bows and arrows kill at a distance. Even with hand weapons like the sword and halberd, you thrust outward to cause injury. Fighting with a dagger can only be done when two people are close. When a dagger connects, your hand will practically touch flesh and because the blade is short, one has only two defenses—attack or flee."

Mairead swallowed and Hamish could see fear in her eyes. Her look comforted him to a degree. She needed to understand that what he was telling her was nothing like what she had been doing with the sword. That was to satisfy some need for physical challenge. What he was going to show her now was about life and death. "The best defense against a dagger is just not to be there. When you see one, you leave. But if you are the one wielding the knife, use it and without hesitation. If an attacker sees you waver, he will snatch the blade out of your hands and use it against you." He paused. Mairead's eyes had been locked with him the entire time, but it was critical that she grasped his meaning. "Do you understand what I am saying? Because you cannot protect yourself with a *sgian dubh* or even a dirk. Deflecting attacks with a small blade is not feasible and you have neither the weight nor the strength to fight a man. Defending yourself with a dirk means you must know how to *fight* with one. It's close and it's bloody."

Mairead tilted her chin up in reaction to the challenge. "I understand." Her eyes narrowed but did not waver. "Just show me where and how to aim."

If Hamish had any doubt before that Mairead wanted this training, the look in her hazel eyes erased it. "Here, here, here, and here," he said, pointing to his kidneys, liver, stomach, and heart. "Do *not* go for the chest. These blades glance off ribs easily, and while they do damage, it would not be enough to stop a man before he was able to attack back. Then you will lose whatever advantage you have. Now point to the areas I just showed you."

Mairead did.

"Give me your blade." Hamish reached out and wiggled his fingers, beckoning her to hand over the weapon. When she did, he gave her a short but thick stick. "Grip this and pretend it's the blade." Mairead did as instructed. Centered in her palm, the branch was not visible on either side of her fist, but it still gave her the feeling of what it would be like to hold the black knife. "Now close your eyes, count to three, and when you open them, show them to me again, but use the side of your fist."

Mairead did so and found that Hamish had moved to the side, but she quickly acclimated herself and pointed to the vulnerable spots.

"Again, but this time move faster and don't punch, but slice. Pretend the blade is in your hand. If you don't make contact with your thumb, you missed."

Mairead closed her eyes and when she opened them, lunged for all four spots, but the awkward angle made it difficult. They tried several more times before Hamish mumbled something under his breath about wasting his time. "You are thinking too much before you act. If your life is in danger, you have no time to think and strategize. If you move slowly, you might as well just concede and not fight at all."

Hamish knew he was being harsh, but he had to be. Time was not on their side. She needed to learn these moves in the next few days and then practice them over and over. They had to become second nature.

Hamish also knew that he needed his anger to remain at the surface, affecting everything he said and felt. Without it, his other emotions would take over—desire, doubt, passion, stress, longing, misery, guilt, fear—all of which he felt when near Mairead, and none that he could control.

Mairead closed her eyes, determined to increase her speed. She counted to three and this time used her other senses to know where he was, rather than just her eyesight. It worked. She was able to lunge almost immediately and her aim was true. However, she still struggled with getting her fist to make contact as it would in a fight.

"Again. But in a different order."

Mairead nodded each time as Hamish ordered her to attack him. She did it again and again, until she was finding him and making contact without hardly thinking.

"Good. Those are the vital organs, but they are not the only places you can attack. There is the arm"—he showed her where to slice the upper forearm—"and the back of the knee. And remember, each time you make contact the result will be bloody, so grip the handle hard, else your blade will slip through your hand."

Mairead nodded and once again they started repeating maneuvers over and over after he demonstrated them to her. He showed her how to come in at the side, from behind, how to deflect attention, and use her size and femininity to her advantage.

They continued to work as the sun started to sink. Despite the air temperature dropping by several degrees, Mairead was sweating. She was putting everything into this session and Hamish was impressed. She was nowhere close to being competent at any maneuver, but that she could repeat some of them at all was amazing. Her abilities with a sword were a tremendous advantage. She understood how to balance her body and thrust and move.

If anyone had come upon them, their close proximity would have been seen as intimate, despite there being nothing intimate in Mairead's touch. Tension ran throughout her entire body and except for the beginning her mind had been completely focused on what they were doing and why. She was not having fun. Everything about her demeanor cried out that Mairead didn't *want* to learn how to use a knife. She *needed* to.

Mairead sidestepped and aimed her fist for his liver, but Hamish twisted out of the way, tripping her. Mairead fell, but then targeted the back of his leg and he could feel her muddy fist swipe the back of his knee.

He chuckled to himself, wishing everyone he trained learned as quickly as she did. "I'm impressed," Hamish said, offering his hand to help her up. She said nothing and dusted the sand off her gown.

Mo chreach, Hamish wanted to know just who it was threatening her. At first he thought it might be Ulrick, but Mairead knew that Hamish would not leave as long as he was a threat. And Mairead was not Ulrick's type, Hamish had reminded himself repeatedly. He had seen Ulrick around women. He liked them wanton and sleazy. No, it had to be one of Ulrick's men, someone Mairead was afraid might remain at Foinaven even after Ulrick was gone. That was why she had pressed to know his plan. Mairead had wanted to know who would stay and who would go. What she would soon learn was that it didn't matter. Whoever she was afraid of—and he *would* learn his name—was not ever going to be in a position to threaten her again.

"We're done," Hamish said, gathering his things. "We'll meet here again tomorrow. And I will tell you how to best avoid a blade."

And tomorrow, you will tell me the mac na galla's *name.*

"Today, your real training begins."

Mairead quirked a brow. She did not say it aloud, but she could not keep her face and her body from showing her frustration. Just what had they been doing all day yesterday? She had returned to Foinaven exhausted but exhilarated. She knew that she would have to go over and over what Hamish showed her so that she could do the maneuvers without thought, but she had *learned*. Really learned. She had fallen asleep with a peaceful mind that actually held hope.

Hamish had been demanding, but he was also clear, conveying how to pivot and twist, and the advantages and disadvantages of each tactic. He had pushed her to do more than she thought she could at times, but in the end, she had surprised herself by performing all that he had asked. Her motivation was not meeting the challenge or even to make him proud. She was doing this for her.

"Yesterday was about learning how to defend yourself *with* a blade. Today is about defending yourself when you don't have one." Mairead pursed her lips together in understanding. Hamish was not teaching her how to use a dirk like she had asked. He was preparing her for what might come. He had seen her fear and even though she had refused to tell him what was its cause, he had guessed. But had he guessed who?

Hamish got out his dirk and held it like he was going to attack. "Now that you know how to attack and the movements used, it will be easier to learn how to throw an attacker off balance and use their weight to your advantage."

Mairead's eyes brightened as she understood Hamish's teaching strategy. Yesterday had been just about offense and how to attack—or so she had thought. Hamish had actually been teaching her how to defend herself all along.

He handed her a *sgian dubh* that was sheathed. Attached to the scabbard was a long, thin strap of leather. "Cut the hem of the pocket in your dress and then strap the blade to the outside of your thigh where it will be hidden but not uncomfortable." When she looked at him dubiously, he said, "If you are attacked, it's doubtful you will have a dagger just sitting in your hand. Therefore, you will need to have one on you that you can get to and remove quickly."

Mairead licked her lips and bobbed her head in agreement. "That makes sense." She found the pocket in her gown and ripped a hole in it. She liked pockets and most of her bliauts had them. By the end of the week though they all would, and every one of them would be unusable as pockets.

Mairead then turned around, hiked up her skirt and the chemise underneath, and tied the *sgian dubh* to her leg. How *glad* she was that she had not insisted on a dirk. It would have been impossible to wear like this. The black knife, on the other hand, could be kept hidden and gave her a means of defense at all times.

"You are going to learn only three moves today. And like yesterday, we are going to go over them and over them until you can do it without thought. Muscle memory takes a while to build, but the more you do these moves, the faster and more natural your movements will feel. So practice them daily and when possible, several times throughout the day."

Mairead tapped the side of her leg, feeling the small knife through the material. "I'm ready."

For the next hour, Mairead practiced what to do if facing an attacker, whether they were armed or not. Then Hamish made her lie down, to learn what to do if she was asleep when ambushed. Lying on the damp sand was unpleasant and cold, and when she suggested on top of a rock, or even some of the drier grass, Hamish had refused. She could see his point—that she needed to be able to focus regardless of the conditions—but she really hated sand in her hair and quickly figured out how to unsheathe her blade while prone. She just had to commit. Hesitation was the enemy.

The third and final move was the most difficult. It was when Hamish came up from behind. She was getting frustrated and knew that she was doomed if an attacker grabbed her. She was just not strong enough to get her hand free to access the *sgian dubh* and get an advantage.

"Relax," Hamish murmured softly against her cheek. "Relax your entire body."

Tension rolled over her. The last thing Mairead could do was relax. She hated the feeling of being out of control and Hamish whispering in her ear did not help. Yesterday had been all about stabbing and slicing. It was harder to keep that level of focus with Hamish's arms around her. "I can't."

"Aye, you can. Don't think of it as a lack of control, but a way to gain it back. A body that is completely limp is very difficult to keep ahold of, let alone dominate. An attacker will have to let go to get a better grip, giving you a chance to get to your knife."

Mairead took a deep breath and forced her limbs to ease. When she could feel them respond, she told her body to go limp. When it worked, she shrieked, "I did it!" instead of remembering that she was fighting off an attacker.

Hamish chuckled and again it was next to her ear. "Aye, *aingeal*, you did it. But I still have you."

Mairead tilted her head to the right and cracked her neck. Then with a nod, she said, "Again."

Hamish smiled hearing her use the word. Mairead struggled for a minute and then all at once went limp. But she took too long going for her knife. She needed more seconds than that one maneuver would allow. "Remember, even at your size and weight, you can fight using more than just a knife. An attacker will be focused on using his own blade and expecting it to create panic. Use that to your advantage. Stomp your heel down on the top of the foot. Does that make sense?"

The only hint that Mairead was about to demonstrate just how much sense it made was her smile. It flashed just as her heel came down on his toes. Hamish winced and fought the desire to hop around and moan in pain. He thought Mairead would at least look apologetic, but all she said was, "Be glad I didn't aim for your groin."

Hamish did moan then. "You do that and training will be over."

Mairead bit back a smile and turned around so that he could grab her again. She went limp and then surprised him by stomping on his foot again. He had not been expecting her to aim at the same foot and was mentally berating himself for underestimating her. "That was, uh, good. But you stopped. Once free, kick again and anywhere that is vulnerable—the shin, the calf, and the knee. You obviously already know about where you can cause the most pain, but you need to kick hard. Remember, the point is to give you enough time to get your knife free."

Mairead narrowed her gaze, unconvinced that he really meant for her to do that during training. "But I'll hurt you."

"No, you won't. I won't let you, but you need to try."

Mairead arched her brows and shrugged her shoulders. Hamish held her once more. "Now, use anything that can move to your advantage. Your fingers can stab eyes or—"

Mairead understood what he meant and had an idea. She rammed her head under his chin, slamming his jaw shut. Hamish immediately let go. "Ow!" And before he realized it Mairead had the blade in her hand and was ready to attack.

When she saw him rubbing his chin, grimacing, she immediately put her arm down. Worry overtook her expression. "I'm sorry."

"No," he groaned, wiggling his jaw. "That . . . that was good. Just not hard enough. If this were real, try to break it."

Mairead's eyes grew wide as saucers. Rebellion shined in the hazel depths. "We are *not* practicing that!"

"No. We certainly are not."

Mairead waited a minute until Hamish looked like he was feeling better. "Can we do it again? And this time, I want you to try hard. Really hard to keep me from getting free."

He had expected her to ask her to quit. That she might have been too afraid of hurting him to want to continue, but Mairead was driven by fear and it was overruling every other emotion. It was a cold reminder that she was not doing this for a lark, but that she truly thought this might save her life. "You'll bruise."

"Then bruise me."

Hamish nodded and she turned around. A second later, he had a hold on her, pinning her arms and body against his chest. Mairead instinctively began to squirm. The more she struggled, the tighter his grip became. She flailed her logs and tossed her head around. She tried to bite but could find no flesh and then without any warning, she collapsed and slipped right out of his grasp.

Immediately she jumped to her feet and reached into her bliaut for her knife while at the same time going for his foot. He shifted and she missed, but she used the momentum to swing her leg around and connect it with the back of his thigh. An inch lower, it would have caught his knee and he would have gone down. But it didn't matter, his momentary shock gave her enough time to free her knife. Mairead spun around to face him, ready for his next move.

Hamish smiled, enjoying the challenge, and unsheathed his own dirk. Mairead kept her gaze locked on his eyes, ignoring how he was palming the blade. She slowly began to move in a circle to the right. He followed suit. He knew she was not going to attack. She may have known some moves, but none well enough to feel confident in them. But Mairead was quick and she had picked up how to guard against a frontal attack extraordinarily fast. And she knew it.

Hamish lunged, but Mairead had seen him shift his weight and had been prepared for it, easily stepping aside. "Good," he said with a hint of condescension, "but remember, all of this will feel much different when you are scared."

Mairead glared at him. She knew he was right just as she knew Hamish was not going to attack her for real.

Hamish and Mairead resumed their slow circle as they faced each other. "Who are you so scared of, *aingeal*?"

Tension ran through Mairead. "After today, I won't need to be scared of anyone, will I?" she quipped.

"Is it Ulrick?" he asked. His breath stuck in his throat as he waited for the answer.

"You are trying to distract me."

Hamish gave her a half grin. "Coming from an expert, that is a compliment."

Mairead's brows furrowed, but her concentration did not waver. "What do you mean by that?"

"Yesterday?" he answered in an effort to sound light and playful, but it rang untrue. There was something dark about his tone. "Or when you were sparring the other day? All that flirting?"

"You sound jealous." Mairead smiled. She couldn't help it.

"Of a muddy creature like yourself?" He cackled. "Maybe you would like to take a dip in the cool waters."

At the same time, he faked a lunge, but Mairead had easily avoided the maneuver. She knew he was trying to distract her just as she knew that she was also *very* dirty. "Do not worry. Before I left today I told the servants to have a bath waiting for me."

"Kicking everyone out of the kitchens again?"

Mairead attempted a withering gaze. That had been the only time she had ever bathed anywhere but her chambers, but she knew he would never believe her. So instead of going on defense, she decided to poke back. "With you as chaperone?"

"Of course," he replied without delay.

"Then I'll decline. I think I should just continue bathing in my room and let you bathe here, where it's cold."

Hamish grinned, showing off his dimples. "What can I say? I hate dirty feet."

"Then you must be miserable right now."

He just shrugged.

Mairead knew that this banter was not working. Any minute he was going to say something that *really* distracted her to get the advantage. She needed to do it first. "Are all the McTiernays married? Even Conan? I understand that he *is* the most attractive brother."

Hamish froze for a second and Mairead immediately lunged. It was far from perfect, but it might have worked if his instinct had not kicked in. She frowned and he knew that her frustration was mounting. "What do you want to know about Conan?"

Mairead shrugged, refusing to give up. "Just wondering if what I heard about him is true. He is supposed to be the smartest of the McTiernays as well as irresistibly good-looking. I would love to personally see if the rumors are true."

Hamish stumbled at the image of Mairead and Conan together. He would eventually get bored with her as he did with all women, but by then he would have enjoyed her kisses and much more many times.

Mairead tried to take advantage of his misstep, but she had been just a fraction too slow, giving him a chance to recover. He knew she was goading him, but now she knew it was working. But her words were hard to ignore. It rankled that the McTiernay brothers did not even have to be present to get a woman's attention.

They were back to facing each other.

"If you have heard rumors about Conan," Hamish began, "then you also know that he is a pain to everyone, but to women, he can be unfeeling and even cruel."

Mairead shrugged. "It is sad, really, for even a very smart man could learn a lot from a woman."

"Conan is a *very* smart man. By far, the smartest I have ever met and he applies that intelligence every time he wields a weapon."

Mairead licked her bottom lip slowly, sensually. "But you could beat him."

Hamish swallowed. He could beat Conan. The second to youngest McTiernay was fast and accurate, but Hamish was stronger and had more stamina. He practiced with weapons daily, while Conan no longer did. In a fight, that would matter. "Aye, I could, but you need not inflate my ego." This time Hamish lunged unexpectedly and with all the speed he would use against a McTiernay.

Mairead saw it at the last moment and spun low. Hamish had been prepared and aimed down. She moved to avoid his thrust and had almost succeeded in getting out of the way when the edge of his blade caught her upper arm. It sliced through the thick material of her bliaut and it felt like it went deep.

Mairead cried out and fell to her knees, clutching her arm. Hamish flung the blade down and pulled her close to him. *"Ó dhìol! Murt! Gabh mo leisgeul!"* he cursed, and did so again upon seeing blood begin to seep through her fingers.

Mairead knew Hamish felt guilty, but he had given her what she wanted. What it would be like if he did not hold back. "It's not bad, Hamish. Really."

"Let me see, *aingeal*." He tried prying her fingers off her arm but was afraid to hurt her any more by forcing her.

Mairead shook her head and wiggled until he let her go. She rose to her feet and with everything she could muster, she let her arm go and waved it around. "See? It barely hurts. It is probably just a scratch, but I probably should get cleaned up and make sure." Mairead picked her fallen *sgian dubh* and did her best to sheathe it without wincing. "If I'm wrong I'll let you know. Stay. Bathe. I know you are dying to clean those feet. Besides, we shouldn't return together, especially in the filthy state I am in. Would cause too many questions." Mairead knew she was rambling, but she made sure that she was also smiling. "I'll see you at dinner!"

"At dinner, *aingeal*." His tone was laced with promise that if she was not there, then he *would* find her.

She flashed him her biggest and brightest smile. "Dinner." Then she left, praying that the pain receded some, else she was going to have to put on her best performance to convince him that she was fine.

* * *

Hamish knocked once and then pushed open Mairead's door. He had noticed the other night that she did not bar it, and remembered her saying at dinner one night that little Rab often came into her room to cuddle when he was scared.

He closed the door and slid the wooden bar into place to prevent anyone else from doing what he'd just done. Entering her chambers without permission. But he really did not care if he was caught. He did not care if Selah came by or even if Rab called out, forcing his presence in Mairead's chambers to be known. She had not come down for dinner and after lying awake for hours, Hamish knew he could not wait until morning to ensure she was well.

Mairead was asleep on her bed. Her hair was down, and sleeping on it unbraided, it was a mess. Her arms were exposed and he could see that the left one was wrapped. She was wearing only a chemise, which was tangled up to her knees, leaving her feet and calves exposed. Hamish just stood there, ogling her in the firelight. She was so beautiful that she took his breath away.

He took another step toward her and the sound caused her to stir. Her eyes opened and she blinked as if she could not believe what she was seeing. "Hamish?"

He nodded. "Aye." He was about to give her an angry lecture on the hell she had put him through when he saw her wince as she pushed herself to a sitting position. "*Mo chreach,* Mairead. You *promised* to tell me if this was more than a scratch."

"It is a scratch."

Hamish sat down beside her and began to unwrap the bandage. He could see from the amount of blood on the cloth he was removing that it was far more than a scratch, but he was not going to argue. "How bad does it hurt?"

"Just a little, Hamish, really." Her words said one thing, but the fact that she was not fighting his efforts was not a good sign.

"Then why were you not down at dinner tonight?" He tugged lightly on the last bit, which had partially dried to her injury, and she fought from crying out. Tears, however, escaped her eyes. Hamish brushed them with his thumbs and then kissed her forehead. He was relieved. There was no fever. Hopefully, he was in time and there wouldn't be. "You will feel better soon, *aingeal*. I promise."

Mairead watched as he picked up a very small bag that he must have put down when he sat beside her. "What is that?"

"Something for you."

Mairead recoiled. The cut was painful and it was longer than she had thought, but it thankfully was not very deep. However, she was not certain that Hamish would agree. If he had a needle and thread in that bag, there was no way she was going to let him touch her.

Hamish could see the spirit of non-cooperation grow in her eyes. "I'm going to only *look* at it, *aingeal*, so you might as well *yield* now."

Before she could stop him, Hamish reached out and grabbed her waist and pulled her back toward him. Mairead squirmed to get free. "*Mo chreach-sa a thàinig*, Mairead! You are hurt and I *will* be taking a look at that arm."

Mairead pointed to the small sack with her good arm. "*What's in the bag?*" she demanded with bite.

Rolling his eyes, he let her go and opened it. He pushed it under her nose so that she could smell it. "It's just some herbs that Laurel gave me before I left. It's something she uses to patch up all the McTiernay soldiers and we carry it with us because you never know when a blade might get you. I'm not sure what it is, but I can tell you from experience that it speeds the healing and usually keeps any fever away."

Mairead swallowed. "That's all. Herbs and no . . . needle?"

He looked at her questioningly and back at her arm. It did not seem that deep, but if she was scared that it needed to be stitched, perhaps it was. "Do you need one?"

"No! I absolutely do not!"

Hamish smiled. Mairead was scared of needles. Hell, he did not like the damn things either. "No needles," he promised.

He went to the small bowl on the table and poured some water in it. He grabbed a small square cloth next to the bowl and waved it. "Have you used this for anything?"

Mairead shook her head. "It was just laundered."

He nodded, dipped it in the water so that it was saturated, and then looked around. There was a mug on a table. He sniffed it and was glad it held water, not ale. He dumped the contents and shook some of the herbs into the mug before adding fresh water. He swirled it with his finger. "Where's some clean cloth I can wrap your arm in?"

Mairead pointed to an open chest. In it were several strips of linen cloth. He grabbed one, the wet cloth, and the mug, then moved to sit beside her. He dabbed the wound and examined it further. It was not as deep as he feared, but if Laurel were there, she'd probably insist on stitches. He didn't think they were necessary. The poultice definitely was though and it would help reduce the chance for fever. He quickly smeared the paste on and then used the strip of linen to redress the wound.

Mairead moved her arm. It felt a lot better. She had bandaged it earlier by herself and had made it too tight. "Thank you."

Hamish tucked a piece of hair behind her ear. "I'm so sorry that I hurt you, *aingeal*."

Mairead looked at him. Her eyes were large and he could see no anger, no resentment. "I'm not. What you did . . . what you showed me, it means a lot, Hamish."

Hamish swallowed. It was time to stop denying the truth. When she had not answered him during the standoff he knew without a doubt whom Mairead was afraid of. "What did Ulrick do to you, Mairead? Did he hurt you?"

Mairead stiffened. "Ulrick didn't do anything."

He did not believe her. "Then tell me who."

"I cannot." She tried to scoot away from him, but Hamish would not let her. "And it probably will not matter in a few weeks. Your plan will work and all will be fine."

"And if all is not fine?"

Mairead looked down at the blanket she was twisting in her right hand. "Then I can now protect myself."

Hamish wanted to say, *There will be no need. I will protect you.* But he couldn't. It wouldn't be true for he was leaving and he would not be coming back.

Suddenly Mairead turned her head and looked at him straight in the eye. "Kiss me, Hamish. One last time. Kiss me so that I never forget what it feels like to be in your arms. Please. Just one more time."

She was ripping away all his carefully constructed defenses. He wanted Mairead. He wanted her more than he had ever desired anything or anyone. But to touch her and know her the way he did in his dreams would trap them both. One kiss. That is what they said last time and it had been almost much, much more. And yet he could not bring himself to leave her side. All he could think was that if Mairead never wanted to forget him, then he would make sure she never did.

Mairead's lips parted in anticipation. When he caught

her face between his hands, her breath stilled as she waited to feel the warmth of his lips against her own. And when they did, they sparked an ache deep inside her that she knew would never be extinguished.

Hamish was not soft and gentle. His mouth was voracious, his tongue plunged inside, tasting, teasing, drinking in the essence of her. This kiss was not intended to melt her insides when fondly remembered. It was blatantly erotic, demanding everything she had and Mairead surrendered to his claiming. Her entire being vibrated with desire. Her mind was awash with need and could only form one word—"more."

Her hands stole around his neck in an effort to get closer. Hamish complied, deepening the kiss as his own hands moved from her cheeks to the side of her neck where his thumbs caressed her wild pulse. Her soft moans were both a salve and a torment to his soul. They were doing nothing more than kissing, and yet her innocent but eager response to his every touch was torment. He never wanted to stop. He needed more. Craved more. He wanted to know what it was to have a woman completely fall apart in his arms. To revel in his touch and think of nothing else.

Slowly he moved his hand down her nape, brushing her soft skin, until at last he found her breast. He cupped it tentatively, almost reverently, detecting the hard bud through the thin material of her chemise. His thumb stroked it as his tongue mated with hers. The double sensation wrenched a moan from both of them.

When Hamish covered her breast with his hand, Mairead's whole body quivered in response. Then he began to tease and flick each nub in turn, causing the ache between her legs to intensify. Her skin ached for his touch and she instinctively arched into his palm, demanding more.

Hamish continued his double assault until he could feel Mairead growing mindless with wanting more. She was not alone. Deep down, he had known that a kiss would not be enough. It would never be enough. He dreamed about her every night. Kissing her, touching her, tasting her. She was better than his most vivid fantasies. And he did not need to pretend. Mairead was here, with him and could be with him forever if he would just accept what she was offering—herself. And he wanted to. God how he wanted to.

His kneading fingers were sending currents of longing throughout her body. Her nipples were growing painfully hard under his palm and the pressure was no longer enough. Mairead did not know what to do with the on-slaught of sensations consuming her. She felt everywhere, places she did not know she could feel. It almost seemed too much, and yet the idea of ending this was unfathomable and she moaned as much between kisses.

"Not yet, *m' aingeal*," he whispered against her cheek and pulled her onto his lap, so that she sat across his legs.

Mairead closed her eyes as she felt his lips caress her ear, then slowly move to the responsive spot just below. She forgot everything except that he was kissing her, giving herself up to the sensations he was creating. Knowing he did not want to stop with just a kiss, she arched her back, requesting more. Hamish complied.

He buried his face in the waves of her freshly cleaned hair and inhaled. *All mine.* There was no scent like hers. Nothing as intoxicating. Then slowly, his lips trailed down the veins of her neck as his hands edged aside her chemise, exposing the curve of her shoulders. He kissed her there, lightly, and then slipped his tongue under the neckline to trace the upper part of her breast. She was perfect and having her in his arms, knowing that he was never going to let her go, was almost overwhelming.

Mairead held her breath when Hamish paused. She was afraid he was hesitating, uncertain on whether he should continue. Somewhere inside a piece of her said that what was happening between them could be perilous—not to her body, not even to her future—but to her heart. But it also said that this could be just the beginning. That if she fought hard, Hamish could be hers, for she was already his and had been for a while. Hamish had her heart, completely and forever.

"Please don't stop," Mairead whispered, trembling in anticipation.

Hamish then began to move once more. He slid his mouth a little lower and just before he enveloped the beckoning nub, said, "I don't plan to."

He dipped his head and took one hard nipple in his mouth. She gasped as he ran his tongue across the tip. The sensation was almost overwhelming. Never had Mairead felt so much pleasure. She arched against him and thrust her fingers into his hair pulling him closer.

Hamish groaned with barely leashed need as she began to writhe in his lap, grinding her hips against him. He swirled his tongue over the taut peak and then suckled harder. Feeling her, tasting her, it was torture on his control. Replacing his lips with his thumb on the swollen nub, he moved to the other breast, kissing a soft line to that nipple, before flicking it with his hot tongue and then pulling it fully into his mouth.

The desire coiled so tightly in Mairead's body since Hamish first kissed her was now spinning out of control. Her body was screaming for more. Shivers of anticipation raced over her skin.

Hamish hungrily nipped at the soft flesh of her bosom as he returned to her other breast, replacing the caresses of his thumb with masterful strokes of his tongue. "You're so beautiful . . . so very beautiful . . ." he murmured over and over. "No woman can ever compare to you."

Mairead made another soft moan that drove him to the brink of insanity. The passion building within her was continuously growing, and Hamish reveled in it—the arch of her back, the innocent but demanding pressure of her hips as they kneaded his groin. He wanted to lavish kisses over every inch of her skin. Know her intimately as none other ever had. To brand her to him for all time.

Momentarily he raised his head and he stared into her passion-filled eyes. She was so beautiful and she was all his.

He lowered his hand down to her leg to palm her calf.

"Please . . ." she begged, her voice a sighing whisper, her hands entangling in his thick curls, pulling him back down to her heart.

A satisfied grin spread across his face as he lowered his hand down to the calf of her leg, under the hem of her gown. Mairead was unaware of what she wanted so badly, but he knew and before she could sense what he was doing, his fingers caressed up the side of her thigh until they met the heart of her own fire. Tonight he would give her a hint of what they would share once they were married.

Mairead suddenly became aware of his hand and just where it was. His fingers lightly brushed the soft hair of her mound and she began to shake. "Oh, God," she moaned. Blood pounded in her veins and her entire body arched against him as it trembled with never-before-known desire.

Then she felt his mouth against hers and once again she was drowning in his kiss. It was long and hot, flooding her with sensations so that she could not pull away. He pulled her tighter against his torso, and Mairead could feel the throbbing mass of his erection, but instead of scaring her, it filled her with feminine power. Hamish wanted her— *her*—little Mairead, Selah's sister, the woman forever attached to a place he wanted to forget—he still wanted her.

Lacing her fingers through his auburn locks, she met his driving tongue, thrust for thrust, taking and giving back in turn.

Hamish felt the shift in their kiss. It deepened. It was as if she knew that every kiss before was a mere prelude to what was about to follow. When he broke away to look at her, all her shyness was gone. Her hazel eyes had turned an incredible shade of gold and were filled with longing for him. Mairead was who he had been seeking all these years. Someone who looked at him with trust and desire that was only for him. Someone who looked at him with love.

Hamish temporarily moved his hand to cup her cheek. "Stay with me, Mairead. I am about to take you to the heavens."

Before she could answer, his mouth crushed on hers once more. Mairead felt completely claimed as he kissed her with so much desire and passion, it completely consumed her.

Once again his fingers found her thigh and moved upward, skimming over her warmth as his tongue teased hers. He felt her shiver in his arms, but she did not pull away. Instead, she pressed into his palm, her body demanding relief.

Hamish was controlling every wild pulse, every sensation. He would not rush this. Mairead deserved much more than what he could give her. But she had chosen him over everything—her home, her sister.

Mairead's blood raced in the shock of his touch, her soul ready to permit him every advantage. But when his palm once more pushed against her sensitive core, the pressure was no longer enough. Unable to stop herself, she rocked her hips against his hand until slowly he parted her with one finger, sliding into her. She went completely still.

"My God, Mairead," he said with an almost painful groan as her tight sheath clenched around his finger.

Mairead couldn't believe the pleasure streaking through her. No one had ever touched her like that, but Hamish had only begun.

His mouth claimed hers just as his finger began to move within her liquid warmth. Ever so slightly, he stroked her outer flesh with a careful thumb, loving how she melted into his broad shoulders.

Mairead was overwhelmed and yet full of a growing but unfulfilled need. When she felt a second finger enter her, she stopped trying to rationalize what was happening and just surrendered to the almost painful pleasure.

Rocking her against him, Hamish kissed her mouth, neck, and then ear as he began to move his fingers. Her body was quivering and his own throbbed excruciatingly, but there was nothing he wanted more than this. A blissful, soul-searing reward that she was giving him. Her surrender in this one and only siege.

Mairead was undulating her hips to his torturous fingers and their maddening movements along her sex. Something was building within her, making her breaths short and fast and her heart pound against the wall of her chest. She wanted to scream out her feelings for him. To let him know that memories were no longer enough. That she needed him and wanted a future with him. To tell him the truth—everything—and have faith that he would find a way to keep everyone safe. But no words would come out.

Hamish continued his onslaught as she clung to him.

He heard her utter his name, but he remained merciless as she writhed in his arms. Then reality disappeared as her body tightened. Hamish swallowed her cry as she shattered into a million glowing stars.

Breathing heavily, Mairead leaned back, seeking the heat and strength of his body. Hamish's thick arousal pressed into her buttocks as shudders continued to pass through her. Only when he heard her ragged sigh did he reluctantly ease his hand away from her.

Mairead curled on his lap and nestled her cheek into his chest. Hamish closed his eyes and he relished the sensation. His loins throbbed with want and it took everything he had not to lay her down and bring her to even greater heights of ecstasy. Nothing had felt so right as Mairead being in his arms.

"Are you all right?" he asked gently. He brushed her hair with his hand, his dark green gaze searching hers soberly.

She nodded and smiled at him. "Thank you. I never knew."

He kissed her forehead. "We need to talk."

"Aye, we do," she said dreamily. "Now you cannot leave me."

Every muscle in Hamish seized simultaneously. He had been a fool to think Mairead would be willing to leave her life and all that she loved for him. Did she think that their passion would somehow enable him to tolerate working under his brother? She had to know that would make him miserable. Did she not care? Did she really think that his feelings for her would make him a fool? Hamish forced her to sit up. "This cannot happen again." He tried to keep his tone from sounding bitter. "And the only way to ensure that is if we no longer see each other.

At least not privately." He shifted her off his lap and onto the bed. He rose to his feet.

Mairead felt her throat close off. "But you said . . ."

Hamish forced himself to look into her eyes, glad that he had not revealed what he had been feeling. "And I meant all those things, but it doesn't change the facts. Robert's in charge and I cannot work for him. We are too different. Your home is here at Foinaven and you've made it clear that you never want to leave, and nor should you."

Mairead could feel her perfect world start to shatter. This couldn't be happening. She had to be wrong. "But what we just shared, you cannot leave me. . . ."

"You may be less naïve, but you are still chaste, Mairead." She looked at him. He misunderstood what she had meant and she wondered if it was not intentional. "Soon you will forget about me, marry, and your husband need never know what happened here tonight. And I promise to never return and remind you."

Mairead reached out and clutched one of his hands in her own. "Please don't go, Hamish. I need you."

Hamish closed his eyes. Her "please" was almost enough to make him want to stay. But in the end, that would make them both miserable. "Don't ask me that, *m' aingeal*. I can't." He opened his eyes and looked beseechingly at her. "Not even for you."

"Then don't stay, just . . ." Her voice trailed off as she thought everything she wanted to say. That a future with him meant more to her than her home, than her family. That he was all that she had ever dreamed *if* he loved her in return. But if he did, then he would be begging her to be with him. Hamish had said he didn't have the ability to love anymore. What if he had been right?

"Just what?"

Tears fell down her cheeks. "Just be happy. I want you to be happy."

Her soft whimper was killing him. "And that is what I want for you, Mairead. More than you know." He freed his hand, stepped forward, and bent down to give her a final kiss on the forehead. Slowly he straightened and then headed for the door. He removed the bar, opened it, and then paused. "This is not good-bye. Not yet," he lied. It was good-bye and they both knew it. They would see each other at dinner or in passing in the courtyard. Maybe even other times when Selah and Robert were around, but never again alone.

Mairead watched the man who held her heart walk out of her room, and probably her life, forever.

Chapter Eleven

Mairead threw her covers aside and stepped onto the cold floor. She ran over and grabbed a piece of firewood and tossed it into the hearth. After several seconds, the dying fire caught the new fuel source and a minute later, the heavy log was ablaze. She then went and grabbed a blanket, threw it around her shoulders, and moved to stand in front of the fire to warm her fingers. The moment Robert was well again and Selah no longer needed her chair in his room, she would ensure it returned to her chambers. She understood Selah's need, but she really missed her chair.

This was the second night in a row that she had not been able to sleep. Hamish plagued her thoughts. She had not seen him since he had left her room. He had eaten with his men, leaving her to dine with little Rab, Robert, and Selah. Mairead was glad to see that her brother-in-law was finally on the mend, but she had been a poor conversationalist. Robert had remarked about it and Mairead feared Selah might seek her out, looking for an explanation. But what could she say? *I fell in love with a man who doesn't love me.* But that was not true. Hamish did love her.

Just not enough to want to take me with him.

Mairead hated it when she answered her own questions. It was like she had a surly, wizened aunt who lived in her head, possessing no tact, few supportive words, and little kindness. Besides, her inner voice was wrong. She *had* given Hamish a reason. She had given him her heart and he had dismissed it.

No, you didn't.

I did so.

You gave him your body. You've never once told him anything about your heart.

I haven't? Mairead thought back.

Think about it and then apologize for calling me wizened.

Mairead ground her teeth together and tried to recall her words. She knew she had not on the way back from Davros's, but two nights ago, she *had* to have said something. She definitely had *thought* the words, but Hamish had rendered her unable to speak. Was it possible she had never told Hamish that she loved him?

Telling yourself doesn't count.

Telling Hamish might not be either, though. More than once he had alluded that he did not even believe himself capable of the emotion. What if she bared her soul only for him to reject her again?

What if you live your whole life wondering what would have happened if he knew the truth?

Mairead began to pace. She had been hurt and shocked by his declaration. *And* he had told her what she felt. Hamish had assumed Foinaven and her sister were paramount in her life, but he had never asked.

What was he supposed to think when you begged him to stay?

That I wanted him, of course.

But you didn't ask to be with him—you asked him to be with you.

Mairead sank onto the bed as she realized her hated inner voice was correct. "But I did," she muttered in denial. "I had to of . . . I asked him not to leave and . . ." She sucked in a deep breath. *"Oh my God."*

She had not been asking him to stay with her at *Foinaven*. She was asking for him to stay with *her*. Not to leave her behind.

Mairead scrambled back out of bed and raced over to yank on her bliaut. She quickly laced up the sides and then took a brush to her hair. Grabbing a strip of leather, she hastily tied her hair back in a loose ponytail and then slipped on her shoes. Snatching the blanket off the bed, she wrapped it around her and exited her room.

A minute later, she was at Hamish's door. She knocked and there was no answer. She peeked out into the courtyard. She had heard a couple of scurrying feet in the direction of the kitchens, but it would not be long before the courtyard would be bustling with activity despite the fact that the sun would not rise for several more hours.

Mairead knocked again and when there was no answer she knew there would not be one. He had already left for the valley. Mairead bit her bottom lip and debated going back to her room. She pushed on the door and when it opened, she decided to stay. He had successfully avoided her for two days and she was *not* going to let it happen for a third.

She grabbed a torch, went into the room, and looked for a candle. She found a stack of them on the table and a partial one in a holder. Lighting the candle, she returned the torch, stepped back into the chambers, then closed the door and looked for a place to sit.

There was no chair, but there was a bed. She sat down

and huddled in her blanket, wishing she could light a fire. But doing so would not only block Hamish's ability to return, but it would let him know that she was there waiting for him. It was not a stretch to guess he would slip back out and take extra means to avoid her.

That nonsense was over. They started a conversation two days ago and despite what Hamish thought, they had to finish it.

Hamish snuck back into his chambers. It was pitch-black for he had neglected to light a candle before he left. To do so was pointless for it was almost always completely melted by the time he returned. Using only his sense of touch, he found the outside edge of the mantel and leaned his sword and targe against the wall. Taking a step forward, he reached out for the table, found it, grabbed a candle, and went out to light it from one of the tower torches, taking care to evade being seen by those working around the castle. He stepped back inside, put the candle on the mantel, and began to undress.

It was as if the weather sensed his mood and matched it. Yesterday, the temperature had dropped several degrees— so much so that if the dark clouds dropped their contents, it would come down as slushy ice. Not snow, not rain, just some miserable state in between.

Hamish unhooked his belt and tossed it on the table. As usual, he had become dirty and had stopped to quickly bathe in the river before returning. It was bad enough he had to wash outside in icy water, but now, because he had trained Mairead at the very spot he bathed, the area was filled with memories of her. And his irritation had only been made worse when he realized that he had forgotten to grab a clean leine and plaid when he left that morning.

He had had no choice and had been forced to put back on his filthy clothes. He was desperate to change into clean ones. He just wished he could change out his heart as easily.

It had been nearly two days since he enacted his self-imposed withdrawal from Mairead's presence. And he had missed her more than he had thought possible to miss anyone—let alone a woman. He missed her laugh, her sarcastic looks and statements, and much more. He missed her ability to see at the heart of him. To just know what was bothering him and either argue with him about it, or concede that he was right. Simply put, he enjoyed being around her. She had been able to make him happier, more at ease and strangely more confident.

But that was then.

Now, she was like a curse. He had not seen Mairead even once, and yet he had been able to think of nothing else. It was to the point he had almost considered staying, telling himself it was the only way he could ensure Mairead would be safe from Ulrick. But it was not the truth. When he left, Hamish would have instilled so much fear in the man that he would never go near Foinaven or Mairead again. Ulrick might have designs on Mairead, but the man valued his life above all.

Hamish dropped his kilt onto the floor and was about to remove his leine when he heard a moan from behind him. He spun around and was rendered speechless. Mairead was asleep in his bed. She was dressed, so he doubted she came to seduce him, but she was nonetheless a feast to his eyes.

Mairead shifted, moving the cover and exposing how her gown had traveled up past her calf. His mind envisioned that lovely leg draped over his body in the most gratifying way. Her head would rest atop his shoulder, allowing her tawny mane to fan out around them. After drowning in her eyes of infinite tenderness, he would open his mouth and envelop hers, brushing his tongue ever so gently across her savory lips. She would moan and he would roll her over to her back so he could have access to her breasts, the soft skin of her stomach, and lower. He would touch and kiss and savor until both of them were writhing with uncontrollable need before burying himself in her sweet warmth.

Hamish curled his hands into tight fists and began to search for his clean leine and kilt. Sophie had a habit of putting them in a different spot every day. He finally found them lying over a storage barrel in the corner and was about to get them when Mairead began to thrash around.

Afraid that she was feverish from her wound, he went and sat on the edge of the bed, cursing at his shortsightedness. He should have at least given her the herbs to make a new poultice. He touched her forehead and exhaled feeling the cool skin. She was just having a nightmare, but from the looks of it, it was a bad one. "Mairead, wake up," he said gently.

She began to pull at the covers, struggling with them as if she thought they were hands holding her down. "No! I won't let you!" she mumbled, then did so again, much louder.

Hamish grabbed her shoulders and Mairead began to kick violently and shouted, *"Never!"*

Disturbed by her growing disquiet, Hamish gave her a slight shake and more forcefully said, "Mairead, *wake up*."

Without warning, she shot straight up, opened her eyes, and screamed out his name. Not in fear, but just the opposite. She was crying out for him to help her. Rattled,

Hamish began to rock her in his arms. "Wake up, *m'aingeal*. I'm here. I'm right here."

Mairead clung to him. She was shaking, but it had nothing to do with the chill in the room. "You cannot leave me," she pleaded with him, over and over again. "I need you. I won't let you leave me. Please, please. I won't let you go."

Hamish was unsure if Mairead was still asleep or was awake. He tried to pull her out of his arms to look at her eyes, but she only tightened her grip. "Mairead?" She snuggled her head into his chest and finally started to calm. He stroked her hair. "*Aingeal*, you had a nightmare."

Mairead was still in a fog. Her cheek was against something warm. She knew it was Hamish and instinctively turned her head to kiss his check in the opening of his leine. "I did?" she murmured, still half asleep.

Hamish gritted his teeth. He needed to put her away from him. And he would. In another minute. "You did," he finally managed to get out. "It seemed to be a bad one."

Mairead kissed him again. Her lips were velvet torture. "Mmmm . . . I get them all the time."

Hamish stroked her hair, concerned. What he just witnessed was not just a simple nightmare but something far more severe. "Do you remember what it was about?"

Mairead shook her head. "Last thing I remember is coming down to your room and . . ."

Hamish knew the moment she was fully awake. Her whole body tensed and she slowly pulled back to look at him. Her eyes were wide with alarm. "I . . . I'm so sorry. I didn't mean to fall asleep. I just wanted to see you. To talk to you. To tell you that—"

"Mairead, you have to leave," he said, not letting her finish. "If someone finds you here . . ."

"Someone already did," came the curt reply from a voice that typically was soft and sweet.

Hamish swiveled around and his gaze clashed with Selah's. Anger shot through him as he realized what she was thinking. He rose to his feet and glanced back at Mairead, who did not look at all shocked to see her sister. Only mad. Had this been staged with Selah interrupting them prematurely? Had Mairead intended to be in a truly compromised position before her sister barged in on them?

"Did you plan this?" he accused Mairead. He was so angry, the vein stood out on the side of his neck.

Mairead's eyes left her sister and landed on Hamish. "*What?!*"

"You intentionally snuck into my room," he sneered. "Then 'happened' to fall asleep. Then, just as I was about to leave, you conveniently have a nightmare to draw me to your side."

Mairead's jaw tightened. "You think I *planned* all that. To what end?"

Hamish's scowl became colder when she did not deny the accusation. "I will not be forced into anything, Mairead. Not into staying and definitely not into marriage."

His tone had never sounded more hostile and cold. It fed Mairead's own anger. She pointed to his clean leine and plaid on the empty storage barrel. "Then leave."

Hamish gave her one last pointed look before snatching his clothes. He stomped toward the door and, feeling the weight of Selah's icy stare, stopped and turned around to issue her a glacial glare of his own. "You and my brother may rot in hell before I am forced into marrying your sister for something *that did not and will not ever happen.*"

* * *

Selah stared at the empty doorway for several long seconds before swinging her gaze back to her sister. She was totally unfazed by what Hamish had just said and clasped her hands in front of her. "Everyone heard you scream," she said, to explain her unexpected appearance.

Mairead got to her feet. The explanation made sense but did nothing to calm her ire. "Aye, but did you have to come in here?"

"Aye, I did."

"Could you not have just knocked?"

Selah shook her head. "More than one person heard it and recognized that it came from Hamish's chambers. Or would you rather have had the blacksmith running in here seeing what I witnessed?"

Mairead shook her head, collapsed back down on the bed, and then dropped it in her hands. Tears began to fall. "I've ruined my last chance."

Selah went and sat down beside Mairead. She smoothed out the covers and helped pull the blanket back around her shoulders. "You love him."

Mairead nodded, no longer wanting to deny it. She had just wished she had been able to tell Hamish. "Very much. But it no longer matters. He wants nothing to do with me now."

Selah smoothed back a lock of Mairead's hair. "Lucky for you, he has to."

Mairead scoffed. "You think because you caught Hamish comforting me that he is going to be compelled to marry me?"

Selah tilted her head. "He does not have much of a choice, Mairead. Too many people heard you scream and know you are in here. But when he just marched out of these chambers half dressed, carrying his clothes, he had to know what would happen."

Mairead wanted to disagree. Hamish had been too angry to think about the consequences of his dress. But it did not matter if he had or not. Mairead was not about to marry anyone who felt coerced into doing so. "Hamish thinks I tried to manipulate him, Selah. That I am dishonest and like the woman he almost married last year."

Selah put a comforting arm around Mairead's shoulders. "He doesn't really. He just lost control of the situation for a moment and reacted poorly. When he calms, he'll realize the truth. Deep down, Hamish knows that you would never try to threaten or deceive him."

Mairead swallowed. She could not admit to her sister that she *was* capable of all that. She had proved it over and over. No, she would never do something like this, but Hamish had been hurt and betrayed by women so much in his past that he most likely would never believe the truth.

Selah patted her hand. "I will talk to Robert and let him know what happened. He will speak to Hamish about wedding plans and whether or not we should wait for the priest."

Mairead stood up and stared down at her sister. "You and Robert *really* don't understand Hamish at all. The man lives by a code of honor, which you and your husband should know better than anyone after what Hamish gave up for the both of you."

Selah squared her jaw and crossed her arms. "It really doesn't matter whether I *understand* him or not, Hamish is honor bound to marry you. Your reputation is at stake. He would not dare refuse."

Mairead threw her hands up in the air. "Oh, he most certainly would dare! And even if Hamish did capitulate to your demands to restore my reputation, *I would not let him.*"

True anger flashed out of Selah's hazel eyes as she rose to her feet. "Aye, you would. I am your older sister by several years and the last of your family. You *will* marry Hamish and you will do it soon."

"I will not."

Selah held Mairead's glaze. "*You* created these circumstances. You entered an unmarried man's bedchambers and, based on the state of your appearance, you fell asleep. Hamish did not do this to you, you did it to him and you *will* take responsibility. He should have left the moment he saw you and because he did not, he too will pay the price. You are just fortunate that you both are in love. But let me make this clear, *it would not matter if you weren't.*"

Mairead knew her sister was right on all accounts, except two. Hamish was never going to marry her and under these circumstances, she would *never* agree to marry him. "To agree would only sentence me and Hamish to a lifetime of misery. His anger of being forced into something he did not want would only grow and it would kill anything there was between us. So *no*, I will *not* marry Hamish. Not today, not tomorrow, *not ever*. And nothing you say can change my mind."

Selah watched with an open mouth as Mairead marched by her and out the door.

This had *not* gone quite like she had hoped. Catching the two of them in a compromising circumstance was supposed to ensure their union. Not ensure that it never occurred.

She prayed Robert would know how to fix this mess, because when Ulrick finally arrived, it was critical that Mairead be by Hamish's side. If she wasn't, then all their futures would be in jeopardy.

* * *

"I will not, Robert."

Hamish sat across from Robert in his dayroom and lifted his leg to rest his right ankle on his left knee. He was glad his brother was doing better, but his outer calm was not indicative of what he felt.

His anger had been enormous when he had left his bedchambers hours ago. The idea that Mairead had tried to manipulate him into staying with her by forcing him to marry her had filled him with a fury unlike he had ever known. He had not thought her capable of such deceit. And deep down, he still did not believe it.

Mairead just did not operate in such a manner. She openly admitted her machinations when she had them and was never ashamed of them. Selah had probably heard Mairead's scream, which brought her to investigate, and then used the situation to force a union upon not just him, but Mairead. Robert and Selah knew he would never wrench her from Foinaven and they were doing what he had accused Mairead of: forcing him to marry in order to keep him at Foinaven.

It was never going to happen, especially as Mairead was not compromised, and Robert and Selah knew it.

"You must marry Mairead and you know it," Robert countered.

"I *must* do nothing of the sort," Hamish scoffed, unaffected by the genuine urgency behind his brother's statement. "Nothing happened between us. Mairead can arrange to marry any other man she pleases because it won't be me."

Robert shifted in his chair to a more comfortable position. He was feeling better, but his energy had yet to return. Still, he was glad not to be having this conversation from his sickbed. "Is that what you think? That Mairead *arranged* for Selah to interrupt you? I can assure you that she did not."

"Selah interrupted nothing." Hamish scowled at his younger brother, but his voice kept that same icy, calm tone. "Furthermore, I no longer believe that Mairead staged what happened, but nonetheless you three are trying to use *something that did not happen* to your advantage."

"The *three* of us are using?" Robert scoffed. "You could be no more wrong. Mairead is also refusing to marry. Just before you arrived, Selah was in here telling me that her sister will never marry a man being coerced into it."

Hamish sat with pursed lips at the surprising information. He had mixed feelings about hearing Mairead's resistance though it did reaffirm his gut instincts. But it did not matter because the reason he refused to marry Mairead had nothing to do with coercion. It had to do with his not being enough. He was not enough to leave everyone and everything she loved.

"Selah is convinced you two are in love. I suspect she is right if Mairead is running to you for comfort in your chambers and you are giving it to her."

Hamish rolled his eyes and dropped his foot to the floor. He leaned forward on his elbows. "Mairead runs to me for many things—answers, details of my plans, training—*comfort* is not one of them. And of all the things that would *not* bring her solace in the long run, marriage would rank high among them."

Robert started to speak, but a hacking cough overcame him and it took a second for him to catch his breath. The cntire time, Hamish's expression had remained unchanged. "You don't realize what is at stake."

"I'm speaking fairly simply, Robert. I will not marry Mairead and I will not be forced to remain here. Can you look me in the eye and swear that you hold no desire, that you have no expectations, plans, or otherwise that I would stay?"

Robert's brow furrowed. "I think you are afraid," he said calmly, refusing to answer Hamish's question. "Maybe it's love that has you so scared that you cannot allow yourself to grab hold of a chance at happiness."

"*I'm* afraid?" Hamish barked. His temper flared back to life and something dark came over him. "Don't you *dare* accuse me of being afraid when it is you who walks the path of fear every day, Robert. I'm not the one who is afraid of people resisting being in one clan, afraid of confrontation, *afraid to lead*. You won't even sleep in the solar, Robert! It is your right! It is a symbol of who you are to these people. Without it, they have no loyalty to you or this clan. People look to strength to guide them. Someone they can believe in. They don't need someone to manage the clan, they *need a laird*. Maybe you need to ask yourself just what has *you* so afraid."

Robert's green eyes bore into Hamish's. He was a hard man to anger, but inside he was seething.

Hamish knew his brother was mad, but he did not care. Robert brought him in his room to talk about Mairead and Hamish still had more to say. "As far as what I *feel* for Mairead, you might want to remember that I was once in love with your wife. And there is no denying all these years later that we would have been miserable together. I will not condemn Mairead to the wretched fate Selah escaped. I am giving her the same chance to find someone who can make her happy."

Robert rose to his feet and shoved his anger to the side. He was not nearly as wide as Hamish, but he had the same height and wanted to look him in the eye. "Here's the harsh truth, Hamish. You left, Father died, and *I was the one* who kept this clan together. I helped it to grow by giving the people what they wanted. I was here when they needed me. And I am still here. I *was not* and *am not* running away, *afraid*."

Hamish glowered and Robert suspected he was in danger of being punched. But he did not back down. "And aye, I am pushing you to marry Mairead, but not because I want to use it as a noose to keep you here. I am doing it for the same reason you are refusing. *I am trying to save her, you ainmhíde*. Mairead needs your *protection*, not your sense of honor. Why do you think I created the situation that compelled Ulrick to leave with every good soldier we have? *To get you here.* For you to see for yourself that Mairead was in trouble and take her away. Because God knows, she is as stubborn as you and would refuse any other way."

Hamish stood completely still for at least a moment, digesting what Robert just said. He believed his brother . . . and yet he did not. "You expect me to believe you arranged everything so that I would come back, get ensnared in a situation, and be forced into agreeing to marry? If you did, you far outshine the McTiernays when it comes to strategy."

"Of course not. I wanted you to come and do what you originally agreed and send Ulrick away. But like Mairead, I had thought you would be bringing men and that perhaps one of them might have appreciated her enough to want to stay. But I also knew that even if neither happened, it would not take you long to realize that Mairead was scared and needed to be taken from Foinaven. You both falling in love was not planned, but it *was* welcomed. And given the way you both feel, *you* must be the one to marry her."

Hamish's jaw twitched. "No, what *I need* are answers. Mairead doesn't need me to marry her. She needs me to know the name of the man she is so afraid of."

Robert sighed and sank back down into his chair. "Can you not guess?"

"I asked her if it was Ulrick and she denied him ever harming her."

Robert shook his head. "Ulrick's ultimate desire is not Foinaven or this clan. It's Mairead." Hamish stared at his brother unblinking. But he could feel his heart begin to beat harder and faster. "Ulrick has wanted her since he first saw her and her rebuffs only stoked his obsession. Mairead doesn't know I am aware of this, but he threatened her at Epiphany. They are to marry when he returns and if she refuses, then he will find an unpleasant way to make her change her mind. Those were his words."

"Mo chreach-sa a thàinig." Everything now made sense. "Mairead had wanted to know if I was going to kill him," Hamish muttered.

"Now do you understand why you must marry her? It is the only way she will know—that Selah and I will know—that she is safe as long as Ulrick is alive."

Hamish looked his brother in the eye. "If Ulrick touches her, I will take his life and I will do it slowly."

Robert gulped. He did not think that was necessary. Ulrick just needed to accept that Mairead would never be his. "But what if he agrees to leave Foinaven? We need to talk with him. Explain to him the situation. For to kill without provocation . . . that's murder. Once he is gone we can figure something out long-term to protect Mairead." Hamish's right eyelid flickered. "What are you going to do?"

Hamish scowled. "I don't know," he said simply, and then left.

Chapter Twelve

Mairead pulled her fur blanket tighter around her shoulders and adjusted her position on the sloped granite outcropping. The morning air was warmer than what it had been the past couple of days, but the clouds overhead and the even darker ones on the horizon hinted that by mid to late afternoon, the icy rain would once again be upon them.

The gooey sounds of footsteps on the soggy ground made her head snap around to see who was coming. A second later Hamish came into view.

Mairead waited until he saw her sitting there. "I've been waiting for you."

Hamish studied Mairead for a moment. She was cold and had probably been sitting there for a while in an effort to catch him. He glanced at the river bank behind her and said, "I'm dirty and I want to bathe. We can talk when I get back to Foinaven."

Mairead shook her head. "We need to talk now. Here. Where no one can hear or interrupt us."

Hamish smiled, but there was no humor in it. "Then you will be speaking to my naked backside."

Hamish sauntered over to a rock closer to the water and

dropped a bag. He then unbuckled his belt, freeing it and his tartan. He laid them both on the small rock and then, without another word, he headed straight into the water, keeping his leine and raw leather shoes on. He strode quickly in without pausing, as if he were strolling into a pond heated by the summer sun. She knew he had to be freezing. "Is this bravado I'm witnessing or do you actually enjoy icy water?"

Hamish did not answer. He was waist deep and dropped himself down into the cold depths until his head was submerged. He hated the cold and wading slowly in only prolonged the agony of washing in a river this time of year. The only reason he even bathed was because he hated the feel of grime on skin and mud between his toes. How Craig McTiernay had loved to tease him about it, but Hamish had not cared. Especially since he knew they enjoyed being clean almost as much as he did.

Under the water, he brusquely rubbed his scalp and then stood up. Quickly he removed his dirty leine, wrung out as much of the grime as he could, and tossed the shirt onto the shore. When he did so, he caught her staring at him. "Like what you see?"

Mairead did not turn away. If Hamish thought he would intimidate her into shielding her eyes, he was highly mistaken. They had shared a very intimate moment and if that did not make her unfit for marriage, then seeing Hamish unclothed would not either. "I do," she finally answered, catching the shift in his jaw.

She had been staring at him not to prove a point, but mostly because she had wanted to see the rippled muscles she had only felt and envisioned in her mind. She was not disappointed.

The strength in Hamish's upper arms and broad chest had been clearly noticeable under his leine, but this was the first she had seen of his stomach. It rippled as he moved, firing her blood and making her heart pound. There was not an ounce of fat on him anywhere.

Free of clothes and mud, Hamish sauntered back to shore. Mairead was still looking at him, but he noticed that her eyes were locked to his. She was cheeky, but only to a point. It was another aspect to her character that he liked. Marriage to her would never be dull and he was starting to find himself looking forward to it.

Mairead kept her focus on his face even as he leaned down and pulled out a clean leine from his bag. As he tugged it on, she decided to delay their conversation no longer. "I wanted to tell you some things that I should've said, meant to say, the other night. I came to your room to tell you them, but we got interrupted. So I'm here now because when you leave I don't want to regret never having told you. I don't want you to put me in that same category with all the other women you've ever cared for."

Hamish grabbed his plaid off the rock. "Since meeting you, I've not been able to put you in any category of any woman I have ever known. I doubt that will ever change."

Mairead could not help but smile. God, how she loved him. And though nothing would ever come of it, he deserved to know. "I love you, Hamish. I think I have for a while. Spending time with you has changed me and only for the better. I want to thank you for that."

Hamish paused his efforts to pleat his tartan with frozen fingers and looked at her. She was earnest. She had not said it to gain a response from him in return, to secure information or even protect her from a scary future. She simply loved him. Him. Hamish MacBrieve. The man whom all women liked, but none wanted for their own.

Mairead MacMhathain loved him. And the idea terrified him to his core for never had he felt more vulnerable.

Getting control over the onslaught of emotions, Hamish finished belting his plaid.

Hamish's green eyes had held hers for a long time. It was as if he was searching her soul, seeking the truth. Only when he had looked away was she able to continue. "I am not telling you to tie you to me or create any guilt. I know that you soon will leave Foinaven, but I never wanted you to think that I was like the other women you have known. You need to believe that there *is* love out there for you. I fell in love with the real you and if I did, so can someone else."

Hamish heard the trip in her voice at the end. Mairead did not like the idea of his being with another woman and he liked the idea far less. He knew there was no one out there for him. He had searched for too long to think that there was. Mairead was a miracle. She really was his *aingeal*. "From what you are saying, Selah has not told you of my decision."

Mairead looked at the clasped hands in her lap and with a sneer said, "Oh, I heard. My sister was extremely eager to tell me about it last night. She was also quite upset when I made it clear that it did not matter what *you* had decided for *I* also had a choice in the matter. And I've made it." She looked up and, catching his eye once more, said, "I will not marry a man in order to save myself from Ulrick. I doubt I will have a need, but just in case, I now have other ways to convince him to look elsewhere for a wife." She patted her outer thigh where he knew the *sgian dubh* was hidden.

Hamish narrowed his gaze. "I'll admit that you picked up the basics of using a knife quickly, but Ulrick is a seasoned warrior. *That*"—he gestured to her thigh—"is no protection. You have only one choice, Mairead. We will handfast tomorrow."

Mairead stood up and squared her shoulders. "I will not. Marrying you is no doubt the best option I have to protect myself against Ulrick, but—and I hope you can understand this—I want more than just protection when I promise myself to someone. I don't want to be locked to a man who married me out of pity or was forced into it by my family. Neither do I want to be with a man whose honor compelled him into agreement. Any *one* of these reasons would make me say no, and your rationale for marrying me involves all four. I am not someone you want as a wife and you made that very clear the other night."

Alarm shot through Hamish. Mairead just admitted to loving him but was at the same time refusing to marry him. And *he* was the reason why. Hamish was not sure how to handle the situation, but he knew one thing. That he might have wanted to marry Mairead before, but now that he knew she loved him, there was nothing anyone— including Mairead and her stubborn pride—could do to stop it. "Then what do you plan to do?"

Mairead shrugged and gave a shake to her head. "I honestly do not know. I'll probably look to find someone Ulrick would not want to tangle with. Maybe I'll marry a Mackay. It would be better than . . ." She stopped speaking just in time.

"Than what, Mairead?" Hamish asked. His entire body racked with tension.

Than to tie myself to a man who did not love me, but Mairead could not say the words. Hearing Hamish admit out loud that what he felt for her was less than her own declared love would shatter the few pieces of her heart she had left.

Hamish's eyes never left her and she knew he was waiting on an answer. "Than marry you and make us both miserable."

Anguish ripped through him. He felt more pain than he had ever known in his life. He could feel it gnawing at his vitals, eating him alive. Losing Selah, finding out about Wyenda's betrayal, being constantly overshadowed by McTiernays—they were *nothing* compared to the pain her words inflicted. "Then you leave me no choice. I'm leaving," he bit out. "The whole reason Robert even brought me here was for us to meet and marry."

"What! You can't leave!"

Hamish's jaw clenched. "Aye, I can. My reason for being here no longer exists."

"But . . . but . . . but Foinaven, Robert, the clan, *they need you*!"

Hamish shook his head. "They need me no more than you do."

"You're wrong."

Hamish walked over and grabbed her hand. "You are coming with me."

Mairead stumbled after him. "But . . . but it is going to rain!" she yelped.

"Then you will get wet," he snapped, and led her to where he had left his horse.

Without warning, he put his hands around her waist and plopped her down in front of his saddle. He then freed the reins and threw his leg over the horse and pulled himself up. Wrapping an arm around her middle, he pulled her back against him and he yanked his mount to head just where he had come from.

They were riding fast, but it was evident that Hamish knew the way by heart. Soon they were in the woods and she was ducking to avoid branches and limbs as they made their way to *the* valley. After almost an hour of riding in silence, they arrived at its edge.

Hamish gestured to the scene below. "Do not worry about your home, my brother, or even various clans that live under his protection. I have prepared so that they will be fine."

Mairead slipped off the horse, her mouth gaping at the sight before her. She had not known what to expect. She had thought Hamish might be working some of the village boys that he had ridiculed in the great hall, and they were there—along with five to six dozen other men. Many she recognized. Like Amon, they had either left the guard or had been forced out by Ulrick. But she had not seen them since and had assumed they had left the area completely. But they were there. Training in preparation to face Ulrick when he returned.

Mairead stood there for some time, just watching everything. As soon as they arrived, Hamish left her without a word where she was and rode down to meet with some of the men.

He carried himself with a commanding air of self-confidence and all the men, even those older and highly skilled, listened as he spoke to them. Their faces radiated awe and respect. It was now clear what Hamish had been doing in the mornings. He had been out finding people of like minds, who were still willing to fight for Foinaven, for the safety of this community . . . but not for Robert. They were there because of Hamish. And when he left, she suspected so would they.

How she wished she could simply agree to Hamish's marriage request. But she could not muster the will to change her mind. She loved him, even more so now after seeing all that he had been doing for her, his brother and her sister. But she would not tie him to her this way. She always wanted what her sister had with Robert—a deep, forever-binding type of love. And from the few conversations they had, Mairead knew that Hamish longed for the same, otherwise he would have wed some nice, willing girl long ago. He wanted to be loved. Well, so did she.

"So he finally told you his secret, did he?"

Mairead jumped and spun around. Two women were walking up to her.

"We saw you standing here when we brought food out to the men. We thought we would bring you some as well and join you for a bit," Lynnea said with a smile.

Mairead returned it, glad to see Amon's wife. She had not seen her since Amon and Ulrick had their row and split company. Her farm was fairly self-sufficient and had no need to exchange goods and food on market day. Mairead suddenly realized she had missed the older woman's company.

Jeán pulled her into a quick embrace and then pointed to the group of men below as echoes of metal clashing reached them. "I know you *had* to suspect something like this."

"I really didn't," Mairead denied. "I thought for a while that Hamish might be training some of the village boys, but never this," she said, waving her hand out to the sight in front of them.

"Then why don't you seem happy?" Jeán asked. "I would have thought seeing a small army would give you the peace of mind you have been seeking."

Mairead sighed. "You are right. It should."

"Ahhhh," Lynnea said, and then mouthed to Jeán, *You were right.* "You love Hamish."

"I do, very much."

Jeán winked at her. "I told you the kiss would work. Hamish told Amon this morning that you two are to wed. Or handfast until a priest can be coerced into coming this far north."

Mairead grimaced. "Just because Hamish is willing to marry me, does not mean he wants to. Look out there, Jeán. *That* is what Hamish wants. He wants to protect me and Robert has convinced him that the only way he can do that is by marrying me. Hamish doesn't want me. He certainly doesn't love me and without him returning my feelings, I cannot agree to marry him." Using her chin, Mairead gestured to where Hamish, Amon, Davros, and two other men were talking animatedly. "I have a feeling that he is telling them that he is leaving."

Lynnea started chuckling and Jeán joined her. "I doubt it."

"When I refused to marry him, Hamish said that there was no longer any reason to stay. That his army would handle Ulrick and his men when they return."

Both women started laughing in earnest now.

Mairead gave them both her harshest glare, which again caused their laughter to increase. That they thought so little of what she was saying bothered Mairead. She had thought to have their support, not their derision.

Jeán wiped the tears from her eyes. "I'm sorry, Mairead, but the idea that Hamish doesn't love you, is well . . . laughable."

Lynnea nodded. "The man is completely besotted. It makes Amon's stomach turn."

Mairead's brow furrowed deeply. "Hamish said he loved me?"

Lynnea made a dismissive gesture. "Of course not. He's a man. He has no idea when he is in love."

Mairead wanted to believe what they were saying, but she knew that they were wrong. Hamish was not the type of man who denied being in love. He was just the opposite. "Hamish cares for me. He's told me so, but that is all. And I don't even think he feels that for me right now."

Jeán pointed out to the field. "I might not know Hamish well, but I do know when a man is in love."

Lynnea nodded her head. "From what I can tell, Hamish is much like my Amon and I too doubted his feelings for a long time."

Mairead looked at the kind face of the older woman, unable to hide her disbelief. "Anyone can see how much Amon loves you."

"Aye, *now*," Lynnea agreed. "But not at first. He was a soldier and my father was pushing him to a life of farming that he did not want. He thought that I wanted the same thing as my father and actually *left*. Thank goodness my mother was still alive. She urged me to go after Amon and tell him my feelings. That Amon was not the type to pour out his feelings without some assurance that they were returned. He had risked exposing his heart by coming to the farm and that it was my turn to be vulnerable. I think the same is going on with you and Hamish. I doubt he has even admitted to himself how much he loves you, but trust me, love is the *only* thing that could have made him willing to want you for his wife."

Mairead shook her head, this time more vigorously. She had not wanted to reveal Ulrick's involvement to anyone, but it seemed several people already knew and she wanted Jeán, as well as Lynnea, to understand what was happening. "Hamish agreed to marry in order to protect me. Ulrick has been threatening me for months and he warned me that I would become his when he returned.

Hamish doesn't love me and he doesn't want me for his wife. He just believes there is no other choice."

Jeán rolled her eyes and pulled her own blanket tighter around her. "Do you really believe Hamish incapable of finding another way to free you from Ulrick's threats? I imagine there are a hundred ways Hamish could ensure the man never bothered you again, and yet he chose marriage."

Lynnea nodded her head. "What Hamish offered was not just protection, Mairead, but *permanent commitment*, which is so much more. You would be the mother of his children. You would help him create his legacy. Such things are important and I cannot believe Hamish would just give them to you out of a warped sense of honor and to give you some sort of security."

"He loves you," Jeán reiterated. "Don't wait for an idyllic setting or for perfect words to be said at the ideal time. Take hold of what you know is true. The rest will come and Hamish will tell you what he feels. Not as soon as you may want it or even when you want it, but the words will come."

Mairead's eyes grew large and she bit her bottom lip. "But . . ." she groaned, and closed her eyes. "How? I've hurt him. And you should have seen his face. I did not want to be like the other women who had hurt him, but I am. He thinks I am just like them."

Jeán tilted her head and winced. "If you did hurt him, remember you have something those other women did not have." Mairead looked at her friend pleadingly for some kind of hope and direction. "You actually do love him and Hamish needs that love more than he probably realizes. And despite what you said to him or vice versa, I cannot see that man letting you go if he knows you don't want him to."

Mairead looked back down at Hamish. He clasped hands with one of the men he was talking with and began to head her way. Amon and Davros followed. Mairead watched as the three men approached. The stern expression Hamish wore completely hid the fact that he had the most beautiful dimples. She wanted to see him smile at her and make him laugh in return. This man was everything she ever wanted, and if Jeán and Lynnea were right, *he loved her*. He loved her so much that he was willing to promise himself to her for life, despite all she was connected to—Selah, a lairdship that should have been his, a home of his own. He wanted to have a life together. A family. How she wanted to raise a bunch of little Hamishes. Was she really going to give that up because of the circumstances behind his proposal?

The answer was no.

The six of them spoke for a second and then headed to Amon's, who lived the closest to the valley and all the activity. Lynnea and Jeán prepared the midday meal while Mairead kept the children occupied.

"I cannot believe the improvement you have made with the unskilled lads I sent you earlier this week," Hamish said.

"They are good boys." Amon knew exactly to whom Hamish was referring. "They actually knew how to handle a sword. One though was a natural archer and Davros is working with him. But they will need far more than a few weeks to be ready for battle."

"Hopefully, it won't come to that."

"But if it does, it is hard to know how they will react. More than half of the men out there have never seen battle. What we need is experienced men. The others will look to them for confidence and direction and mimic their actions."

Davros nodded. "The mercenaries Ulrick is gathering are going to be hard men and very comfortable in battle. But their loyalty is not to any man, but to power and coin," he said, and then noticed that Jeán was coming with food.

All three men moved their arms out of the way for the plates being served at the table. Mairead went to go get mugs and the pitcher of mead while Lynnea offered food to the children and told them to eat near the hearth so that the adults could talk.

Davros bit off a chunk of meat. "Excellent. Thank you for this," he said to Lynnea in particular. "It is much appreciated." Then to Hamish, he said, "If you need experienced men, I know a couple of brothers who live an hour's ride farther east who might be able to bring another dozen men. They were never part of the Foinaven's ranks and refused to serve under Ulrick when he approached them."

"Are you talking of the Kyldoane brothers?" Mairead asked.

Amon nodded. "I rode out there a couple days ago. They listened, but promised nothing. I think it will take you, Hamish, meeting with them directly for there to be any possibility of them joining us. But they would give us the numbers we need."

Hamish grimaced and glanced at Mairead. There was only three to four more hours of daylight left and a possible chance of rain.

Mairead knew he was factoring her into his decision. "We should go."

Hamish shook his head. "*We* won't go. I will. You will stay here where it is warm and dry."

Mairead shook her head. "I not only know the Kyldoanes, but I also know where they live. They are proud people, the men especially. But I have met with their wives and when they first came to the area I made sure they had food and shelter until they were able to get settled and live on their own. The men don't know you, but their wives know me. They will at least make them listen to what you have to say."

Hamish ran his tongue along the outside of his teeth. Mairead knew he was contemplating what she said, but he was still not convinced. "If Davros and Amon say you need to meet with them, then we should go. If we leave now, we could make it there and back before the sun goes down, but even if we have to travel the last part in the dark, I know the terrain, Hamish. And I trust you to keep us both safe."

Hearing that last comment, Hamish studied her for several seconds. Then he inhaled and released it with a single nod. "We need to leave immediately then. And you"—he pointed at Mairead—"need your own horse."

Amon elbowed her and said, "I have just the one you can borrow."

Less than twenty minutes later, Hamish and Mairead were on their way.

The last of the sunlight disappeared only a half hour ago, but visibility was the equivalent to the dead of a moonless night. The expected rain had come and with more force than normal. The wind was steadily picking up and the initial drizzle had gone from annoying to a flood. Mairead was soaked and cold, but yet she felt oddly triumphant. The afternoon had been very successful.

When they arrived, the Kyldoane brothers had not been eager to listen, believing they had heard everything already from Amon. But Mairead's presence had been as important as she predicted for it kept the first brother they encountered from ordering Hamish to turn around and leave. And that was all that Hamish needed. He only spoke a few words, but they drove right to the honor of a man and forced him to continue to listen. Mairead had felt herself similarly pulled in, wanting to hear more.

Soon the man had sent for his elder brother, who called to their cousins and some others they thought might be interested. One by one, they listened to the benefits of ridding the northern territory of Ulrick and his kind as well as the benefits and the quality of life that a peaceful Foinaven could bring to them and their families. It had taken longer than Hamish had planned to convince them to join Amon's training, but in the end they all agreed to participate at least until Candlemas.

Deep down, however, Mairead knew that much—if not all—of the reason they agreed was because Hamish, not Robert, would be leading them. The moment Hamish left, she knew this collaboration would end. It would be up to Robert as the leader to keep them together, to rally them as Hamish had done, and encourage their loyalty and support, but she doubted it would happen. Robert just did not inspire men like these soldiers.

Mairead pushed back such thoughts and focused on the present. She had enjoyed talking with their wives and visiting with their children. Before they departed, the women made sure they left with some dried meat and drink for their journey back.

She and Hamish had made good progress at first. The path was familiar so they had thought to still make it back to Foinaven despite the darkness. But when the weather hit, it forced them to start looking for alternatives.

"I remember an empty cottage being near here," Hamish shouted over the pelting of the rain.

Mairead did not even try to respond, but she knew the one Hamish was talking about. It was not a cottage, but more of a one-room hovel traveling merchants used when in the area. However, it was shelter and more than likely had dry firewood in it from its periodic use. Mairead pointed a finger in the direction she thought it was. Hamish nodded and twenty minutes later he was helping her off the horse and inside.

The inside was pitch-black, but Hamish somehow managed to find the fireplace, kindling, and wood and then got a fire started with some flint. Now able to see, he glanced over his shoulder and took in the place. It was just a single room, but it was larger than he had thought it to be when he had passed by it a few times riding in the area. In the corner was a stack of dry wood he was relieved to see. The one window had shutters that were closed and the roof seemed to be withstanding the storm, which alleviated his second concern. Next to the hearth was a square small table that Mairead had already used to place the bundle of food she had surprisingly been able to protect using her body and furs. Beside the table was a narrow bench, which looked to be the place's only sitting area. And across from the fire was a bed. It was of a good size for a cottage this small, but it was still meant to only sleep one. It had been stripped bare, which was to be expected, but then his eye saw that whoever had used it last had just shoved the blankets off the end.

Seeing Mairead's failing attempts to hide how cold she was, Hamish grimaced. "You're shivering so much your teeth will fall out if you don't get warm soon." He threw two more large logs on the fire. "Come closer and take off your clothes."

Mairead advanced a step, seeking the heat, but shook her head about the clothes.

Hamish frowned. "You've made your feelings about me and our future clear, but you need to get warm. If you don't undress yourself, then I will do it for you."

Mairead could see he was serious, plus she was freezing, so she slipped off her sodden shoes and then struggled with the ties of her gown. Her fingers were too numb to get a firm grip and Hamish came over to help her. Quickly he yanked on the ties, loosening the bliaut. He then went and grabbed one of the blankets off the floor and handed it to her. "I'm going to check on the horses and get the rest of our things. Take that off," he said pointing at her wet gown, "and get dry."

Mairead nodded and the moment he stepped outside she quickly pulled the bliaut off her shoulders and then laid it over the makeshift chair. She considered taking off her undergarment as well but decided the chemise was thin, would dry quickly, and she needed its pathetic protection. She then wrapped herself in the dusty MacBrieve plaid and sat in front of the fire. A moment later, Hamish reentered and she could see his face relax a little seeing that she had done as instructed. "Your turn," she said, and quirked an eyebrow to let him know that she was serious.

"I'm fine."

Hamish turned to open the door and Mairead realized he was planning to sleep outside. "Are you crazy? You will freeze if you go out there!"

As if to emphasize her point, a sudden burst of wind shook the cabin. Hamish looked back at her, his dark green eyes unfathomable. "The weather is far from agreeable, but I've slept in worse." He had, but it was not often. Part of the structure was a stable. It had a roof, walls, and enough room he could create a small fire to keep from freezing. It would not be warm or comfortable, but it would provide a measure of protection from the wind and rain, and he could not trust himself to stay inside.

Mairead stood up and the blanket she was holding shifted. Hamish could see the chemise slide off her creamy shoulders as she reached out. "Please stay, Hamish. Do not go back out."

"If I do that, I cannot promise to stay away from you."

"I'm not asking for promises."

"No, you are asking me to walk away. And I won't be able to do that if I stay with you tonight."

Chapter Thirteen

Mairead knew what she wanted, but she also knew that after her emphatic decree by the river it was not going to be as easy as saying "I've changed my mind." However, she was determined and fate was on her side. It had given her rain, protection, and this chance to claim her future. "Then just sit for a while and at least get warm."

Hamish hesitated, but he was chilled to the bone. He had mentally compartmentalized the cold, but now that they had found shelter and had a fire, the need to get warm was pressing at him.

They sat for several minutes, both staring at the flames as they flickered and curled. With the room being small, the temperature was quickly growing more comfortable. Mairead let the blanket pool around her waist and untied the leather strip that was keeping her hair from tumbling free. She used her fingers as a makeshift comb and worked to get some of the bigger knots out of her hair.

Silence filled the room. Normally, Mairead was content to just listen to the crackle of wood as it burned, but she had a feeling that at any moment Hamish would announce he was warm enough and leave her alone. They needed to talk, but she worried that discussion on any topic—especially that of love or marriage—would drive him out the door faster. There was one, however, that would not.

"Ulrick did not just promise to make me his own when he returns." Mairead knew Hamish heard her, but he just continued staring into the fire. "I did not know that Robert and Selah knew anything about Ulrick's threats, but I realized yesterday when she told me what they overheard that they are unaware of their extent."

Hamish did look at her then. His dark green eyes narrowed. "There's more?"

Mairead studied her fingers, which were intertwined on her lap. "Ulrick knew that I might take steps to prevent him from doing so. He promised to kill anyone who intervened— Robert, Selah, and even little Rab. And if I dared to marry someone when he was away, then he would take great pleasure in gutting them alive." She looked up then and saw that Hamish was watching her.

Hamish tensed his jaw, remembering her threat to marry a stranger rather than him. "What about your great plan to snatch a Mackay?"

Mairead frowned at him. "I was never serious about marrying a Mackay. I don't know them and what little I do scares me." Hamish knew Mairead was right to be scared about the Mackays. Under the leadership of MacHeth, Iye Mor Mackay, and now Donald Mackay, Clan Mackay was known for their strength, courage, and skill in soldiering. Their warlike reputation was echoed in their motto, "with a strong hand."

Hamish stared at Mairead. Her hair was a mess and her chemise clung to her curves. He had never seen a woman looking more beautiful. If Mairead had gone to the Mackays, she would have found a champion there. More than one most likely and the idea caused his eyes to grow cold and unfeeling. "The plan has merit. Ulrick would not want to face the wrath of the Mackays to get to you."

"What about the wrath of the McTiernays?" she posed, her eyes wide and serious. "Wouldn't they protect me just as fiercely?"

Hamish narrowed his gaze. His heart was starting to pound at the implication and he was afraid to assume that she might have changed her mind. "Does it matter? I thought you would never tie yourself to a man who you believed had been compelled by honor and sacrifice."

Mairead swallowed, hating her own words being parroted back at her. "It matters. Would they?"

Hamish studied her for several long seconds, nothing in his expression giving away the turbulent emotions he felt inside. "Aye. More fiercely than any clan in Scotland."

Mairead sat still for several seconds. She needed to finish telling Hamish everything, but she needed to know one thing first. "Why would you agree to marry someone you think would make you miserable?"

Hamish scowled darkly. "Those are your words, not mine."

Mairead's chin jutted out. "Only after you begged me to let you go that . . . that day," Mairead challenged softly, unable to say the words "when you made love to me." "You said that my 'please' would cause you to do something that would make us both miserable."

Confusion infiltrated Hamish's implacable features, causing them to soften as he realized his role in her refusal. "That is because leaving Foinaven, your sister, and even Robert and Rab, *would* make you miserable."

Mairead closed her eyes. Hamish did not believe *they* would be unhappy; he feared taking her from her home.

She shared that fear and it was time he knew why. "I love Foinaven and consider it my home, but that has not been why I have been so reluctant to leave it." She had his full attention then. "Ulrick threatened to kill all I loved if I was not here when he returned."

Hamish breathed deeply as the desire to kill Ulrick once again consumed him. He did not want to scare her and rose to his feet. Rage was erupting inside him, racing along his every nerve. Part of it was aimed at Mairead for trying to handle the burden by herself. She claimed to love him, but not once had she trusted him enough with the truth.

Hamish turned and Mairead could see that he was once again preparing to move outside. She reached out and grabbed his arm to stop him. Her breath caught in her throat when he looked down at her. His green eyes had grown dark and were smoldering with a mixture of anger and a possessive intensity that made her heart flutter. Jeán and Lynnea were right. Hamish did not just want her. He loved her. He may not say the words, but at this moment it did not matter. "Do not leave me."

"I will only be outside."

"That is not what I meant. I want to marry you."

Hamish's jaw twitched. "There is no need, Mairead. I will make sure that Ulrick will never be a threat to you or anyone else you love."

Mairead's brow furrowed and she rose to her feet, forgetting that she was in only her chemise. Her full focus was on Hamish. "That is what you think? That I'm using you to ensure my safety and that of my family?"

Hamish fought to keep his desire in control and his expression emotionless. "I can give you other options. Ones that can offer you a future of your choosing, not one you were forced into accepting."

Mairead's heart almost stopped. Then it began to pound furiously. There was only one *option* that could ensure her happiness. Now that she had accepted that fact, it was time that Hamish did too.

"You asked me to marry you. Was that only because you wanted to save me? Because if so, then we really do need to discuss those other possibilities." Mairead rose to her feet. Her question was more of a challenge, a declaration, a promise. "But I think they were an excuse. I think you *want* to marry me. And would even if there was no Ulrick, danger, my sister, or the choices made twelve years ago."

A shadow crossed Hamish's features as raw emotions warred inside him. Mairead wanted to say yes to his proposal, but she was waiting for declarations of love— something he could not give her, possibly ever. Every time he came close to voicing the emotion, things went wrong. Actual proclamations resulted in disaster. He may not be able to say it out loud, but Mairead was his, no one else's, never had been and never would be.

Mairead found herself suddenly pulled against his chest. His eyes burned down into hers. "No more games, Mairead. No more delays. We will marry tomorrow when we return."

Mairead grabbed the front of his leine, refusing to let him go back out into the cold. "Then stay with me."

Hamish shook his head and his hands enfolded hers. She squeezed her fists tighter and he closed his eyes, seeking the fortitude he needed to walk away. He wanted her, but he needed them to be bound together first. "When we marry, I want no one to ever doubt that it was our choice. Yours and mine. Uncontrolled passion will not have a part in dictating our futures."

To his surprise, Mairead nodded, genuine agreement

sparkled in her eyes. And yet she did not let go. "You said no more delays. I agree. I pledge myself to you right now. There is no priest anywhere near Foinaven. A handfast needs no witnesses. Only you, me, and God. There is no reason to wait."

Hamish blinked down at her. "Just you and me?" he asked, a mixture of confusion and a need for reassurance in his voice. "You do not want your sister to be a witness?"

Mairead shook her head. "I am tired of letting others influence my actions and decisions. I don't want to worry about Selah and Robert and their reaction. I don't even care about Ulrick and his threats. We can handle whoever dares to try. All I know is that I love you and I want to be yours and more than anything I want to know that you're mine."

With those words of love and trust, Hamish felt the cracks in the wall around his heart begin to break. It scared him. He was already vulnerable and she had too much power over him as it was. But he would never love another woman as much as he did Mairead. His arms came around her, pinning her to his body, possessive, certain, his hold unbreakable. He closed his eyes, savoring the feel of her against him and the fact she wanted him back with the same intensity.

"To pledge now, to God, even without witnesses, would be just as binding," Hamish agreed. "But know this, as soon as there is a priest, this union will be made permanent. We will not be revisiting this decision in a year and a day."

Mairead smiled up at him, her face full of longing and complete assurance this was what she wanted. Some allowed that handfasting was a temporary union and either party could elect to dissolve it after a year and a day so that it was as if it had never happened. "Nothing will get me to let you go, Hamish. Not even *you* and your arrogant, *flirtatious* ways."

For the first time, Hamish felt completely reassured. "Determination and persistence. Such fantastic qualities," he said as he smiled down at her, flashing his heart-stopping grin that broke hearts wherever he went.

Mairead reached up to trace his incredible smile with the pad of her finger. Jeán was right. A girl had to love a man with dimples. It was an unfair advantage and he knew it. "I take you Hamish of the clan MacBrieve to be my husband. I make this pledge to you and to God."

Hamish swallowed the emotion threatening to choke him. It was rare to marry this way. Handfasts were still common as priests were difficult to find in many of the more remote areas of Scotland, but usually the ceremony had witnesses. However, they were not necessary. It only made the marriage easier to prove. A couple only needed to exchange their consent for a union to be just as legally and bindingly married by the law of both church and state. "I take you Mairead of the clan MacMhathain to be my wife. I make this pledge to you and to God."

With a groan, Hamish cupped her face and claimed her mouth with his. The moment he said the words, his control left him and the need to kiss her, to have her taste in his mouth, to feel his desire returned in her embrace, became nearly crippling. He kissed her hard. His tongue plundered into her accepting mouth. Mairead responded with a feverish intensity that ignited in him a passion that had been dormant too long.

Hamish forced himself to slow down. His body was on fire and she was so accepting, trusting, and willing that he had to fight the desire to bury himself inside her, then and there, without preliminaries. For tonight nothing would stop him from making Mairead his, claiming her so that she could never leave him for another. But he also wanted her to feel treasured. With a gentleness he had not known he was capable of, he pulled back, tracing the contours of her lips with his own.

After a moment, Mairead relaxed into him, her lips softening. Hamish was kissing her. Thoroughly. Completely. It held such tenderness and longing that it melted her insides and brought unexpected tears to her eyes. He loved her.

Mairead wrapped her arms around his neck and caressed him lovingly. She enjoyed this gentle side to him, but he had lit a fire in her two days ago that had yet to be extinguished. She needed more and greedily swept her tongue across his lower lip, darting it inside when he opened to her. Hamish moaned and slanted his head. Mairead mimicked him as he succumbed to her enticement to deepen the kiss.

A low rumble of satisfaction escaped from deep within him. His right arm began to drift lower and palmed her buttocks, pulling her closer, loving the feel of the curvaceous woman in his arms. Mairead raised her head in surprise and then recaptured his lips with a moan as she tunneled her fingers into the russet-brown waves of his hair and held on.

Hamish moved his hand up, cruising gently over the thin material of her chemise until it reached her breast. He began to knead the flesh in a sensual, torturous way, flicking his thumb over and over her nipple, relishing her response.

Mairead moved against him restlessly, her nipples pushing erotically against the thin material and into his palm. Her body began to vibrate with liquid fire as waves of desire beat at her. She could only cling to him, a safe anchor in a storm of growing, turbulent emotions.

When her hips began to grind against his own turgid arousal, Hamish could scarcely breathe. He had only just begun and he was not sure if he would last much longer if she continued her sensual attack. "Do not . . . do that," he whispered huskily.

Mairead ignored his plea and her hands, of their own accord, found the hem of his leine and began to push the material upward. Without argument, Hamish helped her. With enormous eyes, she watched as he pulled the shirt over his head. Then his green eyes held hers captive as he freed his belt. His plaid hit the floor.

He stood naked in the firelight, but she was mesmerized by his eyes. They were filled with such intensity and hunger. And it was for her. Only her.

He reached out to touch her hair, which fell in tangled waves over her shoulders and down to her waist. The movement broke the spell of his gaze, letting her eyes drift over him. She could finally see the muscled breadth of his shoulders, the classic V of his torso, and his lean hips. When her eyes fell on his long powerful legs and what was between them, she stared. Her blood became hotter as her pulse raced. Hamish was huge. She knew she should be terrified of what was about to happen, but all she could think about was that she wanted him. God, how she wanted him.

Hamish's hand let go of her hair and he stepped in close to her. He dropped soft, persuasive kisses into her hair as his fingers went to her shoulder and began to edge the sleeve of her chemise down her arm. Mairead splayed her hands over his broad chest, drinking in his strength as she entrusted herself to a man for the first time in her life. The chemise fell to the floor and her exposed breasts tingled when they came against his hair-roughened chest. Her hands started to explore the hard lines of his back, his waist, and hips. She loved to feel the hardness of his muscular body, but when his hands moved up and cupped her breasts, she could only hold on and close her eyes. She quivered.

With her body finally free of any garments, Hamish's fingers brushed her silky skin, his thumb stroking her nipples into hard peaks. He murmured *"sonuachar"* before he lowered his mouth to taste the creamy offering.

At the first touch of his tongue and the scrape of his teeth, Mairead's legs almost gave out. Hamish held on to her, keeping her from falling as he drew her into the moist heat of his mouth. Her body became boneless, liquid, aching. Then, without warning, Hamish swept her into his arms and the small points of her fingertips dug into the back of his neck and shoulders as he carried her across the room.

Hamish paused at the bed and kissed her intensely. Then he lowered her down, stretching out beside her, his larger, heavier frame dwarfing hers. "You're beautiful," he said with awe in a ragged voice.

He slid a finger down her cheek. She looked wildly desirable, framed by her magnificent mane of tawny hair. He was completely entranced by the softness of her skin, the curve of her hips. She was his own *bean bhàsail*, with seductive creamy thighs and pearly skin. That she did not know it made her all the more dangerous to his soul.

Hamish let his finger drift lower, along her throat, through the valley of her breasts and then splayed his hand across her flat stomach. He could not get enough of her.

The more he touched, the more he needed. She took his breath away.

"I think of you constantly." His breath was uneven with wanting her, needing her, burning for her, and knowing that he no longer had to fight his ever-growing desire.

Then, unable to delay another moment, he leaned down and pressed his lips to hers. Mairead moaned and tilted into his embrace. He knew that she was gifting him with her body to show her undying love and devotion. It stirred something within him, something primal and his mouth became aggressive and more possessive.

Mairead was caught in a whirlwind of emotion and sensation. His kiss made her feel desired, beautiful, and more cherished than she could even describe. Her breath quickened and her breasts heaved in expectation with the increased fervor of his kiss. The outside storm also grew in intensity. The downpour's rhythm created one in Mairead and she wrapped her arms tightly around Hamish, kissing him and whispering her love.

Hamish's hands moved over her urgently. He needed to touch every part of her, to feel her crushed against his body and the soft fullness of her breasts against his chest. Mairead was so soft. Soft and sweet and vulnerable. And she offered herself without reserve.

He covered her body with his, bringing them slowly into full contact, and she moaned in pleasure. He once more aggressively claimed her lips as her hands skimmed over his large frame, pausing periodically to massage and pull him closer. It was as if she wanted to touch him and explore his body as he was doing with hers. Never had he felt this much desire, this much longing and need from a woman.

Hamish caressed her shoulders in fluid strokes, tracing the contours of her breasts, her ribs, and her belly. He allowed his hands to linger, cradling her breasts as he tore his mouth away and began to press hot kisses down the column of her neck. Unhurried, he moved down the curve of her throat, tracing her collarbone and bending lower.

A tremor started between her heated thighs and Mairead arched her back, desperate for his touch.

Her body curved toward him and Hamish smiled with satisfaction. She writhed as he delayed addressing her soft pleas, letting his fingers tease, pinch, massage, and stroke her breasts into a delirium. Then, unable to wait any longer, he licked one tight nipple, curling his tongue about it before drawing it into his mouth.

Mairead cried out softly and closed her eyes. He suckled, deep and deeper, eliciting sounds of pleasure and pain. Her breathing became erratic as undefinable sensations caused by his mouth and tongue coursed through her.

With a last flick of his tongue, Hamish shifted to her other breast, leaving his hand to continue the sensual on-slaught as his mouth devoured her other peak.

Mairead clung to him. Heat was radiating from his skin. A hot tide of passion raged through them both as he continued to suckle while his hand began to slide lower.

His hand trailed down her stomach and Hamish pulled away to look at her. His hand found her soft curls and then, with a low, husky groan, he closed his fingers pos-sessively over her. Mairead gasped and he was more than gratified at the sight before him. Her entire face was flushed, her mouth swollen, and her eyes were heavy with passion.

Then he touched her, exploring her with a deliberate possessiveness that made Mairead quiver. She was burn-ing, hot silk in his arms—her body pliant, liquid heat. Another shudder went through her as he slipped a seeking finger inside her. He went lower still and dizziness swept over her as he found the sensitive flesh just below her soft, wet channel. There he drew an exquisite little pattern that nearly drove her over the edge.

Mairead closed her eyes and clung to his shoulders as he introduced another finger into her, crying out as he began to slowly separate his fingers, stretching her gently. He seemed to know exactly where to touch her, how lightly, how slowly, how deeply. She moaned as he dove deeper. He stroked her into ever-growing flames. Her body was on the precipice. She wanted more of him inside her and lifted her hips against his hand.

Hamish smiled a satisfied, possessive smile. He was so hard he hurt, and his imagination was going wild, thinking of all the things he'd like to do to her. But seeing her writhe wild beneath him was worth the wait.

With his knee, he urged her thighs wider. As slowly as he could manage, he settled himself in between and lifted her hips. She was slick with need, hot, tight, and velvet soft. He could wait no longer and began to penetrate.

He struggled against his need to thrust deep and hard. Mairead needed slow and gentle. Her eyes had closed tight.

"Put your legs around me." He groaned the instruction. His face fell against her neck. When he felt her move to obey him, he plunged forward. Mairead cried out in pain and he shouted in pleasure.

Her body was made for his. Tight. Hot. Silken. He never wanted this feeling of euphoria to end. He only wanted to bury himself deeper into Mairead, and for her to feel as consumed by him as he was by her. But her body needed an opportunity to adjust to his size.

With painful control, Hamish kept still and kissed her gently. "The pain will soon be gone," he assured her, kissing away her tears, "and when it is, I promise to give you more pleasure than you have ever known."

Mairead had thought she had been prepared for him. She had seen him. She had known he was big, and she had even known there would be pain, but she had not realized that entering her would be so excruciating. Tears formed in her eyes. She was not sure she could endure a future of this.

Hamish began to move and Mairead resisted, fearing more pain. But as he moved the ache began to dissolve into the pleasure just as he had promised. Mairead felt him opening her, stretching her, making a place for himself in the very heart of her. His size and length were no longer to be feared, but welcomed. She arched her hips causing him to fill her completely.

Fully inside her, Hamish threw his head back. His eyes were shut tightly, teeth clenched, and a sharp groan escaped his throat. Slowly, afraid to hurt her again, he eased out and back in, trying to keep himself from bucking too hard.

Now that her body was adjusting, Mairead did not want him to move slowly. Her desire was strumming and rapacious. She became insistent, impatient, and began to set her own pace.

Hamish tried to calm her with kisses and caresses. If she didn't relax, he was going to climax before he brought her pleasure. And he had vowed she would know ecstasy the first time she lay in his arms. "Mairead, you must slow . . ."

"No, no, no . . . I can't." Mairead rebelled at his delay, wanting it all.

His body began to cave to her demands. Moving within her, he thrust again, increasing with speed, plunging harder, grunting with the effort. Mairead moaned long and low, digging her nails into his back, her ankles gripping his buttocks and pulling him deeper within her.

Hamish basked in the exquisite feel of her soft flesh completely surrounding him. It was even better than he had imagined. Mairead's eyes were half closed. Her legs were around his back, drawing him in farther as he immersed himself in the feel of her soft, warm body. He leaned down and claimed her mouth.

How he had longed for this moment; he almost could not believe this was real. Moans escaped her beautiful lips. This was how it was meant to be between a husband and a wife. He finally had found what he had seen been given to McTiernay brother after McTiernay brother. He had a woman who loved him—fully and unconditionally.

Hamish caught her hips in his hands and set a faster rhythm, using hard, sure strokes that drove deeper and deeper. As his pace increased, she matched him, raising her hips to his every thrust. Then suddenly Mairead gasped and then cried out, bowing her neck back, her hands curled into tight fists. Every muscle in her clenched and unclenched in small spasms.

Her soft cries of sensual fulfillment were the most incredibly exciting sounds Hamish had ever heard. He could no longer pace himself. The small convulsions squeezed him demandingly. "Mairead!" He barely heard his own muffled, exultant shout. His body surged deeply into hers one last time and then he was erupting inside her.

Mairead clung to him. Her mind was overwhelmed with new, erotic sensations flooding her body. But she knew one thing.

Hamish was hers.

From this moment forward, he belonged to her just as surely as she belonged to him.

* * *

Hamish slumped on top of her, holding himself up by his elbows so as not to crush her. They struggled to catch their breath. Mairead's legs were still wrapped around him, her hands rubbing his arms, his chest, and his back. He rolled to lie beside her and pulled her against him. He could not get enough of her touching him.

She nuzzled her face into the crook of his neck as their legs intertwined. "I love you," she murmured with a sigh against his chest.

Hamish closed his eyes. "I thought about what it would be like with you every night since I first laid eyes on you. But I had no idea," he murmured.

Mairead smiled. She had hoped for words of love, but though she received none, she had no doubt of his feelings. Hamish loved her and someday he would no longer fear saying so. Until then, she would listen to what he did.

Hamish tucked her head underneath his chin and held her close. He was close to tears and did not want Mairead to know. He finally understood what Conor had been telling him about Laurel. If something pulled him and Mairead apart, Hamish would become a shell of a man, uncaring of anything and potentially dangerous to everyone.

He had not been numb for all those months from a broken heart. It had been frustration, wounded pride, a feeling of hopelessness that had caused him to shut down emotionally. But he had never once had a broken heart. He knew that now because he had never really loved anyone before. And he loved Mairead. With all his soul. And yet it scared him to think, let alone whisper the word. Nothing good had ever come from his saying it aloud, but he silently vowed to show her his love. He would be good to her, keep her safe and make such sweet love to her that thoughts of ever leaving him would never enter her mind.

Mairead raised her hand and stroked the line of his jaw, caressing the soft growth. Her hazel eyes locked on his, a faint smile touching her mouth. "What are you thinking about?"

Hamish propped himself on an elbow and looked down at her. He did not want her to know how vulnerable he felt and bent his head to kiss her. Two small fingers stopped him. "Was it Robert?"

"Aye," he lied, only somewhat relieved that for once she had not guessed the truth to what he was thinking.

Mairead shifted to her side and reached out to caress his dimple. "I know the reasons behind your desire to keep your army secret, but at some point we really do need to explain your plan to Robert and Selah."

Hamish caught her hand and slowly kissed her fingers. "You still as of yet don't know my plan."

Mairead frowned and tugged her fingers free from his grasp. She suddenly realized he was correct. She saw several men training, most of whom looked skilled, but using them went against the bloodshed he warned her about. If he had any army, it was for a purpose beyond what she considered and she very much wanted to demand he tell her what that was. They were husband and wife.

The challenging gleam in Hamish's eyes silenced her demands. He fully expected her to plead for an explanation. Well, she refused to. She would not give him the satisfaction. She now had the luxury of trusting Hamish and she was going to do just that.

Well, for as long as she could.

"What if Ulrick comes after them?"

Hamish twitched his lips. "He won't." He was going to make sure that Ulrick came after him. And Hamish looked forward to it.

"Then, is it a long-lasting solution? Will it prevent someone else from trying what Ulrick has planned?"

Hamish grimaced and fell back onto the bed. He lifted his arm and rested the back of his wrist on his forehead. "The army will give my brother the means to protect himself and Foinaven, but if he chooses to wield them poorly, then . . . no. Robert must protect this clan. Nothing I leave with him—not even an army—can do it without his leadership. And I cannot predict what he will do once we are gone."

"Aye, you can."

"And so can you," Hamish replied with a note of finality, for they both knew the truth. "There are always those seeking power and it will not be long before Robert's weaknesses are exploited."

"*You* wouldn't be exploited."

Hamish sighed heavily. "No one is infallible. But I prefer to handle things the McTiernay way. Anyone who tried to destroy them, their reputation or their clan, would most likely die in the attempt. Everyone knows this, so no one tries."

Mairead bit her lower lip. "Perhaps, with the men you have gathered, no one will try against Robert."

Hamish brushed his hand roughly over his face. "It takes more than just men, Mairead. Just as there are ways to effectively use a weapon, there are rules when dealing with those who oppose you." Mairead tipped her head to one side, her hair falling in a slide over one shoulder. He tucked it back behind her ear and studied her expression. Her interest was earnest, prompting him to continue.

"First, never show your true emotions to your enemies. Keep them guessing about what you are thinking, and you'll have the upper hand. Next is stability. An inconsistent leader lacks control. Anything out of control is considered weak. Therefore, when confronted, a leader needs to appear to have the situation under control, even if they don't."

"Is that all?" she asked, bending down to kiss his right dimple and then his left. "Just the two rules?"

Hamish caught the mischievous glow in Mairead's eyes. She moved against him provocatively and he knew instantly that she was questioning his own ability to remain in control. He grinned at her and began speaking, implicitly accepting her dare. "When confronting an opponent, there are two more basic ones."

Mairead leaned over and whispered, "Go on. I'm listening." She began to nibble on his ear and he felt his exhausted body flare back to life. "One must also, uh, be aware of their surroundings and, um, remain cautious at all times. One should not feel safe"—swallow—"because those around them tell them that they are. A . . . a good strategist follows, uh, their instincts and, uh, anticipates situations and their consequences. If at all possible, one should never face an unknown."

"Makes sense," Mairead murmured, dipping down to kiss his chin, then shoulder and chest.

Her hands were everywhere, working their magic, soft and hypnotic, but Hamish refused to let her win. "And then, um, last," he grunted, and then moved over her in a single fluid move. "When dealing with someone—even allies—never let them believe they are smarter or know more about what is going on."

"Dealing with *someone*," she repeated teasingly, and rose up to kiss his chin. "Does that include your wife?"

His *wife*. How much Hamish enjoyed hearing her say that. It was time he proved again that was exactly what she was. His. Forever. His mouth came down on hers for a long, soul-searing kiss.

When he finally freed her lips, Mairead smiled blissfully up at him. "You think like a McTiernay and not a MacBrieve."

Hamish returned her grin with a wicked, sexy one of his own. "How would you know?" he asked, catching her wrists, holding them beside her head. "You have never met one."

"I disagree." Undaunted, Mairead pulled up and recaptured his mouth with her own. Hamish complied and ravished her with his lips and tongue. "Not only have I met a McTiernay," she murmured, when he finally released her, "I married one."

Hamish cocked his head to the side. "Perhaps. I've always felt more like a McTiernay than a MacBrieve. Robert is the tinker, the builder, the mason—not me."

"And perhaps for the good of the clan that is all he should be, Hamish."

Hamish knew what Mairead was hinting at. She wanted to stay at Foinaven. "Mairead . . ."

She put a finger to his lips. "Not to protect us. Ulrick is a short-term difficulty that I know you will address. Nor do I want you to stay as commander. But as laird, there are many clan problems you could fix. These are *your* people, Hamish, and they need you. Not a leader unwilling to make the hard choices."

Hamish closed his eyes and touched his forehead to hers. She was asking him to overthrow Robert. It did not matter that it was supposed to be his. He had given it up and now had another life—a good life—with the McTiernays. "I thought you understood."

Mairead blinked up at him. She saw his frown and his

warring thoughts. She knew that it was not just loyalty, or
a desire to protect Foinaven and its people, that had caused
Hamish to invest so much of himself the past couple of
weeks. He had an innate desire to lead his people. He just
did not know how to do so without hurting his brother
and her sister.

Unfortunately, neither did she.

"I love you and I will always support you."

Hamish swallowed. The way Mairead looked at him
turned his heart over, melting his every resistance. "Do
not ever leave me, *m'aingeal*," he said, almost choking on
the words, releasing her wrist to cup her cheek.

"Never," she vowed. "I will be with you always."

The green and gold of her eyes swirled with passion.
For a moment Hamish was held spellbound. What he felt
for her was far more consuming than anything one simple
word conveyed. Being with Mairead was not the sweet,
longing romance he had been seeking all his life. It held
much greater power. The kind that could build and destroy,
that could drive a man to succeed or lead him to failure.
His heart swelled with the sheer enormity of it all—of his
love for her and the endless possibilities of their future
together.

He lowered his head and captured her lips in a long,
gradual kiss that contradicted the raging need building
below his waist. Her lips met his gently, searching, seeking, and welcoming him without question and without
reservation. The barriers of his control fractured and the
kiss went from tender and reverent, filled with gentle
emotions, to one of fierce need. He deepened their kiss
and lay more of his weight on top of her. His hands mem-
orized every inch of her as he feasted on her lush mouth.

Mairead made love to him with unrestrained enthusiasm and after they regained their strength, he once again

brought her to the heavens. When he at last drifted off to sleep, listening to the rain finally begin to ease, her body was draped over his in the most gratifying way. One leg was entwined with one of his. Her arm was folded over his chest, and her head rested atop his shoulder with her dark gold hair fanned out behind her.

His last thoughts were that he had found heaven.

Chapter Fourteen

Hamish waited for Robert to speak. His brother had taken the news of his and Mairead's union as expected, with mixed emotions. He had been pleased that Hamish and Mairead had finally "yielded and done what was right." But he was also disappointed that they had done so alone and without witnesses. Mostly because Selah was going to be upset that there had been no ceremony, no celebration, and most of all—she had not been there. But Robert had yet to say anything about his feelings on the army Hamish had pulled together.

Robert coughed into his hand and considered his words carefully. His voice was still a little raspy, but he no longer sounded as if he were gasping for air. He was dressed, out of bed, and ready to be more active in clan affairs, but Selah had made it clear how much she hated the idea of his leaving the keep. Thankfully, he was regaining his strength quickly and would soon be able to take on all his responsibilities—including this unexpected army of Hamish's. "We agreed there would be no bloodshed."

"And I have no plans for any. But to appear weak to Ulrick would give you no leverage in your negotiations."

Robert frowned and rubbed his head. "Seeing you, with all those men, might incite Ulrick into battle, not discussions. Aggression is not always the answer. A peaceful path might be the best way to achieve what we all desire. Ulrick will not fight unless he thinks he must. We must show him that is not his only option."

Hamish hung his head and curled his fingers into fists. He could not believe what he was hearing, though he knew he shouldn't be surprised. His brother truly thought that a display of strength was a type of weakness. Robert would rather bow and kiss the hand of the enemy in the misguided idea that it built trust and goodwill, when to men like Hamish, it just made him look weak, foolish, and ripe for attack.

"If you wanted a puppet to do your bidding then I can point you to one or two of your guard. They are more than capable of helping you with this peaceful strategy of yours. Meanwhile, Mairead and I will say our good-byes and wish you luck."

Robert scowled at the sharp rebuke. "Don't threaten me, Hamish, just because I am acting like the leader you want me to be and making decisions you don't like."

"I don't mean it as a threat, Robert, but a warning. I've been told what Ulrick said to Mairead. You may ignore the risk your *decision* poses to Selah and your son, but I will *not* stay and put my wife in danger because you refuse to accept the truth. I wish you were right and that the world did not need weapons or deadly soldiers with my skills and experience, but that is not reality. Pretending otherwise is not just unwise, but as a leader it puts innocent lives in danger. Lives beyond that of your family and you are sworn to protect them as their leader. Without the willingness to *fight*, the peace you seek will only result in tyranny. All because of a foolish belief that the best response to someone who clearly seeks war is placation. You claim to be these people's leader, Robert. So *lead*! At the very least, let me do what I know to do to keep them safe and defend them against Ulrick. But the plan should not begin and end with a plea for peace."

"But neither should it discount it!" Robert argued back just as vociferously.

"Of course not!" Hamish agreed. "Negotiation and a peaceful resolution should always be the objective, but you refuse to prepare for the alternative!"

Robert's dark green eyes locked with Hamish's own deep green pools. Both swirled with an almost palpable intensity. "You don't want to be just prepared, Hamish. You want to flaunt it. You want Ulrick to be well aware of the strength he faces. That blatant show of aggression is *exactly* what I'm against."

"You see it as aggression, Robert, when to all others it is a display of strength. And not just enemies use perceived weaknesses against their foes—but allies, friends, and even those who you consider to be most loyal would take your peaceful stance and use it to their advantage when the time is right." Hamish's voice dropped dangerously low. "And it is usually those closest who inflict the most damage, because one never expects their weakness to be used against them by someone they trust."

"That is your world, Hamish, where fighting is a norm. We are far north, away from the conflicts you see in your part of the Highlands."

"What about the Mackays?" he barked. "And the Keiths, Rosses, Gunns, and Sinclairs? They live and fight all around you! Even the Sutherlands participate in endless battles."

"They ignore us because we pose no threat," Robert said smugly.

"They ignore you because you have a stone castle and assume you are like our father," Hamish countered. "But things would be different if they knew your castle had no *gate*." His tone was one of disgust.

"You and Father are so driven by war and defense. He wanted a gate as well but died before Foinaven was completed. I opted not to see that part of his vision."

Hamish inhaled sharply. "Father would have *never* left Foinaven to you if he knew that you would go against his wishes in such a way."

"*Father* gave me nothing. *Menzies MacMhathain* did when he died and I married Selah."

Hamish balled his fists. Menzies had not bequeathed *Robert* Foinaven through his daughter. Robert had not even fought in the deadly battle. It had been *he* who had held the dying man's hand and made a promise to marry his daughter in order to protect his people. But it was too late to change things back to the way Menzies and his father had intended.

Robert was not finished. "And you are wrong about Father. Before he died, I made a vow to him to lead these people and do what I thought was best and right for them. And I have done just that. I made Foinaven a safe haven for *all*—not just for some—by making other clans feel welcomed, not giving them a reason to fear us. And time has proven the validity of my approach. We have not been attacked; we have *grown*."

"I understand the importance of inviting the needy and giving them shelter and opportunity. *Murt!* Conor Mc-Tiernay gave that to me twelve years ago and I am grateful every day. But what you speak of is unnatural growth that imports ideas and cultures. These clans you opened your arms to are not personally invested in everyone's welfare. Without that investment, there is only a false sense of loyalty. The moment Foinaven no longer gives them what they seek, they will turn and flee somewhere else for a better situation. They will not fight because they consider nothing theirs. This is not their clan. They do not wear the MacBrieve tartan. And this castle is simply a place. I may be a MacBrieve by birth and I kept the name to honor my father, but when I am with the McTiernays, I proudly wear their tartan, displaying to all that I am not just there, I am *with* them."

Robert was not swayed. "You were not here, Hamish, for the winters, for the illnesses that came, the bad harvests. These people *have* had hard times and they did not leave. You make assumptions and assume the worst."

Hamish speared his hand through his hair, a frown creasing his forehead. "Perhaps you are right, Robert. I should have more faith in people. Perhaps these people do see themselves as a unit and not separate entities, but if that is so, then they have even more of a right to be protected and not have their futures jeopardized the way you are planning."

Robert threw his hands in the air. "Then do it! Tell the guard to return to their farms, their previous lives, and replace them with this new army of yours. Declare to the whole world that you are here and Foinaven is a fortress of doom and death for whoever dares to attack it!"

Hamish slammed his fist on a nearby table, causing it to rattle. "I am not laird here, Robert! You are!"

"Then you have heard my decision."

Hamish glared at his younger brother. Five dozen fighting men might protect Robert and his family against Ulrick, but soon afterward it would dissolve and his brother would be vulnerable again. If Robert was going to truly protect this clan, it would take a fundamental shift in his thinking, which was unlikely from ever happening.

"And you have heard mine," Hamish said coldly. He turned and left. He headed straight for the stables, giving word to Adiran to tell Mairead that he would be back most likely after nightfall.

Meanwhile, Robert sank into one of his chairs and warmed his hands by the fire. A minute later, Selah stepped in, visibly rattled.

"Sit, my love. All is well."

"It did not *sound* well."

Robert grinned at her, but the smile was not reflected in his eyes. "It was not supposed to."

"Is Rab really in danger?"

Robert closed his eyes and sighed. He would not lie to his wife. "Aye, as are you, but only if my plan falls through and Hamish leaves."

"And if he does?"

He opened his eyes and stared into her large, hazel orbs. He had been drowning in those compassionate pools since he had first seen them. "Then you and Rab will go with Hamish while I stay and do what must be done." She was about to argue and he grabbed her hand. "It *won't* come to that, Selah. Hamish *will* stay. You will see."

"I hope you are right about all this."

"I was right about Maircad and Hamish."

Selah sighed and tilted her head slightly in acknowledgment. "True, but that was easy to predict after seeing them argue that one night."

"But who was the one who told them to stay away from each other?" Robert prompted, a note of pride in his voice. "It was a stroke of genius for getting together two of the most stubborn people this world has ever seen."

"What about now? Are you still so assured of your genius?"

"When it comes to Hamish?" Robert's voice no longer held the confidence from just a moment ago. "I know in my heart that I must stay the course," he said softly, grabbing her hand for reassurance. "I truly believe that negotiations are the way to handle conflict."

"As do I." Selah's voice was soft and supportive, as it always was. "I also know that you have your doubts."

Robert nodded. "I have long been plagued by them."

Selah leaned over and kissed him softly on his cheek. "*That* is why your plan is the right one."

Robert smiled, this time more sincerely. "We will see."

"When Hamish and you were talking, Mairead and I were just across the hall."

"She heard the whole thing?" Robert asked.

Selah nodded. "The *whole* thing."

Robert chuckled. He suddenly felt much better. "Then very soon it should get real interesting."

Mairead sat in her chambers in front of the fire, glad to have a chair once again. She had had another one from the great hall brought up for Hamish. She had thought he would insist on staying on the bottom floor, but he had simply shrugged and said, "It served its purpose. Besides, your bed is much bigger."

Hamish entered the room and watched Mairead tug a brush through her hair, causing the waves to glisten. He could see the action was not one with the goal of removing tangles, but as a way of releasing frustration. They had been married for only a day, but he knew that asking her what was wrong would be pointless. His wife would speak about what was bothering her when she was ready.

Mairead waited until Hamish had unbelted his plaid, removed his shoes, and sat down beside her. She had undressed earlier, but feeling exposed just sitting in her chemise, she stood and donned a robe. She was glad for she saw a gleam in his eye when she turned back around and she did not need him to be distracted right now. They needed to talk.

"I cannot believe you allowed Robert to make the final decision on how to handle Ulrick." Mairead waited for a response, but Hamish just sat there, refusing to defend his actions. "You *know* that your brother is completely out of his depth. He knows nothing about dealing with the man he will be facing. Allowing him to dictate how to handle Ulrick's return goes against everything you told me last night. The safety of my sister, our nephew, and many innocent people are depending on you, for only *you* know what to do," she lamented.

"Your trust in me seems to have vanished quite quickly," he snarled. Mairead sucked in her breath sharply. His tone was one of anger, but his eyes were wounded. Her accusations had hurt him deeply. "This world is harsh, but my *responsibility* is not to Foinaven or its people, but to *you*. I exhausted what little obligation I had to Robert when I told him of the danger he is in and then gave him a way to not only handle Ulrick but ensure the security of his family and this clan in the future. Robert chose another path. He knew what that meant and so do you."

Mairead shook her head in disbelief. "But we cannot leave."

Hamish's jaw twitched, refusing to be dissuaded. "The

men I pulled together will ensure your sister's safety from Ulrick far more than your continued presence."

"I did not mean that."

"I'm not staying, Mairead. I am a commander with a brother who refuses to let me command."

"You are right." Her voice was hesitant, as she chose her words carefully. "You cannot stay as a commander, but there *is* another choice. You have come to know these people. You know more than anything they desperately want a leader and already look to you as such. How can we leave knowing that? How can you?"

Hamish's eyes darkened dangerously. "I made that decision twelve years ago and you made yours last night. When I go, you go." He took deep, slow breaths and stared at her, his eyes arctic cold. He believed she was on the verge of breaking her promise. "You vowed to stay with me."

Mairead immediately moved from her chair and knelt in front of him. She gathered his hands in hers and squeezed. "If you leave, Hamish, have no doubt that I will be at your side. I chose you and I always will choose you. But I also know that leaving is not the only choice you have. Not when there is another way." Her lashes fluttered against a sudden spurt of tears. Mairead hated arguing with him but some things had to be said. "I love Robert. I do. But he never earned the title of laird and to leave knowing *your* own clansmen deserved and wanted better—it is akin to running away."

"You think I ran away twelve years ago?" he spat, rising to his feet to pace in front of her.

"No!" Mairead denied vehemently. "I never believed that. But when you left then, it was not as it would be now. Twelve years ago, your father was alive. He knew how to be a leader and keep the clan safe. And as much as you may want to, you cannot abandon these people—and a brother and nephew you love—when you know the danger that is coming."

Hamish's mouth was a firm, unyielding line. To most, it spoke of a total lack of emotion, but Mairead got just the opposite impression. Hamish had heard her and he was thinking.

"Do you truly comprehend what you are asking me to do, to not just my brother but your sister and their son? This is their *home*. To take that away could tear us apart as a family. Can you live with that outcome? Are you really willing to risk never talking to your sister again on the chance that I might be a better leader?"

"Aye, but I hope it would not be like that," she whispered. Mairead looked away. She pulled her knees to her chest as tears flowed down her cheeks and gave him a yearning glance from under her long lashes. "Why does there have to be only two options—stay and replace Robert or leave? When I thought you had no plans at all, you said you had several. Contingencies for contingencies. Is there really no way you can work with Robert?"

Hamish studied the flames in the fireplace, contemplating her question. He had been so frustrated with Robert, then so surprised by Mairead's insistence on their staying that he had instinctively resisted, shutting down all other possibilities. But McTiernays never had only a single strategy to winning a battle and neither did he. He *had* created options soon after his arrival and even put some of them into play for just such a situation.

Hamish pulled Mairead to her feet. "Aye. There are other options. Even one that would allow me to do what I was originally planning while playing to Robert's sensibilities."

Mairead threw her arms around Hamish and fastened her mouth on his. "I knew it," she said full of the unwavering faith that she had in him. "I never stopped trusting you. I just needed to help you to remember to trust yourself."

A slow smile curved Hamish's mouth. "Trust myself?"

Mairead nodded her head and then laid it on his chest. Hamish may believe otherwise, but she knew if they stayed, there could still be those consequences he warned her about. And while they were for the benefit of all, she hated the pain they might cause. She just prayed that by the time Ulrick arrived, Robert finally would be ready to actually lead the clan. For the same honor that forced Hamish to leave twelve years ago could also bind him to Foinaven forever.

She just prayed Hamish did not hate her for it.

She felt him kiss her hair and looked up. He framed her face in his hands and kissed her tenderly. Soon fierce longing and desire began to build within them both.

Hamish pulled away and smiled. His eyes were sparkling with promised passion. "You know," he drawled, "I didn't just learn strategies and plans from the Mc-Tiernays."

Her eyes returned his twinkle with a mischievous one of her own as her fingers ran up his leg, taking his leine with them. "They weren't?"

He shook his head. His face brimmed with anticipation. "I learned that the best part of fighting is the making up."

Selah curled up next to Robert's side in bed. It felt so good to lie next to him. He was almost completely well and growing stronger every day. It was nice to lean on him again. She needed him, right now more than ever. He had a plan, but this part of it was causing her anxiety to once again grow.

"They've finally stopped fighting," she whispered. The whole keep had been able to hear Mairead and Hamish argue with each other. She and Robert had disagreed over the years, but not on the second day of their marriage and *never* had they raised their voices to such levels. She had been afraid what little Rab might think if he awoke, but Noma assured her that he was blissfully unaware of the anger waging so close to him.

"That means they are making up," Robert offered in an attempt to comfort his wife's fears.

"What if you are wrong? Maybe one of them left."

"We would have heard the door slam shut," he teased.

His attempt at banter did not mollify her. "There was so much anger," Selah mused solemnly. "I know you expected it given their personalities, but Robert." She paused rising to one elbow to look down at him. "Is it moral to use such means even if our intentions are for the greater good?"

"In this case, aye, it is," he reassured her.

"I just wonder if our personal plans are worth making Hamish and Mairead so unhappy."

"We are not doing this for just you, me, and Rab, but for everyone—including my brother and your sister." Robert's voice held no doubt. Neither did his eyes as they gazed up at her. Selah nodded and lay back down. "Twelve years ago Hamish may have believed he knew what was best for my happiness, but I was not a lad when he left and I sure as hell am not one now. I've had a lot of time to think and plan and design a solution to our family's problem." He caressed her cheek. "You know there is no one better at designing something and making it come to life."

"True," Selah acknowledged. Robert could see things as he wanted them to be and somehow make it transpire.

But this was not mason work. This was people's lives. And he was trying to help his older brother, who had no faith in him as a leader, negotiator, or tactician. "Hamish believes you are a fool."

Robert chuckled. "That is fine. We can disagree. It changes nothing."

"You stake much on your memory of Hamish. He has changed."

"Time changes all of us, love, but we need not be worried that Hamish has changed in the way you fear. He has been living with the McTiernays." He bent his head and kissed her hair. "Everyone is born with gifts. Your kindness gives comfort to even the most damaged soul. I create and build, and Hamish . . . he just has a way with people. Since we were young he always knew the right thing to do. He recognized when to come on strong and when to back off. When to get involved and when to just stay out of things. It is only the emotions of what happened twelve years ago that prejudice his judgment. Soon he will be faced with a decision. He will know what he must do."

"Why can you not announce how much you hate being laird? Just tell Hamish that it is his responsibility as it should have been and let him do what he wants with Ulrick and his army."

"I wish it were that simple." Robert squeezed her arm, in light admonishment. "For I would have done that long ago if that was all it took for Hamish to take over. But knowing my brother, he would refuse. And even if I am wrong and Hamish accepted the responsibility, he would always doubt himself and the reasons he was laird. Hamish may think other clans and power-seeking men are the ones to watch for, but from my experience, doubt is a leader's biggest enemy. It eats away at you and cripples your ability to make decisions. That is why I cannot just give this responsibility to Hamish, for it is not mine to give. It is his. It always has been. He was a born leader and he was always meant to have this role. Hamish just needs a little more time to believe it for himself."

Chapter Fifteen

Hamish stood looking out a window in the great hall, observing all the activity happening across the courtyard. Massive, long, thick logs of wood were coming into the courtyard and Robert was directing where they were going as well as ensuring nothing got smashed before they got there. One log teetered and Robert barked an order. Several men scattered into action as a result.

His brother was a different man when in his element. Unlike his actions as a laird, when working as a master mason, Robert had confidence and felt completely comfortable taking charge of those around him.

When he had come to Robert a week ago about building a protected path from the gate to the tower, he had been prepared for another argument. But Robert had just asked a couple of questions. Would there be a portcullis? No. Was Hamish asking to fortify the gate? Aye, the desire was there, but no, not if Robert did not wish it. All Hamish wanted was a protected path built out of stone that led from the gate to one of the main tower's two entrances. It needed to be wide enough to allow a large group and strong enough that it would not crumble if struck repeatedly. The tower had been built for massive storage and both its doors were wide enough for carts to drive through. Those at Foinaven could still enter and leave without restriction, but the walls directed their path, enabling one to better control the flow of traffic and observe who was coming and going. Understanding that, *and* learning that Hamish had already seen to it that the rocks had been gathered and were waiting in large piles by the gate, Robert had readily agreed.

By that afternoon, he had not only selected several men to start working on the walls, but he had changed the plans to make them a tunnel. Hamish had been concerned about time, as he was worried that it would not be completed before Ulrick's return, but Robert casually dismissed his fear. The fastest solid stone castle ever erected had just taken fifteen months. While uncommon, an entire solid stone tower could be and had been built in two weeks. A simple stone passageway would take far less than that.

Hamish had been foolish to doubt his brother. The weather had been favorable and it had rained heavily only once; Robert had taken advantage of their good fortune. When it came to masonry, Robert's placating manner was nonexistent. He knew what he was doing and demanded those working for him performed to his specifications and quickly As a result, the tunnel was going up much faster than Hamish would have thought.

From outside Foinaven, nothing looked different. But when the gate was open, no longer could people just enter and amble in any direction. Within three days, thick walls had been erected and they had withstood the tests Amon and Davros devised. They themselves pounded on the walls and even got several men to join them, to see if they would tumble. Robert had done nothing to stop them and there was a reason why. Not a rock moved. That was when he told Hamish that he was not done. The passageway was going to be covered with an arched stone roof.

Hamish had thought such an endeavor unnecessary and feared it might collapse, but Robert countered with all the benefits a roof provided. If left unprotected to the weather, the walkway would collect water and take several days to dry out. With enough rain, like the kind they endured during winter, the path between the gate and the tower would oftentimes become unpassable. Hamish believed him but also worried that it would take too long. Robert assured Hamish that he could have it done by Candlemas and now, seeing parts of it take shape, Hamish vowed not to doubt his brother again.

Robert barked another order and Hamish shook his head in bewilderment. He left the window and exited the hall. He had moved around some barrels and several huge logs when he bumped into Selah.

She beamed at him. "Robert's over that way," she said, gesturing in the direction he already knew his brother to be. "Please tell him I love him, but I must be off." Before he knew it, she had darted around him, stating something over her shoulder about needing to find Mairead.

Hamish continued toward his brother, staggered once again how so much had changed so quickly. A happier Robert meant a happier Selah. She was incredibly proud that her husband was getting to show off his skills and had hinted more than once that when Hamish had left twelve years ago, he might have given up a lot, but so had Robert. That both brothers were very much alike.

Hamish just wished that a happier Selah made for a happier Mairead. Every night, in the privacy of their bedroom, his wife grumbled that while he, his brother, and her sister might be delighted with all their plans, she was not.

Unlike Robert, Selah had not undergone any similar miraculous transformation. Her older sister still refused to hear anything that she did not like and Selah had decided that Mairead and Hamish needed to marry for a second time. She did not care that they already considered themselves bound together in the eyes of the Lord. There was going to be another ceremony and while a priest was not available to preside over it, there at least *would* be witnesses. More specifically, her!

Mairead did not want the ceremony. She had thought it unnecessary and had looked to Hamish to stop the proceeding, but he had been—and still was—fully in favor of the idea.

Hamish welcomed the idea of proclaiming Mairead as his wife to all. He did not want any doubt that she was his and had said so one night at dinner, which only encouraged Selah and her efforts. He had no idea those efforts would collide so violently with Mairead's preferences. Hamish was still not sure exactly what the problem was. Something about Selah's ideas on the vows and her dress—things that were rather unimportant. He still felt being upset about such stuff to be inane, but he had learned the hard way to keep that opinion to himself.

Hamish reached the construction area and went to stand by Robert. "I honestly thought you were aiming for the impossible when you said this would be done by Candlemas."

Robert shaded his eyes and watched as the men carefully laid the stones down where he instructed. "Two more days I think," he said, his gaze never leaving the work. "That gives us a day to spare." The men went to get more material and Robert shifted his gaze to Hamish. "It would never have been possible if you had not ordered those lads to gather up all those rocks. I must admit that I was surprised when one of them informed me that I had been paying them to do so."

Hamish shrugged unapologetically. "I knew you would need them. If not for this, then for repairs. There are several places that could use your attention."

Robert nodded in agreement. "It has been so long since I have done this work, I forgot how much I enjoyed it. It was hard . . . really hard . . . when the castle was completed. I think I avoided the repairs to spare myself the grief of seeing it end once again."

Hamish was surprised to hear longing in his brother's voice. Master mason was something few achieved, but it was a very hard job and the life was not a stable one. It required a willingness to continually uproot one's home and family. The idea of roaming the country and setting only temporary roots was for single men like Conan Mc-Tiernay. His brother had little Rab and Selah, and both required sheltering. He was fortunate to have Foinaven as his home. Still, Hamish knew what it was like to appreciate what one had and yet still long for more.

"What are those?" Hamish asked, pointing to several indentions in the walls.

"Ah, those," Robert said with a smile. "I may not like the idea of portcullises, but as a mason I cannot design a stone entrance structure and not plan for the day they may be needed."

Hamish walked along the wall, taking a long look. Robert had created two spots where a portcullis could be installed—one near the gate and one near the tower entrance. It would not be simple, but it could be done without dismantling a huge portion of the wall to do so.

Robert brought him inside the passageway, stepping around three men who were focused on reinforcing the tower door leading out into the courtyard. "Is this what you wanted?"

Hamish studied the door and nodded. The men were not done, but by the time they finished, it would not be easily broken through. Hamish wondered if Robert understood how all that he was doing was in direct contradiction with his concept of strength bringing violence, but was afraid to ask in case it prompted Robert to cease being cooperative. It was more than likely his brother knew of the contradictions and had just mentally pushed them aside, deciding to let his love of building temporarily displace his stance against aggression.

Robert craned his head to look up. Abe and Seamus had returned a couple more times to relieve their frustrations and now several holes about the size of a small platter were scattered along the ceiling. "You sure those don't need to be repaired?"

"You have enough to focus on. Besides, they provide light."

Robert rolled his eyes. He knew they served a purpose, but Hamish was right. He had enough to do and worry about if he was going to be finished by Candlemas. And he had to be, not for Hamish, but for Selah. He had promised her that all the village could come and witness the second handfasting of Hamish and Mairead. Selah wanted nothing to mar the day, and that included the noise and dirt from construction. Besides, the feast marked the midpoint of winter, halfway between the shortest day and the spring equinox end of winter. The next day nearly all his labor would be in the fields, preparing the land for first planting, and he would no longer be available to help.

They stepped back outside. The large, thick logs of wood were being stacked just outside the bakery, which was away from all the construction. "What is the lumber for?" Hamish asked. "Because it looks like they are building a bonfire."

Robert nodded. "One here and one on the other side as well. They are insurance." His brother produced a dimpled grin. "I doubt the rain will cooperate with us much longer and I've promised Selah this will be done by Candlemas. I cannot do anything about the rain, but I can create light when the sun goes down."

Hamish was secretly glad that Robert was so motivated for while he knew that his brother anticipated Ulrick to return mid-February, Hamish predicted the man would arrive much sooner. "Well, I will take no more of your time."

Robert gave him a brief nod of acknowledgment and went to go inspect what the men had done during his brief interruption. Hamish too had things to do. He returned to the keep and found his chambers unsurprisingly empty. He peered behind the door to grab his sword, but it was not there. He searched the room, looking anywhere Mairead might have moved it.

"Are you looking for this?"

Hamish spun around and saw Mairead with his sword. The tip was on the ground for it was too heavy for her to hold upright for any length of time. "Aye. Why do you have it?"

Mairead moved so that he could grasp the handle, relieving her from holding up its weight. "I have a better question. Why do you need it?"

"Why do you think?" he retorted.

Mairead gave him a light, painless punch in the arm. "I *knew* you were still training with the men."

"I never said that I would stop." His tone was slightly

defensive. "I only agreed that not all of them were needed to confront Ulrick. I promised to give Robert the opportunity to try to talk peacefully with the man and I intend to keep that promise."

Mairead jutted her chin to the window. "And what is the purpose of that then?"

Hamish closed his hand around the back of her neck and brought his mouth down to hers. He kissed her slowly, lingeringly and with deep possessiveness. "That," he said catching his breath, "is one of *your* contingencies."

Mairead blinked, her expression full of mock incomprehension. "I have no idea what you mean. I am sure that tunnel out there is not *my* idea, nor is it my brother-in-law's. I happen to know that it is the brilliant concept of my husband's."

Hamish bent down and gave her one more quick kiss and then opened the door. Just before he walked through, he turned back around. "Thank you."

This time Mairead truly was puzzled. "What for?"

"I always wanted to know what it felt like to be a Mc-Tiernay. Now I do."

"I still don't understand." Hamish had always been a leader, warrior, and a skilled strategist so it made no sense that he only just now thought he was like them. "You have always been one of them."

Hamish shook his head. "I was missing the one thing every truly successful McTiernay has." Those who spent time with the McTiernays did not remember them for their abilities with a sword, or even their skills at strategy and battle. What the McTiernay brothers were really known for were their feisty, beautiful, intelligent women. It had been the thing Hamish had envied the most.

Mairead put her hands on her hips and this time

prompted him in a voice that required a better explanation. "Which was . . ."

"You, Mairead. To be a true McTiernay, I need you."

Robert called for more ale and all the mugs in the small gathering to be refilled. "Tonight we will enjoy good company and friends, but tomorrow will be the real celebration. It will be a Candlemas like we have never had before. Davros and his men have brought us more than enough birds and game for the largest feast Foinaven has ever seen." He paused to nod to the falconer and his wife. "*And* the stone passageway is complete. On time, as promised, so that all may come in and join the festivities," he finished with a wink to his wife.

Hamish glanced at Amon, who only shared his slight grimace. "I'm not sure such a large crowd is a good idea. Perhaps we should minimalize the revelry."

Selah balked at the suggestion. "Absolutely not! This year's Candlemas will be the most memorable in Foinaven's history for you and Mairead are to be married!"

Mairead shook her head. "We already *are* married, Selah." She had been watching Hamish. He was visibly tense and it was clear that he was uncomfortable with another wedding ceremony. Mairead feared that by pressing for one, Selah was asking for more than Hamish was willing to give. He still had not admitted his feelings and Mairead worried that putting him through a ceremony where people would expect them to proclaim their love and devotion might push him away, not bring him closer.

Selah's jaw tensed. "Not with witnesses you weren't." Her voice was clipped and brokered no argument.

"Still, with such a large gathering, it makes it difficult to prepare for certain eventualities." Hamish did not want to damper the mood. He wished he could just relax and enjoy the celebration and the idea of announcing to the world that Mairead was his and his alone, but his gut was screaming caution.

Robert waved a dismissive hand. "Ulrick would not dare try anything untoward on a holy day."

Hamish knew otherwise. A day all were drinking and unprepared for an uprising was *exactly* the time he would dare to return.

Amon smiled at his friend. "*Two* ceremonies?" he whispered in an effort to lift Hamish's mood. "You must *really* be in love to be so eager to marry twice."

"I doubt I will have the chance," Hamish replied, keeping his voice low.

He wanted to ignore the possibilities, but he found he could not. He grabbed his mug and downed several gulps of ale. "When we leave here, send four of our most reliable men to the two lookouts you and I discussed earlier. Tell them they are to remain until they see Ulrick. When they do, have one ride back as quickly as he can with word. If I'm right, I doubt they will have to wait for long."

Amon frowned. "On this, I agree with Robert. Ulrick might be willing, but he would never convince his men to attack on Candlemas."

Hamish huffed. "If he has mercenaries riding with him, they would. They would be enticed to attack Foinaven when its guards appeared most vulnerable and unprepared. That's tomorrow."

Amon sighed sorrowfully. "I'm sorry, my friend. I know you wanted to wed your pretty wife again and I would love to witness your joy."

Hamish took another swallow. "Just send the men, Amon. And make sure you know where Lumley, Jollis, and Ulrick's other two spies are at all times. When he gets here, I want nothing to deprive them of their reunion."

Hamish then stood, prompting Mairead to stand with him. They wished the group a good evening and retired to their rooms. He said little, not wanting conversation. He only wanted to hold Mairead, make her his, and forget the world for a little while. As he lay beside her, about to fall asleep, he prayed his fears were unfounded.

An hour before the first rays of sunlight broke over the horizon, there was a knock on the door.

Ulrick had been spotted.

Chapter Sixteen

Hamish listened to what the messenger had to say and then closed the door. He threw on his leine and began to pleat his plaid. He looked back at Mairead to make sure she was not just watching him, but also getting out of bed. He was surprised to find her already in her bliaut, tying up its sides. In the firelight, he could see the concerned look on her face. He wished there was something he could say to erase it, but the only words that would work would have been lies. "When you finish, pack a small bag. Make sure Selah packs one for herself and for little Rab. Then I want the three of you to wait in my old chambers. Bolt the door and do not open it for anyone but me."

Mairead's brow furrowed with confusion. She noticed Hamish was not packing anything and had the uncomfortable feeling that if she was forced to leave, Hamish would not be joining her—possibly ever. "This is not the way it is supposed to be."

Hamish ignored the soft tremor in her voice and forced himself to focus on what needed to be done. First on that list was ensuring Mairead's, Selah's, and Rab's safety. "If you hear fighting, do *not* open the door. Do not check on things or attempt to help anyone you think might be injured. And that includes Selah. Neither should you wait. Just use the exit through the hearth and make sure you close it behind you. Ian Kyldoane and his brother are posted at its exit and have sworn a blood oath to me that they will get the three of you to McTiernay lands and into Conor and Laurel McTiernay's safekeeping."

"I am not leaving you behind," Mairead stated emphatically.

"I do not plan on it coming to that," Hamish retorted, trying to sound both sincere and lighthearted. "You know how I like to have contingencies." He had hoped his levity would calm her just a little, but instead a cold silence enveloped the room. Hamish finished with his belt and chanced a glance and knew instantly that Mairead was not in the least amused. She was staring at the logs in the fireplace, gripping the back of one of the chairs, her knuckles white. She was scared and it was not for herself, but for him. Of what he was saying might happen.

He went to pull her back to his chest and hold her in his arms. "You knew if we stayed there could be consequences. This was one of them," he whispered into her hair.

Mairead continued to stare at the red embers. Aye, she knew there would be consequences, but her running away as Hamish fought for his life and for Foinaven was not one of them. If he was going to fight, so should she. This was her home and everything that was about to happen was because of her. Hamish must have sensed where her mind was reeling. "I need you to do this. I cannot split my attention between worrying about you and what needs to be done. You said you trust me. Now more than ever I need you to mean that and do exactly as I ask."

Mairead could not speak. Tears streamed down her face as she leaned back into his embrace and nodded her head. "I will do everything you said, but I need you to do something for me."

Hamish grinned in her hair. "I promise to come back to you."

Mairead turned around and pulled his lips down to hers. Just before she claimed them and reminded him of all that he had to live for, she whispered, "Know that the only reason I married you was because I love you."

Robert shook his head, anger shining in the depths of his green eyes. "You agreed that there would be no show of aggression."

Hamish returned Robert's glare, but where fire boiled in his brother's veins, his had grown ice cold. "I will not argue on this. I agreed to let you try negotiation and to keep the majority of the men out of sight. But I never agreed to conceal *all* my men."

"I'm the one responsible, Hamish, and this is *my* decision," Robert hissed.

They were in the great hall with the few men to whom Hamish had revealed his whole plan. As of yet, Robert was not one of them. Hamish decided his brother would learn about his latest thoughts at the same time Ulrick would. Hamish knew his men were looking to and waiting for directions from *him,* not Robert.

Hamish glanced out the window. The sun was rising, but it was still dark outside. The clouds were thickening, making it more difficult to tell how much time was passing, but Hamish suspected they had no more than an hour longer to wait.

The lookout had said Ulrick had only stopped to eat. No shelters were erected, which most likely meant they planned to ride through the night, hoping to surprise Robert. And it might have worked if the lookout was not a Kyldoane and intimately familiar with the land. He had shown Hamish a more direct route back to Foinaven, shaving off hours of the journey. And it was one that could only be traversed single file and impossible for an army— even a small one—to use.

Bryan Kyldoane had not stayed to make a definitive headcount, but from what he had seen, he guessed Ulrick was riding with approximately seventy to eighty men— and no priest. Based on what Hamish had learned from Mairead and Amon, Ulrick had taken with him almost sixty soldiers—close to the numbers Hamish had been able to enlist. That meant Ulrick had persuaded approximately twenty mercenaries to help his cause. Most, if any, would not want to stay at Foinaven after it was secure. They were only there to earn their money and then disappear south. They were not loyal to anyone but themselves.

Hamish ignored Robert and looked at Davros. "Get your men into position in the tower and make sure none of them fire unless I tell them to. Understand?" The falconer glanced at Robert and saw that he was not the only one who understood Hamish's implication. Robert was no longer making the decisions when it came to this confrontation. Hamish was. And if it had been the other way around, Davros would have taken his men and left, choosing not to die for a man who did not respect the value of their lives.

"You, Amon," Hamish continued, getting his old mentor's attention. "Make sure all the men are in position. Then take the dozen we discussed and wait by the gate, just outside the wall. Also, I need two sentries on each tower. Make sure they are from Foinaven's guard. They need men Ulrick will recognize but who will follow my lead."

"What about Ulrick's spies?"

Hamish twitched his lips and flashed the older man a smile. "I think Lumley and Jollis should help guard the inside of the tower in order to be ready to welcome their commander. Have the other two inside the tunnel."

Amon returned the smile and then waved to the other men in the room, gesturing for them to head for their assigned positions and wait for Ulrick. It would not be long.

Robert stood still as everyone left and only he and Hamish were in the room. He did not quiver under Hamish's quelling stare and crossed his arms over his chest. Anger poured out of him. Every vein was popping on his neck.

Hamish was unapologetic. "I know you want to try negotiations first, brother, and we will. But when I made that agreement, you will remember that I also made another vow. That I would protect Mairead. She, Selah, and Rab . . ."

Hearing the names of his wife and son, Robert exploded. His hands slammed down on the table. *"Where are they?"*

"In my old chambers. I saw them enter and the door is bolted. If negotiations do not work and if my plan fails, I have made arrangements for them to be taken to Mc-Tiernay lands where they will be protected and safe."

Robert eased back. "I should have been informed."

"*You* should have made the arrangements," Hamish threw back at him.

They both knew that it had not occurred to Robert to protect his family in such a way, that he knew no one he trusted enough to protect his family outside of Hamish. "Thank you."

Hamish felt his own anger begin to lower. "I *will* give you the opportunity to negotiate, Robert. And despite what you think, I hope it works. But I will be prepared in case it does not."

"Then let us go to the curtain wall. I doubt we will have to wait long."

Hamish shook his head. "Not you. Just me. I will offer Ulrick the chance to talk, but you need to be ready when he takes me up on it."

Robert's expression became dubious. "I thought you believed only aggression would work with someone like Ulrick."

Hamish threw his head back and inhaled deeply. "I never believed that. All sides lose in battle for everyone experiences loss—even the victors. I explained this to Mairead soon after I arrived. Sometimes it is necessary to prevent total loss, but fighting should be the last option considered and definitely the last taken."

"So you *do* think Ulrick might be interested in negotiation."

Hamish clapped his brother on the back. "Oh, I think he will pretend to be interested enough to get in the castle gates." Hamish moved to open the great hall's doors but stopped just before he stepped through. "But once he is inside, *my* plan is to convince him not to just listen but *accept* your terms."

Robert opened and closed his mouth several times, before finally keeping his lips shut. He had planned almost every aspect of everything that had happened in the past month, with the exception of getting ill. But even that he had worked to his advantage. Mairead and Hamish falling in love was a twist, but Robert had never doubted that his brother would protect her in some way. The impromptu addition to Foinaven had also been something he had not expected, but ultimately, it did not change the fact that Hamish would be forced to fight Ulrick.

Robert was opposed to an army for all the reasons he had stated. He did not want massive bloodshed. But mostly he needed Hamish to stand up and fight for Foinaven. It was the catalyst to getting him to accept his rightful place as laird.

Never had Robert considered that he might *actually end up negotiating with Ulrick*.

It did not ruin everything—Mairead was safe *and* happy. And he and Hamish were no longer estranged, but *his* happiness, and the happiness of his wife and child, were suddenly at stake. All because he had not realized just how good a strategist Hamish was.

All is not lost, Robert told himself. He had a little bit of time and a lot of ingenuity. Before the day was out, Hamish would finally be back home and for good.

Hamish stood on top of the curtain wall adjacent to the wooden gates. Most of the servants had family in the village and the few who did not were told to remain behind closed doors either in the chapel or in the storage rooms of the small anchor tower that was attached to the stables. Foinaven, which was normally a hub of activity, felt strangely abandoned it was so quiet. But not to anyone approaching the castle. To them, the only thing amiss was that the large gate doors were uncharacteristically closed.

Hamish's demeanor was relaxed as he watched the large group of men approach, all holding weapons as they were ready to battle. Bryan Kyldoane's estimate had been a little low. Ulrick's army was closer to a hundred men, not eighty. It would make things tight, but the deadliest men were in front with Ulrick, who, being unafraid of what he might find, was leading the way.

It had been several years since Hamish had seen the man and aside from his pitch-black hair graying along his temples, he had changed little. Like most Highlanders, he was a large man, wide and muscular from hours wielding weapons and besting opponents. His face was somewhat flat and wide with a granite jaw and thin lips that looked like they were snarling even when he smiled.

Ulrick stopped in front of the gate. He paused and assessed Amon and the eleven men with him. None were on horses nor were they blocking the entrance. They were standing to the side in some pathetic display of strength. "I see Robert has recruited you and a few others." Ulrick looked behind him to his men. "So have I."

Amon cracked a genuine smile that caused a questioning brow on Ulrick to arch. Amon said not a word. He just looked up.

Ulrick followed his gaze up the wall to where Hamish was standing. Upon recognizing Hamish, his expression changed to one of understanding. He smiled and then returned his attention to Amon. "McTiernays always make one feel invincible. But I know that Hamish is not a real McTiernay." Then Ulrick returned his eyes upward. His gaze remained cold and unafraid. "Let me in, Hamish."

Hamish crossed his arms and instead used his chin to point to the men behind Ulrick. "Robert has agreed to see you, but *only* you and without your weapons. He wants only peace."

Ulrick's grin widened. "This can be done peacefully, Hamish, something I'm sure your brother is eager to see happen. Just tell Robert to hand over leadership and Foinaven to me and show me where he keeps the money, then no blood will be shed."

Hamish pursed his lips and looked at the two sentries placed on every tower, then down to the courtyard. He nodded his head as if he was receiving instructions. Then Hamish returned his attention back to Ulrick. "I'm not the one you need to negotiate with and Robert asks once again that you come in and negotiate with him. Just without your weapons."

Ulrick slid down off his horse. "Unless you brought a McTiernay army along with you, I have the numbers to take Foinaven. You know it; therefore, Robert does as well. One does not negotiate when the other side has nothing to leverage. I'm entering through these gates, my weapons are coming with me, and so are my men."

Hamish studied Ulrick for a second and then again looked down at the nearly empty courtyard. He nodded his head several times.

"Stop delaying, Hamish!" There was a snarl in Ulrick's voice, emphasizing his contempt for anyone and everyone associated with Foinaven and its weak leader. "You know as well as I that Robert is not fit to be laird and you left this life long ago. Leave again right now and I vow that no one will harm you."

Hamish uncrossed his arms and placed his fists on his hips. "You don't need a hundred men to negotiate, Ulrick. Leave half of them out here."

Ulrick waved his sword at Hamish. "I will decide how many men I need to negotiate. And I say I need them all! Now open the gates!"

Hamish pointed to Ulrick's army. "There is not enough room."

Ulrick glared at Hamish. Foinaven's courtyard was large, but not enough for a hundred soldiers on horses. It had plenty of room, however, if they came in on foot. And looking at the quivering, scared sentries on the towers,

Hamish was still using pathetic guards he had left behind. If there was a battle, it would be quick and one-sided.

Ulrick signaled to his men to dismount. Most did as told, but a few mercenaries hesitated. "If Hamish was foolish enough to have convinced some of the guard to fight for him, then we may have to teach them a lesson. The horses are a disadvantage."

Seeing his logic, the mercenaries slid off their horses. Ulrick then smiled back at Hamish. "There. I've negotiated."

"One more thing before you come in," Hamish stated casually. "Robert offers no ill will to you or anyone in your group, but before he agrees to open the gates, he wants a simple promise."

Ulrick knew that Hamish was baiting him, trying to incite him into doing something foolish. He refused to show he had been riled. "If it is a simple promise," he said with the same singsong indifferent tone Hamish had taken.

"He just wants you to promise to be willing to talk to him about a peaceful resolution."

Ulrick laughed out loud and then turned around to the mercenaries who were keenly following the exchange. None knew Hamish, but some had heard of him. All knew of the McTiernays though. "Seems Robert found a commander even more pathetic than himself."

One of the mercenaries stepped forward. His eyes were hooded and burned with doubt. "I don't trifle with McTiernays," he said, and then grabbed the reins of his horse and left.

Ulrick could see several others were going to follow and shouted out, "Hamish is no McTiernay! He is a *MacBrieve* who ran away from a wife and a lairdship over a decade ago." A few paused. "Leave and you return with *nothing*," he reminded them. Their hesitation ceased and

Ulrick knew he had regained control. But he was done waiting. "I'm done talking. Open the gates or I will burn them open."

Hamish shrugged as if he did not care, then waved his arm. A moment later the doors slid slowly to the side. Seeing them open, Ulrick raised his sword and ran inside. The mass of men behind him followed him and he was several steps in when he realized his folly. It was too late to stop. A hundred men were plowing down behind him and if he stopped, he would be run over. He had no choice but to continue. But when he and his men exited the tunnel there would be hell to pay.

Ulrick continued through the tunnel, which forced him to enter the bottom floor of the main tower. The torches on the wall were unlit, but the holes above gave enough light for him to see Jollis and Lumley standing guard by the tower's now only door. They were so incompetent he had almost kicked them both out of his guard before he left, but they were also the kind who were loyal to those with power. So he had given them the grand assignment to observe what happened while he was gone. It never occurred to either fool that telling him about the tunnel *after* he had secured Foinaven would be meaningless.

He waved his sword at them. "Well, don't just stand there, open the door!"

Jollis jumped and tried the door. It did not budge. He began to panic. Hamish had told him to guard the door and be prepared to open it for Ulrick when he returned. He had thought it an ideal assignment at the time, and that all the gossip about Hamish being this great warrior and strategist had been unfounded. With each kick and shoulder he threw against the barred exit, he became aware of just how wrong he had been.

"I know it works," whined Lumley, who was beside

Jollis throwing everything he had against the solid door. "I saw Robert's men working on it when they built the tunnel."

Ulrick grabbed Jollis's shoulder and flung him aside. With all his might, he kicked the door and knew instantly it had been seriously reinforced. "Robert did not *fix* the door, you fool. He blocked it." His army was still piling in and the little room he had to maneuver was dwindling. He let go a string of curses.

This was Hamish's plan. He should have known the man had something prepared, but it did not matter. Ulrick had not planned on hurting and killing the villagers to achieve his goal, but the moment he got everyone to go back out, he was going to torture every last one of them.

Ulrick bellowed for everyone to leave as they had come in. He waited, but the mass did not move. If anything, the numbers crowding the bottom of the tower had grown.

Ulrick was about to yell out again, this time with threats of death if they did not move, when he heard a clanking above him. Once again he was looking up at Hamish's face. This time through a large hole. No longer did he have no quarrel with the man. The pseudo McTiernay was living his last day on Earth.

"Your men cannot leave," Hamish said with a mocking apologetic tone. "Amon and his men are blocking the way."

"Twelve men cannot hold a hundred."

Hamish looked to ponder the statement and then shook his head. "These twelve probably could. And if I am wrong I am sure I can find more to help them."

Ulrick knew then that Hamish was not nearly as unprepared as it had seemed from outside the castle. If there had been no guards outside the gate when they arrived, he would have been suspicious. Seeing the dozen armed men, Ulrick had just assumed that they were all there was.

Hamish might have him at a disadvantage, but he was not the person in charge. Robert was. And Robert hated violence of any kind.

"I would like to talk to Robert now."

Hamish stood on the first floor of the tower and gestured to his younger brother. Robert wanted a chance to negotiate, and Hamish had arranged it so that Ulrick would be accepting his terms. But Robert said nothing. He just stared at Hamish, looking helplessly lost.

Hamish was furious and knew he was not alone. Davros and ten men he had personally trained had their bows and arrows ready to fly into every hole and the tension was growing. If a peaceful resolution was going to be made, this was Robert's chance. "You wanted an opportunity to speak with Ulrick before any blood was spilled. *This is that time*."

Robert took a deep breath and looked down into one hole. At least forty angry, violent men were below his feet and they were ready to kill, not talk. He looked back at Hamish. "What should I say?"

"Mo chreach!" Hamish swore. "For once be a laird to these people," he hissed. "Negotiate with Ulrick or kill him, I don't care which you choose, but make a decision and *lead*, Robert!"

Robert's face closed down, a dark shadow crossed his normally kind features. "I know how to build towers, not how to use them. I can work with any reasonable man, but they," he said pointing downward, "are *not* reasonable. They want war and nothing I say is going to change that. There is only one option that will prevent bloodshed."

Hamish stared at his younger brother, completely appalled at what he was hearing. Robert was going to give up though he was in a position of strength rather than risk having to fight.

Twelve years ago, Hamish had done the honorable thing and left. Mairead had convinced him that this time his honor required him to stay. Had she known it would come to this? Possibly. Did it matter? No. Because she was right.

Robert was a good man and Hamish loved him, but he had no more right pretending to be a laird than Hamish had at professing to be a master mason. If his brother wanted to build and fix and create, then that is what he should be doing. But no longer was Hamish going to watch him destroy and endanger those around him.

"I want to speak to the laird!" Ulrick bellowed again in an effort to needle Hamish.

Hamish signaled Davros. "Shoot him in the shoulder. Everyone else, make sure those men down there understand the disadvantage they are currently in."

Before Ulrick could register the order, something whizzed through the air. He cried out and the crowd started murmuring. In each hole, an arrow appeared, and in the dim light it was impossible for them to see exactly who was being targeted.

Ulrick stood back up and yanked the arrow from his shoulder. He had been injured on the battlefield before. Any pain that was not lethal could be compartmentalized and temporarily dismissed. "Robert, best kill me now or I promise I will kill you and take your place later."

"Killing Robert will gain you nothing, Ulrick. He is not the MacBrieve laird. He never was. That title goes to the firstborn MacBrieve and unfortunately for you, he just decided he wants to assume his birthright."

A deep, scraggly voice cried out. "You aren't going to kill us any more than your brother was willing to."

Hamish caught the attention of one of the mercenaries who had almost decided to leave when it became known that McTiernays might be involved. "Ulrick is right. I am not a McTiernay." Hamish's voice had lost all its playfulness as well as all its anger and in its place was something cold, menacing, and full of promise. "But I do consider Conor McTiernay a close friend, and in a way, family, like an older brother. I've been one of his elite guardsmen for years and during that time, he taught me much about fighting . . . and, well, obviously strategy."

A growling voice of another man called out. "I've heard of you McTiernays. And if this is how they fight, then they are cowards."

Hamish flicked his wrist and a second later an arrow was lodged in the man's throat.

Hamish waited until it became quiet again. "I do not need to fight in hand-to-hand combat to prove my honor. Something that man would have known if he had allowed me to finish, for I was about to explain that Conor also taught me how to win. Hopefully, you all now realize that I am more than willing to apply everything I learned from the McTiernays against those who oppose me, threaten my clan, or endanger my wife, *Mairead*."

Ulrick's head snapped up and if possible the fury in his eyes grew to new levels. Mairead was his. *His!* And she *knew* what would happen if she tried to avoid him through marriage. And the malevolent look that Hamish was sending him made it clear that he too was fully aware of Ulrick's threat.

"In a moment, I'm going to open the tower door and let you out one at a time. Be prepared to hand over your weapons. Refuse and you will end up like your comrade with an arrow in your throat."

Ulrick shifted so that a dozen men had exited the tower before he took his turn. And again, he was surprised to find that Hamish had been prepared for the tunnel approach not to work. The courtyard was filling with soldiers. Only a few he recognized from being forced out of his guard, but all of them looked comfortable holding a weapon. And there were more coming out of the kitchens, the keep, even the stables. They just kept coming.

Ulrick suspected he still had the numbers, but more than half of his men had no battle experience and were from the original Foinaven guard. It mattered little now. His current attention needed to be on getting out of this alive.

Hamish had just proved he *was* willing to kill, and yet he had not yet killed him.

Why?

Robert filled his mug once more with ale and raised it to the small group of men in front of him. "I saw it. I was there, but I still cannot believe it worked."

Davros swallowed a large gulp and sent a questioning look to Hamish. "I still cannot believe Hamish named Amon his commander." Amon gave the wily falconer a withering glance that both knew was only in jest. "Just know that is because he knew I would not accept."

Amon laughed. He could not help himself. "I cannot believe Hamish gave them their weapons back," he drawled, referring to the mercenaries.

Despite their large numbers, it had not taken long to disperse Ulrick's fickle group of would-be, power-hungry raiders. Every mercenary had taken the option to get their weapons and their horse and leave, never to return. One of the Kyldoanes was following them, but he had already sent word that they looked to be true to their word. All were leaving and none looked like they had any intentions of returning.

Almost all the guard who had followed Ulrick had no real particular loyalty to him. They had just wanted to avoid being on the wrong side of the man when he took over Foinaven. Once it was clear that was not going to happen, their allegiances had quickly shifted to Hamish. However, a quick promise was not enough to be trusted as a guard. All lost their weapons and most their mounts, as the horses had been provided by Ulrick with MacBrieve money. But they had been allowed to return unharmed to their families with three messages.

Leadership had changed. Hamish was now laird. Expectations would be higher, demands would be greater, but in return they would have a leader who understood their needs, respected their skills and their sacrifices, and was willing to make those same sacrifices for them. That announcement had brought cheers, even from those who had just hours before been intent on helping Ulrick take over Foinaven.

The second message had been a surprise. The new MacBrieve laird was no longer going to offer support with very little expected in return. Loyalty would be assured for at least one male member of each family had to devote a minimum of one day a week to the guard and learn how to master one or more weapons. The murmurings on this point indicated there was not much dissention. Jaime and the others who had joined Hamish's guard had been spreading the news of just how good and just how different this army would be. Several families with multiple eligible sons were arguing over which one of them would serve.

It had only been a few hours, but the feedback on Hamish's third and most solemn message was not as positive. No longer was Foinaven going to be a safe haven for a motley assortment of clans. Hamish's promised support and provided protection would only be for those who swore an allegiance to Hamish and accepted the Mac-Brieve name. Those who refused had to leave by spring.

The men and women affected had no issues with living near and among MacBrieves, but those who did not already have the name did not want it. They did not see themselves as tinkers and masons or even judges like those from the original line of MacBrieves on the Isle of Lewis.

Hamish understood their viewpoint, but it did not change his decision. He refused to lead a community like Robert had done. As laird, he intended to oversee a single clan and if possible, help it grow into a powerful one that would be respected and feared as much as the McTiernays.

Amon clapped Robert on the back. "Of *course* Hamish's plan worked! It was brilliant! The only tricky part was getting Ulrick and his men off their horses and so riled up that they charged through the gates, not paying attention to what they were charging into. Once that happened, the result was inevitable."

Robert shoved Amon's hand away, his expression smug. "Not *that* plan. *My* plan."

"And what plan was that?" Ian Kyldoane asked. He was the only fair-haired man in the group and he and his younger brothers resembled the Vikings who had invaded Scotland hundreds of years before. He was quiet, but when he spoke it always cut right through to the matter. And he was the best tracker Hamish had ever seen.

When he and Hamish had first met, Ian had known Hamish was coming long before he came into view and had laid a trap. Because of Mairead, the trap had not been deadly, but it almost had ensnared them both. But Hamish had not only seen and avoided it, he had done so without alerting Mairead to its existence. Both men had impressed each other that day and their mutual respect had only grown in the days since.

Ian had refused to join the cause and support the continuation of Robert's leadership, but he had vowed to do whatever was needed to keep Mairead safe, if necessary. He was glad it had not been necessary, but nevertheless, he still had procured a promise that Hamish would come to his aid if he ever needed it. That vow just became even more powerful, for Hamish was not a guard for the McTiernays. Today, he had become a laird.

Amon nudged Robert. "Do tell us. What part of this plan of yours worked so well?"

Robert waited until he had Hamish's attention and then with a knowing nod answered in a low voice, "The whole damn thing."

He had Hamish's full attention now.

Neither brother had had a chance to talk privately about what had happened earlier that day. Hamish was not sure what he would say when he did. He just knew that if it were all to happen again, he would make the same decision. It was the right one and he would not apologize for it.

"It was what I wanted, Hamish." Robert's voice was low and calm. "It was what I've always wanted. I never wanted to be laird," he added, confirming that he had guessed what Hamish was thinking. "But you wouldn't come home. You refused to return and assume your birthright. And when I finally did force your hand after twelve years, you made it clear during our first meeting that you thought being laird was something I was proud of and wanted to be. Simply telling you the truth would not have worked.

You would have believed it an attempt at reconciliation or worse, a desperate ploy to force you to stay."

The lively room had grown quiet. Hamish's expression had turned cold as he digested everything Robert was saying. His brother was right, but it infuriated him to know he had been manipulated. His great plan had actually been only a component of his brother's larger one. He was not the great strategist. Robert was. "And Mairead? Was she part of this *plan* of yours?" he spat out softly.

Robert shook his head. He was unfazed by Hamish's anger and had even expected it. But Hamish needed to know the truth. "Only Selah knew what I had in mind, for she, just as much as I, wanted to be free of Foinaven and its burden."

The teeth in Hamish's jaw ground together. "What about our marriage?"

Again Robert shook his head. "You surprised us on that one. Our main concern was Mairead's welfare, but we knew that you would ensure her protection, even if the rest of my plan failed and you left Foinaven—especially once you knew the particulars." Robert knew they had an audience and suspected that Hamish had only confided in Ian the level to which Ulrick had been threatening Mairead. A door opened behind him and he heard several footsteps approach, but he ignored them. "But you and she falling in love? Not even *you* could have predicted that."

Selah's hand slid over Robert's shoulder and she bent down to give him a brief kiss. "I did. I recognized it from nearly the beginning."

Mairead, who had also entered along with Jeán, Lynnea, and Tyra, Ian's wife, stopped beside Hamish. Her body, which had already been tense, went rigid. She glared at her older sister. "You did not!"

Robert inclined his head and with a wince said, "Aye, she did. And when I saw you fight that night, I knew she was right."

"You said that it was obvious there was nothing between us." Hamish remembered it vividly.

"No," Robert corrected. "I said that I was satisfied."

Selah sat down beside Robert and clasped his hand in hers. "I know that you are angry with us. I just told Mairead what we did and she is furious right now."

Mairead sucked in a sharp breath and looked at the men in the room. All were quiet. Hamish had yet to say a word since she had entered the room, but she could feel the anger rolling off him in waves. "You made fools out of us."

Hamish snaked a long arm around her waist. For some inexplicable reason, Mairead's anger helped quell his own. Robert, however, was indignant at the accusation. "We did not!" His voice was firm and allowed for no argument. "I never manipulated either of you. The only time I came close was when you both refused to realize you should be married, and that was not done through veiled attempts but only pressure." Robert's gaze bored into Hamish's. "You were brought here not under a false pretense, but an accurate one. *You* made the decision to stay, no one forced it upon you. I only kept quiet about my own motivations and much of that was because I did not want it to be a factor in your decision. I never wanted you to think that you did not have a choice. You and everyone here know that you *chose* to be laird. It was not thrust upon you begrudgingly. You have earned their trust and loyalty as well as mine. Not for just what you did today, by saving my family and Selah's home, but for what you did twelve years ago. You were the honorable man then; I just wanted the chance to be that in return."

One by one Hamish captured the eyes of each person in the room and saw no pity reflected in them. What shined in their depths was respect, admiration, and a hint of fear that all their hopes were in jeopardy. He shifted his gaze to Mairead, who despite Robert's eloquent speech was still angry. But he knew now it was mainly for him. She feared that he would think less of what he accomplished, and for a moment, he had.

"What would you change?" he asked her softly, and pulled her onto his lap.

"What?" Mairead was befuddled. She *knew* Hamish would be even more furious than she was at learning Robert and Selah's grand scheme. And yet he no longer seemed even mildly upset.

"Because I would change nothing." Then in front of everyone he kissed her.

"You stop that right now!" Selah jolted out of Robert's lap and went to grab her younger sister. "There is at least an hour before the sun sets and we have not just Candlemas to prepare for, but your wedding. We may not have a priest so it will still have to be a handfast ceremony, but this time *there will be witnesses*!"

Mairead fought unsuccessfully to avoid being pulled out of Hamish's embrace. She glared at Selah, but with exasperation. "Tell her, Hamish. Tell her that it is unnecessary and that you don't want this!"

"But I do want it." Hamish grinned, flashing his dimples.

Several hours later, after much merriment, drink, and food, Hamish swept up his newly announced wife in his arms and carried her to the top floor of the keep. And there in the solar that had been cleaned and prepared for them, he brought her pleasure over and over again.

With Ulrick's arrival no longer looming over their shoulders, Mairead had responded with complete abandon. In return, he had completely let go of his fevered need, trusting in what he had found in her.

Mairead lay on her side and slowly slid her hand down Hamish's chest then stomach, then lower. She felt fully satiated and yet she was not ready to roll over and fall asleep. Hamish had brought her to new heights and she was determined to see him just as out of control as she had been.

Hamish had released himself quite powerfully and thought himself incapable of responding to her touch, but he was wrong. "Damn," he said through clenched teeth.

Mairead lifted her head and saw that Hamish's jaw had gone tight and fierce need blazed up at her. With a wicked smile, she pushed against his chest and crawled onto him. Straddling his thighs, she traced his lips with her tongue before easing into his mouth, seducing him, rekindling his need for her.

When she felt one of his hands sink into her hair, pulling her against him to deepen the kiss, she pulled back, but only just slightly. Slowly she let her mouth trail down his neck, then chest, and paused to nip his navel. She could feel him tighten with anticipation as she let her fingers once again caress his growing erection.

Hamish reveled in the soft brush of her hair against his skin, which was followed by the moist heat of her breath. She withdrew and for a long moment he thought he would go mad with anticipation. And then he felt it, the searing heat of her tongue licking him from root to tip.

Hamish lay there unable to do anything more than grip the blankets in both his hands. Fear was choking him, fear and an almost intolerable desire as her mouth tortured him with sensations. He had given her his heart, and his body, but now she was asking for something more.

A moan erupted from somewhere deep within him as she took him fully inside her mouth. That she was new to this made him feel even more possessive of her than he already was. He thought he would die from the pleasure if she continued and die from the lack of it if she did not. He had lost control before in her arms, but it was nothing like this. Here she had all the power. He was completely at her mercy.

Being in charge was a whole new experience for Mairead and she found herself loving the fact that she was the reason behind the constant shuddering that rippled through him. It encouraged her to continue. She gripped the base of his length with one hand and slowly stroked up and down until she felt Hamish's hands tangle into her hair. Unable to stop himself, he began to thrust. "*Ó dhìol*, Mairead! You're killing me."

Mairead moved faster, weakening him, torturing him, just as he had always done to her. She knew he was desperately trying to regain some sort of control, but his sensual agony only encouraged her to continue.

Abruptly Hamish pushed her away. "No more," he cried out, and in a deft maneuver flipped her over and onto her back. Before Mairead had time to do anything other than open her eyes, he slammed into her. She arched forward and met it and the one thrust that followed. He began to take her so hard and fast that Mairead could do nothing but wrap her arms and legs around him and hold on.

Hamish moved his hands over her breasts, felt her nipples tighten against his palms as her muscles squeezed around his erection. Nothing in this life had ever felt so right. He knew then that he could not ever lose her.

"God, Mairead, I think I'm going to—" He clenched his jaw, cutting off the words. He wanted her to come with him, but it was too late. His face was contorted as he came with such force he had never before experienced or would have thought possible.

Hamish collapsed and for the next half hour they lay in each other's arms, kissing, their mouths melding together, conveying feelings that neither could express with words.

Chapter Seventeen

"Hamish, come over and take a look at these changes."
Robert's voice echoed in the great hall. Seeing that he
finally got his brother's attention, he and Davros once more
bent over the plans for the new gatehouse Hamish wanted
built onto Foinaven. It was not something he wanted as a
leader, but as a mason, he was eager for the challenge.

Two weeks had gone by and the transition of responsibilities from him to Hamish had been surprisingly
straightforward and simple. Mostly because Robert did
not want them. He answered questions and helped Hamish
learn some of the less exciting but critical things to running Foinaven and keeping it financially solvent.

Robert would have thought the transition of responsibilities from Selah to Mairead to be even simpler, as
Mairead already knew the staff, what needed to be done,
and had been doing a majority of the work for some time.
But he had been very wrong. His only comfort was knowing that Hamish was as mystified by the situation as he
and also lacked the insight into knowing how to respond.
For no matter what either man said to his wife, it was the
wrong thing.

No longer restrained by Selah's approach to handling the staff, Mairead had immediately gone in and made sweeping changes. In Mairead's mind, they had been long overdue and some of the benefits—especially in the quality and flavor of their fare—had drastically improved. The servants were now punctual, competent, and less apt to voice a surly opinion. They understood their responsibilities and that they would be accountable for them. As a result, things were cleaner, fireplaces were always prepped and ready for use, the rushes had been replaced, and the well had been cleaned out.

Selah, however, saw what the pain of such drastic decisions had created, for several men and women had not just changed positions within the castle but lost them completely. They have been forced to leave Foinaven and return to their families to seek other means to provide for them. When Mairead refused to listen or even discuss the problem, Selah was incensed. She had listened to Mairead for years and incorporated her counsel into her decision-making. The least Mairead could do was offer her the same courtesy!

Hamish and Amon had just joined Davros and Robert to look at the gatehouse plans when the doors opened. Heavy footsteps caused both men to look up. Ian Kyldoane was approaching and with him his youngest of four brothers, Dryan, who looked grim.

When he had ended Ulrick's reign of tyranny, he had surprised everyone by not killing him but offering him the chance to leave and join the few guards who had opted not to stay and swear allegiance. Hamish had warned Ulrick that if he were ever to be found on MacBrieve land, his life would come to a painful end and without mercy.

Amon had been furious and Ian had a look of betrayal in his eyes and both only calmed later when Hamish told them why. He did not want Ulrick to die by another man's hand and certainly not swiftly with an arrow in his throat. He also *knew* Ulrick would not be able to stay away. And when he returned, Hamish would keep his vow and end his life, painfully and slowly.

They were further pacified when they learned Hamish had sent Bryan, an expert tracker who was unmarried and had no family waiting on him or farm to tend, to follow Ulrick and send word when the man made the mistake of returning.

Hamish had not surmised it would take long, but he had thought Ulrick would need more than two weeks to muster the ability to fight back.

"I bring news." Bryan was like his older brother Ian and did not mince words. "Ulrick joined the Mackays and is telling them that you are now laird and are growing an army with the intent of increasing MacBrieve's reach and rule. Laird Donald Mackay has begun to gather his own men in response."

Hamish stood still for several moments considering what Bryan had just told him. He had hoped to meet Donald Mackay sometime later in the year and assure him that although he was now laird, he had no intentions of trying to alter the boundary marking their two territories. He had known for the past week that Donald Mackay would not be willing to listen. Until now he had not known why.

Seven days ago, one of the newly promised clansmen came to visit him. He lived farther out, not east where the village and Davros lived, but to the west where his farm bordered Mackay lands. He had heard rumblings the Mackays were gathering men and seen an increase in activity. He had been worried they were about to attack.

Hamish had assumed Donald Mackay did not like the idea of what was once a collection of smaller, inconsequential clans banding together into a large one with a laird to rule them. That he especially did not like that this clan was directly on their eastern border. But it seemed there was much more instigating Laird Mackay's anxiety than simply a new neighbor.

Amon squared his jaw. "We should not have waited when news came of this earlier. We need to act now and gather the men once more." Hamish's permanent guard was becoming fairly substantial as he started including more and more of the ones who had followed Ulrick. Many he learned had not been following power but had been protecting their loved ones. Ulrick, to ensure loyalty, had threatened the family of any guard who was decent with a weapon. As a result, Hamish had allowed several back. From others he had gained the promise that they would return and fight if needed. Amon thought that time was now.

"If Donald Mackay is foolish enough to listen to Ulrick and seek a fight, he will get one!" belted Amon.

Hamish held up his hand. He did not personally know Donald Mackay and was almost certain that Conor did not either. But that did not mean they had not heard of the man. "Laird Mackay is known to be powerful and ruthless, but I have heard that he is also extremely cunning. He may be gathering his men together as a test."

Forced from Moray lands and their home for hundreds of years, the Mackays had been making their way to Strathnaver for many years. They had been massing at Tongue but also had acquired significant stretches of land around Durness. After fighting alongside Robert I, the king of Scotland, they had become both feared and respected as warriors. And all knew that they would fight to the death before letting another clan take what they believed rightfully theirs.

Hamish looked at Bryan. "Besides the gathering of men, were there any other signs of aggression? Such as changes in routes, territory markings, missing animals?"

Bryan kept his face impassive but shook his head no.

Davros sighed and offered insight he was sure Hamish knew but needed to consider when he decided his next course of action. "Ulrick can offer Donald Mackay little value except that of information. He knows Foinaven's strengths and weaknesses and can probably give him fairly accurate estimates on the size of our army."

Hamish nodded. "Aye. Mackay would not have grown his clan into the force it is today if he was either a fool or a mere defender."

Ian nodded and quickly did a summation of the situation. "Mackay will eventually attack. He does not have the luxury of assuming Ulrick is wrong."

Hamish then looked at Robert, Davros, Ian, and Amon and smiled deviously. "Aye, but the real question is when."

None returned his smile.

Mairead continued to pour ale into several mugs as the men spoke. She was not sure if they even saw her enter the hall as she had done so via the kitchen entrance and not the courtyard. What they said unsettled her greatly. She also thought it immensely unfair. Hamish had been laird for barely two weeks and already he was having to defend Foinaven and the clan. She hated to think it, but maybe Robert had a point about appearing weak. People left you alone. Problem was, under Robert's leadership, they had not just appeared weak, they had actually *been* weak—and very vulnerable.

Mairead put the jug of ale down and examined the expressions of many of the soldiers who were in the room, some of whom had ridden with Ulrick but were now sworn to Hamish. They were all listening just as keenly as she was to what was being said and their fear struck her. She could see it on their faces. They were needing reassurance that they had not once again chosen the wrong side. All eyes were on Hamish as if he had the answer. It was his first time to truly lead and he needed their trust.

Mairead put the mugs on a large tray and carried them over to the group standing with Hamish. "I see that look in your eye," she said loud enough for all to hear.

Hamish quirked a brow. Mairead was talking to him, but it was clear that she was addressing the whole group. "I have no idea what you are talking about."

"That look you have when you smile a certain way." She offered the mugs and all of them took one, regardless if they were thirsty. They wanted to hear what she had to say. "Whenever you have a clever plan, you wear that grin. I would ask what your plan is, but I have learned not to waste my time. You will let people know how you intend to handle the Mackays when you are ready. Can you just tell me first?" she said with a wink and then sauntered away

If Hamish had not already fallen hard for his wife, he would have done so just then as he sensed the tension in the hall ease and the men's confidence increase. "Everyone out!" he barked. He had not raised his voice, but his tone cut through the crowd nonetheless and within minutes the hall was vacant with the exception of Mairead.

She had put down the empty platter and was biting her bottom lip, glancing up at him. Her hazel eyes were sparkling with smug satisfaction. She knew what she had done and was waiting for an appreciative kiss. But he also knew that she was trying very hard not to be worried over what the men had been saying about the Mackays.

"Don't worry, Mairead. I have things under control."

Mairead gave a little shrug of her shoulders. "I'm not in the least concerned. I know you will think of something."

Hamish wrapped his arms around her and pulled her back against his chest. "What makes you think I haven't already?"

Mairead spun around in his arms. She was about to kiss him when she saw that his lips were smiling, but his eyes were not. "You have a plan, but you do not think it will work or . . . you don't like it."

"I still cannot decide whether I like it that you can read me so well."

Mairead playfully slapped his arm. "You like it."

His eyebrows shot up. "I do, huh? And aye, I do have a solution to the Mackays. I just wish I had more time to get to know my clansmen, and gain their confidence and trust."

Mairead reached up and gave him a kiss that despite its brevity, conveyed her love and faith in him. "You have more than you realize."

Hamish pulled her close and rested his chin on her head. "I hope so. I've always known that as a leader, there are things one must do, decisions one must make. The one I'm facing now comes with long-term consequences. But stewing on it any longer will change nothing."

He released her and went to leave the great hall. The last thing Mairead heard was him calling for a herald.

Chapter Eighteen

Mairead entered the great hall to see if she could learn more about what was happening. Every day Hamish left early and came home late. He would grab something to eat and ask her about Selah. She would lie and tell him things were much better between them and then Mairead would try something new to get him to reveal *anything* about his plan. She could not decide whether she was pleased or frustrated that her attempts to get Hamish to admit even snippets of what was going on continued to fail. She knew Hamish enjoyed it immensely and was probably the main reason he would say nothing. She would have been angry, but she *was* having quite a bit of fun trying to get him to divulge his secrets as his wife. So far though, none had been successful.

Her best source of information came not from Hamish but others. During the day, she would listen for snippets of information from the soldiers who were coming and going, but what she heard was usually more confusing than illuminating. And the few times Hamish had been around, he had done nothing to keep her from blatantly eavesdropping. The frustrating man *knew* she would not understand, only that *something* was definitely being orchestrated.

Mairead went to stand by Hamish, who glanced down briefly at her but did not stop Ian, who was talking, or suggest that she leave.

"We moved that stretch of rocks three feet, just as you ordered," Ian stated. His tone, as usual, flat and impossible to read.

Hamish nodded. "Wait a day and then move them another three feet into Mackay land."

This time Ian arched a brow but said nothing. Mairead would have thought she had misheard, except that she had been hearing similar instructions all week. He had told Amon to have the fishermen come in just a little farther up the bay. Not to actually violate where the Mackays moor their boats, but to make it uncomfortable.

Every Highlander, especially those clansmen who lived on the border of their territory, knew every stone, tree, road, and stream of their area. Encroachment changes like the one Hamish was ordering were blatantly incendiary.

"Amon, have Jaime partially block the stream where it bends near his farm. Tell him not to block it entirely but to just impede its flow. And make sure the stones can easily be removed, but only from MacBrieve lands." Every word Hamish spoke was of a request for another provocative activity. It was like he *wanted* a fight with the Mackays.

Knowing Hamish would only give her an innocuous, empty answer, she elbowed Amon and gestured for him to follow her to the other side of the room. Once there, she whispered, "Can you tell me *why* Hamish is seeking to start a war with the Mackays?"

She held her breath, afraid that Amon would tell her to

ask Hamish, but instead he beamed with pride. "A war with them was going to happen regardless. When Ulrick joined the Mackays, it became inevitable. What was impossible to predict was *when* Donald Mackay would decide to attack. That left Hamish, our *laird*," he said with pride, "a choice. He could wait for Donald Mackay to choose a time to attack that was optimal for him—probably spring, giving him enough time to gather men from Durness as well as Strathnaver—or Hamish could accelerate that timeline to one that won't allow Mackay the time to amass his full force, making it much more favorable to us."

Mairead's mouth hung open. "Hamish is actually *goading* the Mackays into attacking us?"

Amon nodded, his grin still in place. "If they don't, their laird looks weak. Donald Mackay cannot afford that."

Mairead was not sure that *they* could afford a fight any sooner than spring. That precious time was needed for Hamish to train at least a few more men. Even then, based on what Hamish had told her, they would lose. Mackay had twice the numbers they had, plus, unlike the Mackays, most of Hamish's soldiers had never seen battle.

She was about to mention this fact to Amon when Abe and a lookout came in, each clearly arriving with news.

Hamish advanced toward them. "Speak," he said, looking at the soldier.

"The Mackays are starting to mass their forces near the western border."

Abe pressed his lips together, knowing his news was even worse. When Hamish looked at him, the farmer swallowed. "Ye've got another army coming from the south and it be almost on top of Foinaven. They're riding from where them mercenaries went. I rode as fast as I could to tell ye," he said, hoping this was a sign that he had meant his allegiance.

Mairead felt her heart begin to pound. She was finding it difficult to breathe. The mercenaries had returned in force?

She turned to ask Amon a question, but he had left to rejoin Hamish. There was a flicker of concern on his face, but nothing like what should have been there considering they were not facing one but *two* armies. Even if they had been able to scramble the numbers to fight Mackay on one front, there was no way they could defend themselves against two.

Seeing her distress, Hamish came to her side and pulled her into his arms. He slid his hand up and down her back soothingly. "Where did your faith in me disappear to, *aingeal*?"

Mairead pulled back, but Hamish would only let her go so far. "You have it all and always will, you know th—"

Before she could finish her sentence, both doors of the great hall swung wide open and with such force one of them banged on the stone wall. Mairead snapped her head around to see just which soldier was announcing his arrival in such a brazen way.

But the man was no mere soldier. He was enormous and at his side was an incredibly beautiful woman.

The man was very muscular and taller than every man in the room, including Hamish. Next to him was the most stunning woman Mairead had ever seen. Tall and thin, she walked with a gracefulness Mairead longed to have but knew she never would. Her hair was the color of moonlight and it cascaded all around her shoulders down to her waist in harmonious waves.

Mairead was about to ask Hamish for explanations

when he moved from her side and walked over to greet the couple. The first thing he did was gather the gorgeous woman in his arms and hold her in a long embrace that could not be mistaken for anything but what it was.

Whoever this woman was, she loved Hamish and he also loved her.

Chapter Nineteen

Mairead threw another log on the fire and waited for the flames to take hold before finally sinking into one of the great hall's hearth chairs. The past hour or more had been cacophony of activity and Mairead was not sure if she was more angry or grateful that her sister had taken over—without permission—the role of hostess. For it had been Selah who had thought to order Mairead's old room to be cleaned out and prepared for the McTiernays and she had been the one to make sure the kitchens knew that there were more mouths to feed. Many more.

Conor and Laurel McTiernay had not come alone. They had brought their priest, Father Lanaghly, and based on the jokes that Conor was making, a slew of soldiers, including several friends Hamish used to work, train, and even battle alongside. Introductions had felt non-ending and Mairead could not remember a single name. Only that she had gotten several offers that they would be back for her in a year in case Hamish had driven her nuts with his sword polishing by then.

Mairead's mind had been spinning, seeking some kind of explanation for the reason behind Laird and Lady

McTiernay's impromptu arrival. What she had deduced was that their visit was not just a visit. Hamish had sent for them. And that sent an intense wave of fear through her that she could not easily dismiss.

He had been so adamant about refusing to ask Mc-Tiernays to risk their lives for non-McTiernay matters that it could only mean the Mackay situation was truly dire. And yet, both Hamish and Conor seemed to act as if the pending battle was the equivalent of a mild squabble between farmers.

Mairead had nearly fallen over when she heard Conor say, "I take it then that you're thinking about confronting Mackay soon."

Without pause or concern, Hamish nodded nonchalantly. "Aye. Tomorrow if you're up to it. We were waiting on you."

Conor slapped his hands together and rubbed them with glee. "I haven't been this excited about a plan in years. I cannot wait to see how it will all turn out."

Hamish returned his grin. "It should be quite a bit of fun." Conor beamed in agreement. "There's no reason to wait now that you are here. Amon will send the men to the ridge tonight, right in sight of the border. Mackay will have no choice. He's expecting me to make a move and has been making preparations for it."

Conor rocked back on his heels. "I want to ride out there now and see where it will all take place." He elbowed Hamish in the side. "I'm glad this happened for many reasons, but one is Donald Mackay. He's someone I've wanted to meet for some time, especially if everything I've been told about the man is true."

The next thing Mairead felt were Hamish's lips on her cheek as he told her that he would see her later that night for dinner and to save the welcome feast for the next night when all of this would be over.

Then Hamish was gone, along with Conor and all the other men in the great hall. Even Father Lanaghly had decided to ride with them. With a long white beard and warm dark eyes surrounded by wrinkles, he was far from young, but he did not act like it. The man was unlike any priest Mairead had ever heard of. Most stayed in their chapel and away from clan matters, but the McTiernay priest was unnaturally curious to see the grounds where several men might be lying dead the next day.

By the time the great hall doors closed again, only she, Selah, and Laurel remained behind. The sudden drop in noise level was unnerving, but Mairead was the only one who seemed to notice it. When Selah suggested that they sit down by the fire to talk, Mairead had been glad, for her mind had ceased to work. Her husband was out with his old laird and a priest, and they were eagerly planning a war with one of the most powerful clans in the northern Highlands. A war that Hamish had intentionally instigated.

Mairead pivoted and moved to follow Selah and Laurel to the main hearth and the large chairs ready and waiting to be used. She wanted to rest, but more important she had questions—ones she prayed Laurel had answers to.

Mairead waved her hand for everyone to sit down. Laurel glided to the chair next to her and sat down. Selah, however, pointed to the back entrance that led to the kitchens. "I'll return in just a moment. I'm going to see if there is some bread and cheese available for us to nibble on." The McTiernays had arrived just in time for the noon meal, but Mairead had been so overwhelmed, she had not eaten enough to last until dinner and suspected neither had Selah due to the excitement. "I have a feeling dinner might be late tonight."

Mairead bristled. Selah was once again making decisions as if she were still the lady of the castle. Aye, she was proving to be a better hostess, but that role was not hers anymore and Mairead was tired of trying to claim it when it should have been willingly given. This is what Selah wanted! What she and Robert had schemed so hard for! Mairead knew it was hard on Selah—it would be on anyone, but Mairead had respected her position for years. Why could her sister not do the same for her? Mairead was going to have to say something, and soon, but now there were other priorities.

Mairead glanced at Selah, sending her sister a look that spoke volumes, but like the other times, Selah just ignored it. *Now is not the time*, Mairead thought to herself, and took a deep breath to more personally welcome her unexpected guest.

Laurel McTiernay was eyeing her carefully. Mairead knew Laurel had picked up on the tension, but she had said nothing. She was close to Selah's age, perhaps a few years older, but she saw neither judgment nor pity in them. Just simple recognition of what was happening.

It was probably that more than anything that made Mairead yearn to be like Lady McTiernay. It was not that she was the most beautiful woman Mairead had ever seen—though gorgeous, long blond hair and deep storm-colored eyes *were* enviable qualities. So was her wit. From the few pleasantries they had exchanged and what she heard her say to Hamish and the others, the woman was intelligent and kind, yet also comfortable with sarcastic banter. But it was Laurel's calm assurance, mixed with self-confidence and wisdom, that Mairead wished to emulate.

Without any apology, Laurel kicked off her shoes, curled her legs underneath her, and leaned back to rest her head on the back of the chair. She took a deep breath and sighed. "I hope you do not mind me getting comfortable, but is it terrible to admit that after traveling for several days and being on my feet the past hour, that this room, its fire, and this very comfortable chair are just what I needed?" She flashed Mairead a smile that compelled one to return it.

Mairead blinked. "I . . . I . . ." she stammered. She barely knew Laurel McTiernay, but she *really did like* her style. Probably because it was much like her own—direct.

Mairead decided that if the woman could show up at her doorstep without warning, clutch her husband to her breast for several seconds, and then kick off her shoes in front of her fire, then she would not object to Mairead also being herself. "I actually want to do the same thing." Mairead kicked off her shoes and tucked her feet underneath her, no longer feeling anxious about doing or saying the wrong thing.

Laurel waved an index finger at her and said knowingly, "You have questions."

"So do I!" Selah called out from behind them, pulling the small side table that was next to Mairead to be where all of them could reach. She then moved out of the way so that the servants could put down the platter of meat, cheese, and bread. Once they were alone again, she said, "I wanted to ask you about Father Lanaghly."

Mairead glared at her sister. Selah held the glare and then nonchalantly picked up a piece of meat and stacked it on a small piece of bread. Then she saw Mairead's comfortable position, issued her a stern, reproving glare of her own, and waved a finger at her feet. It did not seem to matter to her that Laurel was also sitting similarly.

Mairead fought to calm her temper and ignore her sister. "I *do* have quite a few questions, Lady McTiernay."

Laurel's eyes grew large. "Please call me Laurel, for I think us calling each other by our titles will quickly rankle us both."

Mairead smiled gratefully. "After what I just witnessed, I think most of my questions should be directed to someone else." There was no doubt by the tone of her voice that Mairead was speaking about her husband.

Laurel laughed with delight. "I take it that Hamish did not tell you we were coming or what his plans were."

Mairead licked her lips and gave a quick shake of her head.

Laurel's sigh conveyed her sympathy. "As far as what is taking place tomorrow, you probably know more than I for Conor is still vexed that I not only made him take me with him, but I insisted on stopping to see Cole on the way. As a result, he has decided to keep much of the details to himself as a way to chastise me." Laurel bent over and grabbed a piece of cheese, grinning as she popped it in her mouth. "It's not working," she said with satisfaction after she swallowed. "But here is what I know. We received a message from Hamish approximately a week ago that he had married, assumed lairdship of his clan, and was going to remain at Foinaven. There were no details, just that everything had all transpired amicably and was something that Selah and Robert were comfortable with."

Selah smiled with pride. "Robert actually planned the outcome."

Laurel gave her a quick look of being impressed and then continued. "And that while there was no issue between him and his younger brother, there was one brewing with your neighbors the Mackays," Laurel continued. "Hamish then requested that Conor come join him and while I know there was much more to that part of the message, those are the details that I have not been told. All I know is that Conor is not acting like he does when there is a battle looming, which means he is here to help Hamish do something else. Do not ask me what. Conor loves being cryptic, especially when I rile him. But he should have known that I was *never* going to accept being left behind."

Mairead quirked a brow. She *really* liked Laurel McTiernay. For so long, she had thought a laird's wife needed to be sweet and gentle, possessing the decorum of her older sister. Kindness Mairead could do, but sweet and soft-spoken? She could periodically fake it, but long term it was just not her.

"At least Conor has told you *something*." Mairead sighed, her frustration showing. "Hamish enjoys keeping me in a state of ignorance, but I am aware of the situation our men are facing tomorrow enough to know that it is very dangerous and many lives are potentially going to be lost."

Laurel did not debate the possibility, just tilted her head and said, "We will just have to wait and see."

"I just wish that Hamish at least acted like he understood the threat the Mackays pose. They outnumber us and their army I am sure is far more experienced and skilled. Hamish just has not had the time to build up ours, and yet *he* was the one to pick this fight. Or at least rush it into happening."

Laurel's lips thinned. "McTiernay men have their weaknesses, but strategy is not one of them. I trust Conor."

Mairead's back stiffened into what she knew was a more defensive posture, but she could not help it. "Hamish *is* a McTiernay in all ways but name and your husband proved it when he said that Hamish's plan was a good one."

Selah sucked in her breath disapprovingly at Mairead's harsh tone. But rather than being offended by Mairead's brusque comment, it warmed Laurel's features. "I like you," she said with complete sincerity. "More important, I'm glad Hamish has you. He needs someone who loves him enough to defend him."

Mairead instantly relaxed. "I just wish I knew what was going on."

Selah was shocked by what she was hearing. "Robert and I share everything. We have no secrets."

Laurel turned her head toward Selah. "Then you truly are fortunate you married the right brother, for Hamish would have driven you quite mad. The man adores his secrets. So does Conor and the wicked side of me is so glad he does."

Mairead chuckled, completely understanding what Laurel was saying. "Selah, you should consider keeping one or two from Robert. Ferreting secrets out can be mutually pleasurable."

Selah frowned at her.

Laurel leaned forward. "So you *have* been trying to find out."

Mairead quirked a brow. "I have been quite inventive, but nothing has worked as of yet. Until I heard what I did this afternoon, it had been fun. But I did not know that Hamish was so *eager* to meet danger. It scares me."

"I have been trying as well, but Conor has been unusually impervious to my attempts. I am extremely curious for I have never seen Conor so eager to set out on an uncomfortable journey, especially north in the middle of the winter. I know why I was eager, but I doubt that is the same reason Conor has."

Mairead was curious. "Why did you make the trip?"

"Well, I was not about to let Conor leave me behind and rob me of the chance to meet you, Hamish's *bride*." Laurel sat back and her face took on a look of pure pleasure. "It *was* one of Conor's and my better rows for it lasted nearly a day. What an incredible night. I pray that you and Hamish have several good arguments in your future. They can be *so* much fun . . . in the end."

Mairead nodded knowingly.

Selah just sat there with her mouth agape, her eyes shifting back and forth between the two women. She could not imagine anything fun about having a daylong fight with Robert. When she said as much, Laurel looked at her sympathetically and with all seriousness said, "For two people as passionate about each other as you and Robert are, you would absolutely *love* a good fight."

Several hours later, Mairead scanned the great hall. She had seen it full before, during holidays and celebratory events, such as the birth of Rab, but never had she seen it used to host a visiting clan's laird and his men. It felt right. Robert had built the massive hall to be used in such a way and it was a shame it never had. But what was being served was a crime—and it was one that had been committed by her sister.

Clenching her fists, Mairead looked down at the food on her plate. This afternoon, in the kitchens, Selah had done much more than just put together a tray of food.

Mairead should have known Selah would do something like this.

Since Mairead had assumed the role of lady of the castle, the meals at Foinaven had dramatically improved. She had removed the two men causing most of the problems in the kitchen, one with his drunkenness on stolen ale and the other exceptionally lazy with his belligerence to all, and it had instantly improved things. Hellie's instructions were no longer ignored and drowned out by a constant barrage of loud, snide comments. The young man and woman she had replaced them with were new to the castle, but not to food preparation as they each came from very large families and had been one of the primary cooks. Mairead knew neither family wanted to lose the help, but the wages were needed and they had other children who were eager to take their siblings' role as a cook.

Mairead had made similar changes throughout the castle. Adiran now had two additional stable boys to help him with all the work. The candlemaker finally had two decent apprentices as did the blacksmith. While neither job was a pleasant one, all the young men now employed understood the value of learning and mastering a craft other than being tied to farming and fishing—something the ones before them had not.

The difficulty of making these changes lay not in knowing what to do or even who to choose to dismiss—it had been Selah. Her own sister would speak to the ones she let go and tell them that she would set things to right and speak with Mairead, who was new to the role. *New to the role!* For years, she had been doing most of the duties of lady of the castle. It was not *she* who needed to be set right, it was Selah! And it was past time that it happened.

"How dare you!" Mairead growled. Everyone at the main table heard her as well as the vehemence that had come with those three words. Mairead slammed her fist on the table and rose to her feet. She glared at her sister. *"How dare you!"* Now she had everyone's attention, but Mairead did not care. Her eyes were locked on Selah. "This time you have gone too far. It is one thing to constantly to irritate me with your inability to let go, but it is another when your interference embarrasses my husband, *your* laird, and starves men who are going into battle the next day!"

Selah's face morphed from one of shock to indignation. "I did no such thing!"

"Do you deny that you changed my kitchen staff this afternoon and rehired Einns and Torphin behind my back, without my permission—*without even asking*?"

Hamish felt Robert bristle next to him as his brother tried to decide what to do. Whatever Robert decided, Hamish would not let him interfere. He was thrilled Mairead was finally addressing the problem between her and Selah. She had been keeping it inside for a few weeks now and he had known that at some point she was going to explode. He had not expected it to happen in the middle of the great hall with close friends and visitors, but at this point, he did not care. He was tired of being the one to listen to all her frustrations every evening as she paced the floor telling him of a new counteraction Selah had taken. Hamish had considered telling Selah himself that she needed to stop, but he had been too busy with other matters to get into the squabbles of castle life. So this eruption was welcomed and Hamish was not going to let anyone prematurely end it.

"I deny nothing." Selah's back was straight and she

held her head high. It was clear that she was embarrassed but refused to cave to Mairead's withering stare. She rose to her feet. "Since they were new to the kitchens, I sent the two you hired to help with the cleaning of your old chambers for Laird and Lady McTiernay to use during their stay. And then I asked Einns and Torphin to assume their old duties because *I knew* how much work needed to be done. Just as *I knew* how much suffering both men had gone through since they lost their positions. You would too if you had listened to me."

I knew, Mairead repeated the words under her breath. Well, she knew quite a few things as well and it was time for her sister to learn what one of them was. "Well, *I know* that you gave up the right to make those decisions. *I know* that I am lady of Foinaven, not you, and *I know* that no one but Hamish or I can instruct, counsel, or hire and dismiss any staff within these walls. And that includes you, Selah. This is your home and always will be, but you no longer have a role of authority here. And unlike you when you were in charge of this castle, *I don't want or need your help."*

The silence in the room was oppressive, but both women ignored the eyes and all the held breaths. Robert was the first to speak. "You cannot talk to my wife that way. Selah did nothing to cause this outburst and she certainly did nothing to embarrass you or Hamish. It is your behavior that should be admonished, Mairead. Not Selah's."

Hamish had known Robert was going to say something, but he had not expected his own anger to rise when he did. How could his brother be so blind to the shortcomings of his wife? Of *course,* Mairead was angry! It was most likely her outrage that was keeping him from

also being cross with the situation. "My wife's behavior is
not only *appropriate*, but *justified*," Hamish said through
gritted teeth. "And because of *your wife,* not only do I
have to suffer through another godforsaken tough and
flavorless meal, but those who are visiting do as well!"

Robert's jaw clenched and he reached out to grab his
wife's hand and give it a squeeze. "There is nothing wrong
with this food."

Conor coughed in his hand with surprise at hearing
that Robert was serious.

"And *that* is why I'm forbidding your wife to ever go
near Foinaven's kitchens again." Hamish did not raise his
voice, but its effect was the same as if he had been yelling.

Mairead wanted to throw her arms around him and tell
Hamish how much she loved him while at the same time
run out of the room in mortification. Their first family
fight and they were having it not just in front of others but
the *McTiernays*!

With all the dignity she could muster, Mairead looked
to Laurel and said, "I apologize."

Laurel gave her an encouraging half smile. "You forget.
I love a good row. It's nice to be the spectator. I'm usually one of the participants. And I knew from earlier today
that something was brewing between you and your sister.
It was a wonder that either of you have held out this long.
The quality of food though, that would have done it for me
as well."

Conor picked up the piece of hard, dried meat and let
it drop. "You call this food?"

Laurel elbowed him. "Not now, unless you want to join
this ruckus."

Conor steepled his fingers and let go only a *hrmph*.

Mairead wished Laurel's simple dismissal could allevi-
ate her anger, but it did not. She needed to leave before

she said more to further humiliate herself. "I will talk with Hellie and see if some better fare can be brought out." She would go, but she doubted anything could be found. All had already been prepared and ruined. It would take hours to prep the other fowl and meats, cook it, and then offer it to their guests.

Selah watched her sister leave via the door to the kitchens and without a word, left through the main doors to the courtyard.

Laurel popped some bread in her mouth, completely unfazed. Conor tried another piece of fowl and grunted as his teeth ground the flavorless meat. Robert just shook his head, still stunned. "Over *food*," he muttered. "Who gets so angry over an overcooked meal?"

Laurel looked at the man in disbelief. Robert's features were very similar to Hamish's, but to her, that was where the similarities ended. "Me," she answered unequivocally. "If this had been served to my guests, I'm not sure just who and how many would be injured from my wrath, but I doubt it would be limited to only your wife. If what Mairead said is true and Selah *did* change the kitchen staff without permission, then Selah would be my first target."

Robert's face turned red with fury and Laurel suspected that this was the first time anyone had ever informed him that his wife was not perfect and that she had done something to cause someone's ire. Selah had not been exaggerating when she said that neither she nor Robert had ever raised their voices against each other. As such, neither knew what to do. Laurel felt a modicum of pity. "Your wife definitely has some explaining to do," she began. "However, I am convinced that her intrusion on Mairead's role as lady of the castle has far less to do with missing the responsibility as Mairead thinks, and more to do with something far more personal."

Laurel rose to her feet. "This should be interesting." Then she pointed to one of the platters. "The bread and the cheese are edible, Conor." Then after placing a kiss on his cheek, she turned to leave. "Eat those while I go meddle."

Conor clutched her fingers just in time. "Do you really need to get involved?"

Laurel glanced over her shoulder and blinked at him, surprised he even needed to ask. "Of course I do! How can I refuse such a compelling invitation?"

Laurel found Mairead sitting in front of a fire in a small keep room. By the décor, Laurel could tell it was where both sisters went to sit and talk.

Mairead turned her head and upon seeing Laurel, said, "Lady McTiernay, I am very sorry for my outburst earlier, but I really would like to be left alone."

The use of her title was definitely a hint, but Laurel ignored it. "Not surprising and I would probably feel the same way. It was fortunate that tonight it was just Conor and me, for you are right to assume other lairds might have taken offense by what was served."

"I think your husband *did* take offense," Mairead mumbled, looking back at the fire.

"Conor does love his food and he is not used to such fare."

Selah gasped behind her, feeling the intended barb. Laurel felt no regret at the harsh words. It was important the woman understood that in her effort to prove something to Mairead, there could have been serious consequences. Right now, the men were just going to be a little hungrier than they might have been. Laurel would be more concerned if Conor had not assured her that she would enjoy tomorrow's outcome.

Hearing the sudden intake of her sister's breath, Mairead turned around and saw that it was indeed Selah. She shifted her gaze to Laurel. "As I told you before, Lady McTiernay, I do not wish to be disturbed."

Laurel entered the room and sat down beside her. "Well, fortunately for you I love Hamish like a brother, which makes you family. And as you so eloquently pointed out tonight, families interfere and usually when least wanted."

Selah stepped into the room as well, her arms crossed. Laurel had found her pacing in the courtyard, oblivious to the cold night air. The two sisters were furious with each other and if left on their own it would take them days, if not weeks, to finally truly speak all that was in their hearts.

At this moment, Selah thought what she wanted was an apology and Laurel had hinted that she might get one if she went with her to see Mairead. Laurel, however, was not about to take sides. It might have seemed like she supported Mairead, but she had heard very clearly just why her older sister was in so much pain. *Unlike when you were in charge of this castle, I don't want or need your help.* Ouch.

Laurel waited for nearly a minute for either sister to seize the opportunity to speak. After a minute, it became clear that it would not happen without some prompting. "If I'd known how much trouble cleaning a room would be, I would've insisted Conor and I sleep in dust."

Mairead let go a disgusted snort. Laurel smiled.

Keeping her gaze locked on the fire, Mairead sneered,

"I know you have a reason for what you did, Selah, but I cannot think of *anything* to justify your actions."

"Justify *my* actions!" Selah huffed. "I'm not the one who cut two men and their families off with no support. Both were shocked and devastated when you fired them. More than that, neither has been able to find work on someone's farms or fishing boat. I think it is *you* who need to justify just how you can be so heartless!"

"Heartless? Einns is a mean drunk and working at the castle near the ale enables him to remain inebriated at all times. His family was *relieved* that he no longer had access, but you fell for his pleas that *he* was the injured party." Selah's jaw dropped. Her hazel eyes grew large and tears began to form. It was clear she had no idea. But Mairead was not finished. "And Einns is an angel compared to Torphin. He is lazy and actually *enjoys* causing problems. He grossly insults whoever he works with and threatens and berates them into doing his job. He terrorized people daily and I've tried for *years* to get you to listen to me when you had the chance to fix things. He is made from the same cloth as Ulrick. He is lucky that I only dismissed him from the castle and did not ask Hamish to banish him altogether!"

"I . . . I . . . didn't know," Selah stammered, the tears in her eyes starting to fall. "I was just trying to help."

Mairead, however, was finally releasing all that she had been thinking and was not inclined to stop until she was done. "You were not trying to help, Selah, for you were content to let me do the majority of the work running this castle. Now that you do not have the responsibility, you suddenly crave it and step in every chance you have and try to assert your will over mine. It confuses the staff, it infuriates me, and mostly it creates chaos, causing poor work and embarrassing debacles like tonight's meal."

Selah stood immobile. No one had ever spoken to her so strongly, but then she always prided herself on resolving problems, not causing them.

Seeing her distress, Laurel leaned over and patted her hand. "Everyone reacts differently to pain, especially when inflicted by a family member."

Selah lifted her eyes to look at Laurel and Laurel realized that she had guessed correctly. This was not a play for power. This was a response to how Mairead assumed responsibility and the number of changes she was making. It was an indirect way of saying that for years she had thought her sister had done a poor job.

Selah swallowed and looked back down at her hands. "Mairead is just so eager to change everything," she said to Laurel. It was easier telling Laurel than directing what she was really feeling to Mairead. "I understand that this is now her home, but it was *my* home."

Mairead ignored Laurel, who rose to her feet and left the room. It was a good thing, because Mairead could feel the tension rising in her again and this time she did not want to censor her words. "Do you still want to be the lady of the castle?"

Selah shook her head. It was a relief not to have those responsibilities. She never liked them and always felt jealous that Mairead, who was eight years younger, handled them so easily. "I'm glad you are lady of Foinaven. You naturally know what to do, where I'm a natural peacemaker."

Finally understanding what was at the crux of Selah's actions, Mairead began to calm. "That is a vital part to being a laird's wife, Selah. I would have no hope of knowing how to do that if not for you and your guidance these last twelve years. I was able to make these changes so swiftly *because* I had learned from you how to work with people and be empathetic to their needs. I'm far from good at it, but at least I know to try."

Mairead's concession gave Selah the courage to say what really weighed on her mind and heart. "I thought that every time you made a decision you knew I would never have agreed to, you were intimating that I had done a poor job. That you were looking for ways to show me how I had failed."

Mairead felt her anger dissipate even more. It had been growing for so long it felt like a huge weight was being lifted. She had no idea that Selah felt this way, but now that she was looking at all her changes from her sister's point of view, she could believe it.

"Selah, nothing could be further from the truth. I am so sorry."

Laurel returned with a third chair and a large bag. "I think I filched the chair from your son's room," she said to Selah. "You don't mind?" The elder sister shook her head. Laurel put it near the fire and all three women sat down. "I suspect that if you stopped looking at all the changes Mairead made, you will find that there is a lot more that she kept."

Mairead nodded her head and started listing them. After several minutes of hugs and reaffirmations of love and admiration, Laurel was ready to finally talk about why *she* had insisted on journeying north, for it was not just to meet Hamish's bride but to see them properly married.

"Absolutely!" Selah squealed, the depression previously weighing down on her instantly vanished. "That is what I was wanting to talk about this afternoon!"

Mairead was not so positive. A *third* wedding ceremony? She was lucky that Hamish had been willing to do the first two. A third in such a short period of time would certainly make him rethink things. Aye, they were more than compatible in bed, but Hamish had yet to say that he loved her. And if he did not feel that way by now, she was not sure he ever would. "Hamish was content with a handfast and so am I. I think anything more would be . . . unwise."

Laurel just smiled and would not be dissuaded. "If that is all, then Father Lanaghly will just remind him that *all* McTiernays marry at sunset. It was the whole reason he insisted on coming, after all."

Mairead tried once again to explain that Hamish was not a McTiernay, but Laurel seemed too intent on what was in the bag to listen. "I'm not sure that Hamish will want *another* ceremony."

"What do you mean?" Selah posed rhetorically. "Of *course* Hamish will! He loves you!"

Mairead's eyes grew large at the mistaken claim. "Hamish cares for me, but love?"

"If Hamish exchanged vows with you, then his love for you must be very deep and he must believe you share that sentiment," Laurel answered without hesitation. "I've known him for ten years and he has never come close to marriage. Oh, he flirted with a number of women and pretended to entertain the idea of marrying one day, but he told me once very soon after we met that he was waiting for what Conor and I have. I don't think anything could have enticed him to share vows with you if you had not fully captured his heart."

Mairead smiled and pretended to be convinced, and she wanted to be, but something in her yearned to know why, if Laurel was correct, Hamish did not tell her himself. He had had plenty of opportunities and he had to know how much she longed to hear him say that he loved her after hearing her whisper those words to him so often.

Laurel reached into the bag and pulled out a beautiful gown. Both sisters gasped. Laurel giggled. "And Conor thought stopping by Cole's was a waste of time." She laid out the nearly complete gown across her lap and handed the top to Mairead so she could see the intricacy of the beadwork. "Someday you will get to meet the rest of Hamish's family. Cole is one of Conor's younger brothers and is a McTiernay laird of lands near Loch Torridon." Mairead opened her mouth again to clarify that Hamish was a *MacBrieve* laird, not a McTiernay one, but did not have a chance. "Cole's wife's best friend used to live with us and she does the most beautiful beadwork I have ever seen. Upon my arrival and news that Hamish was going to marry, we focused on nothing else but this gown. We left the stitching open here and here because we were not sure of your size, but I did pummel the herald with enough questions to get an idea of your coloring and height."

Mairead fingered the garment. It was a rich burgundy with pearl beads intricately sewn along the wide collar and sleeves. It was simple and yet with her hair coloring, it would be stunning.

Selah let go a low whistle. "It is a shame that you will not be wearing it very long." She looked at Laurel and added with a wink, "Hamish left his last wedding celebration nearly as soon as it began."

Mairead had a feeling that her sister was right. This gown would make anyone look irresistible. She just wished it had the power to make Hamish admit his feelings.

Laurel ordered her to try it on so that she could mark the hem. Selah left to wake up Foinaven's best seamstress and put her to work.

"I have a feeling this gown will get much use over the years." Laurel looked thoughtfully as she stroked the luxurious material. "There are certain outfits . . . and robes . . . that let Conor know my mood and feelings." It was true. Her robe was an especially useful tool when Conor was being most stubborn about something. "Maybe this gown will remind Hamish that some words—no matter how much the other knows them to be true—still need to be said."

Chapter Twenty

Amon, Conor, and Hamish sat on their horses and examined the campfires not far in the distance. Yesterday afternoon, when the men started gathering on the ridge, they had seen the Mackays begin to make camp. The time had come. In another hour, the sun would rise and he would be facing one of the fiercest Highland lairds. Either they would part amicably and Ulrick would be removed as a presence from the Mackay clan, or blood would be shed. It was a large risk, forcing Donald Mackay to meet him, but Hamish was calm.

Amon lightly pulled on his reins to keep his horse still. If someone had told him at the beginning of the year that he would give up his life as a farmer to be commander of the MacBrieve army, he would have thought them mad. It was not that he disliked being a farmer for it was not nearly as dull as he had thought it would be, but it was not the type of challenge that spoke to his soul. There were many others capable and willing to take over those duties, but that was not the case for Hamish's burgeoning guard. Being a commander was something Amon was uniquely suited for and he had loved every minute so far.

Mostly because he loved following a laird who believed it was more important to be able to outthink his opponents and not rely on outfighting them.

Conor had been amused when Hamish had said his strategic skills came from being with the McTiernays for so many years; Conor knew otherwise. Some things could be taught, but others people were born to. And Hamish was born to lead.

Hamish sat quietly and studied the horizon. He had no doubt his plan could work, but success hinged on one last vital component and it required Hamish to give up something he had protected for years. But if he was to grow this clan like he envisioned, making it strong and formidable, he could not be *like* a McTiernay . . . he needed to *be* a McTiernay.

Hamish looked at Conor, who returned his steady gaze. "Any questions?"

Conor shook his head. "None. My men know what to do."

"Then I just have one more thing I must ask of you, as a friend and someone whom I respect who already has my allegiance," Hamish began solemnly. "I have no wish to meet Donald Mackay as the MacBrieve laird."

Amon froze. He could not believe what he was hearing.

"I wish to meet the man as who I truly am. A McTiernay."

Conor smiled. "A McTiernay laird," he corrected.

Hamish looked him in the eye. "I pledged my sword to you long ago. Let me now pledge my people and my men."

Amon's mouth dropped. He had not been expecting this.

Conor flashed a wide smile, his gray eyes shining with pride. His brother Cole was a McTiernay laird of Torridon and he would be proud to claim Hamish as his own as well.

"I, Conor, chieftain of the McTiernay clan, now address you as Hamish, the laird of the McTiernays of Farr."

In the firelight on a hill where a battle might soon dictate his fate, Hamish swore his allegiance to Conor and the McTiernay clan. Amon, who was still shocked, left soon after to spread the news.

Hamish moved to meet with his lead guards, who he knew would have questions when they were told of the change, but Conor indicated that he needed another moment with him. "There is something about your family history I have been under a vow to reveal to you only now."

Conor's tone was serious and Hamish found himself uneasy. What secret could Conor have about him? Who could have sworn him to secrecy? "I'm listening."

"Your father was not a MacBrieve."

Hamish sat still. He had just promised loyalty to Conor and found it beyond comprehension why he chose *now* to dishonor his father's memory. When he had relinquished the name of MacBrieve, it had not been out of shame, it had been out of acknowledgment of who he felt he was inside. But now he was not so sure.

"Your father was a McTiernay."

Hamish definitely felt like someone had punched him in the stomach. He could do nothing more than sit and wait for Conor to explain.

"Physically, you take after your mother's side of the family. She was the MacBrieve and the only child of your grandfather, who was the MacBrieve laird. Your father served under mine for several years, but upon a chance meeting, your parents fell in love." Conor glanced at Hamish. "I think you and Robert get this propensity to fall in love quickly from them."

That small jibe was enough to rattle Hamish into a

response. His anger was morphing into shock, but also recognition that Conor was speaking the truth.

"Your grandfather agreed to the marriage but only if your father assumed the MacBrieve name and accepted the responsibility of becoming the clan's next laird. Twelve years ago, when we met that day in that skirmish, I had no idea who you were. I thought it was good luck, but your father felt it was fate. When he found out that you had joined my guard, he came down and we met." *That* got Hamish's attention. His father had left the northern lands and yet had chosen *not* to see him? The questions were multiplying as Conor continued talking. "I was reluctant to see him at first but did so out of respect to another laird. He explained his past and asked that I not tell you about his visit or who he once was. He knew you were not like most MacBrieves and would feel a kinship to the Mc-Tiernays. He was afraid such a revelation would give you reason to irrevocably tie yourself to our clan and keep you from coming home, making amends with your brother, and assuming your right as laird. I was uncomfortable with the secret and only agreed to keep it until you had met with your brother, which would only happen when you chose to do so. You have finally released me from my burden."

Hamish sat for several minutes and then a slow, relaxed smile took over his expression. All these years he had fought becoming a McTiernay because it meant he would no longer be what he was born—a MacBrieve.

But it turned out, he had to give up neither.

He was both. A MacBrieve *and* a McTiernay.

Mairead would be thrilled learning that she had been right.

* * *

Hamish signaled Amon and they rode out to join Ian, Davros, and his men awaiting them on the ridge—half were on horseback, the others on foot. His army numbered eight dozen now and in most circumstances, the visual effect they created all lined up and armed for battle would have served as a warning that would have been heeded. But the Mackays were gathered on the other side of the strath, and their numbers nearly doubled his.

And Hamish knew that the number of men each laird had on his side was going to be key to swaying the outcome of what was about to happen.

Hamish rode up and down the line, sitting proud on his horse wearing the McTiernay tartan. Word was spreading throughout the village that their newly formed clan was undergoing another change. They again had a choice—wear McTiernay colors or leave. This time, very few were against the idea. Most had come to peace with the idea of uniting into a single clan and their contributions to its security. But it had rankled many to become MacBrieves. McTiernays, however, that was different. To suddenly belong to one of the most powerful clans in all of Scotland was a mighty gift.

Hamish suspected a few in the village might still choose to leave, but neither would he be surprised if some of the families that had already left decided to return. His guard, however, Hamish had no doubt of their loyalty. They may not all be wearing his colors *yet*, but two hours ago every man had raised his sword without hesitation and swore their allegiance to Hamish McTiernay and vowed to support and fight for clan McTiernay of Farr.

Hamish rode one more time in front of his men, and then with a kick to his mount, he turned and headed out alone to meet Donald Mackay.

Donald Mackay was an imposing figure. He had brown hair that hung loose below his shoulders and sported a dark beard that held hints of gray. His eyes were brown and set above a wide nose that would have looked odd except that every feature of his face was built similarly.

Mackay looked Hamish over with a narrowed gaze. "So you have returned home then."

Hamish relaxed his expression and gave a signal nod. "I have." He did not need to say that he was now the laird. He did not need to say that he had united the clans. It was clear Ulrick had told Laird Mackay the initial changes that had been made.

Mackay pointed to Hamish's men lined on the ridge. "Your numbers have grown considerably in the past several weeks." Mackay then looked behind before returning his gaze to Hamish. "But not nearly enough."

Hamish took his time and let his eye glide over all the Mackay men who were waiting for their laird to give them the signal. "Aye, there have been many changes. But your numbers have also grown in the past couple of weeks."

"Then your spies have misinformed you. I gave Ulrick a place to sleep for a night for the information he provided but that was all. I have not seen him since nor do I expect to. The man has loyalty to only one man—himself. Only a fool would think otherwise."

Hamish grinned. The verbal swipe was not an insult to him, but his brother. Donald was attempting to get a reaction, to gauge Hamish's control over his emotions when slightly provoked. Hamish had to admire the strategy. "I agree. Hence there have been changes. Some of which might have bearing on today's events."

"I always dreaded this inevitability." Mackay's tone was weary, but it held no fear. He knew what was soon to happen, just as he knew that his clan would be the victor. But he took no joy in slaughtering good men. "Your part of the Farr region has always made me uneasy."

Hamish understood what the older laird meant. Multiple small clans in the region created a lack of predictability, but also it meant that an insurgence was unlikely. However, uniting them into a single clan with a burgeoning army posed a danger that pushed tolerance. It was why Hamish knew this confrontation had to happen now, not in the spring when emotions had grown to uncontrollable limits and Mackay had a chance to gather his full force.

"Change does not have to be taken as a threat. It can be a good thing for all those in this region."

"I have not found recent changes all that beneficial." Mackay grimaced. "However, it did give me some pleasure knowing the effort your men had to go through to move all those rock walls. But then I had to endure much grief listening to my men grumble about cleaning out the stream." Donald tightened his fist on his reins. He did not long for war, but when it came knocking at his doorstep, he would not back down.

It was no struggle for Hamish to keep his face calm. He felt no fear and Donald needed to know that. "I knew of no other way for us to meet alone and face-to-face."

A new light of hope suddenly sprang into Donald Mackay's dark eyes. A man facing potential death did not look as calm as Hamish. "I cannot decide whether you are the most foolish Highlander to come to these parts in some time or the most fearless. But I will admit that your ploy was clever."

"You have to admit it was successful," Hamish added.

Donald cocked his head to his side and with a smirk said, "We have met and I admire your mind, but I have yet to hear anything that makes you think this meeting will end in your favor." He paused to grip his sword and in a solemn tone that spoke of no flexibility, he said, "I have no desire to assume responsibility for MacBrieve mouths, but a neighbor who wants to pick a fight better be ready to have one. So either tell your men to lay down their arms or I will signal mine."

"There are no MacBrieves at Farr. Nor are there any MacMhathains, Mhic Eains, Ceiteaches, Faills, Shyns, Largs, or Munros." Hamish moved his hand to flick some dirt off his tartan. When he did, he flung the material, and the color pattern caught Donald's attention. It was not that of a MacBrieve. Hamish then gripped his own sword and waited until he once again held the eyes of the older laird. "I was born to a McTiernay Highlander and this is a McTiernay plaid. The mouths I feed are part of the clan McTiernay under the chieftain Conor McTiernay."

In one smooth movement, Hamish rose his sword and immediately Amon rose his. Within seconds, two hundred battle-experienced, highly trained soldiers came into view and joined the eight dozen Hamish already had on the ridge. In front of them all was Conor McTiernay.

Donald Mackay reassessed the young laird in front of him. Those numbers had been kept well hidden and had to have only arrived in the last day or two. It was clear that the rumors of McTiernay strategy and bravado were not overstated. He sighed. "War it is then."

Hamish shook his head. "I did not come here for bloodshed. I came because I have the same unease about these lands. I also knew that you would never consider an alliance with a small clan that held nothing of value. But one with the McTiernays—you could not easily dismiss that. And your men"—Hamish gestured to the now uneasy

Mackay soldiers—"now that they see a *portion* of the force the McTiernays wield, will not sit in silent disagreement with such a decision."

Mackay inhaled deeply and let it go slowly. "An alliance?" It was clear he did not like the term.

Hamish nodded. "An alliance of two great clans that would ensure peace for both our peoples. I need to lead my people, not have them live in fear. And you would know that not just my men, but all McTiernays—Conor's as well as those from Torridon—would never let what happened at Mornay happen to a Mackay again."

Donald Mackay did not move. Nothing changed about his expression with the exception of his eyes. Hamish knew he was carefully considering the offer. To no longer be alone was a powerful incentive.

"I always heard that McTiernays were brilliant strategists. It would be an advantageous trait to have in an ally."

Hamish glanced over his shoulder and immediately Conor took his cue and rode down to join the two men. His face was relaxed, but his gray eyes brokered no cheer. "Am I greeting a future ally or should I be giving the signal to prepare weapons?"

Mackay nodded his head in welcome. "You are Conor McTiernay, chieftain of the McTiernay clan, I presume." Conor nodded his head. "I always wanted to meet your father and then you, after he had passed away."

"I am somewhat surprised we have not before now."

Mackay glanced over his shoulder. His men were getting antsy. "It is going to take some time to become accustomed to the idea of an ally, especially when my men are itching for a fight."

Conor's impassive face suddenly broke out into a huge grin. "Then I say we have one."

* * *

The courtyard had been a bustle of activity all day, but the sudden increase in the level of noise caught all three women's attention. Selah went to look out the window and nodded. "The men are returning. The games must be over."

Mairead's eyes were large. "I hope the games included finding food. *Three hundred men!*" Her voice cracked at the idea.

Laurel shrugged her shoulders. "I'm more thankful that your buttery is so well stocked. But I do believe our husbands improvised a little to ensure tonight's feast would have plenty of food as well. I believe Conor said that one contest was to see whose men—Conor's, Hamish's, or Laird Mackay's—could erect the most bonfires within an hour. The majority of the soldiers will cook their spoils themselves. So stop worrying about all that. We need to focus on you, not on them."

Laurel tucked the last of Mairead's thick hair into a soft bun that was a complex collage of large and small braids with a scattering of pearls intermixed. "There," she said with a satisfied smile. "All that is left is the dress."

Mairead had just slipped it over her head and was beginning to lace it up when shouts erupted from the courtyard.

"Ale!" came a loud shout from the courtyard.

"Aye! Lots of ale!"

"The hall!" bellowed another.

"Victors get the hall!"

"Then *you* shall enjoy the baily this evening!"

"I need ale!"

"I need food!"

"I need a priest!" said one loud voice.

Mairead held her breath as she heard Hamish shout again, this time calling Father Lanaghly by name. She could not believe it. Hamish sounded *eager* to get married—again.

Hamish must have gotten Conor, Davros, Amon, and every other man to join him for now the walls vibrated with shouts for Father Lanaghly to make an appearance. The old priest must have done so, for now they were shouting for a bride. "We need a bride! Hamish needs a bride! *Maaaaiiiireaaad!*"

Laurel rolled her eyes and looked at Selah. "This is ridiculous. You would have thought they'd been in the buttery for hours the way they are acting." She then turned to Mairead and said, "Your sister and I will go and end their madness."

Selah nodded in agreement. She pressed her hands together and looked as if she was about to cry. "Oh, Mairead. You are so beautiful."

Laurel kissed Mairead's cheek. "Come down when you are ready and not a minute before. We will keep the men at bay."

Mairead watched the two women exit the solar and took a deep, calming breath. She could have left with them, but she was finding herself a little anxious. She shook her hands in an effort to calm herself. It was not like she was not already married to Hamish, but many felt a handfast was not permanent. One could opt to dissolve the union after a year and day. Marriage by a priest, however, that was forever binding.

When Hamish returned that morning with *another* laird in tow, this time the fearsome Laird Donald Mackay, she had thought that would be the most astounding thing to happen that day. Then there was an alliance followed by some very intense Highland games with all three armies competing. But when Laurel announced that the wedding should take place at sundown, Hamish had immediately agreed. There had been no need to persuade him into the idea. The man had leapt to it, announcing that the games would cease early so they could be wed at sunset.

The music started playing and people were singing loudly. The merriment had begun. "And if you don't leave now," Mairead muttered to herself, "you might just miss your own wedding!"

Taking a deep breath, she went to the door and pulled it open.

Her heart dropped. Her eyes grew massive and fear filled her every pore.

Ulrick was standing there waiting for her.

Mairead screamed, but she knew it had not been heard over the deafening sounds coming from the courtyard. Even if it had been, everyone would have thought she was only one of the merrymakers and not someone who was shrieking that her life was about to end.

"I've been waiting for you." His voice was deep and dripped with an evil sickness that had no cure.

Mairead backed up a step and began to fondle the *sgian dubh* that was sheathed against her thigh. She had insisted on the slit in the new gown not because she had thought to need it, but because she was now accustomed to having access to her small knife and not wearing it had felt awkward. Besides, she had always enjoyed the way Hamish had taken it off her leg.

"How did you get in here?" Mairead's heart was pounding so loudly she could barely hear his answer.

"Through your sneaky little passageway. Those Kyldoane brothers use it to deliver messages in and out of the castle without being seen . . . or so they thought."

"Leave now, Ulrick, while you have the chance."

He shook his head back and forth slowly. "I made you a vow. Did you forget?"

Mairead took another step back. She wanted to scream again for help, but the noise from the courtyard had only increased. Another shout would only cause Ulrick to leap forward and she had yet to find her knife through the folds of her dress. Fear was starting to suffocate her, sending tremors through her slender form. "I'm married now. You cannot have me."

He threw back his head and laughed. The sinister sound sent sheer black fright sweeping through her. "I do not care about such conventions. Your promise means nothing to me and what I plan to take from you."

Mairead's fist finally closed around the handle. She took a breath and fought her nerves. She hated fear. Hated reacting to it. "If you touch me, you're a dead man. Hamish will track you down and leave you for the vultures."

Ulrick shrugged. "Hamish would have to find me first, but until he did, he would be tormented knowing that I had you. I tasted you. I *hurt* you."

"I will die first," she hissed.

Ulrick's brows rose and he nodded his head, advancing toward her. "I intend to accommodate those wishes, but I *will* have you." With those words, he lunged forward and Mairead pulled free her *sgian dubh* just in time. She shifted to the right, but Ulrick had anticipated the move and reached out to grab her. But when she had shifted, she had also sunk to the floor. A move that caused Ulrick to hesitate just long enough to give her access to his abdomen.

When Mairead realized she missed, icy fear twisted around her heart. For she also realized that she was not the only one armed. Ulrick had a blade in his hand. A full-size dirk.

Laurel winked at Hamish to calm him. He was a bundle of nerves. He had not realized just how badly he had wanted to marry Mairead. Once she vowed to be his, he would never lose her. A year from now she could not look at him and break his heart and walk away. He knew deep down that would not have happened, but once Father Lanaghly pronounced Mairead as his wife, there would no longer be even the tiniest of doubts.

"Do not worry. She will be down soon. Trust me, it is worth the wait," Laurel said with a smile.

Donald Mackay clinked mugs with a group of men and then with a smile sat down beside him. "I have never been one to think much of alliances, but I am beginning to think you McTiernays are not such a bad lot."

Hamish returned his grin. "You may have won the most games, neighbor, but my men won the most difficult."

"Fine, be proud that your men can throw cabers accurately, Hamish, but *my* soldiers proved they would be the deadliest," Conor claimed as he joined them.

"If we did not need to get this young laird married, the games would have lasted long enough for us Mackays to prove just who is best with *every* type of weapon."

Conor rose his mug. "To future games."

"To future games!"

And all three men downed their ale and signaled for more. "I must admit to admiring some of the skills displayed out there today." Donald paused to wipe his mouth with his sleeve. "I had not realized some of my men were lacking in certain areas."

Conor grimaced. "Me either. Finn has grown lax this winter."

"At least both of yours have experience," Hamish lamented. "I can teach a man to use a weapon, but it is different looking an enemy in the eye who is intent on killing you. Even the most highly trained man can freeze and fail to react in time."

"Or at all," Donald added, and swung his arm out for his mug to be refilled by a servant walking by with a tankard.

Conor swung his arm out as well. "I cannot bring the experience of war, nor do I wish to do so, but I think all of us might benefit from exchanging some of our soldiers."

"Aye," Hamish said, knowing how well it had worked between the McTiernays and Schelldens, Conor's ally and neighbor.

With a twinkle in his eye, Donald chuckled. "I don't suppose an understanding of how your ally works has anything to do with it."

Conor McTiernay just widened his eyes in mock astonishment. "Now that would be another benefit."

"I have nothing to hide," Mackay said. "The spring?"

Hamish considered it. "How many?"

"How about a dozen men go to each in this alliance. Hamish sends a dozen to me and to you." He gestured toward Donald. "I send a dozen to him and you, and you send a dozen to us."

"Agreed, but only if we meet again in the fall. I want to settle once and for all the victor of the games."

"Lairds can participate?" Hamish half stated, half asked.

Donald scoffed. "Of course."

"Then I absolutely agree."

Conor looked around. "Aren't you supposed to be agreeing to something else soon?"

Hamish was about to answer when one of Donald Mackay's men came up to him. "Laird?"

"It better be important," Mackay barked. He was enjoying the conversation and really was not interested in settling bets.

"We were wondering why Ulrick is allowed to celebrate with us since he did not participate in any of the games. The man insulted us. He needs to be humiliated not pampered."

Donald shook his head. "It was not I who invited that *cac*."

Hamish froze. "Ulrick is *here* . . . *inside* Foinaven?"

The man nodded. The castle gates had been opened and there had been much traffic in and out of the tower entrance, but it had been carefully watched to ensure only those approved were allowed to enter. But the tower was not the only way inside Foinaven. And no one was guarding the keep's hearth.

Hamish leapt to his feet and started running. He threw people out of his way and banged through the doors and into the night air. A moment later he was in the keep and taking steps two at a time in a rush to get to his solar where Mairead was prepping for their wedding. She had to be well. She had to. She was delayed because of her hair, her dress—anything but what his heart feared most.

That he was too late.

He rounded the last turn of the stairwell and saw the door open. There was no sound. Was that a good sign? He sprang to the entrance and glanced around. And then he looked down.

Mairead was on the floor, drenched in blood. Ulrick was on top of her. Both appeared to be dead.

"Noooooo!"

Hamish collapsed beside Mairead just as Conor and Donald Mackay arrived at the scene. *"Murt!"*

Conor grabbed Ulrick's shoulders and threw him aside. Donald checked the man and lifted up his leine. There was a seven-inch gash across his abdomen. The man was dead. Mairead had killed him as he took her life.

Hamish gathered Mairead in his arms and held her close to him. "Do not leave, *m'aingeal*." He kissed her head, her cheeks, her mouth. "You promised me. You swore you would never leave me. I cannot live without you. I love you, Mairead. Do you hear me? *I love you!*"

Mairead sputtered and then inhaled as she was gasping for breath. She clung to Hamish as he squeezed her to him. "Oh my God, *aingeal*, you scared the hell out of me."

Mairead began to pound on his chest and he suddenly realized that she was injured and began to look for her wound.

Free to breathe once again, Mairead inhaled deeply. Air, wonderful air. She had not thought she would breathe it again. When Ulrick had charged her the last time, her mind had gone blank and she just reacted, performing the defensive maneuver like she had done dozens of times over the past few weeks. Usually alone, but sometimes with Hamish as a prelude to their night together.

When it had worked and she saw blood bubble from Ulrick's lips, relief had shot through her. But it had not lasted long. When he had fallen, she had been pinned between him and the bed and had not been able to move out of the way in time. He slammed on top of her, knocking the wind out of her. She had tried screaming for help again, but it only made things worse. Her last thoughts had been that Hamish was going to be furious with himself. He taught her how to win a knife fight, but he had forgotten to show her how to survive it.

Hamish could not find her injury. He was in a panic and about to rip her dress off when Mairead screamed, *"Don't you dare destroy this dress!"*

Strong hands gripped his shoulders and he could hear Conor behind him. "Listen to her, Hamish. Mairead is not hurt. She just couldn't breathe."

"I'm fine. I'm not hurt. Really."

"The blood," Hamish mumbled as the fear that had been choking him finally released its hold.

"Ulrick's blood," Donald clarified.

Conor let go, seeing that they needed privacy. He pointed to Ulrick and he and Donald picked up the body and headed to the door. "We will deal with this." The two older lairds left the room.

Hamish clutched Mairead to him once again, careful this time so that her face was not buried in his chest. "God, I love you, *m'aingeal*. If anything had happened . . . I'm so sorry. God, I'm so sorry." Seeing her on the floor, icy terror had ricocheted through his veins. His life had passed before his eyes while crouching beside her, and it was empty and bleak. "I should have killed him when I had the chance. If *anything* ever happened to you, no one would be safe. No one. Not until I joined you."

Mairead rubbed her arms up and down his back. "You did save me. Without your training, I would have died."

Hamish just held her. "I love you, *aingeal*. Never again will I allow danger to come anywhere near you."

Mairead snuggled against his chest. "Say it again."

"I love you." He kissed the top of her head.

"Again."

She looked up at him and he held her gaze. "I would give my life for you."

"I want the other words."

He smiled then. "I will love you forever."

She reached up and caressed his dimples. "And I love you, Hamish. With all my heart and soul. Never doubt that. Never think that I would leave you."

"You heard me."

She nodded. Hamish's hand closed tightly around her fingers that were on his chest. He leaned down and brushed his mouth across the inside of her wrist in an incredibly soft, almost reverent kiss. Then he kissed her lips slowly, lingeringly, and with a possessiveness that left her with no doubt of his feelings. "I have loved you from the moment we met. I just was too afraid to say the words."

Mairead smiled. "You loved me when I was covered in mud?"

"Aye, covered in mud." He looked down at her. "I am *not*, however, partial to blood."

Mairead followed his gaze. "Neither am I. And I *so* wanted to be married in this dress."

Hamish raised his brows and a smile began to grow across his face. "You know what this means, don't you?"

Mairead heard the mischievous tone in Hamish's voice and was instantly wary. "No . . . what?"

He flashed his boyish grin and his dimples came fully to life. When he looked like this, Mairead could deny him nothing and he knew it. "We've missed sunset, so we *have* to wait another day. That will give you time to clean your dress and my men another day to beat Conor and the Mackays at some games. But sundown tomorrow, you best be in front of Father Lanaghly, because I don't care if you are wearing one of Hellie's old gowns, we *will* be wed."

* * *

Hamish swung Mairead in his arms and ignored all the shouts as he left the hall and headed toward the keep. The grin that had been on his face from the moment Father Lanaghly pronounced them man and wife had only grown.

Mairead giggled. "Just *what* are you smiling about?"

He began to march up the stairwell. "I'm married. You are my wife. I'm a McTiernay laird. And if I died an hour from now, I would pass on as the happiest man on Earth."

"An hour from now? Why not now?"

"In an hour, you will have nothing on and I will have made you scream in such pleasure that you have yet to imagine."

"Promise?"

Hamish unashamedly shrugged his shoulders and entered their solar. He let her slide down his body. "I would marry you over and over again."

"I didn't realize how much you like weddings," she breathed huskily.

He bent over and captured her lips in a searing kiss. "I don't," he said a moment later. "I love wedding *nights*."

Epilogue

Mairead reached behind Selah to snatch a water bag that was sliding off the boulder they were leaning against. She took a sip. It usually did not get so warm this far north in late April, but today seemed to be an exception. "How much longer do you think Robert is going to need?"

Selah shrugged. Robert had been walking with Donald Mackay, studying an old Norse fort. The gatehouse being built at Foinaven was not complete, but it was close. Robert and Selah had been discussing his next project and started seeking out inquiries for a master mason. Both had been pleasantly surprised to learn that Donald Mackay was very interested. Like most clans, the Mackays had a large tower that served as fortress, but the Mackays had finally accumulated the wealth to build a stone castle. And the one he wanted built was not like the traditional ones scattered throughout Scotland, Wales, and Ireland.

Most were not only expensive to build but also to maintain. Stone was durable, but it still required upkeep. Robert had learned a technique that did not include mortar, enabling the structure to last for centuries. When Donald Mackay mentioned that he wanted to build Castle Varrich using this method, Robert quickly dismissed all the requests coming in for his support and accepted Donald's offer.

The rapid beat of a horse's hooves captured everyone's attention. Hamish rode up to the group and quickly dismounted. Mairead tilted her cheek when he leaned down to kiss her. "You are making me nervous."

"Why?"

"Because you are smiling."

Selah had to agree. When Hamish flashed his dimples, it meant that either he was up to something or he knew something.

"A herald just came from the McTiernays."

Mackay stepped closer. "Something going on with Conor?" In the past year, the two men had grown close and Donald now considered Conor McTiernay more than just an ally but a friend. He had met all the McTiernay brothers except for Colin, who lived in the Lowlands.

"Nothing going on with Conor," Hamish answered. "But Conan has been busy."

Mairead wrinkled her nose. She liked Conan. Or at least she did when he was not being insufferable. He was the second youngest of the McTiernay brothers and the most brilliant. But that sharp mind of his made him condescending to others, especially women. It was a good thing he never intended to marry but to travel around Scotland. "I thought he was leaving in the fall to begin mapping clan territories and the coastline. Did he decide to depart sooner?"

Hamish's grin grew. "Better. He's getting *married* in three weeks."

Everyone froze upon hearing the news. They had to have heard wrong. Conan was extremely good-looking, but no woman could even tolerate him for very long. Their opinions never bothered him for he had grown tired of them the moment they opened their mouths to speak. He had been wise enough to be civil to Mairead for Hamish made it clear that anything less would result in bodily harm.

Mairead was the first to speak. "You are not serious."

"The herald assured me that the news was accurate. Laurel must have known we would have doubts and sent an additional message letting us know that she could not be happier for Conan. That his bride was perfect for him and it was only love prompting this union."

Mairead frowned, clearly not satisfied. "Well, that's cryptic."

"Very," Selah affirmed, wishing for more information. What kind of woman would agree to marry Conan? Then again, what was it about her that could make Conan even *think* about tying himself to one woman?

"I agree, but Laurel's message ended my own doubt. I can assume she is beautiful enough to catch his eye. I just hope she is intelligent enough to keep it."

Donald coughed into his fist. "Are you sure this is *Conan* we are talking about?" He did not want to say it out loud, but the only way he could see a woman marrying Conan was if she was forced to do so.

Hamish spread his hands out. "From what the herald said, she is very enamored of him."

Mairead now looked suspicious. "I don't believe it. He is just not the *type* to get married." Hamish let go a small snort. Mairead glared at him. "I mean it. Conan is brilliant, good-looking, and irritatingly arrogant. And he's that way to men he respects. To women? He's the most conceited, obnoxious creature of our encounter."

Hamish nodded. "I have that from many a female,

many a time. And *yet*," he emphasized, "he *is* getting married."

Robert moved around to stand next to his wife. He put a hand on Selah's shoulder and gave it a light squeeze. "I have yet to meet him, but I have heard that he is either liked or hated."

Selah sighed and rubbed her expanding belly unconsciously. "I wonder what she is like," she murmured. "This woman who finally tamed Conan."

"The only way to know is to meet her." Donald Mackay crossed his arms over his chest. "My eldest son will not be pleased as he will have to remain behind, but this is one marriage ceremony that I must attend and see to believe."

"Aye," Hamish agreed. "I'll let Amon or Ian decide who can manage Foinaven in my stead." It would probably be Ian as he was far more reserved and less interested in matters that involved the McTiernays. Amon, however, had come close to several of the McTiernay guards and had encountered Conan several times. All Hamish was sure of was that there was nothing that was going to prevent him from seeing this wedding. Everyone was going to be there. People who never traveled were going to be there. Even Colin, who lived in the Lowlands and had a growing family, would be there. It would be the largest celebration many would ever see, including him.

Robert moved to join the two men. "I've never met Conan, but I've heard of him and agree with Donald. I think I will join you both and witness this wedding in person."

"Both?" Mairead piped in, her brows furrowed together. She turned to Selah and asked her, "Did your husband just say *both*?"

Selah pursed her lips together and nodded. She shifted

to push her bulky body forward. She was not due for another three months, but she was much larger at this point in her pregnancy than she had been with her son, Rab. Mairead, who was a month behind her and had only recently begun to show, was just now able to eat again without fear of becoming violently ill. Both sisters were pregnant, but that did *not* mean they were staying home.

Selah blinked at Robert and smiled sweetly. "Robert, my love, when you said *I,* didn't you mean that *we*"—she pointed to herself and then him—"will join you?"

Robert returned her stare with an incredulous one of his own. He knew what Selah was asking. She wanted to travel with them and the idea was completely absurd. "You cannot be serious."

Selah was still the gentle soul she always had been, but things had changed in their marriage. He had embraced his future as a designer and builder of castles and now had more confidence. Selah, no longer forced to constantly make—or avoid—decisions that she hated, had also grown more self-assured. Neither of them had to constantly re-press negative emotions. As a result, the few times they did not see things alike, they argued. And it looked like this was going to be one of those times, for he was not going to let his beautiful wife travel the countryside while pregnant.

Selah's lips thinned, but her smile remained in place. "You think I'm not serious about seeing the most promi-nent event the Highlands have seen these past several years? I cannot believe you actually considered leaving me behind."

Mairead had left the boulder as well and was facing Hamish. "I hope you are not planning on leaving me behind. I agree with Selah. I'm coming with you."

Hamish's insides clenched at the idea of anything happening to her or his baby. He found it difficult to speak and eventually blurted out, "You're pregnant!"

"The baby is not due for months, so why should that make a difference? You cannot blame the weather. Spring is nearly over. The wet weather is gone and the sun shines nearly every day."

"Mairead, be sensible. Even if good weather does follow us, travel will be uncomfortable and in your condition, it will take several more days for us to get there."

Mairead's face filled with exasperation. "Then we can leave immediately if we must travel more slowly, but I *am* going."

Hamish glared at her, hoping she could see that on this he would not yield. "No, you aren't."

Mairead glared back and came to her feet. Hamish had not raised his voice at all, but his tone was that of a parent talking to a child. She raised her chin, and spoke in a similar, non-compromising voice. "I love that you are protective of me, but *I will* be going. You can either change your mind now or you can change it later, but there is no way I am not going to see this wedding for myself. This event will be discussed for years and *I will not be the only one not to have been there*," she said emphatically. "I am Lady McTiernay of the McTiernays of Farr. You cannot truly think I am not going to a McTiernay wedding!"

Selah stood behind her. "And if Mairead is going, then so am I."

Robert looked to Hamish, who just stood fuming, and then at Donald, who shook his head. It was clear the older laird knew the inevitable outcome. "If we ride together, it would be safer for all. We could depart at the end of the week. It would give us a few days to meet with Conan and see for ourselves this miracle."

"I doubt a soul coming is there to see Conan." Mairead chuckled. "They want to take a look at the woman who not only ensnared Conan's heart . . . but actually agreed to marry the man."

Mackay cocked his head to the right in agreement. He *was* more interested in whom Conan was marrying than the lad himself.

Mairead winked at Selah. "Leave it to Selah and me." Her sister gave her a knowing smile. McTiernay women traded secrets and whoever could tame Conan must have some incredible ones to share.

Hamish saw the exchange and pulled Mairead into his arms. His hands caressed the planes of her back. He loved how she felt against his body and each time he held her close it was a reminder of just how lucky he was. He kissed her cheek softly and then whispered in her ear. "Should I yield now or let you try and convince me to let you come tonight?"

Mairead pulled slightly back. "Tonight," she said with a mischievous smile. "Just as long as you know that you never had a chance."

Hamish bent his head and pressed his lips against hers. His hand held the back of her neck as his mouth slowly glided over hers. A hungry sound escaped him as she opened up for him. The kiss was soft and gentle, melting his bones and making him forget that they had an audience.

No. He never did have a chance.

He had been hers since that first kiss.

More by Bestselling Author
Hannah Howell

__Highland Angel	978-1-4201-0864-4	$6.99US/$8.99CAN
__If He's Sinful	978-1-4201-0461-5	$6.99US/$8.99CAN
__Wild Conquest	978-1-4201-0464-6	$6.99US/$8.99CAN
__If He's Wicked	978-1-4201-0460-8	$6.99US/$8.49CAN
__My Lady Captor	978-0-8217-7430-4	$6.99US/$8.49CAN
__Highland Sinner	978-0-8217-8001-5	$6.99US/$8.49CAN
__Highland Captive	978-0-8217-8003-9	$6.99US/$8.49CAN
__Nature of the Beast	978-1-4201-0435-6	$6.99US/$8.49CAN
__Highland Fire	978-0-8217-7429-8	$6.99US/$8.49CAN
__Silver Flame	978-1-4201-0107-2	$6.99US/$8.49CAN
__Highland Wolf	978-0-8217-8000-8	$6.99US/$9.99CAN
__Highland Wedding	978-0-8217-8002-2	$4.99US/$6.99CAN
__Highland Destiny	978-1-4201-0259-8	$4.99US/$6.99CAN
__Only for You	978-0-8217-8151-7	$6.99US/$8.99CAN
__Highland Promise	978-1-4201-0261-1	$4.99US/$6.99CAN
__Highland Vow	978-1-4201-0260-4	$4.99US/$6.99CAN
__Highland Savage	978-0-8217-7999-6	$6.99US/$9.99CAN
__Beauty and the Beast	978-0-8217-8004-6	$4.99US/$6.99CAN
__Unconquered	978-0-8217-8088-6	$4.99US/$6.99CAN
__Highland Barbarian	978-0-8217-7998-9	$6.99US/$9.99CAN
__Highland Conqueror	978-0-8217-8148-7	$6.99US/$9.99CAN
__Conqueror's Kiss	978-0-8217-8005-3	$4.99US/$6.99CAN
__A Stockingful of Joy	978-1-4201-0018-1	$4.99US/$6.99CAN
__Highland Bride	978-0-8217-7995-8	$4.99US/$6.99CAN
__Highland Lover	978-0-8217-7759-6	$6.99US/$9.99CAN

Available Wherever Books Are Sold!

Check out our website at
http://www.kensingtonbooks.com

More from Bestselling Author
JANET DAILEY

Calder Storm	0-8217-7543-X	$7.99US/$10.99CAN
Close to You	1-4201-1714-9	$5.99US/$6.99CAN
Crazy in Love	1-4201-0303-2	$4.99US/$5.99CAN
Dance With Me	1-4201-2213-4	$5.99US/$6.99CAN
Everything	1-4201-2214-2	$5.99US/$6.99CAN
Forever	1-4201-2215-0	$5.99US/$6.99CAN
Green Calder Grass	0-8217-7222-8	$7.99US/$10.99CAN
Heiress	1-4201-0002-5	$6.99US/$7.99CAN
Lone Calder Star	0-8217-7542-1	$7.99US/$10.99CAN
Lover Man	1-4201-0666-X	$4.99US/$5.99CAN
Masquerade	1-4201-0005-X	$6.99US/$8.99CAN
Mistletoe and Molly	1-4201-0041-6	$6.99US/$9.99CAN
Rivals	1-4201-0003-3	$6.99US/$7.99CAN
Santa in a Stetson	1-4201-0664-3	$6.99US/$9.99CAN
Santa in Montana	1-4201-1474-3	$7.99US/$9.99CAN
Searching for Santa	1-4201-0306-7	$6.99US/$9.99CAN
Something More	0-8217-7544-8	$7.99US/$9.99CAN
Stealing Kisses	1-4201-0304-0	$4.99US/$5.99CAN
Tangled Vines	1-4201-0004-1	$6.99US/$8.99CAN
Texas Kiss	1-4201-0665-1	$4.99US/$5.99CAN
That Loving Feeling	1-4201-1713-0	$5.99US/$6.99CAN
To Santa With Love	1-4201-2073-5	$6.99US/$7.99CAN
When You Kiss Me	1-4201-0667-8	$4.99US/$5.99CAN
Yes, I Do	1-4201-0305-9	$4.99US/$5.99CAN

Available Wherever Books Are Sold!

Check out our website at www.kensingtonbooks.com.

Books by Bestselling Author
Fern Michaels

___The Jury	0-8217-7878-1	$6.99US/$9.99CAN
___Sweet Revenge	0-8217-7879-X	$6.99US/$9.99CAN
___Lethal Justice	0-8217-7880-3	$6.99US/$9.99CAN
___Free Fall	0-8217-7881-1	$6.99US/$9.99CAN
___Fool Me Once	0-8217-8071-9	$7.99US/$10.99CAN
___Vegas Rich	0-8217-8112-X	$7.99US/$10.99CAN
___Hide and Seek	1-4201-0184-6	$6.99US/$9.99CAN
___Hokus Pokus	1-4201-0185-4	$6.99US/$9.99CAN
___Fast Track	1-4201-0186-2	$6.99US/$9.99CAN
___Collateral Damage	1-4201-0187-0	$6.99US/$9.99CAN
___Final Justice	1-4201-0188-9	$6.99US/$9.99CAN
___Up Close and Personal	0-8217-7956-7	$7.99US/$9.99CAN
___Under the Radar	1-4201-0683-X	$6.99US/$9.99CAN
___Razor Sharp	1-4201-0684-8	$7.99US/$10.99CAN
___Yesterday	1-4201-1494-8	$5.99US/$6.99CAN
___Vanishing Act	1-4201-0685-6	$7.99US/$10.99CAN
___Sara's Song	1-4201-1493-X	$5.99US/$6.99CAN
___Deadly Deals	1-4201-0686-4	$7.99US/$10.99CAN
___Game Over	1-4201-0687-2	$7.99US/$10.99CAN
___Sins of Omission	1-4201-1153-1	$7.99US/$10.99CAN
___Sins of the Flesh	1-4201-1154-X	$7.99US/$10.99CAN
___Cross Roads	1-4201-1192-2	$7.99US/$10.99CAN

Available Wherever Books Are Sold!
Check out our website at **www.kensingtonbooks.com**